SKY ON FIRE

SKY ON FIRE

BOOK 2 OF THE ÆTHER SAGA

BY E. K. JOHNSTON

DUTTON BOOKS

DUTTON BOOKS
An imprint of Penguin Random House LLC
1745 Broadway, New York, NY 10019
penguinrandomhouse.com

Design by Anna Booth
Text set in Adobe Caslon Pro

THE LIBRARY OF CONGRESS HAS CATALOGED THE HARDCOVER EDITION AS FOLLOWS:

Names: Johnston, E. K., author. | Johnston, E. K. Aetherbound.
Title: Sky on fire / E.K. Johnston.
Description: New York, New York: Dutton Books, 2025. | Audience: Ages 14 and up. | Audience: Grades 10-12. | Summary: Non-magical, science prodigy Morgan Enni gains attention from a group of rebels for her research, and together they embark on a space expedition, each concealing their true objectives from the other.
Identifiers: LCCN 2024049234 (print) | LCCN 2024049235 (ebook) | ISBN 9781984816160 (hardcover) | ISBN 9781984816177 (ebook)
Subjects: CYAC: Scientific expeditions—Fiction. | Secrets—Fiction. | Magic—Fiction. | Science fiction. | LCGFT: Science fiction. | Novels.
Classification: LCC PZ7.J64052 Sk 2025 (print) | LCC PZ7.J64052 (ebook) | DDC [Fic]—dc23
LC record available at https://lccn.loc.gov/2024049234
LC ebook record available at https://lccn.loc.gov/2024049235

First published by Dutton Books, 2025
First paperback edition published 2026

Manufactured in the United States of America
LSCC

ISBN 9781984816184
1st Printing

The authorized representative in the EU for product safety and compliance is Penguin Random House Ireland, Morrison Chambers, 32 Nassau Street, Dublin D02 YH68, Ireland, https://eu-contact.penguin.ie.

Stay afraid, but do it anyway.
What's important is the action.

—CARRIE FISHER

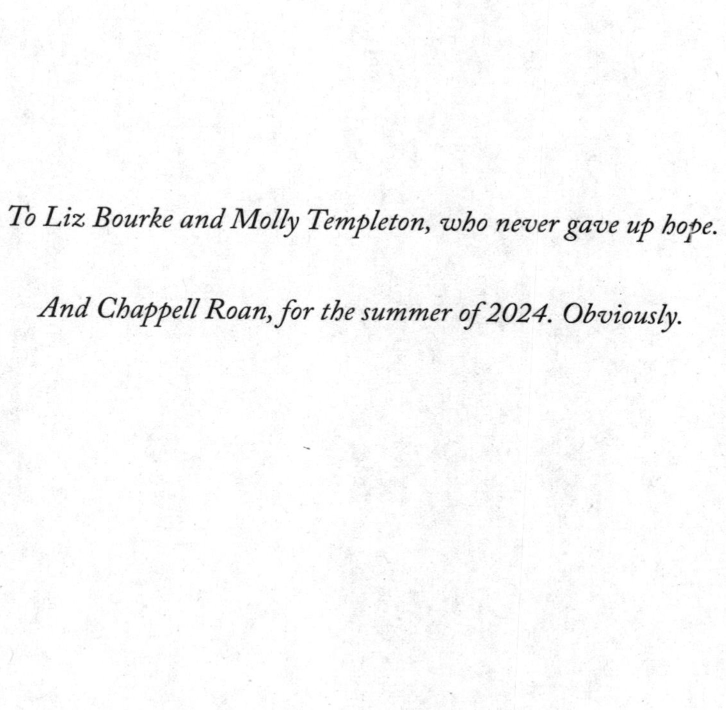

To Liz Bourke and Molly Templeton, who never gave up hope.

And Chappell Roan, for the summer of 2024. Obviously.

SKY ON FIRE

When the Stavenger Empire fell to pieces against the storms of chaos, it fell hard. Reeling from defeat at the hands of the Maritech—who had rejected domination so utterly—and burdened with six space stations that now led to nowhere, the empire writhed in its ruin. Yet it was determined to lock its dying fingers around everything it could as it burned. Their great expansion halted, its endless supply of the protein-rich oglasa exhausted, the Stavengers had almost nowhere left to turn, except inward, on themselves.

Those on the Stavenger home-planets were safe enough, at first. With the security of hard ground to stand on and fresh air to breathe, they did not face the same imminent danger that the rebellious stations did. Against those stations the Stavengers lashed out, determined to exterminate the rebellion before it could make any further steps towards independence. The stations could not run themselves, and there were still resources, however inconsequential, to control; so the Stavengers dug in, hoping to preserve what they could, no matter the cost.

Even that might not have been enough for the empire to cling together. The radicals on the stations were determined to break free. But just when the rebels stood on the cusp of victory, disaster struck. The æther, which gave power to all those who felt its connection humming in their blood, was gone. Between one breath and the next, every æther-worker alive felt their connection to power break. The rebellious stations faltered immediately. With neither æther nor oglasa to support them, Hoy and Ninienne surrendered within days, desperate to take whatever supplies the Stavengers would give them to survive. Skúvoy soon followed, and their allies on Brannick and Katla couldn't stop them. This gave the Stavengers enough time to perform their last great piece of æther-work: securing the station gene-locks, which ensured that only the presence of a ruling family made it possible to operate the Wells and the Nets. With one stroke, the stations were sealed to the Stavengers, and the only cost was an incomprehensible number of calories, hundreds of æther-workers, and the entirety of Enragon Station.

This served the Stavengers just fine. They had enough to deal with at home.

From the ashes of the home-planets came the remnant of the empire—a Hegemony—that rose to power by brute force and sheer will. Without æther, the fight was much harder than anyone anticipated, but it wasn't long before even the alliances between the Stavenger planets were newly welded together. The Hegemony took over, plundering what they could. They were weaker than the empire had been, but they clung to what power they had with a vicious hold. There was no one to oppose them, and so their strength grew.

They did not form alliances with the stations. They informed them what their part in the new order was to be, and the stations complied because the breath of every inhabitant hung on the heartbeat of one or two. Brannick Station was far away, and the Hegemony did not rule them too tightly. Enragon was a dead husk, floating in the void. The smaller stations, closer to the Stavenger solar system, never recovered their full measure of operations. Without the æther and without the oglasa, they had only just enough to sustain them.

After that, the rebels were truly defeated. Without their leaders, they couldn't resist, and it was easy enough for the empire to collect hostages to ensure good behaviour. With the dead example of Enragon Station broadcast into everyone's homes, station citizens knew the penalty for resisting again. The stations themselves, once united as a trade network and by common purpose, became fractured and isolated, protecting their own before anyone else.

Katla Station, with its proximity to a great deal of solar energy, was the most productive of the stations, and the Hegemony allowed them their wealth. The Katla family was resented even by their own station's inhabitants for their collaboration, but there was no other power to turn to. Katla prospered, expanding in size and accumulating money even as the other stations struggled to keep the air circulating. The Stavengers rested easy, thinking they had bought themselves enough time to rebuild.

But something festered on Katla, deep below the ranks of the important operations officers in whom the Stavengers placed so much trust. Katla did not forget. While the other stations loved and lauded their ruling families, Katla only tolerated theirs. The family still had most of the power, of course, but unrest simmered underneath the surface of the common corridors and factory floors. Rebellion hadn't died. It had only gone quiet, same as the æther had.

Generations passed, and Katla remained the shining beacon of the Stavenger Stations. It had wealth and art and scholarship. There was peace and freedom throughout the station, or so it seemed. But if you looked, if you peeled back the shiny surfaces and dug into the nuts and bolts that made the station turn, you would see something else.

Katla had not wasted its time as the dying empire's favourite. When the hopeful and desperate rebels on other stations finally reached out, they found Katla was ready. When Pendt Brannick worked a miracle—and bought her station's freedom from the gene-lock with her own life—Katla stood witness, preparing for whatever came next.

But for what came, there was nothing they could do.

PART ONE:
THE SCIENTIST

IN YOUR HEART SHALL BURN
AN UNQUENCHABLE FLAME,
ALL-CONSUMING, AND NEVER SATISFIED.

CANTICLE OF THRENODIES 5:7
DRAGON AGE

1.

MORGAN ENNI HAD THINGS to do, but in the quiet of Katla Station's designated early morning, she took a moment to breathe.

It was the last time she'd be sleeping in this bed for a while, and she was strangely reluctant to get out of it and start moving around. The bed itself was nothing special, just a simple frame and mattress that she'd purchased from a shop she couldn't be bothered to remember the name of. She hadn't even physically gone to it, electing to shop in her preferred manner: selecting an item from the online catalogue and waiting for the mostly anonymous delivery. It wasn't stylish or, even worse, sexy. It was functional. Her aunt had wanted to furnish the apartment with more flourish and flounce, and had tried to drag Morgan to a whole variety of stores. Eventually they'd compromised and used a public display terminal that offered virtual projections instead. Even then, Morgan had been hard pressed to simplify the decorations, but she had succeeded at least in the matter of the bedroom.

Aunt Vianne meant well. She'd brought Morgan to Katla when she was small and vulnerable, and somehow already too much for her parents to deal with. Katla had much better schools and better teachers for those without gene-sense, Vianne had said, convincing her sister to give up a child she didn't understand. It would be better for everyone. Morgan hadn't been consulted, and at the time she'd been terrified, but as the years passed, she had come to realize that Vianne was absolutely correct. Katla, the most influential of the remaining stations, was the place where Morgan would thrive.

It was just that, on occasion, Vianne tended to surround them both with *things*. Morgan had learned to make herself comfortable in her aunt's home. She had her own bedroom, a proper one, which was a blessing she hadn't had in her parents' cramped allotment, and Vianne was always ready with a new booklet or data-crystal when Morgan was bored with her primary studies. From the time she was six until she was sixteen, Morgan's life was cluttered, but it was good. When it came time for her to move into an apartment closer to her laboratory, she started putting her foot down. A little bit. Particularly in matters concerning throw pillows. Morgan very much enjoyed comfort, and she loved and appreciated Aunt Vianne, but she also liked having space. Space was like quiet: it made it easier to think.

She was surrounded by quiet with some frequency. She worked alone in her lab. She had lived alone in her apartment for two years now. Given any choice in the matter, she'd sit alone in public places with a book or a datapad, and no one to interrupt her. However, there was a special kind of silence to the hours when the people on Katla started to think about getting up but hadn't yet started going about their daily bustle. A waiting sort of quiet, which suited her just fine.

Morgan Enni felt like she had been waiting for something all her life. Test results, acceptance letters, scholarship approvals, ethics committee decisions, and this morning was no different. Once she got out of bed and started making noise, it would be time to face the harder part of waiting. Here, under a sensible quilt, she was at least cozy and could imagine that waiting was comfortable. When she got up, she would have to check her messages, and then she would know for certain whether the thing she had been waiting for the most was going to happen.

Because there is very little dignity in the human form, her bladder made the decision for her.

The humming started as soon as her feet hit the floor. The coffeepot began heating water and a randomized selection of pastries and fruit juices appeared on the counter as the freshseal around them retracted. An overly friendly notification appeared on the counter of her kitchenette informing her how many calories she was advised to consume, based on her previous day's activity. Morgan ignored it and headed into the bathroom. She would eat when she was hungry. Probably. Sometimes work was more important than a grumbling belly.

By the time she was finished with her morning ablutions, the coffee was hot, and cream and sugar had appeared next to the pastries. The calorie notification was replaced by a message reminding her that she would need to reorder several food items if she wanted to have breakfast tomorrow morning. Morgan did not—or at least, not here—so she cancelled the order. An assumption, but she had a good feeling about how her last grant application had gone. She wouldn't be here tomorrow. She was sure of it.

There were several schools and academies on Katla, designated for higher learning or specialized training of some kind. It was these facilities that Vianne Enni had brought Morgan to Katla to take advantage of, and Morgan did not disappoint her. Only the æther-college was selective, requiring some level of gene-sense from those it admitted. Every other college would admit anyone who submitted an application. After that, staying was up to the student's abilities. Aunt Vianne taught in the physics department at Katla's primary university, and so that's where Morgan decided to go. Her aunt had never treated her like a burden, but even as a child, Morgan was wise enough to take advantage of getting free tuition as the ward of an employee.

There were no age restrictions at the university, and the application system tried to be as innominate as possible to give everyone a fair chance with the admissions board. Therefore, many professors were quite alarmed when a small, dark-haired girl-child marched into their classrooms and took a seat in the front row, feet swinging above the floor. At least, they were alarmed the first time. Morgan had quickly proven she belonged, and more than kept up with the fifteen- and sixteen-year-olds the university usually admitted.

The university had been a second home to Morgan from the time she was twelve. In those sterile white rooms and under the too-bright lights, she absorbed every piece of information her instructors had been willing to give her. With Aunt Vianne's encouragement, she took extra classes and attended every guest lecture. Some of them were quite controversial—there had been protests and strongly worded letters—but Morgan went all the same. Politics, history, mathematics, hydroculture, every kind of science, even the theories of æther-work, Morgan threw herself into the black vacuum space of Katla's seemingly endless educational opportunities, and since nature abhors a vacuum, knowledge rushed in.

The problems began when she started asking questions.

The coffeepot beeped loudly, reminding her that her morning stimulant was prepared. Morgan stirred cream and sugar into the dark liquid, and then alternated between drinking it and eating the pastries. She was just beginning the dishwash cycle and programming the freshseal when a lower-pitched hum joined the harmony made by her kitchen implements. The trains were running; the inevitable could no longer be put off. Katla's day had begun.

Morgan fastened a lid on one of the fruit juices and palmed the button on the wall that would flip her apartment over from its domestic setting to its professional one. A frosted glass screen came down to block her kitchenette and the bed folded up into the wall. Her desk unfolded as soon as the floor was clear, and her work-chair rose from its niche in the floor. As she sat down, a series of monitors turned on, glowing softly as they waited for input. A small red circle flashed in the corner of her inbox.

Aunt Vianne had been very understanding when Morgan decided to move out. Young people on Katla had a great deal of independence, and the station was currently in an underpopulated phase, so there were plenty of options. Several of the students

Morgan would have been in school with had she progressed at a regular rate had all sought apartments at the same time. Vianne never for a moment thought Morgan would opt for a co-living situation. Instead, she imagined something glamorous, possibly with an outside viewport, high up in one of Katla's spires. Morgan had the accumulated credit to afford something like that, but absolutely no desire for it.

Instead, Morgan chose a small, compact apartment in Katla's great ring, near one of the main transportation hubs. It had noisier corridors and walkways than the spires did, as people travelled to and from work or school. There was always a variety of street food available, and the shops were stocked with clothes and books that Morgan found suitable, even if her aunt thought they were a little gauche.

If asked, Morgan couldn't have said what drew her to this section of the station. She wasn't slumming it by any means. Katla didn't really have slums, though it did have an underbelly that was not discussed in polite society. She certainly didn't hang out with her neighbours or even meet up with other grad students at the local restaurants and bars, though there were people she saw on a regular basis—picking up dinner on the way home, waiting for the trainway, that sort of thing. It was the oldest part of the station, the part the Stavengers had built to secure the Net and the Well so they could send their ships on to Brannick and ill-fated Enragon as soon as possible.

The truth was that this was the part of Katla that relied the least on gene-sense. There were no arboretums or flashing signs, no view of the stars for those who could orient themselves. The tech was a bit older, the uses more practical. Everything was functional but lacked the flair that gene-mages couldn't seem to resist adding to everything they did. Morgan liked it that way.

It was not that her parents had been disappointed when she was born without a connection to the æther, it was simply more that it was a surprise. Like most people on Skúvoy Station, neither of Morgan's parents was particularly adept. They each possessed enough magic to guarantee a job at one of Skúvoy's many factories, but nothing more. Without gene-sense, Morgan's future employment options on the station were extremely limited, and no one on Skúvoy prized academics. This was not something that bothered her as a toddler. Only when her sister was born did Morgan realize what she was missing.

The baby's reception was far more animated than anything she had seen before. Whereas Morgan had always been greeted with hushed whispers—maybe a coo if she fussed—the new baby was exclaimed over excitedly and passed from person to person like a prize. Morgan was smart enough to understand by then and had retreated into her shell. Now the neighbours all said she was aloof and strange. Morgan had been in the process of shutting down when her aunt Vianne arrived. Her mother's sister was a force to be reckoned with, and she swept into Morgan's life like a rocket.

Morgan could hardly remember what her sister looked like, though she was pretty sure the baby had been blond and cheerful. She'd still been an infant when Morgan left, and there was no telling what she would look like now, more than a decade later. Morgan didn't miss her family, nor did she resent them, nor even hate æther. She just didn't want to constantly be reminded of the family that didn't understand her for her singular difference. Especially when they all shared the same secret, buried deep in the past and kept in their very name.

Vianne probably understood that long before Morgan did herself, and that was why her aunt did not put up much of a protest when Morgan decided to move to such an unfashionable part of Katla Station. Instead, Vianne helped her pack and only quietly grumbled about the ascetic nature of Morgan's design preferences, while trying to discreetly add wallpaper accents to brighten up the kitchenette.

Now, as the message notification flashed on the otherwise inactive screens, Morgan wished her aunt was here. If it was good news, Aunt Vianne would be proud of her. If it was bad news, she'd swear loudly and promise to make disparaging remarks at future interdepartmental meetings. Morgan had outpaced Vianne a long time ago, when it came to brain power and raw ambition. Rather than get angry about it, Vianne had been thrilled. Her niece was now even more of a problem for everyone else on the faculty, and Vianne watched with unfettered glee as department heads courted her niece, while also grinding their teeth over what more than one of them referred to as obstinacy.

Morgan took a deep breath and opened the message from the university. Immediately, three faces filled the screens in front of her. Apparently, the advisory board had felt strongly enough about their decision that they'd recorded a message instead of just writing one. That didn't give Morgan any clue as to what their decision *was*, though. Honestly, it could go either way.

"Ms. Morgan Enni, greetings. We hope this recording finds

you well," the committee chair began. Dr. Argir was an older man, white skin made even paler by a lack of time spent under the solar simulation lamps. "We have considered your research application and are prepared to give our decision."

"We would like to commend you for the changes you have made to your research proposal." This second speaker was Dr. Mattsen, the head of Morgan's own department. She had supported Morgan right up until the moment she started showing initiative. Now Morgan's brevity was unprofessional, where before it had been practical, and her ideas were untenable, where they used to be cutting edge. "It shows a great deal of professional development in regard to your response to critique."

Not enough that they were willing to have this chat in person, or even live. But to be fair, Morgan had called them all some relatively creative names the last time they'd rejected her face-to-face. She didn't really want to meet with them either. She just wanted the courtesy before they gave her the resources she needed to disappear from their orbits for a while.

"We still have a great many concerns about your primary research goals," the committee chair said. "But my esteemed colleague has made several arguments in your defense."

"Morgan, I know how dedicated you are to this idea, even with the doubts expressed by many of my peers." The third speaker was Dr. Morunt, a gene-mage who taught medical cooperation techniques for doctors like himself working with their non-mage counterparts. He had held his position in absentia until recently, when he finally came back to Katla after years off-station doing something Morgan didn't care about. Morgan couldn't stand him, but he had been unexpectedly supportive, and it was because of his recent addition to the committee that she had been given a second chance. "This, in combination with your secondary research objectives, has allowed us to grant you the funding you've requested."

Morgan almost tipped her chair over.

"Effective immediately, you are a Research-Wanderer, with permission to leave Katla Station to pursue your academic goals." Dr. Argir didn't bother to hide his annoyance at the fact that she'd been successful. "Please make sure you sign the attached waivers and file your reports in the appropriate manner."

"Good luck, Research-Wanderer Enni," said Dr. Morunt, a wry expression on his face. If she cared about his opinions beyond his ability to get her what she wanted, Morgan might have been amused by his odd commitment to her cause. He didn't so much as blink as he congratulated and then dismissed her. "I still hope you're wrong."

2.

MORNING ON KATLA WAS a lousy time to go shopping. Most of the stores had only just received their new inventory, which meant the digital system couldn't be trusted, forcing Morgan to visit in person if she wanted to stay on her schedule. At least there were fewer crowds and less of a chance of running into someone she knew who wanted to ask her too many questions. Now she had to deal with the other people on her level who were heading off to their jobs. Morgan always did her best to skip these travel times, but her meeting had pushed her back today, and now she was stuck in the crush with only her clothing as armour, instead of the personal space she'd rather have.

Zipped into a one-piece jumpsuit with a puffy vest overtop, Morgan was far from stylish and stood out a bit more than she liked, especially with the commuters. The jumpsuit had fallen out of fashion several years ago, due to its connection to the working labourers on other stations. Katla residents with station operations jobs wore sturdy trouser-and-shirt combinations that *looked* like a jumpsuit, but weren't, and anyone who worked in an office or shop or anywhere else wore a mixed palette of colours and patterns and fabrics. Even the crews of the ships that docked at Katla didn't wear their shipclothes on the station.

Morgan felt about the clothing the way she felt about throw pillows: after comfort was met, there was no need for excess. The jumpsuit was comfortable and there were a lot of pockets, so Morgan had ordered one in several different colours as soon as she stopped growing. Vianne at least commended her thriftiness.

"Hey, Morgan!" Tasia Furlough, a girl Morgan's age whose family was sizeable and all involved in some manner of food procurement or production, was one of the people Morgan saw on a near-daily basis. To Tasia, that meant casual chatter, but she wasn't pushy about it, and that meant Morgan didn't mind talking with her, either at her stall or while waiting for the lift in the mornings. "If you're up and about already, does that mean you're cleared to head out?"

Morgan had only told a few people that she was going away on a research project if it was approved, and she'd told no one outside of the university what the project was *for*. She didn't remember mentioning it to Tasia.

"Yes," Morgan said, pressing the button that would bring the lift to their level. "I just got the news this morning. I have most things organized, just to be prepared, but there are a few more things I need to arrange."

"Well, if I don't see you again before you leave, I hope you have a successful trip." Tasia was a gene-mage who, amongst other things, served meals at her family's food carts. That was where Morgan talked to her, and it was entirely possible that at some point, Morgan had told her all about the trip while distractedly waiting for her dinner. "You don't have a fish or anything, do you? Something that needs feeding while you're gone?"

"No," Morgan said. There was a pier-cat she occasionally put protein out for, though she was far from the only person who did so. "But thank you."

Together, they stepped into the lift that would take them three levels up and two blocks over. There they would part ways as Tasia took a direct chute to Procurement and Morgan took the more circuitously routed trainway up to the first public level. The ride was quiet, the only sound besides the hum was a newsfeed recording about the new Brannick in charge of his station. The story was a few months old—which was confusing because Brannick had somehow been through two station heads in a short time, so the old one was still "new" when the new one took over—and there were several gaps in it if you listened closely enough, but that was news on Katla for you. The lift doors opened, and Tasia only nodded when they parted ways. Morgan wondered whether the other girl thought she was lonely, but it was more likely Tasia was just happy her weirdo neighbour was quiet. If Morgan had grown up with that many siblings, she probably would have been even more eager to get a place of her own.

The trainway platforms were packed with people, all making their way up into the main part of Katla Station for their day's work. The shifts for all of the mech, tech, and med jobs were set up to overlap slightly, which meant there was no crush of people getting off the arriving train. Morgan stood in the press, holding a handle above her head for stability as the train set out. There were three more platform-level pickups, and then the fun part of the journey began.

The trainway had not been a part of Katla's original design. Under the Stavenger Empire, the station's crew had taken the chutes or climbed up, and this continued after the empire fell. It was only within the last century or so that electro-mages had been able to build the trainway in its current form, and by the time they got around to it, there was no room for the tracks inside the station.

An awed hush swept through the train as it exited through its pressurized airlock and began to climb the station on the outside. It happened like that every time, no matter the time of day or how jaded the riders were. That first glimpse of space was always breathtaking. Some people hid their eyes from the view, but Morgan looked. The stars were so little and far away. It seemed almost impossible to imagine other people living out there or traveling through the void, and yet that was exactly what Morgan was going to do.

The sight of that much nothing made Morgan contemplative. She thought back to what Dr. Morunt had said, that he hoped she was wrong. Not unsuccessful—he wasn't petty—but *wrong*. She was starting to think that her work might seem threatening to æther-workers specifically, even though she was only chasing pure data at this point. Maybe she should have worded her research proposal more nicely, but at the same time, Morgan wanted to be taken seriously. She wouldn't water anything down so that it was more appealing.

The train re-entered the station, the lights coming back up. Everyone relaxed infinitesimally. There was always danger in the void, and it was safer to be inside. Most of the riders were going up higher in the piers than Morgan was, so she was one of only a few to get off at the train's first stop.

She was almost certain that whoever designed the public spaceport to be dingy and old-fashioned hadn't done it on purpose. It just wasn't high on the list for updates or renovations as long as everything was still working properly. That was the only explanation for why the public docks looked like something straight out of a holo-drama. The lights even swung, somehow, in a wind that had literally never existed.

Morgan made her way past stacks of crates and overloaded dollies until she reached the admin hub. She entered her code, and a list of ships appeared in front of her. She was in luck: the captain she had pre-negotiated with was still in the docks. Morgan double-checked the number and then headed off to the appropriate port.

"We meet again, I see," said the ship's captain as soon as Morgan climbed down to the loading bay. "Good news, I hope?"

"Yes, Captain." Morgan realized she had forgotten the woman's name. Chorus, or something like that. "I have been cleared for departure and my route approved. If your ship is still available, I would like to hire it."

"Wonderful," the captain said. "I don't mind hauling cargo, but I think you'll be a bit easier to clean up after, eh? The last time I had grain spores, and I think I was cleaning them out of cracks in the bridge decking for days."

"You were cleaning?" said a crew member from nearby.

"Oh, be quiet," the captain said.

It was this camaraderie that had drawn Morgan to the ship. She didn't want some captain whose crew was afraid of them. She'd heard stories about those kinds of ships, where everything was controlled down to the gram. If the crew felt free to sass the captain a little bit, it was probably going to be a better trip.

"When do you need us to be ready to go?" the captain asked.

"I have a few more things to arrange," said Morgan, "but I'm hoping it will be before the end of the dayshift."

"We'll have her ready," the crew member said, patting the hull fondly. "Captain Choria always follows the schedule."

Choria. Morgan tried to carve it into her mind.

"Don't suck up," Choria said. "And send me the kitten. I have a new job for him."

Choria caught the surprised expression on Morgan's face and laughed, but not unkindly.

"It's what we call the newest hand," Choria explained. "On account of how he doesn't know how to use his eyes, and he's a bit clumsy. But he learns well! I have high hopes for him."

"I'll see you in a few hours, then." Morgan turned and made her way back to the trainway to make it to her next stop.

The bookshop had everything she wanted to download, including the latest in the murder serial that Morgan was following. She liked her work, but she knew she wouldn't do it all the time. Vianne did not consider reading for fun as a break from reading for work, but Morgan enjoyed sinking into the familiar format of a crime or romance story. Plus, it all fit on the same device as her textbooks and research sources, so it made packing economical.

The one thing she wouldn't cut corners on was food. Captain Choria would include her in their water ration, but it was strongly encouraged that Morgan bring along any extra calories she might require. This was, she realized, actually more applicable to æther-workers, who used up calories when they did magic and had to replace them. Morgan wouldn't need the extra calories as much, but she wanted to be polite, and it was only fair that she provide for herself. Also, in staying on Katla to help her, Choria had undoubtedly passed on a better paying job. Morgan wanted to be considerate of that, even if Choria said it was fine because Morgan herself was low maintenance.

She filled four crates with standard rations, and then two more with fresh produce and protein. The crew would appreciate that, even if they had just been on station themselves and had restocked. On a whim, she ordered one last crate and had the shopkeeper fill it with sweets. That would make the æther-workers on board happy, along with anyone who had a sweet tooth. She paid the bill and sent the crates down to the spaceport so that she could move on to her final destination.

Morgan's lab was a forgotten closet in the lowest levels of the university physics complex because they didn't know where else to put her. Her work took the concept of "multidisciplinary studies" a bit further than the university bureaucrats could handle. Also, no department really wanted her because, while they all wanted credit for her genius, they thought she was too eccentric to be useful.

The room itself was not so bad, even if the location left a bit to be desired. It was near a maintenance hatch, which meant that Morgan could take Operations transit to get there, and that was always more direct and less crowded than the public ways. Also it was quiet. No one ever came down this far, unless they wanted to touch the hull, and Morgan could lock the door to prevent her space from becoming a tourist destination.

The most important part of the office was that it was hers. The second most important part was that she'd charmed the janitorial staff into only cleaning it on her say-so, which meant she could leave her notes and experiments lying around without worrying that they'd be messed up or that she'd block someone from mopping the floor. Accordingly, when she opened the door, she found everything exactly as she'd left it.

She took a few moments to tidy up. There were a few long-term experiments that she'd leave running, but she'd left notes explaining what was not to be touched along with four tickets to an upper-pier theatre production for the staff's trouble. Everything else was put away or packed, and her office was the cleanest it had ever been, when someone knocked on the door.

Morgan jumped, because no one ever knocked on her door, but when the knock came again, she couldn't ignore it. Maybe it was Choria, and something had gone wrong. Maybe it was Aunt Vianne coming for another hug. Maybe it was an undergraduate who had got lost and needed help out of the sublevels before they starved to death.

It was, in fact, two of the maintenance people who worked on this level. Both Meggon and Chari looked very apologetic because Morgan had made sure they were well compensated for leaving her office alone. They were carrying a large object between them.

"Apologies, Ms. Enni, but we had to get this down here before you left," Meggon said. "Where do you want the second desk?"

3.

"WHAT?" MORGAN FROZE FOR a moment in the doorway before her manners reinstated themselves and she got out of the way so they could set down the heavy load.

"It's another desk," Meggon told her again. "For your assistant, I guess."

"I don't have an assistant," Morgan said.

This was not from lack of trying. She had filled out an application for a research assistant several months ago, but since she insisted on having a *paid* employee, not some hapless undergraduate volunteer, her application had been rejected. The department had bought an updated stimulant dispenser instead.

"I have the order here," Chari said, handing over a datapad.

Morgan scanned it quickly. It was the application she had filled out all those months ago, outlining the tasks she wanted her assistant to do and how much they would be compensated for doing them. Her ident number was at the bottom of the form, alongside a brand-new red check mark and the ident code of Dr. Morunt, of all people. He'd been back on Katla Station for a relatively short while but had apparently wasted no time at all re-ingratiating himself with university administration. Maybe Morgan should take an extended sabbatical on Brannick Station, if it meant her career would leapfrog like his had.

"Just set it up against that wall," Morgan said, gesturing to the sole clear spot in her office. It was only empty because she had packed up a large portion of her study materials to take with her, but she'd solve that problem later. Or have her assistant do it, apparently. "Make sure they get a decent chair too."

"Already on order," Meggon said. "We're just waiting for the biometrics to make sure it's the right size."

"They don't have biometrics yet?" Morgan said.

It wasn't exactly something the maintenance staff should know, but Morgan had been around long enough to know that it was, in fact, exactly something the maintenance staff *would* know.

"You didn't hear it from me," Chari said. "But I heard from the woman in requisitions said that she heard Dr. Morunt say it would probably be for the best if the assistant didn't actually meet you until, uh, it was determined if they were competent."

Morgan was absolutely certain Dr. Morunt had not said it so diplomatically. But he was probably right.

"I'll go up and talk to him about it before I leave," Morgan said. She had plenty of time left before she needed to get back to Captain Choria. And though Morunt's message had been prerecorded, there was no reason to think he'd be away from his office, unless he was at the clinic, which was also easy to check.

“Have a good trip!” Meggon said, already pulling tools out of the carry case to finish the desk assembly now that everything was in the right spot.

“We’ll make sure nothing gets too out of hand,” Chari said. “Unless your new assistant has really good taste in music. Then we might have to renegotiate.”

Morgan laughed. She was leaving her office in the best hands she could. With a quick farewell, she left the room and headed up the hallway in the opposite direction of the maintenance hatch. Dr. Morunt’s office was in a much more conventional location than hers was, and that meant she had to go through the university corridors to get to him, not slink out through the access tunnels as she would do by her own choice.

Once upon a time, the stark white halls of the university had been welcoming to her. They were blank, but so was she, in a way: ready to learn everything she could. The problems began when her blankness was replaced, when her voice became assertive in conversations and debates, when she stopped deferring to her elders simply because they were old. She still respected them, but not in the way they wished her to. She was bounced around history and radiogrammetry and agroponics, never fitting in perfectly in any of them, even though her field of study required all three and more besides. Her office was the only place she felt welcome, and now she’d have to share it.

It was early afternoon on station time, and the halls were empty because most students were engaged in a lecture somewhere. Morgan made excellent time without having to wait for any of the lifts and quickly arrived in the æther-med department of the æther-college. She still hadn't decided entirely what she was going to say, but her annoyance had cooled enough that she'd be civil. This was the area of the university that she was the least familiar with, so she took one wrong turn before she found the hallway with Dr. Morunt's office. His door was open.

"Ah, Research-Wanderer, come in," he said, clearly having expected her. "Have a seat. Did you have lunch? I know you've had a busy day."

"I'm fine, thank you." Morgan sat in one of the form-plastic chairs across the desk from him.

"I haven't planned an expedition in a while, but I remember it can get complicated. I suppose you've had everything ready, just waiting for departmental permission?" He poured her a glass of water and leaned back in his chair.

"Yes," Morgan said. "I find it easier to be ready to go when I'm allowed to."

"I think it's economical," Morunt said. "It probably keeps you ready for surprises, at least. Speaking of surprises, I assume that's why you're here?"

Morgan ground her teeth before answering. Dr. Morunt was always nice and fair, but she wasn't entirely sure he was kind. You had to have a certain edge to rise in the medical field on Katla, especially as quickly as he had. She knew he had family on Katla and came from several generations of gene-mage doctors, the exact opposite of what Morgan had. His father had been involved in some kind of scandal a few years ago, and that never worked out well for anyone's reputation. And yet here he was, making decisions about her when he wasn't anywhere close to her department.

"Yes," Morgan said. "But in addition, I had some questions for you."

"Go ahead," Morunt said. He braced himself more than she was expecting, but she didn't let that distract her. She didn't have time to think about what he might be worried about. "I try to be transparent when I can."

It hung there for a moment between them, not quite awkward but not very comfortable either.

"Why do you care?" Morgan asked. It wasn't exactly how she meant to phrase it, but it had been a long morning.

"About your assistant?" Morunt clarified.

"No, about my work," Morgan told him. "It's not medical. And though some of my research goals are slightly applicable to your kind of æther-work, they're just as relevant to everyone else. It was never enough to get approval before."

"Ah," said Dr. Morunt. He steepled his fingers on his desk and looked at her over them. It wasn't looming, not quite, but there was no doubt about who was on which side of the desk. At least her feet reached the floor now. "Your research proposal frightens people. They don't want you to be right, so they refuse to let you try."

"Why don't they want to know?" Morgan asked. Her guess was correct, at least, even if she still felt that fear was a bad reason to avoid learning something. "I'm not an æther-worker, but if something was going to happen that burned the æther away again, I'd want to know."

"I am sure that by now, you are aware of how different you are from other people at this institution," Morunt said. There was no judgement in his tone. If anything, he sounded a little sad about it, like it would be better if there were more people like Morgan. That was unusual from someone who was theoretically supposed to be smarter than she was. "They don't want to know. It's too terrifying for them. They want things to continue as they are, the power structures in place and the powers we use to maintain them. They want everything to stay the same."

"But what if it doesn't?" Morgan countered. At least he let her argue like an equal. "The last time something catastrophic happened to the æther, the Stavenger Empire collapsed. How are they going to prepare?"

As soon as she said the words out loud, she knew the answer. No one cared. Denial was easier. Dr. Morunt looked at her, too polite to rub it in now that she'd figured out the obvious answer.

"Why aren't you afraid?" she asked after a long moment.

"Oh, I am." Dr. Morunt leaned back in his chair and rested his palms on his desk. It made him look younger.

"But you want to know." It wasn't a question.

"I do," Morunt said. "And I have also seen things in the last few months that give me hope for the future. That makes me brave enough, I suppose, even if it's only just."

"You found hope for the future on *Brannick Station*?" Morgan said.

At this, Dr. Morunt actually laughed.

"I'd forgotten the way we talk about them," he said. "But yes. I did."

For the first time that day, Morgan felt like she was looking at the full picture. She knew why Morunt supported her, even if it was reluctant.

"And if I'm only half right, I'll find at least a trace of wild oglasa while I'm out there," she said. "That's not great for academics, but it will be nice for Katla's quartermasters."

"That it will," Morunt said. "Never be afraid to take advantage of someone's stomach if it will get you closer to what you want. It does them good too."

She hadn't considered it quite like that before. For her, finding only oglasa while she was on her travels would be a failure. For the station, it would be a coup. A secure food source would further stabilize Katla's economy. There would be fewer things to worry about. It was very civic-minded, she supposed. She still wanted to prove her theory, though. And, because she was stubborn, she wanted her proposal to be approved because her theory was sound, not because she might find some fish.

"So why the assistant?" Morgan asked, finally getting down to the topic that had brought her here in the first place.

"I thought you could use someone to handle administrivia," Morunt said. "If you don't have to fill out grant applications and answer your own department emails, you'll be able to get more done. Who knows, maybe you'll even have time to teach a class and work towards tenure. Then everyone else will have to take you seriously."

Morgan would rather chew out her own liver than teach an undergraduate class, but she had to admit it was a valid point.

"So, you didn't find me a scientist," Morgan said.

"No, I got you a top-notch communicator," Morunt said. "That way you can bury yourself in your theories in peace."

"That doesn't sound half bad. I was a bit worried about what my inbox would look like when I got back," Morgan said. She swallowed like she had a rock in her throat. "Thank you for your support, as unusual as it is."

"You are most welcome, Ms. Enni," Dr. Morunt said. "As I said, I do hope you're wrong, but you know why, and you'll get at least a paper out of it either way."

Morgan stood up and took her leave. It was nearly time for the break between classes, so she walked quickly to avoid getting caught up in the crowd. She wanted to be well clear of the noise. She thought about what Dr. Morunt had said, about getting a communicator because she wasn't one herself.

Morgan had no illusions. Her own mother had given her away because she was weird. Aunt Vianne loved her and encouraged her, but there was frequently a degree of puzzlement in her aunt's face when Morgan did something. And that was her *family*. Of course, the rest of the station—well, the part of it that she dealt with, anyway—thought that she was a bit standoffish. She went to a great deal of trouble to be unapproachable. It was starting to cost her in ways she hadn't anticipated, and she was happy to pay someone to fill in the gap.

The lift took her down to the university trainway platform, and then as the trainway sped around the outside girth of Katla's middle section, Morgan looked out into the void and, for the first time, found it welcoming. She was really going out there. She was really going to find out if her theory was correct or at least do some actual fieldwork in the direction of proving it. Captain Choria was going to take her into the stars, and she was going to learn everything she could while she was there. It would be scary. It would be wonderful. There would be so much science. Morgan let excitement and hope, two things she usually avoided, take root in her chest.

It occurred to her that she probably should have asked Dr. Morunt for her assistant's name.

4.

CHORIA'S SHIP WAS CALLED the *Marquis*, and her surname was Sterling, though no one who served under her ever addressed her as such. Morgan learned both of these things at dinner her first night on board and wrote them down so she wouldn't forget them.

"Do you always take so many notes?" a crewmember asked, passing her a basket of sliced bread.

"When I come to new places, yes," Morgan told her. "You get a lot of things thrown at you very quickly, and if I write it down, I'll remember them better."

"Well, my name's Jonee." Morgan dutifully wrote it under the line that said *Choria Sterling*. "But no one will think poorly of you if it takes you a couple of days to learn everyone's names and where things are."

That would be a welcome change. The university was competitive, and anything that could be perceived as a shortcoming could be used against you. Already, Morgan could see that the crew of the *Marquis* operated differently. Choria was definitely in charge, and everyone deferred to her, but it was because she had earned her place as their leader. Everyone else fell into a pecking order determined by rank, but even that could be related back to a person's experience. Morgan tried to guess who the kitten was, the new member that Choria had mentioned, but couldn't tell. There was teasing from all corners, and no one seemed to get offended by it.

She was going to need more notes.

"Did you settle in all right?" Choria asked, swinging into a seat across the table from Morgan. "We haven't had a scientist aboard before."

"Everything is excellent, thank you." Morgan smiled and slathered butter—a donation from her—on her bread. "I will admit, one of the reasons your ship was at the top of my list was because it would be a little . . . unconventional for scientific travel."

"Oh, a romantic," said Jonee. "You'll fit right in."

No one had ever called Morgan anything besides deathly practical, at least to her face (she knew what the other Researchers, wanderers or not, whispered about her in the common room, even though she rarely went there). She laughed to hear it, a sort of surprised bubble that popped in her chest before she realized what it was. She could be a romantic on this ship if she wanted to. No one knew anything about her, except that she'd hired them to take her and all her gear out to some obscure point in space that no one had visited in centuries. She'd heard about what other students got up to on field trips, and now she was starting to understand the thrill of it.

"I hope so," Morgan said. "I probably won't get very many

other chances to travel away from Katla in my line of work, so I'd like to take advantage of my time here. If it doesn't get in anyone's way, of course."

"The bridge is always open," Choria said. "And the engineers can tell you all the other points of interest, such as they are."

"I'll take you around, if you like," Jonee volunteered. "If you don't mind getting up at the first bell, I can show you around tomorrow."

The ship's cook appeared at the table and the captain looked up, but the cook waved their hand and looked at Morgan.

"I have a question for Ms. Enni, actually," the cook said. Research-Wanderer was a title that was mostly only used on university documents, so it hadn't been on Morgan's paperwork.

"Morgan, please." Morgan had never given someone she'd just met permission to call her by her first name. She'd never wanted to. Fieldwork was a fucking drug.

"I'm Deirdre," the cook said. "I was going through the crates you added to our stores. It's wonderful, thank you. But I wanted to ask: did you think we would ration everything out or eat extravagantly for a couple of days?"

Morgan looked down the table at the crew, who were all trying very hard not to look like they were eavesdropping.

"I don't want anything to go bad," Morgan said. She paused for a moment, trying to read the room. She hadn't expected to be consulted, hadn't thought much past the gifting of the food, and she didn't want to misstep. She hadn't spent so long in academia without learning how to defer to someone else's authority without damaging anyone's ego, though, so after a breath, she continued:

"And I guess you could freeze some of it, but that would defy the purpose. I don't know that much about rationing, but I intended that food to be sort of an extra bonus. I think it makes sense to eat what we can, while we've got it."

"That is exactly what I was hoping you'd say," Deirdre told her, almost bouncing on the balls of their feet with excitement. "I haven't made ice cream in a decade, and there are strawberries and chocolate back there!"

Choria spun the tip of her fork on her plate, collecting a bouquet of noodles that went straight into her mouth.

"They'll all love you now," she said after she swallowed. "You'll be fighting them off with a stick."

Morgan shifted in her seat. Friendship freely offered was weird enough. And this didn't feel transactional, even if Choria suggested the crew's regard was in part a result of the food. It felt as though they would have liked her no matter what her gesture was, because the fact that she'd made one was enough.

"Or whatever." Choria noticed her discomfort and changed the subject. "How long do you think you'll be able to keep us in bread, Deirdre?"

"At least two weeks," they said after counting it off on their fingers. "The fresh stuff will last four or five days and after that we can toast it. And then there's plenty of flour and yeast after that. We'll run out of butter first, but I noticed some jars of jam, so we'll barely notice."

"I did bring some things that were a bit more shelf-stable," Morgan said. "I just thought it couldn't hurt to be a bit frivolous at the beginning."

"It definitely doesn't hurt!" An engineer Morgan hadn't met yet waved his spoon in the air, showing his appreciation. "We might have to name the ship after you."

"Shut up," Choria said. "We only just named it *Marquis*."

"Strawberry ice cream, Captain!"

"Paperwork, you sandwich."

In the rounds of laughter that followed, Deirdre went back to their post, and Morgan finished her remaining noodles. The metal plates and matching cutlery were plain, but it was still the most exciting meal she'd ever eaten.

"Is this your first time in space?" Jonee asked. She phrased it politely, but Morgan knew it was an important question.

"No, I came from Skúvoy to Katla when I was five years old," Morgan said. "I don't remember the trip very clearly, but I know I wasn't sick."

"There's a bit of a difference when you're in open space for a while," Jonee said. "The Well jumps you in fast. The long path can creep up on you."

Morgan hadn't considered that. To her, space had always been there, same as it was for everyone who lived on a station. The idea that space could be different depending on your vessel made sense—it would certainly be horrifying if you were, say, alone in an evac suit—but Morgan's limited experience had prevented her from considering the options. Once, the Stavengers had sent out ships with giant stockpiles of calories so that they could build the station network, linking up the empire with the quick travel of a Well to launch a ship at speed and a Net to catch them safely. Those people had spent decades on board, their great-grandchildren completing the task they'd been assigned. In the face of years, the void outside a ship's hull could only get bigger, and the insides only feel more squeezed.

"I'll keep notes." Morgan gestured to her book, and Jonee laughed. "I take a trainway on Katla every day, so I've seen space more than most people who live on the station. If I start to feel like I'm unspooling, I'll let someone know."

"Maybe you'll be like our captain," Jonee said. "Nerves of steel when she's in space. One time she—"

Jonee cut herself off abruptly, looking everywhere but in Choria's direction. Morgan wondered whether her chosen captain had some criminal activity in her history. A newly named ship. An overly friendly crew. Morgan had done the best she could to run a background check, and Choria seemed safe enough, but Morgan *was* alone out here.

"I've got very good star-sense," Choria said. "It might look reckless to my crew, but I always know where I'm going."

Morgan accepted that as the only explanation she was likely to get.

"You do interstation travel as well as long haul?" Morgan asked, hoping it was a polite question. She was trying to change the subject, but as soon as she said it, she thought it might sound like she was fishing for more information. Around them, the crew was clearing their plates from the table and heading off to wherever they needed to be next. Most of them said goodbye to her directly, and she nodded at each in turn.

"Yes, quite a bit of each, actually," Choria said. "We mostly stick to Skúvoy, Katla, and Brannick for interstation, but we'll do long-haul loops off of any of them, if it's a good job."

"I don't remember Skúvoy," Morgan said. "And I don't know anything about Brannick besides what we hear on the newsfeed."

"You can't always trust those," Choria said. "Katla Station edits their news quite a bit."

"It does seem like that sometimes," said Morgan. The station news always implied that nothing important *ever* happened on Brannick Station, and certainly not anything that was important to people living on Katla. "We don't really pay attention to Brannick."

"Your bias is showing," Choria said, a grin spreading across her face. "If you want to be truly objective, you'll have to work on that."

"I do know some things about Brannick," Morgan said, trying to recall the details of the old story she'd heard in the lift so many times without muddling them up with other snippets she'd caught over the sound of the lift's pneumatics. "One of the twins just died, and some people disappeared."

"Is that what they're saying on Katla?" Choria asked. "Even in less official circles than the station newsfeeds?"

Morgan thought about it. She wasn't usually in a position to hear speculation and rumour, but she'd been out and about around the station a lot more frequently than usual getting all her supplies together. She'd overheard a few things.

"Every story I heard in the markets got more and more outlandish," Morgan said. "I hardly know which of them might be believable. One said that the Brannick twins broke a decades-old human-trafficking ring. Someone else said that the younger twin had gotten married. *Married!* Like we were living in antiquity."

"Oh boy," said Choria, dragging her bread around her plate to sop up the last of her noodle sauce.

"You're not saying it's true?" Morgan demanded. She knew the news was edited, but surely the market rumours couldn't be more reliable.

"The younger twin did get married," Choria said. "It was the only way to break the girl he wed away from her family. Even though marriage does mean he has more rights than usual over her, he'll never take advantage."

"Because he's dead?" Morgan said.

"Well, yes," Choria said after a moment. She blinked. "But the other twin won't be cruel either. It would be hypocritical, since they used the girl to break her family's human trafficking ring."

"I knew Katla likes to ignore inconvenient details. It's why my research took so long to organize, but this level of denial is absurd," Morgan said, already reordering the Brannick section of her thoughts. "What happened to the girl? Is she the one who disappeared?"

"No." Choria's face went blank. "Pendt died too. It was like you said: she rebelled. She was successful, but they couldn't wake her up again after she expended that much energy on her magic."

"What in the world did she do that needed that much æther?" Even if this Pendt girl had been underfed by her family, she should have had access to all the calories she needed once she was legally a Brannick. Her æther-work must have been huge.

Choria looked at her for a long time, and Morgan knew she was being judged. The mess was totally clear by now. The only sounds were the hum of the *Marquis*'s engines and the faint crashes that came out of the galley as Deirdre worked.

"Both of the Brannick twins are boys, but only one of them has a Y chromosome," Choria told her. "Pendt Brannick went into the gene-lock in the stations programming, the parting gift the Stavengers left to maintain control, and changed it so that it would accept either brother, through the X chromosome."

"She freed the station?" Morgan could barely get the words out. Her dinner roiled in her stomach as a wave of surprise swept through her.

"No, it's still tied to the Brannick line," Choria said. "Just made it so that everyone can inherit."

Morgan slumped back in her chair. No wonder Katla had edited the news. If this got out, it would change everything. The Katla family was tolerated, but no one loved them. There hadn't been a truly great station operator in three generations, and patience was growing thin. As it stood, Katla citizens might jump at the chance for a regime shift, even if it only opened up control to some of the further-out cousins, shunted into make-work jobs all over the station.

And, of course, there was the other part. The part that affected Morgan directly. But Choria wouldn't know about that. She *couldn't* know about that. Morgan would never tell her, and the rest of the Enni family would keep concealing the truth as they had always done, all through the line, ever since the male half of the original family had been wiped out in the rebellion all those centuries ago, and the rest of them had been driven into hiding. It was the secret they held in common, even when a lack of gene-sense had pulled first Vianne and then Morgan away from their refuge on Skúvoy. No one in her small family would tell.

And Enragon Station would stay floating dead in space.

5.

IT TOOK THREE WEEKS to reach Morgan's destination. During that time, she had expected to stay in her assigned cabin and work, but the *Marquis* crew seemed determined to include her in every social activity they could think of—and some she was pretty sure they invented just on the spot. Jonee kept her word and showed Morgan the whole ship from bow to stern (which was really top to bottom, because of how the *Marquis* oriented itself, but that was beside the point). Morgan had a standing invitation in the medical bay, the quieter parts of the engineering decks, the crew common room, the bridge, and, most importantly, the galley.

Deirdre was an imaginative cook. All space-going cooks had to be, to some degree, but Deirdre raised it to an art form. They stretched Morgan's fresh supplies out for four days, filling every belly with breads and salads. There were even layered desserts to finish up the meals. Everything was garnished and seasoned and plated with fresh options. When the supply ran out and Deirdre turned to more traditional ship fare, Morgan was not at all disappointed. The new menu was still flavourful and varied. The crisp greens and thick cream were gone, but the protein on the *Marquis* was as good as anything Morgan could have bought on Katla. It's not like it was easy to grow a whole cow on a station either.

"Oh, well, we do our best," Deirdre replied when Morgan said as much. "Even a long-haul ship like this can store a lot of shelf-stable protein and vege-matter. I like to think it takes something special to cook as well as I do, but so far as I know, every ship can do this."

It was reassuring to think that the days of ironclad rationing on spaceships were a thing of the past, even if that meant several lurid and popular stories about desperate cannibalism were wildly out of date.

Morgan was on the bridge the morning they arrived at her coordinates. She couldn't see anything out the viewport, but she had watched Captain Choria navigate for long enough to trust the woman's ability to find a spot when she was looking for it. Finally, when there were just metres to go, the ship turned, and the viewport revealed what Morgan had come here to see.

"Whew, I admit I'm impressed," Choria said. "I suspected there'd be something here, but I had no idea it would be like this!"

"It's incredible," Morgan said.

To be completely honest, Morgan hadn't known what she would find either. Her research had told her about a stable asteroid that had been used in the Stavenger period, but for all she knew, she'd show up and find only an empty rock. The asteroid was spinning slowly, coming in and out of the light of the distant star that held it in place. The dark side was an indistinguishable black spot, but in the starlight, something else was revealed.

It was a factory complex, and it appeared to be intact. The oxygen exchange system would have stopped working long ago, of course, but the buildings and structures themselves seemed to be sealed and solid. Nothing catastrophic had happened, or at least nothing catastrophic enough to destroy the infrastructure. It might be full of desiccated bodies who had choked to death on too much nothing when the environmentals failed, but the factory systems could be made operational again now that æther-workers had returned. It was morbid, but that was history for you. No one had used the asteroid since the Stavenger Empire fell, and Morgan was going to be able to just open the door and walk inside. More or less.

"Is it safe to dock?" Morgan asked. "I have equipment if it's not, but this is way more than my best-case scenario planned for."

"Let me check out a few things," Choria said. "If it's not, we'll be able to lower you in the scoop. While we're figuring it out, you can go suit up."

"Thank you," Morgan said.

She took the lift back down to the deck with her cabin on it and went to the storage area she had been allocated. Inside were three space suits, her tool kit, and a variety of scientific equipment she would use. She had anticipated being able to take cursory scans, and the prospect of being able to set up for a few days instead was exciting.

In this moment, Morgan was particularly grateful that Dr.

Morunt had been correct about her research assistant. In the weeks since they had started working for her, Morgan had received several grants she didn't even know she could apply for. The money would be enough to nearly double her stay on the *Marquis*, and Captain Choria was more than happy to let her. They'd have to stop at a resupply station on the way back to Katla, but Morgan could afford it now. She should have fought harder for an assistant months ago.

"Hey, Morgan!" Jonee's voice rang down the corridor. "I'm going to be your pack mule for the day, if that's all right. You could get someone with more muscles, probably, but I volunteered."

"I'm happy to have you," Morgan said. "I planned all this thinking I'd be on my own, but I'm thrilled to have company."

Three weeks ago, Morgan would have bitten off her tongue before she said anything remotely close to that, but she meant it completely.

Jonee kept up a steady stream of chatter while the two of them got into their suits. Morgan had been on spacewalks before, so she was familiar with getting into the university-issued suit. Her hair was tucked into a cap so she wouldn't accidentally seal an errant strand across her face, while Jonee's was wrapped and secured the same way it was when she was working. Behind them, the *Marquis*'s suits were stored in their compartments, each one bigger than the cases Morgan's suits had been packed in. Safety drills on Katla required every resident be practiced in getting into a suit, and there were additional courses offered at the university that involved extensive time on the outside of the hull. Morgan's suits were flexible and new, each designed for her or someone who was near her size. The *Marquis* suits had to accommodate a variety of body types, which made them bulkier and accounted for the space they took to store. Jonee, who was a little bit taller, could wear one of the suits Morgan brought, but only just.

This would be the most vulnerable spacewalk Morgan had ever done, and she was a little bit nervous about it. Drills and courses could only go so far, especially when Katla always had an emergency rescue vessel deployed during exercises. Morgan would be exposed and mostly alone this time, though she didn't doubt Jonee's competence for a moment, any more than she doubted Choria's. Still, Jonee's one-sided conversation helped Morgan relax and do all her suit fastenings up on autopilot.

"Turn around," Jonee said.

Morgan felt her hands checking the back of the suit for any faults. There were none, and then Morgan returned the favour.

"This is so flexible," Jonee said. "I feel like I could do a cartwheel. Our space suits aren't nearly as nice."

"Yours are much more practical, though," Morgan said. "But I might be able to leave them when I'm done. I can't imagine I'll need one again before the next updated design comes out."

"That's very Katla of you," Jonee said. "The new design part, I mean. The generosity is much appreciated."

Morgan didn't take offense. The crew had made her aware of Katla's general largesse in several ways since that first dinner three weeks ago. The *Marquis* crew were pretty well off, and the ship itself was in top condition, but there was a sense of permanence to everything here: if it broke, they'd have to fix it. Katla wasn't like that any more, even if you weren't in a well-paying job. It was always easier to get something new. Everything was recycled, because a space station was still a space station, but it was much more common to just melt the broken thing down—or whatever—and start again.

Morgan directed Jonee in how to help load all the equipment onto their dolly, and then they went to the airlock to await final word from the captain.

"All hands, prepare for landing," came the call over the intercom.

Morgan could barely contain her excitement. "I've never landed on *anything* before," she said. "I've docked a few times, but *landing*!"

"I've only done it a few times," Jonee said. Her face closed up a bit, as it seemed to do whenever Morgan got too close to that past event that no one on the ship wanted to talk about. "It's certainly something."

"It's too bad the asteroid's not big enough for natural gravity," Morgan said. "Though, I didn't prep my equipment for that, so it might be for the best."

"One step at a time," Jonee said.

The *Marquis*'s engines flared as it began its controlled descent. Jonee would know exactly how much power this was taking, but Morgan didn't ask for details. It was enough to experience it. She could ask questions and take notes later. The ship lurched a little bit, and then there was a very loud grinding sound as the hull-metal met rock. Finally, all was still. For the first time in her life, down was not an arbitrary decision made by the station architects. Down was the rock beneath her feet.

"Come on," said Jonee, a smile on her face.

They pushed the dolly into the airlock, then sealed it behind them. Jonee engaged the descent controls, and the airlock slowly lowered itself to the ground (the ground!) below them.

"Ready?" Jonee asked.

Morgan took a deep breath, even though literally nothing would change about her breathing apparatus once the door was open.

"I'm ready," she said.

With a loud hiss, the airlock's outer door slid open. Morgan engaged her boot while Jonee did the same for her own boots and the dolly. Then, for the first time in her life, Morgan stepped onto solid ground. The shift to weightlessness made walking a challenge, even with the boots. Morgan discovered it was easier to use the dolly for leverage, since its gravity was stronger than anything that could be built into a suit. Slowly but surely, they made their way from the ship to a hatch in the factory wall.

Morgan was sharply reminded that she had no idea what they would find inside, which was a little bit creepy. It was easier to think about desiccated bodies when she was safely on board the *Marquis*. Despite her endless planning, she suddenly didn't think she was emotionally prepared for that. Her heart rate monitor notified her of an increase in pulse, and she got ahold of herself to calm it back down.

The hatch opened smoothly, and they pushed the dolly inside. Now they had a ceiling above them, which lessened the danger of being weightless. It wasn't any easier to move, but it felt safer.

"Don't relax too much," Jonee said. She could see the readout from Morgan's suit for safety reasons. "We're still in space."

"I'm aware," Morgan said. Her voice was even. She was pretty proud of that.

Without a blueprint, it was hard to tell the layout of the factory. Morgan had researched buildings from that time period, but most of them were tailored to whatever rock the Stavengers were attaching them to. The one thing that was usually true was that operations was in the centre of the complex, with the barracks below it and then the actual factory floor spread out around. Choria had got them as close to the middle as she could, and now it was up to Morgan to do the rest.

They headed along the corridor, and Morgan nearly crowed when the hall opened up to reveal what was clearly the control room. This would be a perfect base of operations.

"Do we know what they were doing here?" Jonee said. "I didn't see any signs or anything in the hallway as we came in."

"No," Morgan said. "My research just said the facility was here, not what it did. My guess would be processing, but I don't know the *what*."

"You don't come all the way out here for just anything," Jonee said. "Maybe they strip-mined a planet nearby and didn't want to haul the slag or something."

"This solar system doesn't have a planet," Morgan said. "And the asteroid isn't natural. It was parked here."

"Creepy," Jonee said. "I know the Stavengers did a bunch of weird stuff and a lot of it was bad but moving things around in space seems like too much for me."

"It's strange to think about how moving a rock this size was cheaper than moving whatever they were mining here," Morgan said. "But yes. It makes them seem superhuman, somehow. They were like us. Even their æther-workers weren't more powerful, just different."

"Do you want me to see if I can turn on the lights?" Jonee asked.

It was something Morgan hadn't planned for. She didn't work with a lot of æther-workers because the ones at the university always seemed so smug about it. The crew on the *Marquis* were different. They just did things because it was part of their job or because it was helpful. They didn't rub it in her face.

"That would be great," Morgan said. "It'll save the batteries on the lights I brought for my other stuff."

"You'll owe me one of those candies you brought when we get back," Jonee said, and Morgan nodded exaggeratedly so that her helmet would move.

Jonee looked at the panels and selected one. She put her hands down on the panel, and her brow furrowed as she concentrated on old circuits and an unfamiliar electrical system. Then, with no warning other than a satisfied inhale, the lights in the control room came up. It took a moment for Morgan's eyes to adjust and another to look around at the newly brightened surroundings. She gasped, the sound loud in her helmet.

"Well, holy shit," Jonee said, also looking around. "Maybe this was worth moving an asteroid for after all."

6.

THERE HAD BEEN A small oglasa processing facility on Katla, though it hadn't been used in centuries. Before the Stavenger Empire fell, they imported the bulk of their protein, using the homemade stuff as emergency stock. After the empire fell, well, the fish stock collapsed too, and there was no point in trying to become self-sustaining in terms of protein production. Katla was built for hydroculture, so while they grew most of the food they ate, and even raised actual livestock—primarily for milk, wool, and hides—it was easier to just build their own protein sources. There was even a colony of bees, though Morgan had never been granted clearance to view them in person. Oglasa was a part of Katla's culture and history, but not as integrally linked as it was on other stations. Morgan had only seen the processing plant when she was young, as a museum trip with school. It wasn't really interesting enough for a second viewing.

There was absolutely no doubt as to what Morgan was looking at right now.

There was a window in the control room that looked down over part of the factory floor. It must use the same circuits, because part of it lit up when Jonee activated the control room lights. Stretching out into the darkness was the unmistakable machinery that was involved in processing the best food source the galaxy had ever known, abandoned when the fish became too rare to catch on a large scale. Sealed in all this time, the equipment was pristine. If there was air, you'd probably still be able to smell the processing brine.

"This is insane," Jonee said. "You could buy a fleet with what you could salvage from here. Well, half a fleet, I guess."

"Why half?" Morgan said. "It's Choria's ship."

"Yeah, but you hired us," Jonee said. "Choria puts in the contract that we split any of the salvage. Without that, you could claim the whole thing; or we could claim it from you. This is . . . tidier."

"What the hell would I do with all this?" Morgan asked. She vaguely remembered that section of the contract, largely because she remembered thinking how unlikely it was they'd find anything worth salvaging.

"Anything you wanted?" Jonee said. "You could buy your university and kick out all the people who were dicks to you."

"That is tempting." Morgan blew out a long breath, the sound echoing inside her suit. "We're getting a bit ahead of ourselves, though. I want to take some readings before your crew comes down here and starts prying up the floor."

"Right," said Jonee. "Science now, world-shattering wealth later."

Setting up her equipment in the control room was no trouble at all. With the extra help from Jonee, Morgan quickly arranged the receiver dishes, tuned for various kinds of radiation, and the assorted hardware that would record all the data. Jonee connected everything to the power sources and gave a bit of extra juice to the batteries.

"That's perfect, thank you," Morgan said. "If you want, you can go explore a bit while I deal with the finnicky bits."

Jonee made an immediate exit to the factory floor, taking a large handlight with her, along with some tape to mark any particularly good finds. Morgan missed her almost as soon as she was gone. She always worked alone, even when she was a kid. She thought that's just how she was built, and she'd never been lonely or felt isolated. But there was something about Choria's crew that drew her in. Also, there were a lot of shadows in the control room, and Morgan had a good imagination.

The space suit didn't slow her down too much, even when it came to fine-tuning the receptors on her scanners. When everything was done to her satisfaction, she dug into her crate for one last machine. It galled her, but she knew that the university had only approved her project so that she could scan for oglasa while she was out here. She thought the scans were hopeless, but her professors were determined, and after that first failed research proposal had ended in all that vitriol and name-calling (and one vindictively re-programmed alarm in the ventilation shaft above Argir's office—not that anyone would ever be able to prove that was her), she had reluctantly made it one of her research objectives. She didn't mind doing favours for people, and helping Katla Station secure a whole food source was good too, but she hated the idea of being patronized. Her research should have been enough on its own merit. So, in addition to tracing radiation left by ancient schools of long-dead fish, she was chasing impossible live ones too.

With a grunt, she heaved the bulky machine up onto a clear table in the centre of the control room. She set it up and plugged it in, and then left it to its work. Maybe her new assistant would find her a grant that would cover any future expeditions without having to run errands for other departments.

It had only been about thirty minutes when Jonee came back to the control room. It was hard to bounce on the soles of your feet in grav-boots, but somehow, she was managing it. The roll of tape was considerably diminished.

"Find anything good?" Morgan asked.

"So much," Jonee said. "You?"

"I've only just turned everything on," Morgan said. "It'll be a while before I have enough data to work with. The radiation I was hoping to find is present, though."

"Isn't the whole thing with radiation that it's in most places?" Jonee asked.

"Yes, in very small amounts probably," Morgan said. "That's the problem. Around Katla, there's a lot of background noise. All the way out here, it's quiet. And more importantly, there's nothing *new* here. Nothing's been added on top of what was here when the Stavenger Empire fell."

"That sort of makes sense," Jonee said. "Like, you can hear the music because there's no one else singing nearby, but you can hear specific music because no one else has sung a new song here in forever?"

"Yes," Morgan said. It wasn't a perfect comparison, but it was close enough. "I am all done for now, if you wanted to head back and give Choria the good news."

"I hope Deirdre has saved some of the sugar," Jonee said. "We might need it tonight for celebrations."

Deirdre had, in fact, saved some sugar. They had also saved some chocolate and enough flour to make a cake that was just big enough for the entire crew to share. More importantly, they opened the still.

"To Morgan," Choria said, holding up a cup of alcohol that was so pure, it was illegal in most places. "I thought this would be a nice restful job for us, and it's turned out to be even better."

The crew roared and Morgan smiled until the alcohol burned the feeling off of her face.

"To science!" said Jonee, wavering unstably as she climbed up on her chair. The crew drank again, but Morgan suspected she had already reached her limit and just mimed the action before setting her cup on the table.

Jonee began to sing, some ancient song about fishing and being away from home, and the crew joined in on the chorus. Choria made her way across the mess and sat across from Morgan. The captain's cup was full again, though she seemed as steady as ever.

"Slight change of plan, Morgan," she said.

"I assumed as much," Morgan said. "How long do you think it will take you to get the best stuff out of here?"

"That's not what we're doing," Choria said. "I don't want the hassle of Katla paperwork, which I would have to deal with if I staked a claim right now."

Morgan bit her lip. She really didn't want these people to be criminals.

"It's all aboveboard, I promise," Choria said. "Well, mostly aboveboard, anyway, so you can relax."

Morgan did not relax.

"We're going to register with Brannick Station," Choria said. "I've already started the process, with your name as the co-claimant. We can hash out the details later. A ship will be arriving in a week to resupply us and take over the operations."

"Will my Katla citizenship get in the way of anything?" Morgan asked.

"No," Choria said. "Except the part where the Katla family would almost certainly take a share of your profits. The Brannicks won't do that."

"And there's less paperwork," Morgan said.

"I hate paperwork," Choria told her.

"I don't know what to do with half of a fish factory," Morgan said. "But I appreciate you taking care of my interests along with your own."

"Any time you feel like hiring me to make the find of the decade, I'll be available," Choria said. She was suddenly serious. "This is more important than you know. It will make a difference to a lot of people."

Morgan glanced around the room. Jonee was still singing, supported by the ship's pilot on one side and one of her fellow engineers on the other. They did not look like they planned to stop any time soon.

"I'm happy to help," Morgan said.

Choria raised her glass again and didn't say anything else.

There was a blinking light on the message screen in Morgan's room when she went back to her cabin. She was tired. The strain of everything was starting to catch up with her. Even without the spacewalk, it had been a busy day. She had a lot of work to do tomorrow, and every day for the rest of the week they'd be here. She didn't want to waste time on messages unless they were important. Of course, the last message she'd received had been about a substantial amount of money her assistant had successfully applied for, so maybe it wasn't such a bad idea.

She sat down at her desk and activated the screen. She did have one message from her assistant, but there were four other ones from a sender whose name she didn't recognize. It sounded familiar, though. Maybe a guest lecturer or a student she'd sat next to? But no, there was no reason for anyone like that to message her. The only person she knew who would reach out was Aunt Vianne, and this clearly wasn't her.

Then the location of origin registered. The message was from Brannick Station. It was probably some of that paperwork Choria hated so much, now that Morgan was part owner of a processing plant for a fish that had all but gone extinct centuries before. Morgan opened the message.

It was polite enough, worded professionally and subtly curious about her work, but also incredibly general. A desire to make her acquaintance, possibly even in person if it could be arranged. A mention of another research project that she might be able to help with, fully funded of course, once her current fieldwork was done. Morgan only grew more perplexed as she read the message, until she got to the closing sign-off, five letters that set off every alarm she had in her brain: *Pendt*.

Pendt. From Brannick. The gene-mage so powerful, she had changed the Stavenger gene-lock. Was alive. And wanted to talk to her.

Morgan assumed that a person didn't just fake their death and then announce it to people who found unexpected fish factories attached to random asteroids and filed a claim for them. Somehow, Pendt Brannick was alive. And somehow, she knew the secret that Morgan had carried with her all her life.

Morgan deleted the message, her mind spinning as she tried to come up with a plan. She would have Choria take her off the claim, erase any record of her on Brannick Station records. Surely, Morgan's share was worth Choria's silence. Then she could disappear into Katla once she got back. She didn't need any of this, and they didn't need her. She would do her work and go home.

7.

FIVE DAYS AND SIX deleted messages from Brannick Station later, Morgan looked at the first round of technical readouts she was willing to accept as accurate. There was always going to be some settling-in when it came to the scanners and the other technology, but she trusted her setup now and she was ready to get to the heart of the reason she'd come all the way out here.

Morgan never went to the processing facility alone. If Jonee came with her, then it was a pleasant afternoon of reasonable questions between them. Jonee was endlessly curious about Morgan's work and life on Katla, and Morgan was developing an interest in space travel. Both girls held back. Morgan didn't mention the awkward parts of her life, and Jonee often left gaps in her stories that Morgan assumed were filled by some form of less-than-legal activity. She never talked about how Choria had come by the *Marquis*, for example. Or what happened to the ship before that.

If it was another crewmember, then Morgan was left alone to her work while they explored. The electro-mages on board the *Marquis* had returned basic power to most of the facility now, though the age of the complex made them all reluctant to rely on the air there. The landing parties always wore suits, even though—so far—the seals were holding, and the oxygen exchange was working as well as the lights. Morgan's suit was flexible enough, even the gloves, to allow her to work unhindered, and she happily loaned the extras she'd brought to whoever was coming down with her, which sped up their jobs as well.

When Morgan was absorbed in her research, she rarely stopped for anything. On Katla, she'd just grab food from the vending machine in the Literature department, which was somehow the best, and the walk would count as exercise. Aunt Vianne had long since given up trying to draw her away from a project. Even as a small child, Morgan had been reluctant to leave things like colouring pages unfinished. In space, Morgan had accepted that her time would be directed and limited by her suit: she could only carry so much air, and that air could only be recycled for so long. She hadn't anticipated how eagerly she would look forward to meal breaks.

In stark contrast with her experience in life thus far, the more the crew of the *Marquis* got to know her, the more they seemed to like her. She still mixed up their names and had trouble telling them apart when they were in uniform jumpsuits, but they didn't think she did it because she was snobby. They laughed about it, of course, but in a friendly way.

"Where in the world is she going to put your name?" Jonee had crowed at dinner only two nights ago. "She's only got so much space in that brain, and she's using it for other things right now."

The crewmember Morgan had confused with another had grinned and suggested they all wear name tags until she went back to Katla. It was still teasing, but it was kind of nice.

"How come you knew it was me this afternoon and not now?" one of the electro-mages asked her once.

"Well, I knew who it was in the space suit when I went down to the facility," Morgan said. "And there was no one else. But now there's a lot of people, and they're all moving around and yelling."

The æther-worker nodded, immediately accepting her explanation, even though Morgan had barely understood it herself. She did her best to remember who was who, and she did *know* all of their names. It was just hard sometimes to remember which name went with which person when there were several options present.

Going back to her office on Katla, where she only really saw half a dozen people on a regular basis, was going to be a blessing and a curse. Today it was time for work, and that was taking up all of her focus.

"How is it looking?" Well, maybe not *all* of her focus.

Morgan glanced up as Captain Choria came into the control room. The captain had made a few trips down to the facility to check out her claim, but so far, she had left Morgan alone. They hadn't really spoken since the celebratory dinner in the mess five days ago.

"We have definitely come to the right place," Morgan said. "You know I had hoped to find pre-Stavenger-fall levels of a particular kind of solar radiation here. I thought if I was lucky and got the right calibrations, I'd be able to get accurate readings from that time period, without all the added noise, but this is way better than I had planned for."

"Do you mind telling me about it?" Choria asked. "I know academics are protective of their intellectual property, and I respect that, but I'd be happy to hear anything you're comfortable sharing."

"Usually, people tell me to stop talking because I am boring them," Morgan said. She grinned when she spoke. It didn't hurt any more, not with the crew. It was something she could laugh about these days, when she knew her listeners were genuinely interested in hearing what she had to say.

"I promise not to fall asleep in my suit," Choria said. "If only because I hate sleeping when my boots are what's holding me to the floor."

"Okay, so, as you know, the Stavenger Empire fell for three reasons," Morgan said. She wasn't using a lecturing voice, like she would if Choria was a student. It was more like a story this way, even though it was still factually sound. "First, they lost their invasion in the Maritech solar system. Without more resources to exploit and more worlds to conquer, the empire had painted itself into a corner."

"That's still a pretty big corner," Choria observed.

"They were very ambitious," Morgan agreed. "Anyway, the second reason is that the oglasa were overfished and the stock collapsed. Without a ready source of stable, calorie-rich food, the Stavengers were limited in the range they could explore and the æther-work they could do, until the stations became self-sustaining."

"And at the time, the stations weren't interested in sustaining the empire," Choria added.

"Yes, exactly," Morgan said. "The third reason is that there was some kind of disaster. No one recorded exactly what it was, and we don't have very much information about what happened because everything was in chaos, but we do know the result."

"The æther was gone," Choria finished.

"Exactly," Morgan said. "With those three things working against them, the Stavengers fell. Now we don't have to worry about the Maritech invading, which is good, because the Stavenger Hegemony would absolutely not be able to handle them, and the stations would fall immediately. We can't do anything about the oglasa that we haven't already started doing, like trying to farm them and converting areas on all the stations to food production."

"But we aren't ready for a disaster," Choria said.

"No," Morgan said. "And we don't even know what it was. I'm doing all of this because I want to see if there were warning signs last time, and if I can find them again in the present."

"You think the æther will fry again?" Choria's face was pale. Her ship didn't completely depend on the æther-workers in its crew, but everything certainly ran easier with them. Her own pinpoint star-sense was hard to replace, but other captains made do with less.

"There's no reason to think it won't," Morgan said. "That's how nature works, in cycles."

"Well, that's terrifying," Choria said. She leaned against one of the ancient tables that Morgan wasn't using.

"People keep telling me that," Morgan said. "And the university wanted to actively ignore my research to maintain their ignorance. I would rather know."

"I would too," Choria said. "But when you have large groups of people, like a station, that kind of knowledge can spiral into mass hysteria. The people in charge have to decide what's more important, panic or preparation."

"How can they prepare for something they don't understand?" Morgan asked.

"People are very stupid sometimes," Choria said.

Morgan was inclined to trust Choria's reasoning more than she trusted anyone on the advisory board. Dr. Morunt had made it sound like it was a matter of money.

"Well, I've found the radiation I'm looking for, in any case," Morgan said. "I don't know for certain if it's the correct one, of course, because I haven't traced it to the source, but it's ancient."

"How do you find the source?" Choria asked.

Morgan thought about it for a second, flexing her fingers inside her gloves.

"Ideally, I would wire my scanning devices into the *Marquis*'s control functions and have the ship scan and follow the trail at the same time," Morgan said. "The research grants I had before we got here only covered the initial part of my fieldwork, which was finding the radiation at all. I didn't think I'd ever get any further. I assumed station operations would take over, as a matter of public safety."

"Well, the bad news is that station operations is never going to do that," Choria said. Morgan felt like a naïf. "But the good news is that you've got a ship at your disposal and a captain who is feeling generous since you very kindly set her up for life by finding this asteroid."

Morgan's jaw dropped open, which was not very comfortable in a suit helmet.

"Are you serious?" Morgan said. "I mean, I already have more funding than I anticipated thanks to my assistant, but I've taken an extra week from your schedule already."

"We're flexible," Choria said. "And . . . I think this is important. I know they've probably accused you of scaremongering and being paranoid, but now that I'm out here, everything back on the stations feels a bit more vulnerable."

"I don't even know what to say," Morgan said. "I'd have to come up with another research plan. And plot outcomes. And—"

"We're not the advisory board, Morgan," Choria reminded her. "You don't need committee approval. You've got mine, and I'm the captain, so that's the only thing that matters."

"In that case, thank you," Morgan said. "It will take me a few more days to finish up here and then transfer things to the bridge."

"It's three days until our resupply ship arrives to take over here anyway," Choria reminded her. "There's no rush."

Boots or no, Morgan nearly floated through the rest of her daily systems check on her scanning devices. By the time she was in the airlock heading back to the *Marquis*, she had devised the first part of her plan. Choria was sending her the bridge equipment specs so she could figure out how to tie her own equipment in. Jonee would probably help, and that would have the added benefit of making sure the circuits were all set up properly in much less time than Morgan could do it herself.

By the time she was back in her cabin, some of the euphoria had worn off, but Morgan was no less excited about the future of her research. She quickly wrote up a message to her assistant, whose name she still didn't know. In her defence, they never signed their name to their messages, and they were communicating with each other via her own university account stream, so she couldn't be entirely blamed for not knowing their name yet. Then she checked her inbox, hoping to find the technical manuals Choria had promised to send her.

Morgan had two messages, neither of which was really a surprise. She deleted one of them, and then settled in to memorize the *Marquis* specs until Jonee inevitably came to drag her up to the mess for dinner. The dragging was mostly a formality at this point. Morgan lost track of time when she was working, but she was less and less reluctant to be pulled away.

8.

THE *CLELAND* WAS a much, much larger ship than Morgan had been expecting. Most supply ships were tenders: quick, small craft with a small crew who ferried supplies back and forth between ships and off-station outposts. The *Marquis* itself was only slightly bigger than what Morgan had imagined, so when a giant vessel arrived on the eighth day of her observations, she was a bit surprised when she saw it out the viewport.

"Well, that's a sight for sore eyes," Choria said. Her expression was almost fond, and Morgan wondered who was aboard the other ship that the captain was so eager to see.

"They did an excellent job with the—er—refit," said Axel, the first mate, shooting a sidelong glance at Morgan before he finished his sentence.

Morgan was too busy looking at the ship to pay much notice. The *Cleland* was obviously an older ship than the *Marquis*. Her lines were blocky, function over form, and the panels that weren't shiny and new were a deep hullmetal black from years of jumping through Wells. She was enormous, almost three times the *Marquis*'s size, and had probably been built for extreme long-haul transportation.

"What supplies did you buy that you need a ship that big?" Morgan asked.

"It's a bit more of a reunion, actually," Choria said. "The *Cleland* is mine. She was having some work done, so I split my crew. It was a bit tight, buying a whole ship, but obviously it was a good investment. I wouldn't be here if we were all waiting in drydock for the repairs to finish."

"And now you'll go back?" Morgan said.

"My officers and I will have a chat," Choria told her. "See what worked and what didn't, and who could be moved around or promoted."

"Do not give me the captain's chair," Axel said. "I am quite happy where I am."

"He only says that because he likes the night shift," Choria said.

"It gives me time to catch up on my reading," Axel replied.

"Anyway, we needed a ship like the *Cleland* because we aren't just transporting goods and food," Choria said. "Since Jonee managed to get the oxygen exchange running, and with the parts the *Cleland* is bringing, we're going to staff the facility."

"For what?" Morgan asked.

"At this point, would you even believe me if I said salvage?" Choria replied.

Morgan sighed and looked away from the viewport to the captain's face. Choria had been so good to her and was such a good captain. It was hard to imagine her doing anything untoward, but the evidence kept stacking up. Choria knew a lot about the Brannick rebels, and Morgan was certain she'd known Pendt was alive the whole time. Morgan didn't object to the rebellion; she just had her own list of things to do.

As resentful as she'd been towards the university for using her research to their own ends, Morgan couldn't muster up the same feelings towards Choria and the rest of the crew. They had been good to her: they gave her half of a surprise windfall when a lesser person might have just airlocked her and claimed the whole thing; and they had made her feel at home in a way she never had before.

"I'm probably better off not knowing the details," Morgan said. "It does remind me of something I've been meaning to ask, though. I was hoping you would take my name off the claim. I could be a silent partner. If the university found out I had access to this much money, they'd never fund me again."

It was a tremendously weak excuse, a polite way of saying "I don't want to be tied to whatever it is that you're doing," but Choria accepted it. Morgan would keep her real reasons to herself. It helped that the weak excuse happened to be true.

"I will change the paperwork," said Choria. "I definitely understand wanting to keep your name to yourself."

Morgan turned back to the viewport and watched while the first shuttles from the *Cleland* began their descent to the surface.

"We really should name it, you know," Axel said. "It's a hassle to say 'the processing facility' every time."

"Morgan, I think that's your call," Choria said. "You're the one who led us here, after all."

"Valon," Morgan decided almost immediately.

It was a place name from a story she'd loved when she was younger. She could remember her mother reading it to her. By the time she moved in with Aunt Vianne, she could read it for herself, and so it was her mother's voice that stuck. Sometimes, Morgan struggled to remember what her parents looked like. They probably hadn't changed too much since she left them. It was pointless imagining what her sister looked like. Babies did nothing but grow.

"Valon it is," said Choria.

Morgan eventually went back to her cabin to work because the view from the bridge was too distracting. Ships came and went from Katla all the time, but Morgan rarely saw them. Neither her apartment nor her office had a viewport. When she did have a view, Morgan always felt a little bit queasy looking at the Well, even though the actual travel did not affect her. This was simpler, though. Tiny silver lights went back and forth like the rumoured bees in the Katla garden levels, gathering supplies and dropping them off. And people, of course. For a purpose she was decidedly not thinking about.

Soon, the crew would begin to transfer back and forth between the ships as well. Morgan was not looking forward to all those new faces and names to mix up. In her most private thoughts, she was also worried that the new crew wouldn't like her or that the friends she had made would leave her alone now that the *Cleland*'s crew was reunited.

"Foolishness," she said out loud. She'd been fine before, and she'd be fine again, even if that happened and she ended up alone.

She turned her face down to her desk and began running the complicated equations she would need for the next phase of her endeavour.

It was just Deirdre and Jonee with her in the mess at dinner, and technically Deirdre was in the galley—they just kept coming out to chat. It was what Morgan had feared, and despite her best intentions, she was letting it get to her.

"Thank god it's quiet," Jonee said, stuffing her face with mashed potatoes made possible by the arrival of fresh produce.

"Really?" Morgan said. "You always seem to like it when everyone is here."

"Well, yeah," Jonee said. "But it's nice to hear my own thoughts every once in a while. The engine sounds are extra loud for me, so when you put people on top of that, it can be a whole party all the time."

"Are you staying on board, then?" Morgan asked.

"Yes," Jonee said. "Two of the team are going back, so I'll actually get a bit of a promotion out of it. And my own room. Plus, I kind of like being a science vessel. Makes me feel nice and pretentious."

"She means that's how she's going to get free drinks the next time we're at Brannick," Deirdre said. The cook brought a large bowl of chopped fruit and three little bowls for them to eat out of.

"I'm economical," Jonee said piously.

"I didn't say it was a bad idea," Deirdre said. "I might try it myself."

"I think I've been hanging out at the wrong bars," Morgan

said. Off Jonee's extremely skeptical look, she added, "Not that I do that very often, but Katla's bars seem less likely to . . . share."

"The bars near the commercial docking ports are better," Jonee said. "It's the ones on the upper levels or near main operations that overcharge for everything."

Morgan had done a lot of thinking about Katla since she left it. The crew were never unkind about it, but there had been a hundred observations about how Katla, for all its wealth and prosperity, wasn't always the best of places. Sure, the people on it were comfortable, but when it was easier to replace than it was to repair, it fostered a very specific kind of community mindset. Morgan had never seen an alternative, and she still didn't think Katla was inherently wrong, but she was starting to understand that not everyone felt the same way.

"I'll check it out when I get back." Morgan was at least fifty percent sure she actually would.

"But that's not for a while yet!" Jonee said excitedly. "Axel told me that you and the captain have worked out our course."

"As much as it can be worked out, yes," Morgan said. "To be perfectly honest, I'm not sure I'd want to try a journey like this without a star-mage like Choria."

"How hard can it be to follow a trail?" Jonee asked. This time, her mouth was full of bright yellow melon that Deirdre had somehow shaped into balls.

"It's not really a trail, in the usual sense," Morgan said. "We have the radiation, but it's very faint. And we're looking for more of the same radiation, so we kind of triangulate in a general direction. There will be a lot of adjustments as we go. And we could always follow our *own* trail back to where we started, but Choria will be able to cut a line straight to Katla, and that will save time."

Jonee nodded instead of trying to agree out loud over the melon balls. Morgan speared one with her fork and looked at it speculatively.

"I don't think I've ever seen one like this before," she mused before popping it in her mouth.

"It's from Brannick," Deirdre said. "That's where the *Cleland* was repaired. The gene-mage there has done a lot of work on their produce to make it stay ripe for longer without going off."

Without being given a name, Morgan knew that it was Pendt Brannick's work she was eating. The girl was inescapable. And apparently a goddamn saint. Morgan lost her appetite and pushed her fruit bowl over to Jonee, who happily added it to her own portion.

"I definitely ate too much of the mashed potatoes," Morgan said. They were probably from Pendt too, packed full of extra vitamins or able to leap tall buildings in a single bound or something.

The comm on the tablet Morgan had been carrying with her while she plotted their course sounded, and Morgan looked down, almost wincing. Fortunately for her sanity, it was not another to-be-deleted message from Pendt Brannick, but a note from her assistant.

"I was able to send a second set of detecting equipment with your supply ship," Morgan read. *"I thought you might like to leave one set on the facility asteroid to continue scanning. —NF."*

A set of initials was not a name, but it was more than her assistant had ever used to sign off before. Morgan was going to feel ridiculous asking their name after working together for so long, but right now, even that impending awkwardness didn't bother her. She sent a silent thanks to her assistant, who had somehow managed to read her mind and organize transport of exactly what she wanted. And it wasn't even being shipped from Katla. She was never letting them go, or revealing how talented they were, because then someone else would poach them.

She sent a quick reply commending their initiative, and then set her tablet down. Jonee had finished eating all the fruit and was making calf's eyes at Deirdre, who was steadfastly ignoring her. Morgan had never realized that a smile could be felt as surely in the belly as on the cheeks, but that was something else she'd learned on board the *Marquis*.

"I'm done being alone," Jonee announced. "Morgan, do you want to come to engineering and watch me do the pre-departure engine checks?"

The old Morgan would have said no. The old Morgan probably wouldn't even have been asked. The new Morgan felt the smile crawl up from her belly to her mouth, making her answer obvious before she started to speak.

9.

BETWEEN MORGAN'S CALCULATIONS and Choria's star-sense, the *Marquis* had no trouble following the trail Morgan's instruments detected and changing course as necessary. The only issue was that the trail didn't lead to anything before they ran out of time and had to head back to Katla. Morgan did her best to hide her disappointment. She had already achieved so much on this trip, almost ludicrously more than she had dared dream for. It just felt like a letdown after so many things had gone her way.

"If you try again, at least you'll know where to start," Choria said after she gave the order to turn around.

Morgan would have to accept it. You couldn't argue with space after a certain point. There was a hard limit, and exceeding it had dire consequences.

"I guess I just got spoiled," Morgan said. "I thought I'd finish everything in one go."

"Well, if you can sweet-talk the university into more funding, go ahead and call me," Choria said. "I've forwarded all of our maps to your assistant so you'll be able to see where we've been when you plan the next trip."

Morgan did not have high hopes of there being a next trip. Maybe if she had discovered evidence of oglasa, but without a tangible target, it seemed unlikely. The alternative was to get station operations involved, but they would probably cut her out if they did. Still, she was seriously considering going to the Katla family directly. Her connections to the station rulers were tenuous, but between that and Aunt Vianne's connections, she might be able to talk to one of the heirs.

"Thank you," said Morgan. "For everything."

It would take two weeks to return to Katla, and the *Marquis* had just enough of everything to make it without running dry. Morgan spent most of the time in her quarters, writing up her report. She called up a three-dimensional model of the map Choria had sent her, which showed the relative positions of Katla, Valon, and the point where they'd been forced to abandon their search. The route they'd taken was unpredictable, which made sense because oglasa didn't swim in a straight line, so it was impossible to project where her target might be with any precision.

When she opened up the field of observation, she noticed that the general direction of the trail led towards Enragon Station. Because of course it did. On Katla, Morgan had gone whole months without thinking about that place or her family's secret, but out here, it seemed to confront her at every turn. It was possible to travel from Katla to Enragon without using a Well, but it took several months, depending on your ship's capabilities, and with nothing at the other end to eat or breathe, it was a foolish venture. They were the only two stations within comfortable traveling distance. It would take decades to reach Brannick, for example. If Morgan wanted to follow her research, she was going to have to get closer to the one place in the universe she never wanted to go.

She made a disgruntled sound and turned off her projection screens. She'd been writing and making diagrams all day. She hadn't noticed it was time for lunch, and for some reason, Jonee hadn't come to get her. Morgan thought the schedule hadn't changed, but maybe she'd just missed hearing the crew talk about it. She had been fairly preoccupied with her work.

Her stomach grumbled, and she decided to go to the mess and see if Deirdre would take pity on her. There was no one in the corridor as she walked to the lift and went down to the galley level. That wasn't impossible, but it was unusual. Off-duty crewmembers used that corridor to get to the common room. Which had been empty, now that she thought about it. That was even more unusual.

The mess was empty too. Morgan went into the galley, but the lights were all off, and she didn't want to mess with Deirdre's things, so she headed back out to the corridor. That was when she noticed the hum.

If she hadn't spent so much time on board the *Marquis* when it was docked over Valon, she wouldn't have been able to tell, but now she knew the difference between how the ship sounded when it was moving compared with how it sounded when it was holding position. And they were holding position. In the middle of nowhere, for no reason Morgan could determine.

She went back to the galley and sat down so she could use her tablet more easily. She called up a 2-D map and then plotted out the course they had taken. It wasn't a straight line to Katla. For some reason, with rations running shorter every day, Captain Choria was taking a detour.

Following a hunch, Morgan took the lift all the way down to the cargo levels. It wasn't forbidden, exactly. Morgan could visit her allotted storage space any time. But it wasn't something she'd done before, and it felt entirely too clandestine. When she read the information board on the wall of cargo bay one, she noticed that cargo bay two had an open airlock.

There was a glass panel that was used as a window between the bays so that people working in one could see the other if they were coordinating an offload. Morgan went over to it and looked through to the second bay. Most of the off-duty crew was there, unloading an unfamiliar shuttle while Choria and Axel watched. The crates were unmarked, but everyone who carried one was very careful about it, setting each of them down gently and not stacking them too high.

Choria opened one of the crates. Morgan couldn't see the contents, but there was no mistaking the soft green glow that bathed the captain's face. They were power cells. A huge number of power cells, and they had come from Skúvoy, because that was the distinctive colour of Skúvoy manufacture.

"The captain wants to talk to you." Morgan jumped at Jonee's soft words. She hadn't heard the door open, or the other girl's step. "She asked you to wait for her in your quarters."

Morgan knew that it wasn't a request. She also knew that Jonee was going to escort her, so she didn't make it any more difficult by pointing out that they were friends, and Morgan felt a little bit betrayed.

Even if only half the crates were full of power cells, it was more than enough to run Valon. The facility had been designed to be self-sustaining, and nothing Morgan had seen indicated that any part of the system needed replacement. The power cells were for something else. And Morgan was rapidly starting to reach the point where she could no longer willfully ignore all the evidence she'd seen but deliberately not thought too much about since she'd selected the *Marquis* as her mode of transportation.

Jonee stood outside as Morgan paced her room, waiting for the captain to finish her work down below and join her. Finally, the door slid open, and Choria came in. She looked the same as always. Morgan felt angry but held herself in check as Choria took a seat. Morgan sat down on the bed.

"You cut into my research time for this," Morgan said.

"It's still my ship," Choria said softly. "In your contract, it does say that I can redirect as necessary."

"And this was 'necessary'?" Morgan asked.

"Yes," Choria said.

Morgan knew she didn't really deserve an explanation, but she still wanted one, and the shortness of Choria's answers got under her skin.

"I wouldn't have reported you," Morgan said. "I've suspected for a while that you were not exactly aboveboard, but I understand that the universe is a complicated place."

"You are the least of our worries," Choria said. "But anything you said might have led certain authorities down a trail I cannot allow. Too many people are counting on me."

The final piece fell into place. This wasn't just smuggling or some kind of thieves' organization.

"You're rebels," Morgan said. This was the point of no return.

"We tried to keep you out of it," Choria said. "But Valon was just too good an opportunity to pass up."

"I found you a stronghold," Morgan said. Then, "You put *my name* on a rebel base?"

"Of course not," Choria said. "The right people at Brannick know, but the actual claim is filed as something else."

"Great, so now I'm involved in money laundering too," Morgan said.

"I had to come up with that part of the plan pretty fast," Choria admitted. "You are excruciatingly difficult to buy, Morgan Enni. You just keep asking questions and trying to share."

"Did you have to convince your people not to shove me out an airlock?" Morgan asked.

"Of course not," Choria said. "Secrecy is one thing, and murder is something else. Besides, we really do like you. Once Valon was secured, I was supposed to try to recruit you."

Morgan put her head in her hands. Of all the times for people to decide they wanted her around, it had to be the rebellion. And just when her research was finally starting to deliver the data she was looking for.

"Look," Morgan said. "I think the rebellion has good points, but it's not how I solve problems. I can't give up everything I've worked for. I can't give that up. I'm too close to a real breakthrough, and real attention to the possibility of another disaster."

"That's what I said you would say," Choria told her. "I respect your work and I think it's important, even if you have to leave us to do it. I just wanted you to know that you have a place here if you want it."

"As what exactly?" Morgan said. Aunt Vianne aside, no one had ever wanted her without a very specific label applied.

"We would figure that out," Choria said. "There are myriad ways to rebel, once you start trying to do it."

Choria stood and opened the door. Jonee was still standing there, her face hopeful.

"It's not for me," Morgan said. "Please, just, don't tell me anything else. I won't say anything to anyone. I'll do my best to forget everything. I just want to go home."

Jonee looked disappointed. Choria clasped her on the shoulder and then walked away.

"I was in a Stavenger prison," Jonee said. Her voice was tight, and her hands clenched at her sides, but there were no sparks. "We had one chance to escape, and Choria made it happen. I'll never forget her face when we were finally on the bridge of the *Cleland* again. We could barely make the jump to safety, but Choria did it. She got us out."

Morgan stared at the floor. She'd let herself get close to Jonee, let Jonee get close to her, only for it to come to this: frustration and anger.

"We don't really have anywhere to go," Jonee said. "We keep moving and do what we can. Valon changes everything, and you gave it to us. I thought that might mean something to you, but I guess it doesn't."

"It was pure luck," Morgan said, desperate to downplay her contribution in the face of her friend's—former friend's?—disappointment. "I didn't *do* anything."

"I'm sorry that's how you feel," Jonee said. She hesitated. "It's probably best if you stay in here for the rest of the trip. It's just a few days. I'll bring you your meals."

"I have work to do anyway," Morgan said.

Jonee didn't reply, just let the door slide closed between them. Morgan couldn't put words to the emotions that crashed through her. She was angry that they'd twisted her up in this, even if they did eventually do their best to keep her name out of it. She was sad that all of her new friendships, so new and so surprising, would come to nothing. She was frustrated that the detour had cost her extra time, and maybe that lucky shot at tracking the source. Tears welled up in her eyes, and she brushed them away. Morgan had never cried in her entire life. She was not about to start now.

She bit her lip, pain giving her focus for long enough to pull herself together. Then she went over to her desk, opened up her screens, and got back to work.

Three days later, they came into Katla Station, and Morgan left the ship without a single word of goodbye.

PART TWO:

THE WITCH

TOUCH ME WITH FIRE THAT I BE CLEANSED.
TELL ME I HAVE SUNG TO YOUR APPROVAL.

TRANSFIGURATIONS 12:4
DRAGON AGE

Hegemony prisons were not the best place to have a birthday, but Choria Sterling was determined that this would be the only one she spent here. This was made slightly achievable thanks to the loose lips of the guards who patrolled her corridor. It was a lights-out period, and theoretically the prisoners were taking advantage of the time to sleep, but the guards never bothered to lower their voices. Usually that was annoying, but today it was like a very nice present.

"I can't wait until I'm done with my rotation in this godforsaken hole," one said. Choria called her Lex, after her least favourite cousin. She was everything you'd expect in a prison guard, but she wasn't overtly cruel.

"At least you get to leave," the second one replied. Choria was pretty sure this guard was an indenture, someone paying off a family debt to the Hegemony. The guard was frustrated about something and mean as a result, and indenture was an explanation. Choria called her Lex 2. She really hated that cousin.

"At least you're on this side of the bars," said Lex.

The Hegemony didn't imprison their own all the way out here. They had firing squads for that. The guards were either low-ranking volunteers in the Hegemony's army or aristocrats being punished for something. It was an interesting combination, but not so interesting that Choria wanted to stick around.

"Hopefully that rebel piece-of-shit ship holds together in the Well," said Lex.

Choria almost fell off of her narrow bunk. She'd seen the explosions. She'd been sure they destroyed the *Cleland* after stripping it, but apparently, they had towed it in. If it was here, she and her crew actually had a shot, however unlikely. The even better news was that there was a wild Well somewhere near the prison, a way to jump that the Stavengers didn't control. They'd been hauled in from the space around Katla, so Choria knew it was possible to make that journey, but she'd much rather travel fast. And she'd *much* rather travel back to Brannick. A regular prison-break attempt wouldn't be able to use the Well, which was probably why the guard here was so limited, but Choria had an ace up her sleeve.

One step at a time, she told herself, and began to formulate a plan.

The focus had to be Ned. She couldn't risk springing her whole crew at the same time. There was too much chance they'd be recaptured before they got anywhere close to wherever it was the prison was keeping the *Cleland*. They had to set a priority, and Ned was the only person who could be guaranteed a landing at Brannick Station. Even if he didn't survive after making the trip, the Net would hopefully recognize his DNA before he died and catch him, and Fisher would realize that something was up. It was cruel to imagine as a worst-case scenario, but it was still their best chance.

The next step she had to figure out was how to get Ned out of his cell and into a ship of some kind. She would also need enough time to do the calculation to make sure he hit the Well correctly. Her star-sense made it easier for her, but she did like having the computer's math to back her up. Whatever, she needed practice doing it in her head anyway.

She would start tomorrow. They were allowed half an hour of time in a common room before being shoved back into their cells. There were always two guards there, but Choria knew her crew. She would be able to communicate with them. After that, it was only a matter of time.

In the end, it took four days to set everything up. Axel was prone to seizures and volunteered to have one as a distraction. It wasn't exactly safe, but they were desperate. With the guards focused on her flailing first mate, Choria and Ned overwhelmed the single guard who remained at the door and made a run for the docking bay.

Their best-chance vessel was an old escape pod that was lying close to the bay doors. Choria sealed Ned in, hoping she wasn't sending him to his death, and began programming the sequence that would take him to the wild Well. The calculations flew from her brain, and she felt the energy being sapped from her body. She'd been saving up some of her dinner every day for this. It made a mess in her pocket, and it had tasted terrible when she finally shoveled it all down, but it was calories, and she felt better the instant the food hit her bloodstream.

With two final keystrokes, she launched Ned into space, watching until the Well sent up its rainbow flare. No alarm had gone off yet. The only sound she heard was the pounding of her own heart and the rasp of her breathing from the run down to the docking bay. She didn't waste time. Choria called up a manifest and scrolled through until she found the *Cleland*. It was on this level. She could get to it right now. But she wasn't about to leave her crew. She just had to not get recaptured.

Choria was not recaptured. For people running a prison, the Hegemony was pretty bad at it, relying on the prison's isolation to do most of the work for them. Choria tracked the guard rotations and was even able to steal food from the galley with no one the wiser. She couldn't get word to the crew directly, but she dropped one of her jumpsuit buttons into Axel's cell. He would guess that it was her—mostly because it couldn't come from anywhere else—and let the others know that they had to wait it out.

After almost two weeks of hiding and waiting, an alarm finally sounded. The comm broadcast a notice that the prison was under attack. It had to be a rebel ship, sent by Ned—or whoever recovered what was left of him. That was the only explanation. No one would just find this place by mistake and then open fire on it. Choria hit the ground running.

She caught Lex in the corridor outside Axel's cell and took

her out without even slowing down. Lex had keys, and Choria used them to free everyone in the row.

"Axel, take them down three levels," Choria ordered. "You can't miss the docking bay, and the *Cleland* is right there waiting for you."

That put some speed into everyone's steps, and Choria raced off to the other side of the lift, where the remainder of her crew was held. She opened each cell but found that Jonee's was already empty. She sent the crew on without her and tried to think of where to look. Lex 2 came around the corner just when she was starting to despair, and Choria was on her, knees on either side of her chest and a hand around her neck, before either of them really thought about it.

"Where is she?" Choria demanded.

Lex 2 made a croaking noise, and Choria loosened her grip.

"She's in depro," Lex 2 managed to say. There was a spiteful grin on her face. "Little bitch was hoarding food, so we shoved her in an even darker hole."

Choria smashed the guard's head against the floor, and she went limp under her grip. As a career spacer, Jonee wasn't claustrophobic, but deprivation was hard for other reasons.

After so many days in hiding, Choria had a pretty good idea of the prison's layout. She knew where the deprivation cells were, even though she hadn't gone near them because they creeped her out. She took the lift down two levels and ran down the dark hallway. There was only one depro cell in operation, and she opened the hatch as quickly as she could.

"Jonee, it's me," she said, not wanting to get punched in the face as Jonee desperately crawled out of the tank. "Come on, honey. It's time to go."

Usually, Jonee had a smart remark for everything, but when Choria hauled her out of the tank, she just stood there, dripping water on the floor.

"I need you to run a bit, okay?" Choria said. "Can you run with me?"

"Yeah." Jonee's voice was hoarse. She'd been screaming. Choria wanted to find Lex 2 and bash her head in. Again.

Instead, they ran for the lift and for the freedom of the *Cleland*. The ship was in bad shape, but she was able to launch. Choria broadcast the rebel frequency so their rescuers wouldn't shoot them down by accident. The other ship was taking heavy fire. Someone in the prison knew how to fight back after all.

"Captain Choria?" came a voice over the comm.

"Ned Brannick," she said. "Am I glad to hear you."

"Fisher's holding the door open," Ned said. "We're just about overrun here. Are you ready to go?"

"We are," Choria said.

"We'll give you thirty seconds to get clear," Ned said, and cut his comm.

Choria reached out for Brannick Station and felt it, sure as she knew which direction her hands were. She threw the *Cleland* into the Well with absolute certainty, knowing someone would catch her when she landed.

10.

THE TRANSPORTATION HUB ON Katla Station buzzed with activity, and Morgan could only grind her teeth. She was waiting. At the moment, she was waiting specifically for the trainway that would take her to Aunt Vianne's apartment level. But more generally speaking, it felt like she was waiting for everything else too, only she didn't know what everything else was.

She'd been back on Katla for a week, and in the time since her return, she hadn't been able to accomplish any of her goals. When she was on board the *Marquis*, everything had seemed so straightforward. She collected the data. She drew the conclusions. She planned the next steps. Now she was home with what she thought was groundbreaking information, and no one wanted to listen to her. She had almost convinced herself that that clarity was the only thing she missed about life aboard ship.

Her meeting with her advisory board upon her return had not gone well. They had been visibly disappointed with her failure to find a new source of oglasa—or anything else they deemed worthy. There was no nebula to mine, not even a puff of usable gas or crumb of ore, and no one could eat a radiation trail. They were especially put out about Valon, because Morgan had ceded her half of the ownership to Captain Choria. This meant they couldn't use it for their own ends. In their eyes, she had accomplished nothing worth further study, and it rankled every part of her soul.

"Will you at least send another team out in a few months?" Morgan asked, one last-ditch attempt to salvage everything she had accomplished. "They could take more equipment, and maybe they'll find something else besides what I did. It could be—"

"No" was the answer, firm and devastating. "It's your outpost, Ms. Enni. If you want to go back, you'll have to get there on your own."

Morgan wasn't in a hurry to return to Valon herself. It was probably for the best that the university wasn't going to send anyone. She didn't think the rebels would be too keen to allow just anyone onto their new base. But it was still frustrating. She had been so close. To validation. To success. To tenure, or whatever it was she was supposed to want. Instead, she had nothing, and she couldn't even tell funny fieldwork stories in the post-graduate pub—a place she had never once stepped foot in, anyway—because all of the stories reminded her of people she thought had been her friends.

Dr. Morunt said nothing at the committee meeting. Morgan had hoped he might argue in her favour, but he didn't even give an indication that he'd read her report. He didn't seek her out after the meeting either. For some reason, that hurt even more. She could have gone up to his office, but she was too angry and stubborn to put herself out like that again. The wounds from the *Marquis* had only barely started to scab over.

This left Morgan with nothing to do but contemplate writing up her study for publication—though she was all but guaranteed no one would publish it—or to go above their collective heads and take it right to a Katla family member. There was really only one person she could talk to about that, so when Aunt Vianne invited her over for dinner three days after her return, Morgan swallowed her pride and decided to ask for help.

Her trainway arrived, and Morgan followed the pull of the crowd on board. It wasn't a shift change, so there were plenty of available seats. The trainways were always busy, but at this time of day it wasn't an uncomfortable press. It was more of a comforting reminder that Katla was full of people who didn't know who she was or who she might be, and who she had never disappointed.

Morgan got off the trainway when it arrived on Aunt Vianne's level and walked the short distance to her apartment. She pressed the chime, and a few moments later, the door slid open.

"I'm sorry about the committee," Aunt Vianne said after a long hug and a short moment where she put her hands on Morgan's shoulders and looked into her face.

"It wasn't entirely unexpected," Morgan told her. "But it was still disappointing."

Vianne was always understanding. There were many kinds of mothers, and while Morgan had a few memories of the woman who'd given birth to her, it was Vianne she thought of in the role. She might have been a little bit distant sometimes and preoccupied with her own work, but, well, so was Morgan.

"Come and sit down," Vianne said.

Morgan followed her to the table. It was already set for two, and several covered containers were arranged between the plates. Vianne could cook, if pressed, but for special occasions, it was far more common for her to pick something up at the market. The table would keep it hot until they were ready to eat, and then for several hours, if one of them was caught up in something and forgot.

"I was a bit worried, you know," Vianne said, dishing out portions of noodles and strips of seared protein. "You did so well on the trip here when you were little, but it's hard to tell how a person is going to do in space."

"Captain Choria's ship was very comfortable," Morgan said, watching as thinly sliced bell peppers were judiciously added to her plate. "It wasn't really all that different from being on a station."

"The food was all right?" Vianne dug in and Morgan followed suit.

"Yes, the cook was wonderful," she said. "Even after we ran through all of the extra supplies I brought, they still managed to make the rations interesting."

"A good cook is probably the most important person on a ship," Vianne said. "Though the captain and chief engineer might argue on that."

"I don't think Captain Choria would," Morgan said. She knew for a fact that Choria thought *everyone* on the ship was the most important. Even her, until it had become too uncomfortable.

"Well, I'm glad you're back, anyway," Vianne said. "I had a small fear that you'd discover you liked exploring, and then you'd be gone all the time."

"I think I've done enough exploring for a while," Morgan said. "It's nice to be home."

The strangest part is that it actually was. Everything on Katla seemed more vibrant, each system more cohesive. The *Marquis* had been good, but Katla was where she belonged. Even if the university didn't take her seriously, she still had a place there, and the possibility of a future. And this is where her aunt was. If her mother or sister ever came looking for her, this was where they'd start. It was for the best that she was back.

"And independently wealthy," Vianne added.

They hadn't talked about Valon yet, except for a brief mention of it in a message. Morgan didn't know what her aunt's reaction would be.

"I think it will be a while before I have anything to show for that," Morgan told her. "I told Captain Choria I'd invest my half in hers. I trust her, but I don't think I'll be rolling in credits any time soon."

"It's nice to have a retirement plan," Vianne said. "Especially if you decide to move into a bigger apartment someday."

Vianne always said "bigger" not "better," which Morgan appreciated.

There was a lot of difference between bigger and better on Katla. It was a space station, after all. They couldn't just decide to expand, so the size of everything was well-regulated. Vianne thought Morgan deserved a place with an actual bedroom, not a convertible day/night setup. Morgan didn't have strong opinions on the matter, even now, but if she was going to put down roots, they might as well be good ones. Maybe Tasia knew of a bigger place that was available. Morgan could always ask next time she bought lunch.

They ate in silence for a few moments. The noodles were Morgan's favourite kind, thick and soft, and covered in flavourful sauce that left just the right sting on her tongue. Then Aunt Vianne set down her sticks, and all of Morgan's defenses slammed back into place.

"Did you meet someone?" Vianne asked. "In the crew, I mean. As a . . . friend?"

Morgan could evade. She had met a lot of people, and they'd all been friendly. But that wasn't what her aunt was asking.

"No," she said. "I mean, everyone was very nice to me and would answer all of my questions about how things worked, but nothing like that."

Morgan had never really been interested in sex, though she did on occasion wonder what it would be like to have someone around who could be relied upon for occasional and possibly metaphorical hugging. At first, she thought it was because she spent so much time studying, but as she read widely for her work, she discovered that was not the case. There was a whole spectrum of asexuality out there, like there was for colours, and there were words for it and everything. What a wonderful thing, to not be alone.

Aunt Vianne still worried, though. Perhaps because she was alone too and didn't seem as comfortable about it as Morgan was.

"You seem extra quiet, is all," Vianne said. "I know it's only been a few days, but I wanted to make sure you were settling back in."

"It is a bit strange to go from living in close quarters back to living on the station," Morgan allowed. "I had my own room, but

I still saw the same people every day for weeks. I guess I got used to a certain amount of . . . boisterousness, or whatever. So, if I'm quiet, it's just because it feels quiet."

It wasn't entirely a lie, which was probably why Aunt Vianne bought it immediately. "That makes sense." She nodded and picked her sticks back up.

"Thank you for asking, though," Morgan said. "If I did have a problem like that, it's nice to know I have someone to talk to."

"You grew up very quickly," Vianne said fondly. "It was a delight to watch you, and I wouldn't change anything, but sometimes I wonder if I should have also encouraged you to spend time with people your own age."

"It wouldn't have made a difference, Aunt Vianne," Morgan said. "I am who I am."

"I love you," Vianne said, a genuine smile on her face.

"Even when I re-catalogued your library while you were at work because I thought my system made more sense?" Morgan grinned.

"Well, maybe not then," Vianne said with a laugh. "But every other time."

They finished their dinner and Vianne put the plates into the cleaner while Morgan wiped down the table and pressed the button that retracted it into the wall. They retired to the large plush sofa in the other corner of Vianne's living room with steaming cups of tea and a plate of little cakes between them.

"I was thinking," said Morgan after her second cake. "What if I went straight to a Katla with my research? Do you think that would get me a better result?"

Vianne set her tea down and laced her fingers together, as she always did when presented with a particularly difficult problem.

"There are two issues with that," Vianne said. "The first is that a Katla could take it from you entirely and turn the project over to operations. You'd have no input. The second issue is finding a Katla in the first place. They don't exactly make themselves accessible."

"I am fine with them taking over the project," Morgan said. It hurt, but it was true. Almost. She could *make* it true if she had to. "If my hypothesis is correct, this is much more important than just getting me closer to tenure. This is actual danger and people losing their livelihoods. Operations probably *should* be in charge of it."

"You really believe," Vianne said.

Vianne had never questioned her studies before. Never given any indication that she thought Morgan was on a frivolous track. But there was a seriousness to the work now that could not be denied.

"I do," Morgan said, something settling in her chest. "Enough to give it away. Enough to take my name off of it."

"Well then," said Aunt Vianne, leaning back into the plush cushions, "I have no idea how you'll do it, but I definitely think it's time for you to take this to a Katla."

There were three Katlas currently attending the university, but Morgan didn't think they were worth cultivating. All of them were younger cousins, not even deemed important enough for the Hegemony to take as hostages. The senior Katlas were all in the upper levels—the ring and operations—and Morgan didn't exactly have quick access to either of those places.

She would have to find another way.

11.

MORGAN WAS ONLY kind of avoiding her office. The market was a good place to think, she told herself. Also it was almost time for lunch. There was a hum here, a bustle. People bought food and new shoes; they laughed and chatted. It was almost like the mess on the *Marquis*, but she got to be anonymous and fade into the background noise. It helped her focus. Her office was quiet. There was too much empty space for thoughts to rush into. Also, her office wasn't just *hers* any more, and for some reason, that was keeping her away.

Her assistant had done a wonderful job managing her affairs while she was gone. Whoever "NF" was, they'd gone over and above her expectations. The funding they'd secured was wonderful, and even though it hadn't been enough to extend her project for long enough to find what she was after, she still wouldn't have made it as far without them. She really should go introduce herself, but it was so much easier to communicate through messages.

"Morgan Enni, you're out in public in the middle of the day and everything!"

As soon as she heard Tasia's voice, Morgan knew that this was what she had been after. This was why she'd been sitting in the market for all this time. She wanted a person who wasn't connected to the university, who thought she was weird but talked to her anyway. Who understood hard work and shared her sense of accomplishment, even though on the surface they had little in common. And now Tasia was here, somehow finding a moment to call out to her even though it was the lunch rush and Morgan hadn't gotten into line yet.

Tasia Furlough had been in school with Morgan until they separated when it became apparent that Tasia was not meant for higher academics. Instead, Tasia had pursued practical agronomics. Now she helped her family run a successful restaurant chain that had recently expanded under her management, so they had stalls on what seemed like every level of Katla. Morgan had started eating Tasia's food because it was convenient and tasted good, and continued because Tasia was personable but didn't overshare. They hadn't been close at school—mostly because Morgan left it so quickly—but that didn't seem to matter to Tasia, as long as Morgan didn't complain about the food being too spicy. Before she left with the *Marquis*, Morgan would have said they were, at best, acquaintances. Now she realized that Tasia probably thought they were friends, even if Morgan was too standoffish to know that.

"Hey, Tasia," Morgan said when she got to the front. It wasn't too busy, and Tasia always talked to people while she worked. That was how she got a read on how many calories would suit them. "What brings you down here?"

It wasn't a question she would have asked before, but now she voiced it as naturally as her polite greeting. She knew Tasia wouldn't think on the same terms, but she felt like she had several years of friendship to make up for, and she was actually kind of pleased to do it.

"With the plebes, you mean?" Tasia laughed. She didn't react to Morgan's new behaviour except to keep talking. "I might be high ranking in the family business, but that doesn't mean I have to like the people up there in the ring. It's nicer down here, and I get to cook more instead of just nodding politely while some operations officer tells me all about their very important job."

Tasia had gene-sense, which meant her portions were always perfect, and she charged by weight, so no one felt like they were being cheated. It made her popular in the ring, but it made her practical down here, and that's why people kept coming back. Well, that and the spices she put on her fried protein.

"I guess I wouldn't want to either," Morgan said. There was a reason she liked her office. "It can get noisy down here, but at least it's a good noise."

"Agreed," Tasia said. She wiped her hands on her apron as the crowd cleared around them and took advantage of the lull to tidy up her workstation.

"How are your mothers?" Morgan asked politely. "You said something about lambs before I left, and I realize I don't know how long that takes."

"Oh, the mums are fine," Tasia said. "And it was kids, not

lambs. We have three of them so far and they're already hellions. But they're cute. Have you tried goat's milk before? I'll bring you some if you like. It's great."

Morgan hadn't been down to the livestock enclosures since she was eight and Tasia's mothers had taken their class on a trip to see what they were like. At the time the station had been near the end of their slow transition from cattle to sheep and goats, on the grounds that they shit more manageably. The replenishable textile source was a more polite upgrade, so that's what it said in all the official government documents.

"I've probably had it," Morgan said. "But not fresh. I'd love to try it."

"Awesome," Tasia said. She finished wiping everything down and laid out all of her serving tools again. "The upper level would rather import cow milk from a rancher flotilla. It makes my dads a fortune, so I don't really complain, but it's stupid and that makes my mothers snippy. Also, can you imagine what it smells like on those ships? The recyclers can only handle so much. This is why grown-protein is better."

"Do you ever see the Katlas up there?" Morgan asked. It was a long shot, but it might be worth it. "On the upper levels, I mean, not with the goats."

"Whew, I mean, I guess?" Tasia blew out a breath. "They don't stop, of course, but I see them go by sometimes. Why?"

"Oh, it's a university thing," Morgan said. "I wanted to talk to one of them about something, but I think it needs to be a central family member, not one of the satellite ones."

"Well, that just sounds like a lot of paperwork," Tasia said.

Then she clapped her hands together. "Oh, you should ask Ned! He's great at paperwork. He got me permits for three new stalls and made sure I got to the front of the line in the bacterial dairy. You know how cheese is."

"Who is Ned?" asked Morgan, who did not, in fact, know how cheese was.

"Are you kidding?" Tasia put her hands on her hips and Morgan felt like she was failing a test she hadn't known to study for. "Ned is your assistant, Morgan. He ate up here a lot, and we got to talking about stuff. He's very helpful, even though it was his time off. Ned Fincher. Or Fletcher. Something like that."

"I didn't meet him before I left." Morgan laughed ruefully. "And he only ever signed his initials. I didn't even know he was *he* until right now."

"Oh, Morgan," Tasia said. She paused. "I know you don't always want to talk, but did something happen out there? You just seem different since you got back, and you never ask about the goats."

"Nothing bad," Morgan said. First, Aunt Vianne had asked similar questions and now this. For some reason, she wanted to tell Tasia the whole truth, but she held her most personal feelings close to her chest. "The ship was nothing like anywhere else I've been. The university is competitive, even if people are professional. On the *Marquis*, it was just fun, sometimes, you know? I guess I realized what I was missing here."

"If it makes you feel any better, I like both versions of you," Tasia said. "It's nice to have someone who is reliably quiet, you know?"

"I do," Morgan said. It had never occurred to her that her silence was an endearing quality, even though it was something she valued. Most people just said she was off-putting.

"You should still talk to Ned, though." Tasia looked at her sideways. "Seeing as how now you know his name and everything."

"What does he usually get for lunch?" Morgan asked. Food was always a good way to start a conversation.

"Oh, perfect," Tasia said. She started moving, efficiently making up a to-go plate of salad greens, goat cheese, bread, and a small allotment of protein. "Tell him I said hello."

"I will," Morgan said, taking the container. "And thank you, Tasia."

"See you tomorrow!" Tasia waved, and Morgan knew she would.

A new crowd surged around the stall, and Morgan wandered off through the market towards the lifts and trainway. She hadn't solved any problems yet, but maybe Ned Fincher-or-Fletcher would have some suggestions. If nothing else, she should definitely introduce herself. Hopefully he wouldn't take offense that it had taken her so long to do so.

"What in the world did you do to my office?" Morgan demanded, instead of saying any one of a number of more socially acceptable greetings.

A third desk was now crammed into the room, leaving barely enough space to walk between what used to be her workspace and the back wall. Datapads were spread across every available surface, and several sets of dirty dishes had accumulated in a pile by the garbage disposal. She was a bit afraid what she'd smell if she breathed too deeply. Her pristine, neatly organized haven was gone.

"Oh my goodness, you're here." A boy only a bit older than she was jumped to his feet. "I'm sorry, I wasn't excepting you today, or I would have . . ."

He trailed off, gesturing to the mess around him.

"I'm Ned," he said. "And you're Morgan Enni."

"Yeah," Morgan said, too surprised to be professional. "I can't believe that someone this messy got as much done as you did while I was gone."

"It turns out that when I am left to my own devices, I'm a bit untidy," Ned said. He knocked over a stack of mugs. "I will clean this up."

"Fine," Morgan said. She remembered why she'd come down here and held out the container. "I brought you lunch."

"Oh, thank you!" Ned took a quick peek. "My favourites. Tasia's great, don't you think?"

"I do," Morgan said. She rocked back and forth on her feet. "I'm sorry, I imagined this going a bit differently, but the state of my office caught me off guard. I didn't mean to be rude. You have done a wonderful job."

Ned sat down and rummaged through a drawer until he came up with a fork. Morgan suppressed a shudder. She wondered whether she had enough good credit with the maintenance crew to get a deep-clean done.

"Anyway, I did have a favour to ask," Morgan continued.

"That's what I'm here for," Ned said around a mouthful of cheese and salad.

"Tasia reminded me that you're unusually good at paperwork," Morgan said. "Do you think you could see if it's possible to arrange a meeting with me and a high-ranking member of the Katla family?"

"Hmmmm," Ned hummed, a forkful of lunch hovering in the air between his plate and his mouth. "That might take me some time? I mean, I have an idea of how to go about it, but I'm not sure if it'll be fast."

"It doesn't have to be fast," Morgan said. "I don't have anything else going on. The university wasn't too enthusiastic about my fieldwork report, but I am hoping one of the Katlas will listen."

Ned did not ask any follow-up questions, which Morgan appreciated. It was too difficult to explain why she needed a non-academic pathway at the moment. Instead, he got to work, and Morgan began clearing her desk.

They worked in companiable silence for a while, Ned tapping away on some message and Morgan catching up on her reading. Just as Morgan was starting to feel like lunch was too long ago to keep working, Ned's desk chimed, and he gave a victorious shout.

"Got it," he said.

"That's your idea of *not* fast?" Morgan asked. "Usually, it takes me a week to make appointments."

"I have my ways," Ned said grandiosely. "It's not an in-person meeting, but Horense Katla will speak to you in about fifteen minutes."

Morgan scrambled to get her notes ready and find a presentable angle of her office to set up the video in. Ned helped by making several quick trips to the trash compactor, and then she sent him home for the day so she could have some privacy. By the time the officious Katla comm signal rang through Morgan's office, she felt nearly professional. She took a deep breath and connected the call.

"It's not that we doubt you, Ms. Enni." Horense Katla's tones were condescending in the extreme, and Morgan was having trouble keeping her cool. "My family simply will not see any reason to investigate something we can't prevent. If we attempted any preparations, as you suggest, it will only cause panic."

"Madame, I think—" Morgan tried one last time.

"I know what you think, Ms. Enni." Horense cut her off. "And you will keep your thoughts to yourself, or you will face the consequences. Katla Station has run smoothly for generations, and we will not have you take all of that away on a theoretical whim. Nor will we allow you to incite panic. My family will not have disorder. We will not allow you to cause trouble. I do not expect to hear from you again."

Before Morgan could answer, Horense disappeared, leaving a black screen behind.

"I hate ruling families," Morgan said.

"Don't say that," said a new voice from the doorway. Morgan spun around and saw an unfamiliar girl standing there. "Some of us aren't that bad."

12.

"YOU'RE NOT A KATLA." It had been a frustrating day, and Morgan was well past polite small talk.

"No," the girl said. "I'm a Brannick."

Morgan recoiled. It was infuriating. What good was ignoring someone's messages if they were arrogant enough to come track you down in person? None of the messages Morgan had deleted after reading indicated that Pendt would leave Brannick Station, even to run Morgan down.

"Look, I'm sorry to catch you at a bad time." It was no wonder why the people on Brannick Station had taken to this girl immediately. She was personable and the sincerity in her eyes was too blazing to be feigned. Morgan could feel her annoyance ebbing, but fortunately she was obstinate enough that it only made her more annoyed. "But I really do need to talk to you."

"Did it occur to you that I don't want to talk?" Morgan snapped. "Or did you think I was not replying to your messages for fun?"

Pendt Brannick took a deep breath and looked around the room. Morgan resisted the urge to fidget. She hated being caught off guard by visitors, but she really hated it when her things were untidy in front of strangers. It was still messy, though Ned had made significant headway in that regard. Hopefully it would be very clear that Morgan was right in the middle of something, even if the call she'd been on was over before she was interrupted. Morgan watched her blow the breath out through her nose.

"Can I make an appointment to come back?" Pendt asked, oozing tact. "I promise I won't take up too much of your time, and then I'll be on my way."

It was politely phrased, but Morgan had a feeling she would not see the back of Pendt Brannick until she gave her at least a little bit of what she wanted. And an appointment would be good. It would give Morgan enough time to come up with a convincing story.

"All right," Morgan said. "My assistant has gone home for the day, but my calendar is around here somewhere."

She did not actually have a calendar.

"I've made arrangements to stay on Katla for a few days," Pendt said. "So, any time you can squeeze me in is great."

At least she was politer in her manipulations than the Katlas were. Morgan opened the calendar function in her personal datastream and waited while it cycled through a few system updates. If Ned was keeping a schedule, it was somewhere else.

"All right, then," Morgan said. "It looks like I am free tomorrow morning, first thing. I usually start work at the same time the day shift starts. Is that too early for you?"

"No, I can make that work," Pendt said. "I grew up on a ship, so I'm used to adjusting to new times quickly."

Morgan entered the time and set a notification on the very slim chance that she forgot. Well, she might forget she had a calendar, but there was no erasing the dread that a ticking clock towards Pendt Brannick summoned up.

"I'll see you tomorrow, then," Morgan said.

It wasn't quite a dismissal, but Morgan certainly meant it as one. Pendt took one last look around the office, a small line forming between her eyes as she glanced at the desk Ned had been using.

"Thank you for your time," Pendt said.

The door closed behind her, and Morgan threw the datapad on the desk. Now, on top of everything else, she had to deal with whatever sedition Brannick Station was stirring up. She'd only just gotten away from Choria's rebel faction, and now another one had ensnared her. What Pendt wanted, she had no desire to give. Now she had a few hours to think about it, and to decide what she was going to say to convince the Brannicks to leave her alone for good.

Her thoughts tumbled over each other. At first, she assumed her primary aversion to the rebels was that she wanted to be left alone to do her work, and that she had been clear about it. Then she remembered Jonee's look those last few days on the *Marquis*. The electro-mage had been angry, but there was resentment as well. Morgan wondered whether she was some kind of coward, and that was her real reason for not involving herself. That would certainly be worthy of resentment.

But it wasn't just her work. The Enni name had shielded her family for generations. If Morgan wanted to go off and be a rebel, she wasn't simply risking her own safety. The chances of the Stavengers finding out her real name grew higher with every moment she spent near Pendt Brannick, and once she was exposed, her whole family would be too. Aunt Vianne would be easy to track down, living on Katla as she did, but it wouldn't take long to find her family on Skúvoy either, even with her mother's new surname.

How was she supposed to let the rebels know that she had a secret when she couldn't even reveal its existence without endangering everyone? Was her past and her safety worth more to her family than her help might be to the rebels? How could she justify lying, even by omission, to people she cared about—a lot, she was coming to realize—to protect a sister she hadn't seen in more than a decade? Who was she to decide who was more important? How was she supposed to get any answers when she couldn't ask the questions?

Morgan put her head on her desk. She almost wished she was a coward. It would be easier than to have all these unanswerable queries. She was a scientist. She needed repeatable data before she could draw conclusions. This was too much, thoughts smashing into each other and careening off into space before she could nail any of them down.

Here were two facts as she knew them: (1) she couldn't tell her family secrets to the rebels; and (2) she couldn't tell the rebel secrets to Aunt Vianne. Morgan was the pinch point, the section where communication, by necessity, stopped flowing. Right now, there was nothing she could do about it. There was no one she could trust without breaking trust with someone else.

Morgan sighed, lifted her head, and looked around her office. It was still a mess, and she was absolutely going to make Ned clean the whole thing up, no matter how much her fingers itched for work right now. When it came to her bigger problems, there was nothing she could do. As hard as it was to admit, she was stuck, and she would remain so until something else fell out of the sky and landed on her. She didn't even want to imagine what sort of thing that could be, nor the collateral damage it might cause.

For now, all she could do was continue on as she had been. Since her return from the *Marquis*, she had been trying to build a new kind of life for herself on Katla, and she was getting more comfortable with it. The idea of small talk with a stranger in real life no longer perturbed her. She genuinely wanted to spend more time with Tasia and her aunt. Even Ned was someone she was looking forward to getting to know and learning to work with. The university might be frustrating beyond all reason, but it was still familiar to her, and it was still a place she wanted to be.

As sad as her memories of the *Marquis* made her, she wasn't about to bury them all because of that. Good things had happened to her, right along with the bad ones, and she was going to use all of that experience as a proper scientist would: to draw new conclusions moving forward. It was hard and it was new and it was more than a little bit scary, but Morgan Enni wasn't the kind of person who turned away from a task when it got hard. She hadn't got through years of group work for nothing.

Morgan would hold her secrets. She would do her work. She would look for answers. And if everything went unusually well, she would make a breakthrough in something before something made a break through her.

13.

"WELL, IT DIDN'T GO quite as smoothly as I'd hoped," Pendt said to the screen in front of her.

The dim glow illuminated her face, or maybe that was just the absolute peace and contentment she always felt when she was talking to Fisher. She hadn't turned on the main lights in her rented quarters because she wanted her body to sleep. Katla ran a different schedule from Brannick, and while the part about growing up on a ship was true, she was a bit out of practice when it came to adjusting. Once upon a time, a mattress and pillow this comfortable would have kept her awake out of sheer novelty. Now she just needed her body to calm down. She propped herself up on her elbow, the screen resting against the wall.

"You knew she might be resistant," Fisher said, his voice soothing even across the void. "She did ignore all the messages you sent her."

"I thought seeing me in person might help," Pendt grumbled. "I probably shouldn't have started with a joke."

Fisher laughed, and the sound reminded her why she was out here. They were going to change everything. They just needed some help to get to the next step.

"I wish you were doing this instead," Pendt said. "You're much better at it than I am."

"It will be fine," Fisher said. "Just re-evaluate what you want to say and try again. Remember she's a scientist. Maybe you can appeal to that."

"She definitely doesn't seem interested in the politics," Pendt said.

She rolled onto her back on the narrow bed, taking the screen with her so that it hovered above her face.

"That's just because she doesn't know you yet," Fisher said. "How's Katla?"

They would never be able to come here together, not unless Pendt succeeded in breaking the gene-lock. Fisher wasn't much of an explorer, but he did like learning about new things. Pendt had a bit more freedom to travel, but she didn't like the idea of being away from him for long. Space was too big.

"Shiny," Pendt said. "I keep worrying that I am going to leave fingerprints on everything, and they'll toss me out an airlock."

"They won't do that," Fisher said. "As soon as they scan you, they'll realize you're a Brannick."

"Thanks," Pendt said dryly. "I thought Brannick had a lot going on, but compared with Katla, Brannick feels more like . . ."

She didn't say the name of the ship, but they both thought it.

"Just in terms of size and activity, obviously," Pendt said, then quickly changed tack. "There's food everywhere. They actually keep livestock, in addition to the synthesized protein. I think I ate an actual goat for dinner."

"Did it feel different?" Fisher asked.

"Not really," Pendt said. "Maybe it was a bit more stringy? That's not really the point. People on Brannick are stable. People on Katla have a surplus."

"Did you ride the trainway?" Fisher asked.

A few weeks after Pendt had changed the gene-lock, they found the original plans for Brannick in the station's computer. Brannick was supposed to be much bigger, and it was meant to have a trainway like Katla. Fisher would clearly love to build it, but it simply wasn't practical.

"Yes," Pendt said. "It goes outside at one point. I was not prepared, but it was very pretty."

"That sounds so cool," Fisher said. Pendt could imagine him doodling Brannick's external rails on the outside of the station's hull, even if nothing would ever come of them.

"Once I remembered to breathe, it was pretty neat," Pendt allowed.

"Anything else happen?" Fisher asked.

"Not really," Pendt said. "But would you talk to me for a bit? Morgan set our meeting for an ungodly hour tomorrow, and I'm way too keyed up to sleep."

"Of course, love," he said.

Pendt fell asleep about thirty minutes later, and Fisher disconnected the call.

Morgan had intended to pick up dinner on her way home and get a good night's sleep before planning her next step, but with the sudden appearance of Pendt Brannick and all of the crushing uncertainty that came with her, everything changed. She was way too hyped up to sleep. The best way to quiet her mind was to work, so she scoured through the drawer where Ned had found the fork earlier until she found a few protein bars and set to it.

She couldn't go back to Valon. She couldn't hire another ship right now. But she could replicate the experiments in her own lab. Now that she knew what she was looking for, it should be much easier to filter it out through all the background noise. Morgan began tinkering with the gear she had in her office, making a list of what was missing as she went. Ned could take care of that. Or maybe she'd do it herself and get to know more people on the station like Tasia, who might be a friend. She'd go to shops instead of requisitioning things from the university. She would talk to people. It would be great.

It would not be great, but she'd do it.

Four hours later, long past the end of the swing shift and well after her projected bedtime, the third desk in Morgan's office was covered with most of a second set of detection equipment. Morgan yawned. At least that had helped wear her out. If she was well into her work by the time Pendt arrived the next day, she'd have an excuse to cut the conversation short. Maybe she could engineer an explosion.

She yawned again. There was no point in doing anything else tonight. She was finally tired, and her brain had settled down enough to sleep. Morgan locked her office door—not for security, but so that maintenance would know she was in the middle of something—and headed to her apartment. It was quiet at this time of night, which she liked. The station still hummed, same as always, but this one was a more soothing type. This was the loneliness she used to revel in, before she knew that it was possible to have moments to herself and people she liked spending time with.

The trainway was mostly empty, and before she knew it, Morgan was standing in front of her door. Inside, she set an even earlier alarm than usual, wincing slightly when she realized how few hours away it was, and programmed her breakfast and coffee. She was asleep almost as soon as her head hit the pillow.

Whatever Pendt had been expecting Morgan's office to look like in the morning, this clearly wasn't it.

"Did you do all of this last night?" Pendt asked, gesturing to the new gear on the desk.

"Yes," Morgan said shortly. She didn't look up from the wiring she was soldering into place. "You have about fifteen minutes."

"Right," said Pendt. She took the only other available chair in the office, even though it had not been offered. "I'll make this as quick as possible, then."

Morgan said nothing, though she did set down the soldering iron and look up.

"Okay, so you know I was trying to contact you," Pendt said. "I understand now that you were on a research trip, so I totally get that I wasn't your priority. I'm glad to make my case in person, though.

"I'm not sure how much you know, so I'll give you a quick summary," Pendt continued. "I'm a gene-mage—a powerful one. I escaped off a generational space freighter at Brannick Station after I learned my family had some nasty plans for me. While there, I made a deal with the Brannick twins that involved some genetic manipulation they needed done."

That was an evasion worthy of Morgan's admiration, for sure.

"Eventually, this led to me attempting to change the gene-lock on the station, so that control was attached to the X chromosome in the Brannick line, not the Y," Pendt said. "I was successful, though I did die a little bit. But that turned out to be useful, because since I'm officially dead, my family won't come back for me."

There was a tightness to Pendt's tone that indicated she didn't entirely believe what she was saying. Morgan realized that by coming here in person, Pendt was exposing herself to being recorded or recognized. It was a risk, and she'd taken it just to talk to Morgan. With an entire station in play, that wasn't really a surprise, at least objectively. Morgan wasn't used to being important. But Pendt was taking a considerable risk and putting all of Brannick at risk by doing so. It wasn't exactly the same as Morgan's concerns about her own family, but if she *did* decide to tell Pendt the truth, at least they'd both have a lot of skin in the game.

"What I really want to do, though, is *break* the gene-lock," Pendt said. Morgan's head snapped up. "I can't do it on Brannick, because if it doesn't work, everyone will die. So, I thought I'd try it on Enragon Station. That's where you come in."

"That's where I come in?" Morgan said, as tonelessly as possible. She braced herself.

"Yes," Pendt said. "I understand from your records here that you're a top-notch researcher, and the university said that you'd always been interested in strange topics. I'm hoping to use your research as a cover. You'd still do what you're doing, but in addition you'd help me find an Enragon heir."

"You want me to *find* an Enragon heir?" Morgan asked. She held her breath.

"Obviously there aren't a lot of male ones left, or the Hegemony would have tried already," Pendt said. "But if I can find a female one, we can take the long way from Katla, and I'll change the lock from Y to X when we get there so that she can make the station safe for us."

She didn't know. Morgan worked to keep her face blank. Pendt didn't know *who* Morgan was.

"I might be able to help with that," Morgan said carefully.

Pendt smiled and was about to say something else, when the door breezed open, and Ned strolled in. He took three steps and stopped dead in his tracks. The only sound was the door closing behind him.

"Pendt!" he said, a giant smile splitting his face.

"Ned!" she replied, a smaller but no less genuine one on hers.

"What?" said Morgan.

14.

THE THREE OF THEM stared at one another, and then Morgan's temper finally gave out on her.

"How do you two know each other?" she demanded.

"Pendt is my wife," Ned said. "Except everyone thinks I'm dead."

"Technically, I'm his widow," Pendt clarified. "Though, as I said, I am also officially dead. So he's my widower?"

"None of this makes any sense," Morgan said, putting her head in her hands and slumping over her desk. "It is too early in the morning for this."

"I brought breakfast," Ned said, eyeing the work detritus on her desk. "Coffee too."

"Wait." Morgan held up a hand. "If she's your widow, that means you're a Brannick. That means you're *Ned Brannick*."

Ned had the decency to look bashful.

"Well, yes, I am," he said. "At the time, faking my death seemed like the best option, though it turns out it's very inconvenient for making travel arrangements."

"Tasia said your name was Fincher," Morgan protested. "Or Fletcher."

"The name I gave Katla Station is Ned Fisher," Ned explained. "Not the best cover, admittedly, but it was the first thing I thought of."

He set a container that smelled of eggs and cheese in front of her and passed the one he'd clearly intended to eat himself to Pendt. Then he set the coffee down. The smell almost made her forgive him.

"If you're a Brannick, why are you getting my coffee?" Morgan said. "Even dead, you'd still be a great asset to the—"

Ned winced and stole some of his own eggs back from Pendt.

"You're a spy," Morgan said flatly. "You were spying on me."

Suddenly, all of the fortunate breaks she'd had recently seemed hollow. She hadn't earned any of them. The rebellion had been behind it all along. It wasn't a coincidence Choria had been here. It wasn't any merit of hers that had made Ned's grant applications on her behalf successful. If it weren't for the rebels, the committee never would have let her go in the first place.

"We were made aware of your research," Ned said. It was vague, but probably necessary. Morgan didn't want to know. Knowing would only make her feel worse. "If you're right about the collapse, it would be devasting for the rebellion along with the Hegemony and everyone else. But if you're correct about being able to detect the disaster before it strikes, then the rebellion might be able to use it against the Stavengers."

All of the fight went out of her. It had all been a setup.

"Does it really matter who bankrolled you?" Ned asked. "I mean, the rebellion respects your work. Isn't that the same as if the university did?"

"No," Morgan said. She wanted to scream at him, but she couldn't even cry. She didn't want to be an Enragon—not really—because all she'd had to do for that was be born. The university, her academic track record and career, that was *hers*. And now it wasn't. "No, it isn't anything like the same. I have fought these people for years trying to establish credibility. I have worked so hard to disprove any doubts they had in me, and to secure my place here. And now you're telling me that the thing I wanted the most didn't come from them. It came from you."

"I'm sorry," Ned said. Morgan wasn't ready to hear it.

"Why did they send you?" Pendt asked, redirecting the conversation to give Morgan a moment.

"It's relatively low stakes, at least until Morgan gets the proof," Ned said. "Also, I know how stations work, so the filing was second nature."

"That's how you got me fifteen minutes with Horense Katla," Morgan said. Even *that* hadn't been because she was a threat to station security.

"Yeah," Ned said. "I still have access to the comm protocols, so it was easy to spoof . . ." He trailed off.

Morgan opened the box with her breakfast in it and began eating mechanically. It was Tasia's, she could tell from the first bite. The eggs were fluffy, even after spending time in a carryout container, and the cheese was salty and sharp. There was even a little packet of fruit juice included to clear her mouth when she was done. None of Tasia's stalls were on the route from where Ned lived to her office. He'd gone out of his way. It had been bad enough thinking that Choria was able to use her by chance. To learn that she had been manipulated from the beginning hurt even more. And Ned was still being *nice* to her. She thought she might actually hate him.

This was why she avoided most people. She'd tried on the *Marquis* and everything had fallen apart. When she got home, she'd let her guard down just a fraction, letting Aunt Vianne and Tasia closer than she had in years, and this was the reward. She'd been used as a pawn in a game she didn't want to play, and now Pendt Brannick wanted her to take on a more involved role.

The eggs made her feel a little better, in spite of herself.

"I'm sorry that all of this got thrown at you at the same time," Pendt said. "I didn't know Ned was here, obviously, or I would have coordinated with him."

"I don't think that's better," Ned said ruefully.

"We don't have time," Pendt reminded him. "The Stavengers haven't really retaliated yet for what happened at Brannick. Fisher worries every day that they'll use your parents to get back to the Net and attack us. The rebellion is barely holding on. And for some reason, Morgan seems to be at the centre of everything. We need her."

"Well, you haven't got me," Morgan said, pushing her chair back to stand up. Both heads turned to her immediately. "I told Choria I didn't want any part of this, and it's not my fault she didn't tell you. I thought I'd be happy here even if I only had my work, but you've taken that away too. You don't get to have me. You just don't."

Neither of them tried to stop her as she left her own office and disappeared down the corridor.

Morgan went all the way up to the ring. It took forever at this time of day, but she didn't care. Lost in the crowd, she let it pull her along until she was standing in one of the public parks that the ring boasted. There was grass there and a variety of flowers. There were even a few very carefully tended trees. None of it was practical, except that it made people feel better, and Morgan needed as much of that as she could find.

She wandered along the path, staring blankly ahead and letting the green smell work its magic on her. Æther was what made all this possible, of course, and sometimes that annoyed her. Today she didn't care. She wanted someone to make the vines grow around her and pull her into hiding forever. Instead, she found herself standing next to one of the ponds, watching brightly coloured fish swim around in circles, waiting for the next time they'd be fed.

"Morgan?"

She could not take any more familiar voices today. Too many of them had betrayed her. She turned around slowly and saw Dr. Morunt sitting on one of the benches by the pond. He had a flower in his hand, and it was opening and closing, twining new blossoms around his fingers as he used æther on it.

"I missed this place," he said deliberately, "while I was on Brannick."

And there it was. The final piece of the puzzle.

"You too?" she asked, even though she already knew the answer. "You're a r— You're one of them too?"

He set the flowers back in the dirt, re-establishing their roots in the soil before brushing his hands clean and giving her his full attention.

"Not in the way you're imagining," he said. "I did something once, while I was on Brannick, that was very selfish. It did not turn out the way I had hoped. Now I try to help people, to make up for it. I saw what you were doing as soon as I rejoined the faculty here, and I knew who would want to know about it."

"You had no right," Morgan said.

"No," Morunt said. "I didn't. Sometimes the right thing is hard and uncomfortable."

Morgan stared at the fish.

"I didn't know they'd send Ned Brannick," Morunt said. "I assume you just found out somehow."

"He told me," Morgan said.

"He's painfully honest," Morunt said. "His brother is worse."

"I really thought I was onto something," Morgan said. "That finally everyone at the university would have to respect me, not just tolerate me because I'm some gifted freak."

"I respected you," Morunt said. "And your work. I had to be a bit unorthodox about it, maybe, but I am a senior member of the faculty. Why did Ned tell you? Did you figure it out?"

"No," Morgan said. "Not directly, anyway. Pendt Brannick showed up, and everything kind of fell out all over the place."

"*Pendt Brannick* is here?" Dr. Morunt said, and Morgan knew instantly that whatever it was he had done, he had done it to her.

"Yes," Morgan said. "She wants my help for a different reason."

Silence settled between them for a time. The water frothed as the food dispenser released on a timer, sending the fish into a frenzy as they ate. It was a riot of colour and muted sounds, an ever-changing kaleidoscope of patterns that Morgan could lose herself in for a little while.

"I know it's probably the last thing you want," Morunt said, "but if Pendt needs your help, I would think very seriously about giving it to her."

"Just because she's a Brannick?" Morgan asked. She didn't even try to keep the bitterness from her voice. It hurt even more because Morgan was every bit as much station family as any of the Brannicks were, but if she wanted to have that power, she'd have to give up her anonymity and endanger her family. Ned and Pendt were both technically *dead*, and they still couldn't get away from the Stavengers and their legacy. Morgan wanted nothing to do with any of it, but no matter how hard she tried, family legacy seemed all too keen on sweeping her up one way or another.

"No," Morunt said. "Because she very rarely asks for anything, and when she does, it's because she's also willing to put herself at considerable risk. She almost killed herself to help the twins, and yes, she got something out of it too, but that's not the reason she did it."

"You don't even know what she wants me to do," Morgan said.

"I don't," Morunt said. "But I do know that if she's asking, it's because she can't do it herself and it needs to be done."

The fish stopped writhing at the surface of the water, only snapping at each other occasionally when some stray morsel of food drifted past them. Slowly, they returned to their original movements, circling the pond endlessly, waiting for the next release.

That would be Morgan. Sure, her pond was bigger, and she had more control of it than the fish did of theirs, but if things stayed the way they were now, she'd be chasing the unobtainable forever. The university would never change. The Katlas would never change. She could throw herself at them for the rest of her life, and all she'd end up with was bitter repetition and an endless cycle of defeat.

Ned had said it earlier: did it matter who believed her, as long as someone did? Was her pride worth never knowing for sure that she was right? Was the fear of change that held back both the Katlas and most of her advisory board enough to prevent her from finding the trail she *knew* was out there somewhere, waiting for her to find it?

She knew, now, who she was working with. And she knew at least one thing they did not. She still heard no call to fight a rebellion, and certainly she had no desire at all to reveal herself as the very heir Pendt was searching for, but now, knowing what she did, maybe she could work with them.

She'd find the trail again. Her equipment was almost set up in her lab. It wouldn't take her very long to get back to work, tracing the path of æther burning out in the stars. She wouldn't work *for* the rebellion, but she could let them fund her. No one else cared about her findings, so she would tell them about it, and they would do what they could to prepare. It wasn't what she wanted, but maybe she could make it work. She'd just lay down some ground rules this time. Ned could even stay if he wanted to. It would be nice to have a direct line to her patrons, and he was, after all, very good at being a research assistant.

And as for Pendt, well, she'd see what came of waiting. It would cost her nothing to look for her own distant cousins. She'd keep the Brannicks away from her own family, at least. There had to be *some* other Enragons out there, some branch that couldn't be traced to her mother, aunt, and sister.

"I'll think about it," said Morgan, even though she wasn't sure Dr. Morunt was listening any more.

Around her feet, the flowers bloomed.

15.

MORGAN WAS ACTUALLY HAVING a pretty good day. She had felt refreshed when her alarm went off, even though it was absurdly early again. She thought the fruit she had for breakfast was unusually flavourful. Her coffee was the perfect temperature the whole time she was drinking it. Every shop she went into after the market opened had what she was looking for at a price she could afford.

Things didn't start to go pear-shaped until after lunch.

Morgan spent the morning in her office, happily tinkering away with the remaining pieces of equipment she'd acquired to complete her setup. Ned did not appear, and neither did Pendt. It was almost like it was before all of these shenanigans had started, except for the extra desks cluttering up the floorspace. Morgan put it out of her mind. They would come back or they wouldn't, and she would make her decision then.

Once all of her gear was assembled, tuned, and retuned,

Morgan connected the final circuits and the whole apparatus hummed to life. It wasn't quite as good as the machines she'd left behind on Valon, but she hoped that the knowledge she had gained since then would fill in the gaps. She tried to be patient as the data began to stream across her screen. She'd need to let it collect a bit before she could start filtering through it.

She was able to get rid of the main communication channels immediately, though. She hadn't built anything to detect them specifically, but they were powerful enough, especially the ones that originated on Katla itself, that she picked up overflow. She made adjustments and watched with some satisfaction as the background chatter disappeared. Next, she would try to filter out machine noise, and then eventually radiation from sources she could identify. It would take time, but that's what science was: time and repetition and observation.

Her stomach rumbled, and she realized that it was well past the time when someone who ate breakfast so early should be having lunch. She didn't want to leave her lab. Logically, she knew that her presence wasn't actually doing anything at the moment. By the time she got back, there would be enough data to work with again. But she was reluctant to look away now that she was calm and focused and working again.

The old Morgan, the one who hadn't been on the *Marquis* and wasn't trying to be more personable, would have stayed and just gone hungry for the afternoon. The new Morgan, raw around the edges from yesterday, wanted something hot and comforting.

It took almost twenty minutes to get to the closest of Tasia's stalls. Morgan only half expected her to be there. She had a whole business to run, and there were plenty of other things that might require her attention. But her good luck held on just a little bit longer. Tasia was behind the cart, cheery apron around her waist, handing out perfect portions to customers.

By the time Morgan got to the front of the line, she was the only person waiting for food. Tasia started making up her plate before Morgan even ordered anything.

"So, it went poorly with Ned, then," Tasia said with no preamble. Morgan watched as she added extra protein and a healthy squeeze of sweet sauce before rolling up the donair and putting it in a container.

"It kind of did," Morgan said. "What did he tell you?"

Morgan wasn't exactly sure Ned would want Tasia to know *everything* they had talked about.

"He didn't say anything," Tasia said. "He just looked like someone had kicked a kitten and made him watch."

Morgan made a pshaw. "It wasn't that bad," she said. "And he was the one keeping something important from me."

Tasia made a face.

"University politics?" she asked sympathetically. She had guild competition and union busters to deal with, so she could kind of understand.

"Something like that," Morgan said. "Anyway, I have calmed down enough to talk to him again, but I am not in a hurry to do so."

Tasia added a third wrap to the container and then tucked a packet with white liquid in it beside them.

"Goat's milk," Tasia said. "My mother got it this morning."

"Do I really need three donairs?" Morgan asked. She felt hungry, but not any more than most days when she had an early breakfast.

"Physically, no," Tasia said. "You need, like, one and a half. But emotionally you definitely need three."

Morgan's stomach rumbled again at the thought, and Tasia grinned.

"I'm trying not to be completely dependent on my gene-sense," she said.

"Why?" Morgan asked sharply.

"Just because I wanted to." Tasia seemed taken aback by Morgan's sudden intensity. "I mean, I use what I have, but there's no reason not to expand, right?"

"Yes," Morgan said, quieting her thoughts. "Of course. That makes perfect sense."

"Are you eating up here or do you need a hot pack?" Tasia asked, breezing on like nothing had happened.

"I think I'll eat up here," Morgan said. "If I go back down already, I'll just stare at the screens and wish they'd go faster."

"Here you go, then!" Tasia said. "Say hello to Ned for me, unless you need me to kill him or something."

"I'll let you know how it goes," Morgan said, taking the container and picking up a few napkins.

She wandered off into the market, aiming for one of the common areas where people could sit and eat or talk. When she got close to it, she saw that it was jam-packed with other people who, like her, were on their lunch break. Morgan wanted some place a little bit more quiet.

In the end, she found a seat on the trainway and just rode it around the station while she ate. There was a crowd here, but they were transient, and their conversations didn't linger after they got off on their platforms. It took her one full circuit to eat two of the donairs and decide that, emotions or not, the third one might just kill her. She'd save it for later. The goat's milk was a bit of a surprise on the first mouthful, but once she got used to it, she found it pretty good.

Feeling better, Morgan made her way back down to her office.

The first sign that something was wrong came two hours later, when she couldn't crack the background radiation. She knew what she was looking for. It should be easy to find it again. The whole reason she'd left Katla to run her experiments in the first place was because she needed to be somewhere quiet, but surely now that she had done it once, she could replicate the result. And yet she couldn't.

The second sign was a few frustrating hours later, when she got a brief message from Dr. Morunt. It only said "advisory board incoming," so Morgan didn't know exactly what she was preparing for when Dr. Argir let himself into the office without knocking.

"Ah, Ms. Enni, you're here," he said, looking around with a disdainful expression on his face. "I was hoping I wouldn't have to track you down."

"Did you need something, sir?" Morgan asked.

She was seething at the invasion of her privacy, but she held on to her manners anyway.

"Yes, I do actually," Argir said. "We have decided to revoke your fellowship."

"What?" Morgan said.

"You are no longer a Research-Wanderer," Argir said. "You may continue to work privately, of course, but your laboratory will be repurposed."

"Why?" Morgan said. "The whole reason I got this space was that no one wanted it."

"Oh, no one wants it," he said. "We just don't want you in it."

Morgan was speechless. Her mind raced, trying to figure out if it was too late in the semester to secure a good spot in the shared post-graduate lab. She certainly couldn't fit everything in her apartment.

"This is why you don't talk to Katlas, Morgan," Argir said. He'd moved past disdainful and straight into scathing. "You aimed too high, and now you'll fall."

"Did you even try to argue with them?" Morgan asked. She let herself sound as bitter as she felt. She didn't care if he thought she was petulant.

"Well, yes," Argir said. "I don't want them thinking they can dictate university policy. And if you'd found anything that was actually useful, I might have made a stronger attempt. As it is, I will admit that I didn't argue very hard."

Morgan said nothing. There was nothing to say.

"You have until tomorrow, Ms. Enni," Argir said. He was already halfway out the door. "Anything still here in twenty-four hours will be destroyed. Do not ask your friends in maintenance for help. It will end badly for their careers too."

The silence when the door closed behind him was deafening. It wasn't even a proper silence, Morgan thought, because she knew that normal sounds were continuing around her. All she could hear was a mad rushing inside her ears, blotting everything out. She wanted to scream, but to be perfectly honest, she wasn't entirely sure she knew how.

"Morgan?" a voice cut through. She hadn't heard the door open, but her focus slowly came back to her surroundings. It was Ned. Of course it was Ned.

"What do you want?" Morgan asked in a flat voice.

"Pendt wanted to ask you to come out for dinner with us," Ned said. "To talk and maybe apologize?"

Morgan didn't respond.

"Are you all right?" he asked.

One of Ned's gifts, she was starting to realize, was the ability to ask a personal question and then look at the person he was talking to like he cared deeply about the answer. He would accept things like "I'm fine" if necessary, but he was always braced for the full measure of the storm because he knew he could weather it like a rock.

Morgan burst into tears and told him everything. She was furious with herself for crying, but Ned didn't interrupt her when she was sobbing too hard to speak, and he didn't offer platitudes or hollow advice. He let her get it all out, listening to every single word, and then he put his arms around her until her shoulders stopped shaking and she pulled away.

"You might not have noticed," he said calmly, "but I fix things. It's what I'm good at. Do you want me to fix this?"

Morgan considered the offer.

"No," she said after a moment. "Take me to Pendt."

The rooms Pendt was renting were spacious enough that all three of them could sit around the table without being uncomfortable. Ned had messaged her before they arrived, so she already had food delivered for them. The apartment didn't have plates, so they ate straight out of the containers, picking up noodles with their sticks and then racing towards their mouths before they slipped away. It was almost fun.

"What are your terms?" Pendt said, packing away more food than Morgan had ever seen anyone eat in one mouthful.

"I get to continue my research," Morgan said. "You'll get us passage with enough space for all of my equipment and whatever else we need. And in return, I'll help you."

"Passage where?" Pendt said. "Valon or Brannick?"

"Brannick would have the same problem Katla does," Morgan said, "though maybe to a lesser degree. Valon is a possibility. Or at least a staging area. But the real place we need to go is Enragon, as soon as we possibly can."

"It'll take weeks," Ned said. "And even when we get there, it's a dead station. I know you need quiet, but I feel like that's too quiet."

"It won't be quiet for long," Morgan said. She took a deep breath and thought of fish swimming in endless circles and flowers growing as wild as anything could in the cold void of space. "I don't need to help you find an Enragon heir. I *am* an Enragon heir."

It took a moment for it to sink in, and then Morgan could see the exact second when Pendt's brain leapt into overdrive.

"Well then, Morgan Enragon," she said. Beside her, Ned grinned. "We've got work to do."

16.

IT TOOK TWO DAYS to get everything planned out, but that was mostly because they spent the first evening and a good part of the night clearing out Morgan's office. What was clearly designed to be an impossible task for one person became quite doable for three, particularly when two of them had nothing to fear from the Katla family retribution. There were a few things Morgan probably should have left behind, but Ned encouraged her to take pretty much everything that wasn't nailed down. She left the three desks, though. They were heavy.

Pendt's apartment was now crammed full to bursting. Ned was renting some shoebox in the same section where Morgan lived, so he couldn't take anything, and Morgan needed all of her floorspace to pack. Pendt didn't mind.

"I grew up in a tiny room and had basically nothing," she told Morgan as they stacked boxes. "I like things. Things are fun."

By the time they were done moving, it was so late that they

just collapsed, Pendt and Morgan in the bed and Ned on the sofa. Morgan wasn't used to sharing a room, let alone a bed, so when she woke up early, she had trouble getting comfortable again. Eventually she gave up and wandered into the living room. She kept as quiet as she could so as not to disturb Ned, but he was already awake and sitting up on the sofa with a datapad in his hands.

"Hey, come sit," he said, making room for her. "The coffee is set to start in about five minutes."

Morgan sat down. She had slept in her clothes before, usually at her desk, but for some reason she felt weird being all rumpled next to Ned.

"What are you reading?" she asked, mostly for something to say.

"An adventure novel," Ned told her. "It's fun."

"I try to read for fun sometimes," Morgan said. "But I read so much for work that it's hard to relax into it."

"I think that makes sense." Ned leaned back into the cushions and Morgan tucked her feet up under her. "What do you do instead?"

"Honestly, nothing," Morgan admitted. "I've been at the university since I was twelve, and all I ever wanted was to be truly accepted there. I worked, and that was about it."

"Well," said Ned. "We can try some things, if you want. And see if there's something you like."

"You really do just fix things," Morgan said. "It's like you can't stop."

"In my defense, I used to be in charge of an entire station," Ned reminded her. "Fixing things was very useful then."

"And now?" Morgan said. "You just get permits for random vendors?"

"Tasia's food is very good," Ned said. "But yeah, I guess so. I thought joining the rebellion would mean making real change, and we are, on some level, but it's very big and hard to conceptualize. Sometimes I like making something small happen for someone who really needs it."

"I think that's me too," Morgan said after a moment. "Or at least, who I would like to be. When Pendt came here, I was so scared that she was going to drag me to the front of something I didn't want to be part of, much less lead. I think that's why I reacted so poorly. But if I can help from behind the scenes, on a team without being too visible, then I think I'll feel more comfortable about everything."

"It takes a lot of different kinds of people to make something like a rebellion happen," Ned said. "I didn't understand that at first, but now that I do, I think I am much better at it. I leave the big dreams to people like Pendt and focus on the little tasks."

When Ned mentioned Pendt, his voice was full of affection. Morgan had watched the two of them working in close quarters all evening, and she noticed that they seemed to be intensely fond of each other. Yet there was always a respectful space between them.

"So," she said, "you actually *married* Pendt? Legally? No one on Katla has done that for decades."

"It was her idea," Ned said. "I was very uncomfortable about it, but her reasoning was too good. She needed the full protection of Brannick Station, and I needed, well, I needed something she was willing to give."

"Is that why you always give her so much personal space?" Morgan asked.

"Partly," Ned said. "The real reason, though, is that she's in love with my brother, and since I'm technically dead, they can be together without anyone questioning it."

"And you're okay with that?" Morgan asked. It sounded extremely complicated.

"Do you have any siblings?" Ned returned.

"A sister," Morgan said. "But we haven't seen each other since we were five and three. I wouldn't recognise her now, I'm sure."

"Oh," Ned said. That sort of distance between siblings was clearly difficult for him to imagine. "Well, I would do anything for Fisher, especially if it made him happy. Pendt and I probably would have had a perfectly serviceable relationship, a lot like the one we've ended up with, actually. But what she and Fisher have is something else."

"Like an adventure book," Morgan said. She didn't imagine romance very much, but she knew she would be on the quiet side of it.

"Like an adventure book," Ned confirmed.

Morgan leaned back and discovered that her head was resting where Ned's arm stretched out along the back of the sofa cushions. She didn't move and neither did he. A chime sounded, followed by the telltale burble of coffee percolating. Ned stayed where he was for a few more minutes, but eventually he got up to pour cups and set out breakfast. Morgan told herself that she felt colder after he stood up because that's how thermodynamics worked, and not for any other reason.

Pendt clearly loved the Katla markets. Shopping took almost twice as long as usual because she had to stop and look at almost everything. Before, when she'd said that she liked things, Morgan had thought she was being facetious, but it was clearly true. Pendt would talk to literally everyone with goods for sale if they let her.

Morgan was focused on the non-food items they would require. Ned and Pendt both needed space suits, which were easy enough to get. They made their way through the market levels, accumulating more and more of what they were going to need. Eventually, Ned peeled off to run an errand of his own. Pendt had arrived on Katla by passenger transport, so they were going to need a ship. This left Pendt and Morgan with the final shopping list: the food.

"This is a lot of food," Morgan said.

There weren't actually a lot of items on the list, but the number of calories they needed to pack was very high.

"I know," Pendt said. "I overate for almost two weeks straight when I changed the Brannick lock."

Morgan's stomach curdled, and it must have shown in her face, but Pendt nodded grimly.

"It was not a lot of fun," she said. "Still, Katla has access to more concentrated forms of calories. If I can get them through an IV, that would be even better."

"You didn't put a doctor on the list," Morgan said.

"The ship Ned finds will have a doctor," Pendt said confidently. "We'll just use whoever that is."

"I think it might be a better idea to bring someone for you

especially," Morgan said. "What if something happens while you're under? The Hegemony is going to realize what we're trying at some point."

"Who would we even ask?" Pendt said.

"Let me send a couple of messages," Morgan said. "I know you don't have a lot of reasons to trust me completely yet, but I think this is the best idea."

"Fisher agrees with you, about the doctor, I mean. We just didn't have anyone on Brannick to spare," Pendt admitted. "But he tends to be overprotective of us."

"You and Ned are his family," Morgan said.

Pendt opened her mouth and then shut it, clearly deciding that whatever she wanted to say to that could wait. Morgan sent off the message and then returned to her lists.

"You know, Tasia's dads are importers," Morgan said thoughtfully. It was slightly more complicated than that, given the size and complexity of Tasia's family and the reach of their business, but this was the easiest way to explain it. "They're probably the best people to talk to if you want to buy in bulk. Tasia should be able to point you in the right direction, at least."

Pendt nodded, and the two girls set off through the crush of shoppers to find out which stall Tasia was at today. It turned out she was down in the lower habitats, so Morgan took Pendt on the trainway and they ended up pretty close to Morgan's apartment, just outside one of the gas-processing plants. The lunch rush hadn't started yet, so Tasia had some time to talk to them.

"This is a lot of calories," Tasia said. She chewed her lip as she read the list.

"It's for my next experiment," Morgan told her, which was close enough to the truth that she didn't feel too bad about it. "My associate here is an æther-worker, and she's agreed to be my test subject while I study the effect of caloric intake and æther."

"Since when are you interested in æther?" Tasia asked.

"I'm trying to broaden my horizons," said Morgan, which was also true.

"Well, my dads can definitely help you," Tasia said. "They've just secured exclusive contracts on a whole bunch of the new medical-grade stuff. Operations wants it to go to the electromages, but they might be able to set some aside for you."

"That would be great," said Pendt.

"Don't let Morgan work too hard. I only just got used to her remembering to come up for air." Tasia winked. She had copied the request and sent it to her dads. "Do you want lunch while you're here?"

"Yes!" said Pendt immediately. She calmed herself down a bit. "I would like to try a donair, please."

Tasia focused on her for a moment, assessing her caloric needs. Then she blinked rapidly and blew out an explosive breath.

"Shit," she said. "I've never met anyone who could— Who *are* you?"

"It's not important," Pendt said. Tasia narrowed her eyes, but let it pass.

"Thanks, Tasia," Morgan said. "For everything."

"You and I are going to have a talk someday, Morgan Enni," Tasia said. She turned and began to assemble their meals.

"I promise we will," Morgan said, and realized that she was actually kind of looking forward to it.

With a container of donairs and a completed shopping list, they headed back to Pendt's apartment. Morgan hoped that her message from earlier had come through, and that he would be waiting for them there as she'd directed. It was a long shot, but she really did think Pendt deserved her own doctor if they were going to do this, even if it was going to be a bit . . . fraught.

"What are *you* doing here?" Pendt demanded as soon as they rounded the corner and saw who was indeed waiting for them at her door. "Wait, never mind. We did exile you to Katla. What are you doing *here*?"

"This is our doctor," Morgan said. "He's the only one I trust, and he already knows what you're doing."

The door hissed as Ned opened it from the inside, probably to see what all the fuss was about. His kind eyes hardened.

"Come in," he said, the unwelcome clear. "We can't talk about this in the corridor."

Technically, four people could fit around Pendt's table as easily as three, but this time it was deeply uncomfortable. Pendt did not offer Morunt anything to eat.

"I'm here because Morgan requested me," Dr. Morunt said. He was clearly not offended or surprised by the frostiness of Pendt's and Ned's reactions.

"I knew he'd done something you didn't like," Morgan said apologetically. "But I didn't realize it was this extreme."

"'Didn't like' is an understatement," Ned growled.

"Why would we ever trust you?" Pendt asked.

"Because I made sure Morgan went on her original expedition with someone you *do* trust," Morunt said. "Because I pulled the strings that were necessary to get Ned hired."

"That's not enough," Ned said.

"Then because I believe in what you're doing," Morunt said softly. "Because I was there when you tried it the first time. And because you know the Hegemony has nothing they can use to break me again."

It hung there for a hard, painful moment.

"We also don't have to pay him," Morgan pointed out.

Ned looked at Pendt, signalling that it was her decision. It would be her body, after all, and her æther-work that Morunt would be protecting.

"All right," Pendt said. "I will shove you out an airlock myself if I feel like it."

"I don't doubt it," Morunt said.

"We leave in sixteen hours," Ned said. "Get out."

Dr. Morunt left without a word, and the silence that followed his departure had a crushing weight.

"I'm sorry," Morgan said. "I didn't know all of the details. I thought he was the best person, and I didn't even know he was with you the first time."

"You're right, though," Pendt said. "He's the best option. It's just difficult. It's not like we're not asking a lot of you too."

"You get to tell Fisher," Ned said.

Pendt groaned.

"Sixteen hours?" Morgan asked, rising to leave. She had a few last-minute arrangements to make.

"Sixteen hours, and you'll recognize the ship," Ned said.

Morgan froze.

"It's the *Marquis*."

17.

AFTER SURPRISING THEM WITH Dr. Morunt, Morgan didn't think she had much ground to stand on, so she didn't complain about boarding the *Marquis* again. If Captain Choria would have her, she would apologize. She still felt awkward as hell, though. Her last evening on Katla Station was not made any more comfortable, because she also had to have a talk with her aunt.

Aunt Vianne had heard about what happened to Morgan's lab by now, of course. The university was massive, but its gossip networks were efficient. Both of them knew that Vianne didn't have the pull to get Morgan reinstated somewhere, so when she sat down to one last dinner in her aunt's apartment, they kind of already knew how the conversation would go.

"I feel like I just got you back," Vianne said as they finished dessert. "And then I told you to talk to a Katla, and now this is happening."

"I would have done all of that anyway," Morgan told her.

"Neither of us thought they'd react this strongly. Horense Katla certainly seemed content with threats. I wonder if she told someone else, and they're the ones who decided to silence me."

"We're not going to find out," Vianne said, though clearly she wanted to, if only so she could think dark thoughts at them. "What are you going to do?"

"Well," Morgan began, "I was thinking that I'd go back to Valon."

She barely managed not to make it a question. She was long past asking permission.

"I'm not surprised." Vianne sighed. "No one can kick you out of a place you own, and you can do your work there with your own money."

Vianne had taken Morgan into her life for no other reason than she was family, and that Vianne thought she deserved the best education Katla could offer. Morgan hated lying to her, and even though they *were* heading to Valon first, that was sophistry. Protecting the family meant protecting the family, though, and between the rebellion and Pendt's plan for Enragon, Morgan was determined to keep protecting them. The rebellion knew her family secret now, and she had to trust them to keep it. She couldn't force her aunt into the same situation unless she had to. She wouldn't tell Vianne, even if she could.

"It won't be forever," Morgan said. "And I'll be able to come back to visit, at least."

Now she was stretching the truth a bit. She had absolutely no idea what was going to happen when Pendt started messing around with Enragon Station.

"I really am proud of you, you know," Vianne said. "You worked so hard, and you never gave up or compromised when you knew you were onto something. Egos are the worst part of academia, and you never let someone intimidate you, even when you were twelve."

"That means a lot," Morgan said. "The last few days have been stressful, but I learned how to deal with all of this from you."

Vianne smiled. Sometimes Morgan wondered what it would be like to have a mother. Tasia had two, so it wasn't like Vianne couldn't have also assumed the role, but as good and nurturing as she'd been, she was always Morgan's aunt. Both of them had danced around the question over the years, never wanting to hurt the other. Now, on the eve of her greatest expedition, Morgan was so, so grateful that she'd had an *aunt*. Vianne was—and had always been—exactly what she needed.

"When you come back, come back with something big enough that you can get Argir's office," she said.

"That's not a bad idea," Morgan admitted with a snort of a laugh. "I'll keep it in mind."

They talked about so much nothing until Morgan yawned so widely, she heard her jaw crack. It had been a busy few days.

"You should get going," Vianne said. "Before I do something foolish like cry or offer you a history fellowship."

Morgan laughed, and Aunt Vianne hugged her for a little longer than usual. She kissed her aunt's cheek and said her own farewells. It wasn't until she got to the trainway that she felt tears prick her eyes. They didn't fall. But now everything felt real. Even this morning, when they finished packing, their plan was just that:

a plan. Now it was something that was going to happen, and Morgan was going to see it through. In her apartment, she scheduled one last alarm and programmed one last breakfast, and then she went to bed. It took her a while to fall asleep.

The bulk of their gear had been loaded overnight, so when Ned, Pendt, and Morgan stood on the Katla side of the *Marquis* airlock, they were only carrying the personal items they'd need on the trip. Morgan had brought fresh food again, in addition to the other supplies, but it was already stowed in the galley. She hoped the crew wouldn't see it as a bribe. Morunt had gone aboard the previous night to ensure that the medical bay had everything he would need. It was just the three of them left.

Captain Choria appeared in the airlock. Ned gave her a joking salute and Pendt gave her a hug. Then she turned to Morgan.

"Thank you," Morgan said.

"I told you I'd be here if you needed a ship again, didn't I?" Choria said.

"Yes," Morgan said. "But that was before I . . . left."

"Some people come to the rebellion because they're angry," Choria said. "Some, like that idiot Ned, come because they have noble ideas about the right thing. Some, like Pendt, get backed into a corner. It doesn't matter how you got here. The important thing is that you did."

"Just like that?" Morgan asked. It couldn't possibly be that easy.

"Well, no," Choria said. "There are hurt feelings on all sides, I'd guess. Rejecting a person's ideals is a lot like rejecting their self. But that's where you start."

"I can do that," Morgan said. She didn't entirely believe herself. She'd been using what she'd learned from Choria's crew to form other relationships, yes, but she didn't know if she could turn around and apply the same principles to their origin point.

"Good," Choria said. "Because the only place you've got left to go is aboard. Let's get moving."

They cycled through the airlock since the *Marquis* was already pressurized for departure. Once they were inside, Choria signalled up to the bridge that they were ready to go. The route to Valon was already plotted, so the captain wasn't needed on the bridge.

"Ned, your quarters are still there," Choria said. "With the additional supplies Pendt needs, we had to take over the rooms you had last time, Morgan. There's a spare cabin next to Ned's for you two to share. Show them the way, Brannick, then check out the duty schedule."

"Are we on that too?" Pendt asked. Something shifted in her face, and Morgan didn't like it at all. "We don't want to be freeloaders. I can h-help in the galley."

"No." Ned's refusal was instant and adamant, without giving his captain the chance to think about it.

"If you get really bored, we'll find you something," Choria said gently. "But you're passen—*guests* here, and I'm sure Morgan has enough research to keep you both busy, since I'm stealing her assistant back."

"And maybe we can think of ways to get the parts of Katla you liked to work on Brannick," Morgan offered. Pendt was starting to relax again, and Morgan was desperate to keep her from ever having that facial expression again. "Like the goats."

"I did like the goats," Pendt said.

"Come on, love," Ned said, wrapping his arm around her shoulder. Pendt rejoined the group with poise. "Let's get you settled in."

Morgan wanted to know, and she knew with absolute certainty she would never ask.

It took four days for Jonee to talk to her again, and when she did, it was mostly by accident. They were in the mess, Pendt's back firmly to the galley, and Jonee was telling Ned about the first time she had gone through Valon in her space suit to turn the lights back on. She turned and asked Morgan a question without thinking about it, and then froze.

"It was only a couple of hours," Morgan said. She gave her answer as easily as Jonee had asked the question, even though the both of them were walking on eggshells. "The main problem was that Jonee couldn't eat in the suit and needed to refuel. But once she got everything online, we didn't need the suits, and she could explore all she wanted."

There was a long pause.

"I didn't think you'd come back," Jonee said, hurt clear in her voice.

"Neither did I," Morgan admitted. "I was sorry for how things ended here. You were all so welcoming to me, and I wasn't ready for that yet. My life on Katla was very contained and small, I see that now. I wanted approval from people who were never going to give it to me, and who don't actually matter. I was wrong, and I'm sorry."

"It is possible that I was a bit pushy," Jonee allowed. "My loyalty to the captain is personal, and not everyone shares that."

It was a slow beginning, but it was better than no beginning at all. The rest of the crew followed Jonee's lead, including Deirdre, though Morgan never saw the cook when she was with Pendt. It wasn't the same easy camaraderie as before, but Ned smoothed out any number of ruffled feathers. By the time they got to Valon, Morgan had, if not the old relationships she'd developed, then new ones. She and Pendt were invited to tables in the mess, or to sit out of the way in engineering and watch the electro-mages work. Ned worked on the bridge, due to his mild star-sense, but they saw him just as frequently.

The stopover at Valon was brief. Morgan did not get off the *Marquis*. There had been some discussion about whether the last stage of the trip should be made on the fully refurbished *Cleland* instead, but Choria decided that the smaller ship would do. The *Cleland* would follow, if it could, once Pendt was done changing the gene-lock. This meant the *Marquis* was crammed to the gunwales with supplies.

At the request of Valon's quartermaster, Pendt did go over to the outpost. The hydroponics units had been resuscitated enough that a first round of crops had been planted. Pendt took one of the IV calorie bags and Dr. Morunt to see if she could speed that first growth along so that they could harvest and replant. None of the rebellion gene-mages could do it as quickly as she would be able to, and Morunt wanted to see the IV bags in action. Ned went with them, to no one's surprise. When they returned a few hours later, the bag was empty, Ned was eating an apple, and Pendt looked none the worse for wear.

"You're really okay?" Morgan asked as soon as they were in the airlock.

Jonee had kept her company and done her best to provide distractions, but Morgan still worried. Not about Pendt's abilities, mind, but the effect of working with Dr. Morunt again when she was already clearly uncomfortable on board the *Marquis*.

"I'm fine," Pendt said. "Those calorie bags are something else."

"And the IV part?" Morgan said.

"I don't mind Dr. Morunt sticking me with a needle, if that's what you mean," Pendt said. "I still don't like him, and I probably never will, but he knows what he's doing, and if he feels the way he says he does about what happened on Brannick, I am happy to use that."

"And I was there the whole time," Ned reminded them. "We have an understanding."

He put his hand on Morgan's shoulder and squeezed reassuringly.

"Now I'm hungry, which means Pendt is probably starving," he said. "Let's go to the mess and see if there's anything out for dinner yet."

It took a few minutes for them to make their way in from the airlock. Morgan felt like a weight had been lifted off her chest now that they were back on board. It was strange to think that, not so long ago, she hadn't really liked them that much. Now she couldn't imagine being anywhere else.

Pendt stopped dead on the threshold of the mess, and Morgan ran right into her. Pendt lurched forward but caught herself on the doorjamb and held herself physically out of the room. Morgan looked over her shoulder. Deirdre had been using the row of tables nearest to the galley for inventory, which they did every time the *Marquis* was in port somewhere. It was part recipe planning, part calorie management. It required math and æther in equal parts.

"Hey, it's okay." Ned spoke in his gentlest tones and pried Pendt's fingers off the doorjamb as delicately as he could. She let him move her, but it was like watching a ghost. "We don't have to go in. We've got food in your room, remember? We'll go there, and then I'll bring you something hot later, yeah?"

Pendt didn't even nod, but she let him steer her down the corridor until they reached the room she and Morgan shared. Ned let them all in and settled Pendt on a chair before going to one of the drawers for her emergency snacks. Morgan had packed them in case they worked late or Pendt had to do unexpected æther-work, so they were all high calorie. Pendt ate what he gave her without asking what it was, and by the time she was done, some colour had returned to her face.

"I'm just going to contact Fisher before we leave," she said. "Then I'll be okay."

Ned looked doubtful, but he took her up to the bridge anyway, leaving Morgan to clean up the wrappers without an explanation.

Pendt's nightmares started two days after they left Valon.

18.

THE WORST PART WAS not knowing what to do.

Aside from that one night on Katla, Morgan hadn't shared a bedroom with anyone since she was five, and she'd only lived with an adult after that, their rooms separated by a hallway. She knew people had nightmares, vague fears about the dark and sometimes space or, like, public speaking, but Pendt's didn't sound like anything so vague or nebulous as that. Whatever Pendt was afraid of was real, and it was tormenting her.

Morgan considered going to get Ned, but she didn't want Pendt to wake up alone. She didn't know if that would actually be a bad thing, but she felt like it might be, so she stayed. She listened as Pendt tossed and cried out. It was worse when she whimpered, and Morgan heard her flinch back from her own blankets. It was awful when she apologized, voice high and so, so young-sounding. Sometimes Pendt slept through it, horrors subsiding back to restless slumber, but more often she woke up, rolled away to face the wall, and pretended she was asleep even though her breathing was far too ragged.

The fifth night, when Pendt was pretending she had gone back to sleep, Morgan could hear her crying. She said "Fisher" once, so softly and desperately that Morgan's heart ached. She knew what Ned would do, and so she did it. Walking loudly enough that Pendt would hear her coming, Morgan crossed the room and crawled onto the bunk beside her. She curled around Pendt's body, pulling up the blanket that had been thrashed off to cover them both, and then wrapped her arms around Pendt's shoulders.

Pendt cried for a while longer, but it wasn't the awful, hollow sound of still hurting. It was softer, knowing that there was comfort available. When she stopped, her skin was warm instead of nightmare-cold and clammy. She sniffed and sighed, finally relaxing into Morgan's hold.

"I grew up on a ship," she said after a moment. "It wasn't a nice ship like this one."

Morgan had reached the end of methods she knew to make people feel better, so she said nothing.

"On a space station, I can tell where I am. Not star-sense, obviously, I just know I'm not . . . there," Pendt said. "It's big and there's so much going on. I don't remember. But I remember on a ship."

Morgan listened to her breathe, slow and steady.

"You can't tell Ned, or Fisher if you ever meet him," Pendt said. "They'll never let me go anywhere if they know how much it hurts."

Morgan was half inclined to go up to the bridge and demand

they go back to Valon immediately, but Pendt had clearly made a decision to endure, and Morgan respected that.

"All right," she said. "Will you let me know how I can help?"

"This is good for now," Pendt said. She snuggled even closer. Morgan expected to panic or at least feel uncomfortable, but instead she was overwhelmed by a latent memory: downy-soft hair against her nose and the milk-smell of newness. Once upon a time, she had held her sister like this. "I'm exhausted."

There was a song in the back of Morgan's mind, and a voice that wasn't her aunt's. She couldn't remember any of the words, only that they had been sung low and lovely in the dark. The tune came to her, though, and she hummed a few bars. Pendt relaxed even more as Morgan sang, and before long, she was truly asleep again.

Morgan was awake for a while, but not because she was uncomfortable. She was thinking about songs and bodies and proximity, of what a mind remembered and what it didn't. She doubted there was anything good in Pendt's memories of that ship, and she decided that if it was possible, she'd help her make some good memories on the *Marquis* instead. Maybe that would make ships easier, the next time Pendt had to take one somewhere.

She drifted off before she had a concrete plan, warm and close and safe.

Pendt's nightmares didn't stop in the weeks that followed, but their intensity lessened and the dark circles under her eyes went away. She was still uncomfortable and avoided the mess as much as possible. Once when she and Morgan were working in one of the common areas, a group of engineers sat down at the table beside them and started to play a card game Morgan didn't recognize. Pendt didn't notice until one of them had a winning hand, the cards sparking to life as the circuit within them was completed. Pendt jumped liked she'd been burned, and Morgan immediately declared that she couldn't read any more today and wanted to go down to the engine room to ask Jonee when her shift was done. It was a flimsy effort, but it was enough.

Morgan spent more time with Ned since Pendt decided to eat in their room. Jonee had been promoted to the ship's equivalent of the daylight shift, so she wasn't around for breakfast and lunch in the galley. Ned, still on nights, would meet her for one or both, depending on how tired he was. He told her all about Brannick and Fisher, including that their parents were hostages of the Hegemony.

"How long has it been since you saw them?" Morgan asked.

"They went when we were seventeen," Ned said. "I think the Hegemony hoped Fisher and I wouldn't be able to handle the station on our own and would have to make some sort of deal with them."

"What kind of deal would they possibly take?" Morgan asked. The Hegemony was not known for generosity.

"Who knows," Ned said. "Me for my father, maybe? Or a supervisor they controlled? Or maybe a military base. None of the options were good. So, Fisher and I made it work. And then Pendt came along, and, well, you know."

"I don't, actually," Morgan said. "Beyond the fact that you married her. But you don't have to tell me."

"It's not really mine to tell," Ned admitted.

Morgan gracefully changed the subject.

When Pendt did join them for a meal, it was usually dinner. Despite never having officially been introduced to Deirdre, the cook seemed to know all of Pendt's favourite foods. If she appeared in the mess, it was never very long before a plate, piled high, appeared at her elbow. Deirdre never brought it out themself, but the gesture was unmistakably kind.

Dr. Morunt avoided them as much as possible, taking the overnight shift in the infirmary. The crew were pleased, since they'd never had two doctors before, and it kept him out of the mess during regular mealtimes, because the medical shifts were twelve hours instead of eight.

It was tedious, and it seemed unending, but life aboard the *Marquis* settled into a livable routine.

Enragon Station was visible for almost a week before they finally arrived there. It was frustrating, to see the reflected light and know what it was, and yet be unable to get there any faster. Morgan knew how space worked in theory, but practical examples still made her stomach churn. On Katla, it was easy to pretend that everything was stable and solid. Morgan now had some personal experience with how much effort the Katlas extended to enforce that stability, through both mechanical redundancies and propaganda. After all these days on a much less robustly designed ship, Morgan understood the allure. If something happened to the *Marquis*, they would all die while Enragon sat there, just out of reach. That kind of hard line gave spacers a unique outlook, but Morgan had put together enough of the pieces to know that such an outlook had hurt Pendt a great deal.

The light of Enragon grew every day, until a shape was visible, and then the shape grew to reveal details of the station's construction. Where Katla was graceful circles and Brannick utilitarian lines, Enragon could only be described as a decorative hulk. From their direction, the station appeared as five great rings, three above and two below, fused together along a midline. In reality, they were looking down at the top of the station, because humans always had to create direction in the void to maintain their sanity.

The day before they arrived, they were close enough to see the Well and the Net. The Net was inactive, of course, but the Well could be seen rippling faintly, even at this distance. That was the *Marquis*'s way home, at least. A much shorter run back to Brannick, even though the distance was significantly farther. With Ned on board, they were always guaranteed a safe landing there.

Pendt grew quieter as the station grew larger. She had started eating as soon as it was visible, with Dr. Morunt carefully monitoring her intake. The IV bags made her task easier, but she still felt bloated and gross.

"At least this time we don't have to fake my death," she said, watching while Dr. Morunt switched an empty bag out for a full one.

"That will make it simpler, yes," Morunt said.

There was a great deal they didn't say.

Finally, they were close enough to board. The airlock held when the *Marquis* hardened its seal. The boarding party was small: Morgan, Pendt, Morunt, Choria, and two electro-mages. Jonee had asked to come, but Choria decided it was too dangerous and ordered her to stay on the ship. A great many things could go wrong, which was why Ned had to stay on the *Marquis* too. He wasn't happy, but he was their only escape route, so he did it without complaining. Much.

Morunt had decided that Pendt would be put in a wheelchair for the duration of the event. It was an indication of how wretched she felt that Pendt did not argue with him. One last bag was dripping into her arm inside her space suit, and Morunt had a pack full of them for afterward. The electro-mages magnetized the chair's wheels so that the chair could be moved but wouldn't float away if someone stopped holding it.

"I feel terrible," Pendt said as Choria strapped her in.

"You only look sort of terrible," Choria told her, voice a bit tinny through the comms. "But don't worry, I promise to leave this part out when we tell the story later."

"Thanks," Pendt said dryly, but Morgan saw her smile, which was what Choria had been after.

The six of them cycled through the airlock, the first people on Enragon in centuries. They had chosen a docking port as close to the operations deck as possible. On Brannick, it had taken Pendt some time to find the physical location of the gene-lock itself. On Enragon, she was hoping she'd be able to find it quickly, because she'd be on the lookout for genetic sequences. Outside of the boarding party, there weren't going to be all that many to find.

The station was, mercifully, empty. Part of the complete failure of the station involved a total decompression, all doors and ports thrown open wide. The majority of bodies were long gone, sucked out into space in that single, horrifying moment when the gene-lock had been activated while all of the Enragon Y chromosomes were away from the station. Morgan knew they'd have to do a full sweep at some point, but she was trying not to think about it.

It took half an hour to get everyone to operations, because Pendt could not climb ladders, but at last they all stood in the centre of the dead station, surrounded by metal and ghosts.

"Do you need me to put you under?" Morunt asked.

"No," said Pendt, "I can go by myself. Just be ready to get me back out."

"I swear on my sister's life," Morunt said.

Pendt nodded grimly, said a quick goodbye to everyone. When she got to Morgan, she tried to smile again.

"I'll do my best," Pendt said. "I know you don't want to be chained to this place."

"I know you will," Morgan said. "Godspeed."

Pendt closed her eyes and stopped moving. The monitor on her suit indicated that her heartbeat was getting slower and slower as she disappeared into her æther-work. There was nothing any of them could do until she was done and ready to come out.

"How long did it take?" Morgan asked, breaking the silence. "On Brannick, I mean."

"It was hard to tell exactly," Morunt said. He didn't look away from Pendt's suit. "There were extenuating circumstances."

"You had to fake her death," Morgan said.

"Yes," Morunt said. "We had to be sure her family thought she was dead so they'd never come back for her again."

"I didn't realize they'd come back for her at all," Morgan said.

"In any case, between what Pendt's told me and what the twins were able to record, it took her about half an hour to do the actual work," Morunt said. "That includes the time it took to wake her up, but again, waking her should be easier this time, because we're not holding her under."

"Half an hour," Morgan said. "I can do half an hour."

Choria put a gloved hand on her suited shoulder, and Morgan felt better. The electro-mages waited calmly, clearly used to observing æther-work even if this was on a scale that was new to them. Morunt never moved from Pendt's side. Morgan wanted to pace, run, possibly shriek, but she did none of those things. All she could do was watch while a girl who was rapidly becoming a friend changed her life dramatically.

When the connection came, it struck without warning.

It was a horrible awareness, grinding inexorably in her very marrow. Morgan scratched desperately at her suit, feeling trapped in a small space while a bigger one crushed her, and then she pan icked, desperate to make it stop.

"Wake her up!" Morgan screamed. "Wake her up right no

"She's not finished," Morunt protested. "She has to take first step herself."

Morgan keened, an almost incomprehensible noise tha the others scrambling to turn down their comms.

"What's wrong?" Choria asked, shaking Morgan by th ders to get her attention.

Morgan tore herself out of Choria's grip and

sideways into a control panel. She knew exactly which one it was, and exactly which button she needed to activate to ease the pressure in every single one of her senses.

“Morgan!” Choria yelled.

“She’s coming up!” Morunt said as the monitors on Pendt’s suit began to speed up.

“It’s too late,” Morgan said, despairing as destiny inevitably claimed her for its own. She felt like she was going to explode as centuries of quiet shattered in her soul. For some reason, she could only think of one thing that might make it stop.

With absolute surety, Morgan activated the control she’d been groping for, and outside Enragon Station, the Net flared to life, welcoming her home.

19.

MORGAN HAD VAGUE MEMORIES of being shunted to the side, pushed from the control panel, and of falling. Not even her suit could keep her upright, though her boots didn't move thanks to the magnets. Choria caught her before she could hit the floor, and called out for Dr. Morunt, but true to his word, he would not leave Pendt's side. Unable to do anything else, Choria was forced to settle for unlocking Morgan's boots and pushing her down to the deck so she could keep her as still as possible. Horrible shudders racked Morgan's body, and a high-pitched noise always followed. The third time it happened, Morgan realized that the noise was her.

All around them, Enragon was waking up. The lights came on, followed by the cacophonous roar of the air cyclers winding back up. Readouts streamed across control boards, reporting that the hull was stable and there were no breeches detected at this time. Gravity turned on between one breath and the next and caught them all off guard.

Choria lurched towards her, but Morgan was already lying on the floor, so she didn't have anywhere to fall. Her eyes were shut tight, and tears were running down her cheeks. Without seeing, without hearing, she knew everything that was happening as the station came back to life. Because she was an Enragon too, and now they were linked.

Pendt woke up more gently than did the station. Through the comm in her helmet, Morgan could hear Morunt talking to her, coaxing her to open her eyes. She was going to be fine.

"I'm sorry, Morgan," she rasped. "I'll try again."

"You will not," said Dr. Morunt. "This attempt took a lot out of you, literally, and if you try it again, it might harm the baby."

Morgan was hallucinating, or whatever it was called when you heard things that weren't real. She'd been with Pendt for long enough that she'd know about something like that.

"We have to get back to the ship," Choria said. She got to her feet and moved to pull Morgan into a sitting position.

"We can't," Morgan croaked as she was shifted.

She realized they couldn't hear her because they'd removed her from their comms while she was screaming, so she swatted at Choria until she had her attention. The captain brought her back into the comm.

"I can't," Morgan said. This time, at least, her voice was clearer. "I have to stay."

It hung there for a moment as everyone finally digested the enormity of what had just happened—what Pendt had, in spite of her best efforts, shackled Morgan to.

"She's right," Pendt said. "Morgan has to stay."

"Fuck," said Choria. "How much oxygen is left?"

"Three more hours," Morunt said. "If I give her a sedative, double that."

"You can't—" Pendt started, but Choria cut her off.

"And how long until there's enough oxygen on the station for her to breathe without a helmet?" she asked.

The sense of the station was fading, along with the pain, though the latter was definitely lingering. Now Morgan was just exhausted. Even her hair hurt.

"Four hours," said one of the electro-mages, standing over a screen.

"Morgan?" Choria said.

"Do it," Morgan grated out. "Just don't you dare leave me here forever."

Pendt protested but wasn't exactly in a position to stop anything from happening. Dr. Morunt came and knelt by Morgan's head.

"It's just falling asleep like you normally would," he said. "It'll stop you from feeling the pain and lower your vital stats enough to preserve the oxygen in your suit. Okay?"

"Okay," Morgan breathed.

She heard a shuffle and then a thump and a quiet curse. Pendt crawled over, dragging the IV behind her. Dr. Morunt didn't bother to chastise her.

"We will be back the *moment* there is enough air to breathe, you understand?" she said. "Or as soon as the suits are recharged. Whichever comes first."

"I know," she said.

Morgan heard, rather than felt, the hypo connect with the induction port in her suit. There was a hiss, but that was the only indication that anything had changed.

"Deep breaths, Morgan," Dr. Morunt said.

Pendt didn't let go of her hand until she was asleep.

Morgan woke up under different lights and without a helmet on. For a moment, she forgot where she was. Then it all came rushing back—the memories, not the feelings thankfully—and she groaned.

"You're awake!" said Ned, above her. His face was less anxious than she expected, which was probably a good sign. "Do you need snacks or water first?"

"She needs water," Dr. Morunt said. "It wasn't æther-work, so her calories are fine."

Ned held a water packet close to her mouth and directed the straw for her so that she could drink. After a few gulps, she pulled away.

"Does Brannick hurt?" she asked him.

"No," he said. His brow furrowed with concern, and he reached down to hold her hand. "But I was born with it, so maybe that's why?"

"I wasn't," Pendt said.

Morgan turned her head and saw Pendt lying on the bed next to her. They must be in Enragon's infirmary. There was still an IV in her arm, but the bag was almost empty and there wasn't another waiting to be connected. Another device rested on her belly, beeping steadily as it monitored life signs.

"But you married a Brannick," Morgan said.

"And I carry one," Pendt said. "That's how we got around the gene-lock for Ned to leave the first time. Fisher doesn't have a Y chromosome, but the baby does. Now that the lock is changed, Fisher can run the station by himself."

"And the baby's just . . . hanging out?" Morgan asked.

"It's one of my gifts," Pendt said. "And one of the reasons my family was willing to break so many laws to sell me to the Hegemony."

"Right," Morgan said, then: "Wait, if Fisher . . ."

She trailed off, not entirely sure what to say, or even what she was trying to ask.

"I did tell you it was complicated," Ned rumbled.

"You did," Morgan said. "And . . . everybody's okay?"

"Yes," Pendt said. She gestured to include everyone in the room. "Current medical shenanigans not included."

They fell silent for a moment while Dr. Morunt disconnected Pendt from the IV and helped her to a chair that was closer to Morgan's bed. Ned was still holding her hand. It was real and warm, and it wasn't Enragon. Morgan was not in a hurry to let go.

"Has the crew come aboard?" Morgan asked.

"Just a few," Pendt said. "There's us, obviously, and then a few electro-mages checking things out. Once everything is cleared and you're feeling up for it, Choria wants to bring the *Cleland* in."

"I don't know h—" Morgan started.

"I can show you," Ned said. He squeezed her fingers. "I took a look at the control room before I came down here. It's not that different from Brannick's. These two stations must have been built around the same time."

"I don't understand why it hurt," Pendt said. "I was æther-working, and I could still hear you screaming. I just couldn't get out in time. Brannick's never been like that. Is Katla?"

"I have no idea," Morgan said. "I've only ever talked to one Katla, and she was pretty far down in terms of family rank and station power. And our conversation didn't exactly go very well."

"None of them have ever mentioned it to me," Ned said. "Not that we talk much, but there's normal station communications, and it's never come up."

"Maybe it's because I'm not an æther-worker?" Morgan said. "But you don't have to be to work the controls, that was the whole point."

"Maybe it's because everything was broken," Ned said. "I mean, it all stopped in a cataclysm centuries ago, and it's just been sitting here waiting. When it latched on to you, you got some kind of, I don't know, feedback loop."

"That's what the electro-mages guessed too," Dr. Morunt provided. "But they tend to think in circuits to begin with."

"You can't still feel it, can you?" Pendt asked.

"No," Morgan said. "It was already fading when Dr. Morunt put me under. I think Ned's right, and it was just the station waking up."

"Well, I'm sorry for that too," Pendt said. "I got in without any trouble at all, but when I attempted to break the lock, it was too big to move. I tried to come up with something else, but I could feel the calories running out. I had to change it or do nothing, and I decided to change it."

"You couldn't have known," Morgan said.

"I knew it would trap you here," Pendt said. "And I did it anyway."

"Maybe changing the lock will make it easier to break next time," Morgan suggested.

"Next time is a while away," Dr. Morunt reminded them. "And while we're waiting, I think you're both going to have plenty to do. I know you're not going to slow down for anything the moment you step out of the infirmary, so please do me a favour and let me finish up with you."

"And that's why he was our favourite doctor," Ned said. "He knew he couldn't stop us, so he did his best to help."

"Except when I didn't," Morunt said. There was no bitterness in his reminder.

"Except when you didn't," Pendt said softly. "Fortunately, someone else was there to make the final call."

He helped her back to her bed and tucked her in almost tenderly. Ned finally dropped Morgan's hand, and she tried not to let the disappointment show on her face.

"I have to report back to the ship," Ned said. "But I'll be with the first wave once we come on board for good. I'll see you soon."

He stopped beside Pendt to kiss her on the forehead, and then left the infirmary. Dr. Morunt dimmed the lights, and left them as well, the instruction to sleep very clear.

"I didn't intentionally not tell you about the baby," Pendt said. "It just takes some explaining."

"I understand completely," Morgan told her. "For starters, it's not really my business, and also you didn't really know me that well."

"I do now," Pendt said. "And I'm glad you know."

"Are you going to have it someday?" Morgan asked.

"Yes," Pendt said. "With the gene-lock changed, it doesn't matter what the baby's chromosomes are, and we'll have two Brannicks on the station. Fisher is excited to be a dad someday, but neither of us is ready yet."

"And Ned?" Morgan asked. Multi-parent situations on Katla were varied and Morgan didn't know all the legal permutations, but she was pretty sure she'd never heard of one like this. She couldn't imagine Ned not wanting to be involved, no matter his actual relation.

"Ned definitely isn't ready yet," Pendt said. "He never wanted the station, and the baby was his freedom. He'd be a good father if he had to. He takes care of everyone. His main concern when I came to the station was that I'd love him because he was the first person in my life who had ever been nice to me, and in a way, I do. But when their parents were hostaged, it hurt something inside him. I'm not sure if he wants to be a parent himself."

"My parents didn't know what to do with me," Morgan said. "I was born on Skúvoy, but my aunt already lived on Katla. She came for a visit, and she and my mother talked, and the next thing I knew, I was bouncing off the Well. I barely remember what they look like. Aunt Vianne doesn't have pictures. It's not really safe. If the Hegemony found out who any of us were, we'd all be in danger, if only as symbols for the rebels to rally around."

"That's my other motivation for breaking the lock, then," Pendt said. "You don't deserve to be stuck here, and your sister doesn't deserve the target on her back."

“Thank you,” Morgan said. A weight lifted. She had still harboured some reluctance about the danger she was exposing her unknowing sister to, but knowing that Pendt took the danger seriously helped.

“I only had brothers, before,” Pendt said after a long moment. “If I’d had a sister, she would have treated me exactly the same way they did. But I’m glad I have you now.”

“I’m still learning how to interact with people,” Morgan said. “Or, I’m trying to change how I interact with people, anyway. If I’d known you even a year ago, it wouldn’t have been the same.”

“At least we have good timing,” Pendt said. “But we should probably try to sleep before Dr. Morunt comes back and sedates us.”

Morgan laughed for what felt like the first time in an eternity.

20.

ENRAGON STATION WAS SIGNIFICANTLY smaller than Katla, so the basic safety survey only took two days. Mostly, this involved confirming what the computer scans were already telling them: the hull was stable and the seals would hold. Oxygen climbed to a livable level and never wavered. The air recyclers kept up with breathing exchange. Lights came on, doors opened, and gravity kept everything on the floor that was supposed to be there.

Morgan gave up taking notes halfway through the first morning. There were other people more qualified to remember things than she was. For the first time in her life, she was part of a group project where she felt like she could rely on the group. It was surprisingly rewarding.

Morgan brought the *Cleland* in from Brannick on the third day. They couldn't leave the Net on, in case the Stavengers heard rumours and decided to test their strength, so Morgan had to learn to do the timing and coordination that the Net required. She was absolutely terrified, even with Ned and Pendt beside her. The comms units, both on-station and outward, all functioned as perfectly as everything else, so they were able to coordinate without any issues. But a lot of people on that ship depended on her, and Morgan had never felt that sort of responsibility before. The first time she'd activated the Net, it had been instinctive; a desperate hope to cut through the noise that was filling her brain. This time it was deliberate, and much, much more important to get right.

The anxiety that clawed through her stomach was replaced by euphoria the moment the *Cleland* appeared. A cheer went up around her—primarily from Ned, but it was still nice—as the ship activated its manoeuvring thrusters and headed for the port Choria had selected for it. A ship the *Cleland*'s size had to dock in what had been the commercial area of the station, but the electromages had gone over everything with a fine-tooth comb, so they knew it was safe.

With two crews aboard, they were able to do a second survey on the station. This one took longer. First, they cleared out any remains that hadn't been spaced in the original breech. These were brought to the operations level, and Choria held a brief memorial for them. There was no way to know for sure who anyone was. Vacuum desiccation had preserved the shape of the bodies, but explosive decompression had done a significant amount of damage first. Morgan sent them out the airlock herself, with a few whispered words hoping they would find their families out in the void and sleep in peace.

With that done, the rebels began the arduous task of cataloguing everything on the station so they would know what their inventory was. Enragon hadn't been abandoned, and there hadn't even been time for an evacuation to start. There were some signs of looting, but only the most enterprising—or desperate—pirates would have risked the trip. Almost everything on the station remained where it had been when the gene-lock was activated, provided it hadn't been sucked out into space.

It was tedious, necessary work, broken up by the occasional truly wonderful find. Jonee and Deirdre, working their way through one of the holds, discovered an entire warehouse of containers that were still sealed. This protected them from the vacuum, and when the first few were opened to reveal seeds, Deirdre called for Pendt at once.

Outside of the ship, Pendt had no problem working with Deirdre, much to the relief of both of them. Pendt hated offending people who didn't deserve it, and Deirdre hated causing stress. They spent a whole week going through the seeds and then another few days in hydroponics with Jonee, getting everything ready for a first round of planting. It would be a long time before Enragon was anything like self-sufficient, but this was an important step, and not having to acquire starter seeds was a massive bonus.

As more containers of food supplies, medical equipment, and the like were discovered and recorded, Choria increased the number of rebels who were brought in. Morgan spent most of her time in operations, coordinating ships between Enragon and Brannick. She came to know Fisher by the sound of his voice, and working with him made her more comfortable in her new position. Some of the ships merely made deliveries and departed, but a few docked more permanently. Enragon was becoming a true stronghold for the rebellion. The trick now was to get as established as possible before anyone else noticed.

Even though she rarely had time to venture out, Morgan was building a map of the station in her head. The middle line—the joining point that connected all five of the rings—housed operations and served as the main transfer points for the station's internal transport. The two rings between that line and the Net were, logically, comprised of docks and storage warehouses. The three rings "behind" operations were food and oxygen production, habitation, and processing, which included everything from the defunct oglasa facility to electricity generation.

Choria had been assigning quarters to the crews that were staying on. A skeleton watch always remained on each ship, but the rest of the crew were given quarters in the habitation circle. It was a bit of a hike to get there from operations, but the electromages were working on the shuttles.

Enragon had been designed with an automated transport system, but the shuttles themselves were self-powered, recycling their own potential and kinetic energy to move along the tracks. The same powers also controlled operations like the brakes and the doors. This meant that several of the shuttles had trapped their occupants inside when the decompression killed everyone else on the station, but Morgan did her absolute best not to think about what that would have been like.

The main issue, which Ned identified and brought up quietly to Morgan and Choria in operations, was that they didn't have anyone qualified to run logistics on the station. The ships all had quartermasters, of course, and between them, Deirdre and the other gene-mages could handle rationing without taking up any of Pendt's time, but there was no one with experience holding the whole system in their head.

"The rebellion has never had anything this big," Choria admitted. "Even Valon isn't that much more complicated than a ship."

"I don't think we're in danger," Ned said. "I just think we could be more efficient. We're not blundering into anything because the computer databases don't let us, but if we had someone with experience who could run the non-operations parts, they'd catch all the little things I am sure we are missing."

"We can't poach someone like that," Choria said. "Someone else would notice. And we couldn't be sure of their loyalty."

"I have an idea," Morgan said. She was exhausted trying to keep track of everything, and her mind was fuzzy, but she had occasional moments of clarity. "My friend Tasia, her dads. The Furloughs go on trips sometimes, prospecting or whatever they call it, to find new sources for their import business or to barter in person. They could just tell people they were going and be vague on the details."

"Do you trust them?" Choria asked.

"I trust them enough to tell them who I am," Morgan said. "They're no fans of the Katlas or the Hegemony. Tasia could come with them, even bring a few of her sibs. If we gave them some time, her mothers could probably come up with an excuse to come too. Then we'd really be in business."

"How many people are we talking?" Ned asked. "I never really got a straight answer from Tasia when I asked."

"Counting all the kids, eighteen, I think?" Morgan said after a moment to dredge her memory and tally on her fingers. "I don't think there's been a new baby, and Tasia always tells me if someone's been adopted. She's the oldest, so none of them have their own partners yet."

"Well, we've definitely got space for them," Choria said. "I'd like to read over your message before you contact her, though. Just to be sure."

"Of course," Morgan said. "I am still getting used to this whole rebel thing. I certainly appreciate the help."

It was entirely possible that she'd caved because she was exhausted by not-belonging, but somewhere along the way, she'd actually joined them. The mutual benefits were still there, but they were no longer the primary reason for her continued involvement. She still didn't want a major role—including the one she currently had—but she was with them. She grinned, but it quickly turned into a yawn.

"Tomorrow," Ned said. "It's well into the nightshift, and I know you started with the daylighters."

"We all need some rest," Choria said. She gathered up the datapads she'd been working on and headed off.

"Can I walk you home?" Ned asked, extending his arm with half a bow.

"I am home," Morgan said. "I had them put a cot in the corner."

Ned's eyes followed to where she was pointing. He looked disapproving.

"Morgan, even when I was the only person who could control Brannick Station, I didn't live in operations," he said. "And Fisher doesn't live there now."

"Without the shuttles, I can't get here fast enough in an emergency," Morgan protested. "What if someone comes in unannounced?"

"The only people who'd be trying this unannounced are people we don't want," Ned said. "And I don't think you'd have to go all the way back to the habitation ring. There's probably somewhere nearby for whoever used to work here back in the day."

Morgan had not considered that. There was nothing wrong with the cot, but operations did not get quiet at night. She could turn off the lights, but the screens and indicators made noise all the time.

Ned was already calling up the specs, zooming in on the area around ops. They hadn't got to the secondary survey here yet, because the priorities were the warehouses and factories. She saw the empty space at the same time he did.

"There," he said, zooming in. "That's your suite. It passed the seal check; the electro-mages just didn't realize what it was. Let's go. We can pick up some bedding on the way."

Morgan was too tired to protest and let Ned lead her the short way down one ladder and through the corridors to the door of the suite. They stopped at one of the quartermasters' storerooms along the way, and Ned carried the bundle under one arm as they kept walking, his other hand on her shoulder. The door to her new room slid open for her, which was still a bit alarming on a station locked to her genetic code, and the lights came on when they entered.

They were standing in the main living area, which consisted of a long sofa, several poofy-looking chairs and a low table. Across the room was another table, this one higher and with a few chairs around it; clearly the eating area. A short hallway led to a kitchen, and there were two doors off the living room that led to a bathroom and a bedroom.

"Well, it could definitely use an update," Ned said. He poked one of the chairs. "But it's not dusty or anything. Will you be all right here?"

Ever since Dr. Morunt had sedated her so that they could leave her behind on the floor of operations, Morgan had been uncomfortable waking up. It felt stupid, because she hadn't even been scared at the time, and being so uncomfortable about something that had already happened and ended well seemed ridiculous. The upside of sleeping in operations was that someone was always close by.

Ned yawned.

"You know, I am so tired that I don't really want to walk back to the habitation circle," he said, sheer innocence in his every word. "Would you mind if I slept on the sofa? I think we have enough blankets."

Morgan looked at him. He blinked, but didn't give anything away.

"I've slept in worse places, I promise," he said. "And the sofa is definitely long enough."

"You can sleep here," she said quietly.

"Awesome," he said. "I don't snore or anything."

She laughed then—because Pendt had told her that he definitely did snore—and took her blankets into the bedroom. It was a plain little space, but the bed was bigger than the cot she'd been sleeping on, and the mattress definitely looked more comfortable. She pulled off the old bedding, most of it crumbling in her hands, and made up a little nest in the centre of the bed. She curled up, trying not to think too much about who might have slept here before. For an empty station, Enragon held an awful lot of ghosts.

Morgan pulled her mind back from those morbid thoughts and began composing her message to Tasia. It was going to require some interesting wording, to get the right kind of attention and not raise any alarm. She heard Ned snoring in the other room and thought about getting up to write down some of what she wanted to say, but she was far too comfortable. Ned was right. It would all still be here in the morning.

21.

THE FIRST BRANCH OF the Furlough family arrived four days later. Choria had taken the *Marquis* to get them herself, routing through Brannick in both directions to maintain secrecy. They had no way of knowing if Enragon's rebirth was still unknown outside of the rebellion, but traveling through Brannick was the easiest way to prolong their time before the Hegemony found out, because Fisher was trustworthy and knew how to fake the appropriate documentation. Both of Tasia's dads and the six oldest of the siblings had come as soon as Tasia contacted them. The mothers, the little kids, and any number of goats were expected to follow in a few days. Morgan had wondered why Choria was so insistent on making the journey herself, given how much there was to do here. She passed it off as the captain wanting to vet the family in person before she let them on Enragon—until a ninth person stepped off the arrival ramp.

"Aunt Vianne?" Morgan said. "What are you doing here?"

"Captain Choria told me a little bit about what was happening here," Vianne said. "She thought you might need some help, and I want to. It's time we stop being Ennis."

Morgan was caught between crying with relief and raging in fury. With Vianne on Enragon, they could each have a twelve-hour shift. Morgan could sleep. She'd be able to get back to her research without worrying that she'd miss something important and get a bunch of people killed. But Vianne on Enragon was also a target. It locked her in, irrevocably, as an Enragon. On Katla, living as an Enni, she was safe. Enragon was a nascent rebel base that didn't have its defenses in place yet.

"I made the call, Morgan," Choria said, reading Morgan's expression instantly. "It's my job."

Morgan could admit that Choria was objectively correct, but that didn't make it any easier to swallow. It was hard to give up the protection of her family to someone who had multiple priorities.

"I can show you all to the habitation area, if you like," Ned said calmly. Morgan, rather irrationally, wanted to punch him. "And then we can come back up here and start hammering out the details of what everyone is going to do."

"That sounds great," Argon Furlough said, corralling his children behind him while Jenji, their other father, brought up the rear.

Vianne gave Morgan a quick hug, while Tasia ducked under her dad's arm and separated herself from the horde. She made her way over to Morgan.

"I'll be along in a bit, if that's okay," she said.

Her dads had already gone with Ned, so neither of them

protested. Morgan led the way back up to operations. Pendt was there, going over some of the crop projections that the other gene-mages had prepared for her. She wasn't fully recovered yet, though she could do small things like encourage a few plants. This, at least, kept her busy.

"Hi, Tasia," she said when Morgan brought her in. "How was the trip?"

"I've never been through a Well before," Tasia said. "The boys all yarfed, but I was fine."

"I'm glad you're all here," Morgan said.

"Your message was very cryptic," Tasia said, "which intrigued my dads immediately. They know that no matter what they do, they'll never get any higher on Katla than they already are. Even if there's less money coming through Enragon, they'll still be at the very front of it. That sort of thing appeals to them."

"And the rebellion?" Pendt asked.

"Also an easy sell," Tasia said. "My mothers have been brawling with union busters since I was a baby, and my dads have seen a lot of life on other stations. When you combine that with the family ambition—well, we're pretty much perfect, aren't we?"

"Choria had concerns about bringing in more kids," Morgan said. "Which I think is valid. You didn't all have to come."

"Yes we did," Tasia said quickly. "We're a family."

Morgan and Pendt looked at each other. Pendt shrugged.

"Well, my family tried to sell me, and Morgan's family all grew up separated, but we'll take your word for it," she said.

"I'm honestly not all that surprised," Morgan admitted. "I was terrible at paying attention to other people, but I remembered how many of you there were. You must have talked about them a lot, which means you're close."

"And there's always room for more," Tasia said. "Though perhaps not literally, until I get a look at our quarters. I draw the line at sharing a bunk."

"Ned will get everyone settled," Morgan said.

There was a moment of silence between the three of them.

"Did you know?" Tasia asked hesitantly. She looked extremely curious, almost bouncing on the balls of her feet except for the fact that she was clearly trying to contain herself for Morgan's comfort. "About the Enragon thing, I mean?"

"Yes," Morgan said. "It's the family secret. And thank goodness. If I'd been surprised when the station latched on to me, I might have had a heart attack."

"Was it bad?" Tasia asked.

"Everything woke up at the same time, screaming," Morgan said. "So, yes. It was bad."

"I'm glad your aunt is here, then," Tasia said. "Choria took a whole day to convince her, but that ended up being for the best. My dads are excruciatingly methodical packers."

"Just tell me you brought the donair sauce recipe with you," Pendt said.

"That sauce is *my* family secret," Tasia said. "It's no space station, but it's much easier to fit in your suitcase."

Before Ned got back, Morgan and Pendt took Tasia to the galley complex, where Deirdre was in charge. There were several different cooks, but Deirdre was the senior officer, so they did all the planning and delegation. As soon as they realized the extent of Tasia's capabilities, they promoted her to head of the swing shift. She'd be in charge of dinner, which was served twice so that the evening workers could eat before they had to start their shift. The kitchens ran on a six-hour schedule because the work was intense, and so that mealtimes never overlapped with the main shift changeover.

Tasia would have happily got to work right then, except Morgan reminded her that her dads were probably just as excruciating at unpacking as they were at packing, and if she didn't go help them, they would never be done. One of the assistant cooks was done with his shift and volunteered to show Tasia how to get to the habitation circle. Deirdre sent her on her way, loaded down with as much food as they could foist on them.

They had just climbed up the ladder to operations when Ned came back. He was alone, which didn't really surprise them. Choria had been gone for a few days and was probably doing her own check-ins on her people.

"There's nothing else on the schedule for the next six hours," Morgan said. "We can go eat in my room, if you like? The chairs are more comfortable."

"That sounds like a plan," Ned said. He sobered a little bit, and continued. "Your aunt didn't seem affected by the station, at least. Maybe it really was just cranky about waking up."

"That's good to hear," Morgan said. "I knew it hadn't been too bad, but she can be frustratingly stoic when it comes to things like that."

"What an absolutely shocking thing to learn about a person in your family," Ned deadpanned. "I am completely surprised."

"Shut up," Morgan said, because he was too far away to punch.

"You slept on a cot in operations for days before anyone even noticed!" Ned reminded her. "If you were an æther-worker, you'd spend your whole life half passed out."

"I changed my mind," Morgan said. "Ned is not invited."

Pendt giggled, and the three of them headed for the exit that led to Morgan's quarters. Morgan forgot that they would find Ned's bedding still on the sofa when the doors opened and tried to get rid of them as nonchalantly as possible. She was doing fine until Ned found his jacket on one of her chairs and exclaimed rather loudly that he knew he hadn't left it on the *Marquis*. Morgan wished the deck plating would swallow her whole.

"Are you sleeping here?" Pendt asked.

"Well, yeah," Ned said like it was nothing. "If I didn't, she'd be the only person who sleeps out here instead of in the habitation circle. Also, I'm not entirely sure she'd sleep. She's worse than Fisher."

"I am not," Morgan said, deciding to just accept it. "I haven't even started unpacking my research equipment. When I come here, I sleep."

"Except right now we're going to eat," Pendt said.

She went to the table and began parceling out the food that Deirdre had sent them. Morgan genuinely would not have minded going to the mess for her meals, but Deirdre insisted on sending them to her. Ned acted like it was normal, and maybe it was. The idea that her time was too precious to spend walking to get her own food rankled her, but she couldn't deny that there were definitely days when she would have skipped dinner rather than go and get it for herself.

Pendt gave herself a bigger portion than usual, and Ned noticed immediately.

"What are you up to?" he asked.

"I want to go take a look at the gene-lock," Pendt said. "Just a quick check, no tinkering. I promise."

"Is it risky?" Morgan asked.

"Not really," said Pendt at the same time Ned said, "Yes!"

Pendt glared at him.

"I can go look at it without expending too much energy, especially since now I already know where it is. I just have to scan for the Enragon signature, and it's right there," Pendt said. "I know everything is working fine, and Morgan's connection to station functions is good, but I'll feel better if you let me check."

"She will definitely do it without us if we argue about it," Morgan said.

"We shouldn't have let Fisher cut that 'to obey' part out of your wedding vows," Ned grumbled. "Fine, and because I love you, I won't even tell Dr. Morunt."

Pendt ate half of her dinner, and then put her fork down on the table. She put her hands flat against the surface, took a deep breath, and closed her eyes. Morgan didn't think she'd ever get used to watching Pendt æther-work. Tasia and Deirdre, and even Jonee and Choria, did it so casually you'd never notice. But Pendt went deep. No one else Morgan had ever seen had her range, and it was a little scary to watch.

Ned kept mechanically putting food in his mouth, staring straight ahead as though by not seeing it, he felt any less responsible.

It was only a few moments before Pendt's body shuddered and she came back up. She lurched forward but caught herself on her elbows before she could face-plant into the second half of her dinner. Ned put the fork in her hand and refused to let her talk until her plate was clear.

"The lock is fine," she said after making a show of scraping her plate clean and swallowing the last bite. "Everything is stable. I have a better map of it now, and I think I can reason out how to break it before we try again. Which won't be for a while, Ned, so calm down. I was hoping I'd see an easy solution, because I know this whole thing makes Morgan very uncomfortable, but it's not going to be simple."

"I know you're doing everything you can," Morgan said. Pendt needed both hands to eat, so Morgan opened a packet of fruit juice and set it by her elbow. "And your safety is important too."

"There's something else," Pendt said seriously. "I found the lock by looking for Enragon DNA. I took a model from you and used it to scan the first time, but now that I know what I'm doing, I just have to rule out the other samples."

"Like filtering out background noise?" Morgan asked. "You have to know where I am to find the lock again?"

"More or less," Pendt said. "Which meant this time I also had to know where your aunt was, so I did my scan more widely. Morgan, I found Enragon DNA, a living sample, and it wasn't in the room with me, and it wasn't in the habitation circle."

"You mean—" Morgan's voice failed her, and Pendt nodded.

"Dozens of rebels have come aboard," Pendt said. "And it

could be anyone from your line who knows who they were. If I do a more intensive scan, I ca—"

"No," said Morgan. "No, I want you to save your æther-work for hydroponics and your recovery. We can worry about replacing me later. Right now, you have more important things to do."

"Are you sure?" Ned said. "What if it's your sister?"

"I'm sure," Morgan said. "Pendt . . ."

Vianne hadn't noticed she could control the station until she tried. A new Enragon on the station probably wouldn't try for the same reason Morgan hadn't wanted to in the first place. Secrecy was bred into them as much as their station-coded genes were. Also, Morgan wasn't sure how many more new things or feelings she could take.

"I'll be safe, I promise," Pendt said. "I understand wanting to keep other Enragons safe too."

Morgan finished her dinner and tried not to think how close she had been to getting away. The strangest part was, she was no longer entirely sure she wanted to.

PART THREE:

THE PROPHET

FOR YOU ARE THE FIRE AT THE HEART OF THE WORLD,
AND COMFORT IS ONLY YOURS TO GIVE.

TRANSFIGURATIONS 12:6
DRAGON AGE

Once, the fleet had filled the sky, as uncountable as the stars. Their ships had been made from the best materials, taken from worlds that could not defend their resources from the empire's mighty forces. There had been trade deals, in the beginning, alliances and mutual benefits, but when the empire was strong enough, they stopped bargaining. Those early worlds, conquered by signatures on an economic contract, didn't realize the cost until it was too late, and by then, they were part of the machine. It was fight or submit, and the Stavengers always made sure to emphasize the upside of submission.

Once, the fleet had rained fire down upon worlds and brought ruin and silence to the cold void of space. They fought with precision when necessary, subjugating a populace without destroying the resources that made their planets valuable. When they could, they laid waste to whole cities and ripped ships apart to face explosive decompression. That was what most of the stories focused on: the empire's ability to utterly destroy with no regard for the loss of life they caused. Those stories won almost as many battles as the fleet did. The Stavengers might not care about life or sustainability in the personal sense, but if they could win a world without firing on it, they would take that advantage gladly.

Once, the fleet had been in absolute control. A solar system, seven stations, uncountable asteroids, and satellite installations fell under their rule, and still they wanted more. The conquered began to accumulate wealth of their own, and with that growth came the beginnings of rebellious thoughts. Why should the empire, far away and full of its own riches, claim their hard work too? The Stavengers heard those whispers and took the only action they knew: they set out again to conquer, to bring their subjects in line and force them to subject someone else.

That time was long past, the expansion failed, the fleet decimated, the empire in pieces held together by the sheer will of the remaining commanders controlled by the Hegemony from deep in the Stavenger solar system. It was a tenuous situation, ripe for destruction at any moment, though the Stavengers had done their best to ensure that any destruction would be mutual. If they went down, they would take the stations with them, and then everyone else would starve to death in chaos. They guarded their fragile peace jealously, constantly alert for the slightest hint of the rebellion's return. And rebellions aren't generally known for their subtlety.

Rumours had reached the Stavengers, at last. It started with a reliable ship losing a promising resource. It grew to two boys who didn't fear death, which was fortunate, as one of them died. It became a movement, a network of ships and small installations, linked together by an unknown thread of common factors. And now there was talk of something else, something so big that it had destroyed the Stavenger Empire all those generations ago and was returning to do the same to those who fought so hard to maintain that power. It took some time to sort through all of the intelligence, but finally, a pattern emerged.

A lock, a key, a disaster on the horizon.

And so, as they had in the days gone by, the fleet set out, sharp and silent, with conquest and violence at its heart.

22.

WITH AUNT VIANNE ON the station to take a twelve-hour shift each day, Morgan felt like she was getting part of her life back. A small part, seeing as she was still attached to Enragon and responsible for an ever-growing number of lives, but it was enough that she got to sleep regularly, which helped immeasurably.

She resisted getting quarters in the habitation circle. She knew it would be easier in a lot of ways if she did. For starters, maybe she'd stop needing Ned to sleep on her sofa to get any sleep herself. But she was reluctant to leave operations because that's where she had decided to set up her detection equipment.

The only real downside to having Vianne help her was that Morgan had a lot more spare time to think, and once she started, she couldn't stop. Exposing the Enragons to the rebellion had been easier than she'd anticipated. No one resented her secret-keeping, and everyone had been extremely helpful as both she and Vianne stumbled through the basics of station management. What really ate away at her was the possibility of her sister.

Pendt hadn't found any new traces of Enragon genetics when she had gone looking again, meaning that whoever had been aboard was gone now. This was not alarming, since the rebels moved around a lot. At the same time, Morgan found that she was increasingly curious. Watching Tasia's family and seeing the bonds between Ned and Pendt had opened up her concept of what family meant. It might not be beyond the realm of possibility to reforge her connection with her sister, even after more than a decade of estrangement. At the same time, it would endanger her, and that is what kept Morgan from moving forward. Vianne was an adult and could make her own decisions. Morgan's sister probably hadn't had that much freedom, growing up on Skúvoy, and Morgan was determined not to interfere in her life if she could help it.

The two streams of thoughts ran into each other over and over again, creating a feedback loop in Morgan's mind as she tried to reason her way through it. It never got easier, and it never got less intimidating, and Morgan never got anywhere closer to an answer. That only served to frustrate her further, and the thought spiral continued to grow with every moment she obsessed over it.

Thankfully, even when she wasn't on duty in operations, she was eventually able to redirect her concentration into her research. She set up the equipment in an unoccupied corner of operations, after requisitioning a table and some power cells. She could run everything through the main station computers if she wanted to, but a separate system would be easier to set up at the beginning.

If there was already too much noise on Enragon for her gear to detect anything, then it was a moot point, and she didn't want to waste too much effort.

Once her equipment was happily churning out streams of data, she started filtering out the background radiation. It wasn't as smooth as it was on Valon, but after a few days, she had pinpointed the signal she was after, at last. She set the machines to tracking down its origin point, and then there was nothing to do but wait.

Waiting was not her favourite thing. That's when the other thinking took over, despite her best efforts.

First, there was the issue of Ned. This was a new conundrum, and while the fate of hundreds was not at stake, it didn't make getting stuck in a thought spiral about him any better. He was nice and he did things to help her without her asking him, unless it was really important, and then he asked permission. He was still sleeping on her sofa, and more of his things had migrated into her quarters. She'd got him his own storage unit, and he had stocked her little kitchenette with snacks and easily assembled meals. She'd only accidentally seen him naked twice, and he'd never seen her, because he wasn't as absentminded as she was and always remembered to knock.

She thought she might need him. She could imagine a future without Vianne or Pendt close by, only available to talk over long-distance comms every once in a while, and it made her sad, but it wasn't painful. She couldn't imagine life without Tasia, but they'd always been independent of each other, even now that Morgan was making more of an effort to be a good friend. The idea of Ned leaving, though, hurt her in a way she couldn't explain. She knew he had other commitments and a family to go back to, but she wanted him to stay. Which was ridiculous, because *she* didn't even want to stay. At least, not tied to Enragon the way she was.

The worst part was that she couldn't bring herself to be annoyed by her emotional dependence on him. He made her happy in ways she hadn't known were possible, and she liked that feeling. Of course, Ned went out of his way to make everyone happy, so she probably wasn't that special. She decided that she would make the most of the time he decided to give her and not be upset when he left, but it wasn't quite as simple as making that choice. Stupid feelings.

The second issue was her family. Morgan was not a romantic person, so she didn't expect to have a gut feeling connection to whichever Enragon descendant had wandered onto the station for Pendt to detect. Rebels came and left so frequently that it was entirely possible her relative was no longer here. Morgan wondered, though, about if she had been a better person, she would have *known* she had a family member on board. Wouldn't she? Particularly if it was her sister or her mother? She didn't remember her parents as being particularly rebellious. They had worked in a factory. She'd heard enough of Tasia's union stories to know that that didn't exactly preclude political inclinations, but none of her memories of them had that fire she'd come to associate with people like Choria, Jonee, and Ned.

Morgan's father had died when she was ten, five years after Vianne took her to Katla, and while her mother had found a new partner, Morgan didn't know any of the details except that the new husband was better off, and her mother thought she was lucky. Her stepfather had adopted her sister, but there had been no reason to adopt her. She'd never thought to ask Vianne, the person to whom all the messages were sent, if her mother and sister had changed their name.

Her sister would be fifteen or so now. That was probably too young to be an active rebel, though Jonee hadn't been much older when she started, and Ned hadn't yet been nineteen. Morgan didn't know what she'd say to her sister even if they met, but surely she should have *known*.

Pendt was very closemouthed about her family, and so Morgan couldn't ask her for advice. Ned was unusually useless in this situation, since his family all really liked each other, and Tasia was extra useless because she couldn't even comprehend how Morgan's parents had given her up in the first place.

Morgan was starting to feel a little bit lost. She was unquestionably an important part of what was going in the strengthening of the rebel movement right now, but it wasn't due to any of her abilities or her work. She was just the DNA they needed to establish a foothold, and the person who pressed the button to bring more of them in. If Pendt was eventually successful in breaking the gene-lock, she wouldn't be necessary at all, and Morgan had no idea what she'd do then.

It was pointless to think about returning to Katla. With the ruling family working against her, she'd never be able to settle there with any degree of comfort. She didn't doubt for a moment that Fisher would welcome her to Brannick. Every time they spoke—even when it was just a quick chat to coordinate a transport—his kindness bled through in his every word. But she didn't have a purpose there.

It used to terrify her, the idea of being lashed to a station. She remembered ignoring all of Pendt's original messages, the cold thread of fear that had run through her when she even thought the word *Enragon*. She hadn't wanted anyone to use her for the genes she had or the genes she could produce. She wanted to mean something more. And now, despite everything, her genes were all she was, and she clung to that harder than she wanted to, because the alternative was being sent away or left behind.

It made her want to scream or cry or—to her shame—burrow into Ned's chest until he told her it was going to be okay. The most important thing was that no one ever know about it. She would be cheerful when her friends talked to her. She would offer suggestions, even if it was a problem she couldn't solve. She would go to operations every day with a smile and do her job, and when they didn't need her any more, she would be practical about it.

"I'm worried," Ned said to the screen in front of him.

"About the rebellion?" Fisher asked.

"Well, yeah," Ned said. "But also about Morgan."

"Why?" Fisher said. "I think she's settling in very well. Every time we talk, she seems like she's in a good mood."

"That's why I'm worried," Ned said. "I think we're losing her. To the station. The way we would have lost me."

Fisher didn't say anything for a long moment. He remembered those days. Before Pendt had come along, and everything had changed for the better.

"Then don't let her go," he said, like if he said it, it would be that easy.

"What if she asks me to?" Ned asked.

"You don't always have to say yes, Ned," Fisher told him. "It's not always the best answer. Make her ask the right questions."

Pendt had done the calculations several times now, one hand resting on her flat belly, while she ran the numbers over and over again. She needed to talk to Morgan.

When Morgan finally found it, she almost didn't realize what it was. A line on a graph that transposed to coordinates in space. A series of markers to point the way.

Once she filtered out all the comm chatter and identifiable radiation sources, she was left with one thing. The same trail that had led her to Valon was here, leading away from Enragon Station and into the vast nothingness of space.

Or, the vast almost-nothingness of space, in this case.

She had several days' worth of data, enough to plot out a path through the stars. She didn't know what would be at the end of it, but she knew that she was the person who was going to find out.

23.

MORE REBELS ARRIVED ON Enragon every day. By necessity, this required a centralization of command that hadn't existed in the movement since before the Stavenger Empire fell. Captain Choria was not the most senior officer available—by neither age nor experience—but she did know the most about Enragon and Brannick, and so the others deferred to her. A group of ten captains formed a council, and their first act was to promote her to admiral, which she only grumbled about when they weren't listening.

"I know someone has to do it," she said. "But I liked being a captain. Admirals don't go out with ships unless it's really serious. I feel like I'm stuck here."

"Oh no, what a nightmare," Morgan deadpanned. Choria had the grace to look abashed.

Morgan, Pendt, and Ned sat in on the strategy meetings. Morgan because she ran the station, Pendt because she was Pendt, and Ned to represent his brother. Morgan had thought her spatial awareness was pretty good, but as she watched Choria and the others strategize defense manoeuvres in three dimensions, she realized how far she had to go. Choria could plot all directions even if the map was in two dimensions. Morgan forgot about down when the map was flat.

"It's a station thing," Pendt said. "But it makes sense to a certain extent. Down is the floor, and you can't go through it. There's even gravity to reinforce the feeling in your inner ear. If it makes you feel any better, when I got to Brannick, I had to get used to the idea of down as much as you're getting used to this."

That didn't really clear anything up, but it did make Morgan feel better. She started thinking of direction in relation to Enragon's layout, rather than how she was standing in relation to the floor. That would mean the dock and storage rings were at the bottom, for lack of a better word, and the other three circles were at the top. In was towards operations at the junction of the rings, and out was away. She knew there were very old words for direction of spin, but that might be taking it a step too far. When it came to space, they used degrees from an agreed-upon fixed point, in this case Enragon itself. From Morgan's point of view, that meant everything they were talking about was *up*, that her home was now beneath her feet, and the rest of the universe rotated around it.

Ned didn't say a lot in the meetings but was quick to answer questions if any were put to him. Pendt could give reports on logistics but had included herself mostly out of curiosity. Everyone was very polite to Morgan, treating her like she was a Katla. It was off-putting.

She was glad Choria was nominally in charge, however. She was sure the other captains and their crews, including the ones who rotated in and away from the station too frequently to attend council meetings, were fine, but she trusted Choria. That was in no small part why she agreed to make a presentation to the others about her research.

"So, to sum up," she said, hoping they wouldn't ask her too many questions, "the fall of the Stavenger Empire was preceded by a disaster that destroyed the æther. I think it is a cyclical event and I've been tracking down a very old source of radiation that I hope will tell me more about the timeline of the next disaster."

"And then the æther will be gone again?" asked one of the captains. They all looked deeply uncomfortable at her conclusions.

"Yes. We know the Stavengers activated the gene-locks *after* the disaster, but it cost them a tremendous amount in terms of caloric resources, and the stories about it indicate that all of the æther-workers died. The Stavengers might not have suspected that many deaths from their efforts, but I don't think they cared either way, as long as the job was done."

"Which means there's a very small grace period after the disaster begins," said the captain. "But we might not be able to utilize it because we're not willing to kill people."

"Yes," Morgan said. "I am doing everything I can to find out if there will be warnings."

"What do you think, Admiral?" another captain said.

"I've been with Morgan for most of her fieldwork, and I don't doubt her," Choria said. "I also think she is doing everything she can. That said, I don't think a general dissemination of the information is a good idea at this time. We can't really prepare for something when we don't know when it'll happen. We have to go out into space. We have to keep fortifying our position and stockpiling supplies."

The captains grumbled.

"I don't like it any more than you do," Morgan said. "But we can take some small comfort in knowing that the Well and Net will still be operational after the disaster. Those of you who rely entirely on star-sense to calculate your jumps might want to start learning to do it the long way, but the Net will be here."

"Our systems will all keep working as well," Ned said. "The only thing that got damaged in the disaster was the æther. Even æther-workers were fine. Our communications relays and station operations will function."

"The Stavengers will be able to jump as far as Katla." Choria looked at Ned, who winced. "Unless they use a Brannick hostage, but that actually puts them farther away, so I don't think they will. Katla will let them in, and Skúvoy definitely will. If we are extremely lucky, the fleet will be in deep space when the disaster hits and all of them will get lost. If not, we'll have plenty of warning, because I have people in place on Katla who will tell us when they leave. Their ships are faster than ours, but we'll have time."

"The only issue is that you can't spare a ship for me," Morgan said. "Even if I was comfortable leaving my aunt here alone—and I am not. It would be possible for me to brief Jonee and Ned on what to look for, though. Between them, they'd be able to use the æther to track the radiation I'm tracing. But we don't have a ship to spare, so we'll be relying on my data as it comes in."

"Vianne has agreed to work longer shifts in operations, which frees Morgan up to do her work," Pendt said.

"I think that just about wraps everything up," Choria said. "We'll continue to place lookouts and prep the small fighters. The electro-mages will do whatever they can to make Enragon physically stronger. And Morgan will follow the trail."

"There's one more thing." This was from the captain who made the most regular run between Katla and Enragon. "Before I face a general mutiny, could we please decide what we're going to do with the Furloughs' goats?"

The officers left immediately when the meeting was over, but Pendt hung back with Morgan, who had plans to get some work done before she relieved Vianne for a while.

"I wanted to ask you something," Pendt said. "And I'm pretty sure I know the answer, but you're the expert."

"Okay," Morgan said. "Theoretical expert, at least."

"Good enough," Pendt said. "We know the Net and Well will stay active after the disaster."

"Yes," Morgan said. "If they hadn't, all of the stations would have been immediately isolated last time, until the æther regained full strength."

"So, any æther-work that has been done will stay done?" Pendt asked.

"Plants won't ungrow, if that's the sort of thing you mean," Morgan said, thinking immediately of hydroponics. "Rationing will be more difficult, though. You'll have to do that by hand too. And the electro-mages won't be able to jump-start things any more or conduct a current. Æther-workers won't be able to do anything new without a tremendous expenditure of calories and lives."

She realized that Pendt was not really paying attention to her answer, and then several pieces clicked into place in her brain.

"I have no way of knowing," Morgan said delicately. "But I'd guess that the baby would stay in stasis. It would be safe and you'd be safe, but you wouldn't be able to, um, activate it."

"And I'd always be pregnant," Pendt said. "So, five years down the road, I couldn't get pregnant again. At least, not normally."

"That follows, yes," Morgan said. She didn't want to think about the not-normal ways.

Pendt ran her fingers through her hair. She kept it long, and it was usually up in a ponytail or braid, but today she'd just put on a headband and left it at that. Long hair reminded her of many things, and sometimes she needed to feel it on her neck.

"I'm sorry I don't have a better timeline for you," Morgan said. "And even if you tried to do something after the disaster, in that little window, we have no idea how much effort it would take or what the effects would be."

"I'll have a talk with Fisher, then," Pendt said. "We do talk about it sometimes, what we'd like to do when we are parents, but the whole point was that I was supposed to get to choose."

"I'm sorry," Morgan said.

"It's not your fault," Pendt said. "You're the only reason I get any warning. And I do still get to make a choice—it's just got a few more provisos attached."

"That's how I ended up with a station," Morgan said. "And I'm doing okay."

Pendt shot her a long look that indicated she didn't really believe what Morgan was saying.

"Ned worries, you know," she said.

"About me?" Morgan asked. "Why?"

"Because he knows what it's like to not want a station," Pendt said. "He knows what it means to be absolutely required for something you don't want, and to have all those people depending on you for something you don't want to do."

"I'm *fine*, Pendt," Morgan said.

"We're all fine," Pendt said. She had made the next choice, but she wasn't about to announce it. "Until we're not."

It came down to a matter of timing.

First, Pendt had to find a time when the medical-shift change overlapped with a time that Morgan and Ned would be sleeping. Since Ned still slept on Morgan's couch, that part was easy. There were several medical bays throughout Enragon—a few of which they hadn't reactivated yet—but the one she needed was the one on the operations level. That was where they'd taken Morgan when the station latched on to her. That was where they stored the supplies they didn't need for everyday use, like the IV calorie bags.

There was about half an hour at the beginning of every medical shift where the staff were briefing one another and only came into the infirmary itself if there was an emergency. That was the window Pendt needed, and she was just about to seize it when she felt someone tap her on the shoulder.

"You are up to something," said Tasia Furlough. "I have thirteen siblings. I can tell. Also, you've been eating more calories without visibly increasing the volume of your portions, and that's just sneaky."

"If you could help Morgan, would you?" Pendt asked.

"Of course," Tasia said. "I've been her friend since before she knew what friends were. She's weird as hell, but I love her. Why, what does she need?"

"She needs something that I am not supposed to do," Pendt said. "It won't hurt her; I'm just not supposed to do it without supervision. Or, you know, permission."

"I can supervise," Tasia said. "And the other thing you learn with a family like mine is that it's always easier to ask for forgiveness once you've done the thing you don't have permission for."

"In my family that might have got me airlocked," Pendt said. She shook off the memory. "But I see the argument. Will you help?"

"Of course," Tasia said. "Lead the way."

The two girls went into the infirmary through the rear entrance. There were no other patients, and it was quiet. They had about twenty-five minutes before they would get caught. Tasia helped Pendt assemble the IV bags she'd need, and she showed her how to switch them out.

"I'm going to go through them very fast," she said. "I haven't really prepped this time."

Tasia was clearly starting to have doubts about the whole process.

"I will be fine, I promise," Pendt said. "And it'll help Morgan. Just keep the bags coming."

"I knew you were crazy powerful, but this might be literally insane,"Tasia said. She prepped the IV needle and shunt. "Are you ready?"

"Yes," said Pendt Brannick. "Let's go break a lock."

24.

MORGAN WOKE UP SCREAMING, which meant that Ned woke up by falling off the sofa. He was on his feet, kicking free of the blanket, before she stopped, and halfway into her room before he wondered if bursting in like that might scare her even more.

"Morgan, what is it?" He stopped at the foot of her bed.

She was sitting up, ramrod straight with the blankets around her waist, breathing hard. Her face was pale, but not the kind of pale that went with night terrors. She reached for him, and without a moment's hesitation he went.

"Hey, it's okay." He sat behind her with his legs on either side and put his arms around her. She relaxed infinitesimally into his hold.

"It's not okay," she said. Her breathing calmed in spite of herself. "We have to go to operations right now."

He made her get dressed, mostly so she wouldn't be cold in the corridors, then pulled on his shoes. She was in a hurry, and they reached the control room before five minutes had passed.

Vianne was standing in the middle of the room, frozen, and looking at her hands. Jonee, who often spent her free time in operations, stood helplessly to the side. Vianne snapped out of her trance when they entered, and Morgan went straight to her.

"It's gone," Morgan said. Vianne nodded.

"What's gone?" Ned asked.

Choria and one of the other captains, summoned by Vianne before their arrival, poured through the door.

"What happened?" Choria asked.

"Enragon," Morgan said. "I can't feel it. I couldn't really feel it before, but somehow, I know it's different. It's gone."

"Like finding something you forgot, only to lose it again," Vianne said. "You only notice the loss because you noticed the gain."

"We're still breathing," said one of the captains.

Choria was the closest, so she took three steps to the control panel and pressed the button that turned on the Net. It flared to life, and they all stared at it until it went out again. Choria looked at her hands like they belonged to someone else.

"How—" began the captain.

"Where," interrupted Ned, "is Pendt?"

They heard Dr. Morunt yelling from all the way down the corridor as they ran to the infirmary. They also heard Tasia yelling back, though both voices were muffled by closed doors, and it was impossible to determine what they said. Ned went immediately to

Pendt's bedside, while Morgan moved a bit more slowly and took in the room.

There were empty IV calorie bags everywhere. Morgan counted at least a dozen. She couldn't remember how many Pendt had needed the first time she tried to break the lock, but she thought it was more than that. Tasia was struggling to get free of Dr. Morunt's hold, and Morgan soon realized why. The bag currently attached to Pendt's port was almost empty. She must still be drawing calories, and she needed more. Morunt realized what was happening and switched the bag himself.

"I'm not sorry I helped her," Tasia said defiantly. "She was going to do it anyway."

"Her life signs are stable," Dr. Morunt said. "She's recovering, at least."

Morgan looked over at Ned, who had picked up Pendt's free hand and was squeezing it between both of his. There were tears streaming down his cheeks.

Pendt was beyond pale. Her skin was a horrible transparent grey and lay too loosely against her bones. Her veins should have been starkly contrasted, but they were faded too, which was probably a bad sign. Her hair was starting to fall out as Ned shifted her, and her fingernails were falling off.

"Wake up," he whispered. "You promised you wouldn't do this again, *wake up*."

Pendt did not wake up.

"It's my fault," Morgan said, voice so small it barely made more noise than the monitor following Pendt's heartbeat. "We were talking about the timeline. About what would happen after the disaster, and what would change. I told her there was no way to tell when it would come, and that she'd have to make a choice one way or the other, but I thought we were just talking about the baby."

"The baby is unchanged," Dr. Morunt said before Ned could ask. "She decided to go for the lock first."

"And she got it," Morgan said.

Tasia sat down heavily on one of the rolling stools and skittered sideways. For all her bravado, she was glad to hear they had succeeded.

"When will she wake up?" Ned asked.

"I don't know," Dr. Morunt said. "I hadn't cleared her to go under, and she hadn't prepped like she did before. All she had was that one changing the bags."

"I can tell when a body needs calories," Tasia said sharply. "And how much."

"That doesn't give you a medical degree!" Morunt said.

"Enough," Morgan said. "Stop yelling. Pendt is the single most determined person I have ever met. Her plan was probably to change the damn bags herself somehow, and we're all lucky Tasia was here, or she'd be dead."

Morgan turned away from Pendt's bed and looked at Tasia. Her friend was more upset than she was letting on.

"How many calories does she need?" Morgan asked.

"Not more than we have," said Tasia. There were several relieved noises.

"It's going to take a while, though," Dr. Morunt said. "The calories she didn't ingest pre–æther-work are going to be replaced as slowly as her prep time usually takes."

"That's a whole week," Ned said flatly. "Can I take her home at least? To Brannick?"

He meant to Fisher, and they all knew it.

"I would advise against moving her, especially off station," Morunt said. He looked like he had aged a decade since the conversation began. "Even if I was allowed to go with her, any number of things could go wrong."

"My siblings will take care of her," Tasia said. "I can show them how the IV bags work."

"Ned, are you going to be okay?" Morgan asked.

"I don't know," he said. "What am I going to tell my brother?"

Choria and the other council members decided to keep the new state of Enragon Station as quiet as they could for as long as possible. They knew that the Stavenger Empire must have spies within their ranks somewhere, and if one of them were to learn the truth, they could open the Net for the fleet themselves. The rebels' main advantage would be gone. This meant that Vianne and Morgan would still pretend to work shifts, but there were always several people in the control room, and now any of them could activate the Net.

Ned stayed in the infirmary for a bit while his call with Fisher was being set up, and Morgan felt even more adrift than she already had. This was the beginning of the end for her, surely. She'd gone from being absolutely vital to a convenient security measure. She took a moment to look at her data, but nothing had changed since the last time she checked. The trail went on and her machines followed it, but she had no conclusions to offer, and nothing else that she could give. Even Pendt didn't need her, because Tasia's gene-mage siblings would take better care of her than Morgan would be able to.

All her life, she'd never cared about not being an æther-worker. She'd considered it a personal strength, actually. Everything she got, she had earned. It wasn't given to her by her genetics. Now she knew better. Æther-workers put in just as much effort as she did, and not everyone had social connections like she had with her aunt and the university. It was just a different kind of work. With her genetics-given talent no longer required, Morgan was left with nothing. She wanted, more than anything, to have something to give.

Aunt Vianne tried to hug her, but Morgan was not in the mood to be comforted. Vianne hadn't been the one the station reached for when it woke up. She had helped a great deal in the past few weeks, and Morgan was very grateful to her, but Vianne had a life and a job and a purpose on Katla, one that she could transfer to Enragon easily enough if she decided to. Morgan didn't resent her for it, but she didn't exactly want to be close to her right now either.

She didn't view what Tasia did as a betrayal. She meant what she'd said about Tasia probably saving Pendt's life. She also guessed that Pendt hadn't had to talk very fast to get her to go along with it. And that Tasia would help Pendt because Pendt would tell her she was helping Morgan.

Morgan didn't deserve either of them.

There was a crackle of static, an expected identification code, and then a desperate voice filled the room.

"Open the Net!" screamed the comm. "Please for the love of everything, open the Net!"

Jonee was sitting closest to the panel and threw herself on the button instinctively. The panel sparked as her æther got away from her, but the Net flared. A familiar-looking ship crashed into it and rolled free immediately instead of taking the time to get their thrusters online. The ship floated askew in space.

"Close it now!" ordered Choria, who had figured out what must be happening, but Jonee was already moving.

She hit the kill switch, and the Net disappeared. A streak of light blazed through the space where the Net had just been. It didn't slow down at all.

Morgan let out a breath she hadn't realized she was holding. She was not the only one. Everyone's adrenaline had spiked, but now their autonomic functions replaced their instincts.

"I always wondered what that looked like," Choria said. "I really hope I never see it again."

Morgan, half a moment behind, finally realized what she had witnessed. The rebel ship had had a pursuer. They must have been just far enough behind to make the same jump the rebel captain did. That distance had let them mimic the trajectory but gave Enragon the fraction of a second it needed to close the Net. The blaze was a ship, speeding into eternity with nothing to catch it.

"Thank you, Enragon Station." The captain's voice was calmer, but she was still breathing hard. "Admiral, the Hegemony is at Katla. They saw us and engaged immediately. They knew what they were looking for."

"Have everyone recalled to Brannick immediately," Choria

said. "We can't risk them jumping straight here, but once Fisher has had them for a bit, they can funnel in. We've started the clock. Let's get this done."

The captains left to tell their crews, immediately understanding the orders that Morgan was slower to parse. She made her way over to Jonee, who hadn't budged from the panel.

"Nice catch," Morgan said. She tried to keep her tone light. She wasn't sure if her friend was in shock. She knew how she'd felt the first time she caught a ship.

"Holy shit," said Jonee, recovering. "I used a fucking Net!"

"You did," Morgan said. "You really did."

Choria stopped on her way out to congratulate Jonee as well. Jonee was clearly happy to have impressed her captain, though each one was too professional to acknowledge that. Instead, Choria gave her a few words of encouragement, then went below to her staging room.

Jonee was standing at the viewport, watching as the rebel ship docked. Parts of the hull were smoking. They had clearly been under fire. They must have been very outmatched to risk a jump when they weren't entirely sure they'd be caught. If Morgan had still been connected, she wouldn't have known to turn off the system so quickly. She might have let the Stavengers through.

The lock was broken. Pendt was out of commission. And the fight was finally, truly on its way here. Behind her, her equipment continued to scan, almost mocking her at this point. Because the danger was really here, and Morgan couldn't do anything about it.

25.

FISHER WAS NOT HAPPY, but he was also not entirely surprised. Pendt had, after all, taken a great personal risk to help him. She had learned how to be wonderfully, amazingly selfish sometimes, and every bit of that was a hard-fought battle against the demons of her past, but sometimes she fell back on the cold calculations that powered the *Harland* and devalued and dehumanized her.

"Anyway," Ned wound up, "Dr. Morunt says she'll be fine; he just doesn't know when. Tasia, the cook we all like from Katla, is going to take care of her when the rest of us can't be there. And Morgan is throwing herself into station operations even harder than before."

"She's definitely earned a short rest," Fisher said. There were dark circles around his eyes, as always. Brannick had a fixed schedule, but the rebel comings and goings had pushed him to the brink.

"I don't think she'd agree with you," Ned said. "At least not until Pendt's awake and Morgan has delivered her personally to Brannick, so that she can do the same thing for you."

"I will keep her away from here until she's healthy if it stops her from trying this again," Fisher said, but there wasn't a lot of heat in it. He missed her a lot.

In the last few weeks, Ned had learned that people reacted different ways to certain kinds of pressure. For his part, he approached the impending æther disaster with a sort of carefree determination. He couldn't stop it, so he would do what he could before it got here. Both Morgan and Pendt, on the other hand, seemed to fall into the cram-as-much-in-as-soon-as-possible camp. He couldn't really understand that, and assumed they didn't understand him, but he didn't think that made either approach less valid. Theirs was just more immediately dangerous.

"She's worried, Fisher," Ned said. "All the fighting aside, if she loses her connection to the æther, she can't do for Brannick what she did here. I think that's what made her desperate. She had to know."

"I don't blame her," Fisher said. "I just . . ."

"Yeah," said Ned. "I know."

Ned hated being far away from people. It was one of his least favourite things.

"The other news is that a rebel ship came in under fire," Ned continued. "We just got the Net closed before the Stavenger ship followed. I didn't see it, but I gather it's creepy as hell."

"So, they're coming for you," Fisher said.

"Admiral Choria thinks it'll take them about a week to make the trip," Ned said. "Their tech is way better than ours, but our spies were able to at least get a look at it. I think Choria's hoping to take some of the ships as prizes if she can. It would make a huge difference."

"Will you be on the station or the *Cleland*?" Fisher tried to keep his tone light, but didn't fool either of them.

"I don't know yet," Ned said. "Obviously I would rather stay here, but they've put a lot of effort into training me. I can't sit out if Choria asks me to go."

"I wouldn't expect it," Fisher said. "I just feel like I'm not doing anything at all."

"You're keeping us supplied, which isn't nothing. And you're getting our people here safely," Ned reminded him. "Choria would like a few more shipments, after the last of the rebels come through, but then she thinks we should break off communication. The Stavengers will be in range, and if they get wind of how much Brannick helped us, it might get ugly."

Both of them knew that their father could appear in the Net whenever the Stavengers wanted, and that it would probably be the last thing any of them ever saw.

"We've got three of your ships in the docks," Fisher said. "Plus, two more that have volunteered to go. I won't send them if they don't want to stay, but even if it's just the three, that should get you through a siege."

"The Stavengers can't carry that much with them. They don't have cargo ships in the fleet, as far as we know, and you can't fit much stowage on a gunner," Ned said. "Whatever they stole from Katla, they're going to be on tight rations."

"Which limits their æther-workers," Fisher said. "Assuming they don't sacrifice them."

"That's still a limit." Ned made a face. "Even if it's despicable."

"I did have one more question," Fisher said. "It is entirely unrelated to any of our current problems."

"In that case, ask away," Ned said. He regretted it almost as soon as he said it when Fisher's grin turned sly.

"So, Morgan," Fisher said. "Pendt said you've basically moved in with her."

"It's not like that," Ned said. "We sleep in separate rooms."

"Pendt and I used to sleep in separate rooms," Fisher pointed out.

"I am aware," Ned said. "But my point is, she's never given any indication that she wants anything but my help and my presence. And to be perfectly honest with you, I'm okay with that. I like her a lot, but I'm not going to push her into anything. I'll stay as long as she'll have me, but I don't need anything besides what I've already got."

"Does she know that?" Fisher asked.

"Of course not," Ned said. "How emotionally stable do you think I am?"

Fisher laughed, and Ned felt something in his chest loosen. He really did feel fine with the way things stood between him and Morgan. It was just going to be a challenge to explain to people who expected love to mean sex. He'd had sex. He'd liked it, even though it had been very awkward. He was in no rush to ever be that awkward again.

"I'm glad," Fisher said. "I worry about you sometimes."

"I worry about you all the time, so I guess we're even," Ned said. "I better get off this channel. I can see the admiral pacing the hallway outside the room."

"Tell Pendt I love her," Fisher said.

"I will," Ned said. "And I love you too."

Two days later, the fourth and final ship from Brannick arrived in the Net. The fifth captain had elected not to come. Since it was a generation ship with the captain's own family on board, Morgan could understand prioritizing that over honour or profit. She and Vianne had similarly decided it was best to continue ignoring the possibility of more Enragons. There was only one way to test if the Net would still automatically catch someone with their genetic markers, and no one wanted to give the Stavengers that test subject. The safest place for a known Enragon to be right now was on the very station that no longer required them.

Once they had every supply they were going to get on hand, Choria pushed the remaining gene-mages to get the rationing done as soon as they could. It was a careful balance, because using their abilities required calories, but Morgan noticed that even Deirdre had switched over to written calculations at least some of the time. Whether it was practice or preservation, Morgan couldn't say.

The electro-mages were not in a similar position. They had to use their abilities as much as they could, because all of the ships and weapons were needed as quickly as possible. Morgan watched out the viewport as a small armada of ships that Choria called stingers were assembled in near free fall. There were tethers keeping the ships and the suited-up workers from floating away from Enragon, but it was still nerve-racking work. It was no less nerve-racking to watch the bulky ships like the *Cleland* retrofit themselves with armaments, but at least that could be done with the security of a docking clamp.

It was difficult for the star-mages to explain what they were doing. Morgan understood it in theory, but in practice it looked like so much standing around and occasionally glancing at a chart or out a viewport. Every one of them, even those who had only instinctive directional abilities like Ned, was memorizing star positions in relation to Enragon so they would always know where everything was. This would help them stay in formation during a firefight, but it would also help them come up with firing solutions once the Stavenger ships started getting between them and the stellar objects they were memorizing.

With everyone so busy preparing, Morgan was surprised to find herself near the centre of it. Since she was almost always in operations, she heard reports from everyone and helped to coordinate supply depots. She also ended up organizing the noncombatants, from Dr. Morunt and his colleagues in the infirmary all the way down to the smallest Furlough, who was charged with taking care of the goats in the hope that it would distract her from the war going on outside. Morgan fielded questions and found solutions, and it turned out she was pretty good at it. Most of the people on Enragon still thought she was gene-locked to the station, so maybe it was natural that they turn to her for leadership, but it was still good to be doing something meaningful.

She was so caught up in preparing for the attack that she

could be forgiven for letting her attention slide away from her research. She still looked at the data every night before she went to bed, but she wasn't actively thinking about it as much as usual. Her mind was full of things like where to put the gurneys and how many pounds of protein an electro-mage needed before a firefight and why the fuck had she agreed to let the Furloughs bring their goats in the first place.

It was Ned, of course, who was thoughtful enough to ask. They were having dinner in her apartment, actually sitting at the table for a change instead of just eating while they walked to wherever it was they next needed to be. Deirdre continued to send her meals up from the mess, and Morgan hadn't been down to eat a meal there in what felt like forever. Most of the officers ate on their feet in the control room too, so she didn't complain.

She told Ned that she'd been busy, and that while she was looking at the data, she wasn't really thinking about it very much. And then saying that made her think about it all the time. For a day after they had dinner, she turned her data over in her mind when she was supposed to be doing something else. There was something she was missing. She was sure of it. And now that she had noticed it, she couldn't stop until she found it, even if other things were going on.

Morgan forced herself to pay attention to all the briefings that day, digging her fingernails into her palms or biting the inside of her mouth to make herself listen. She focused on the coming fight for every single minute she was required to, determined that no one would think she was giving less than everything.

The moment her shift was over, she went straight to her

equipment. Tasia brought her dinner, but recognized the expression on her face and just left it for her. Morgan absently thanked her, but didn't even look up to see what was on her plate.

It was right in front of her. She could feel it. Something so big and so obvious that she should have noticed it days ago, only she hadn't, because she'd stopped being an academic researcher the moment Enragon had latched on to her. Now she had other responsibilities. Now she had to interact with people. Now she *liked* interacting with people. But she still had this work in front of her, and it was still important.

When she finally found it, she almost shouted in triumph but held back at the last minute. It was big and it was obvious. Her equipment was good, but it wasn't top of the line. She'd made most of it herself. Even after she filtered out every possible bit of radiation that might be muddying her readings, it shouldn't be this clear. She couldn't tell them. Not until after the current crisis was over. Her work was important, but it was still vague. The Stavenger fleet would be arriving practically any moment.

The signal she'd been tracking was way too strong. It wasn't a remnant or the residue of some long-dead oglasa from back when the last disaster had happened. She almost laughed. The university—and the Katlas—had let her go, and now she was going to make them regret it. Assuming she survived the Stavengers. Because this was *current*. And it was much, much closer to the station than she'd originally thought.

26.

"THERE'S SOMETHING I DON'T like about their formation," Choria said, staring at the display screen.

The Stavenger fleet had been visible on it for several hours, giving them time to get crews onto ships and pilots into stingers. Choria had been fixed on the screen for almost as long, waiting for the fleet to shift into their attack pattern. Morgan could tell she was itching to be at the helm of the *Cleland* or the *Marquis*, but the other captains needed the admiral in operations, and so that's where Choria was. The Stavengers were almost in firing range, and they hadn't moved yet. It was putting everyone on edge.

"What could they do in a formation like that?" Morgan asked.

To her, it seemed pretty simple. There were smaller fighters, maybe fifty of them, in a three-dimensional wedge that stretched out to cover the three dozen frigates behind them. Those were in a straight line on the same axis. Behind that were ten gunships and more fighters. The rebels were very outnumbered.

"We've never engaged a battle group this large," Choria admitted. "But our style relies heavily on a bunch of independent, cut-and-run attacks. This just gives us more space to peel away."

"I'm getting a report from Captain Leynar," Ned said from his station. "She says that the gunships are flying normally, but the frigates are in some kind of lockstep. They're not making any adjustments, and they're all firing their engines at full instead of slowing down for an engagement approach."

"Firing," Choria said under her breath, then straightened and called up the comm channel that would carry her voice to every rebel ship. "Attention all ships, all ships. The frigates are fireships. The fighters will cut a path for them, and the frigates will explode as soon as they're fired on. They cannot be allowed to breach the station's perimeter. The Stavengers will fire on them themselves if necessary. Repeat: the frigates are fireships. They must not approach the station. We can't engage them here. New orders are to intercept and engage in space."

Morgan watched as the small rebel units broke their defensive formations around the station and set new courses. She kept looking out the viewport, but they were too far away to see with her own eyes. The screen was the only way to keep track of them, without star-sense. They were flying up, away from the centre of Enragon. Away from her.

Ned was carrying on several conversations at once, coordinating the new flight plans as they came in. Choria was still staring at the map, as though she could divine from it, and Morgan knew she was realigning her æther-work to be as precise as possible. Tasia had come up to operations to monitor the mages and pressed a protein bar into the admiral's hand. It was already unwrapped, and Choria ate it without even blinking.

"How big would the blast be?" Morgan asked. "From the fire-ships, I mean? How far away do our ships have to stay?"

"We won't know until we blow the first one up," Choria said grimly. "But those fighters are hanging in close. And the frigates aren't that far away from each other. Either they know the blast won't reach them, or they know they're going up with them."

There were a lot of things the Hegemony could promise a pilot in return for a suicide run, not the least because those promises were unenforceable.

Morgan watched her screen, hardly breathing as the first group of rebel ships made a run on the Stavenger fleet. Captain Leynar's group went for the wedge on the 270-degree side, taking the frigate farthest from the middle on that flank. Two of the enemy fighters broke to engage them, attempting to sandwich the rebel vessels between two Stavenger lines. Captain Leynar was too canny for that and had two of her stingers swing in behind to take the fighters out. The first shots lit up the screen, but Morgan's attention was turned to the main rebel ship as it punched through the wedge.

"Come on," said Choria. "Come on."

The explosion was visible from the viewport, but the screens showed the true bloom of damage. The frigate went out in a ball of fire, but it wasn't until the sensors cleared that they could gauge the full radius.

"They're in one piece!" Ned announced. "They've taken some damage and they lost two stingers, but they've still got five more. They're going for the next one."

Choria exhaled a gust of air and pressed her palms into the table. On the screen, two more rebel groups engaged, from 90 and 180 degrees. They lost more stingers but took out four more frigates. On the fourth explosion, one of the bigger rebel ships got caught in the blast and was lost with all hands. The stingers fell back, awaiting a new deployment order, and a new battle group engaged to seamlessly fill in the gap. The mood in operations was grim.

"Can damaged ships fight the gunners?" Morgan asked.

"Not for very long," said Choria. "They're making us fight for everything and they're not giving anything away. Ned, get me the third and fifth battle groups."

Ned rushed to comply, and soon had both the ships networked in.

"Captains, I want you to drop below the Stavenger formation and come up on the gunships from behind," Choria said. "You'll be outmatched, but they have to keep moving forward and they can't get any closer to the fireships. Use that to your advantage. You'll be much more flexible than they will be. Hurt them as much as you can. Focus on the guns. You won't have time to board."

"Understood, Admiral," came the replies.

Third and Fifth were the biggest of the nine groups the rebels had remaining. Each had three retrofitted haulers, like the *Cleland*, and ten stingers. Their guns were ramshackle, but their flying was very good. Morgan watched them circle the Stavenger gunships like annoying satellites, trading fire and dodging away from the worst of the hits. It didn't slow the gunships down, but it did take out a significant amount of heavy weaponry. Two dozen Stavenger fighters were pulled out of the wedge to defend them. The whole underside of the fireship line was exposed.

"Can we get electro-mages close enough to shut down the fireship engines?" Ned asked.

Choria had already been reaching for the comm again and gave him a feral grin.

"Groups Six and Eight, your window is open," she said.

The *Cleland* and the *Marquis* were the heavy ships in Group Eight. Morgan could hardly breathe as they took positions under their target. If any of the Stavenger pilots decided to fire or to destroy themselves in a suicide run to blow up a fireship, the rebels wouldn't be able to get away in time.

"You can do this, Jonee," Morgan whispered.

The port engines died first, immediately sending the frigate into a tailspin. The Stavengers reacted, but it was already too late. Rather than focus on one ship's whole engine system, the electro-mages had split themselves into smaller groups and only gone after the port side of any given ship. *Four* frigates were listing, and the two lead gunships didn't have time to change course.

This explosion Morgan was positive she *felt*, even though it was still so far away that it was only a quick flash in the viewport. The sensors on the screen were out for several seconds, but when they cleared, a cheer went up around operations. Three gunships were gone, only half a dozen frigates remained, and the enemy fighters were scrambled.

"Groups One and Two on the frigates," Choria ordered. "Everyone else, on the gunships. Board as you can."

The frigates cost them four more ships, one heavy and three stingers, but the inexorable crawl of fire towards Enragon was extinguished. Now the real fight would begin.

27.

JONEE'S ADRENALINE WAS SURGING, which meant her æther was surging too. Those Stavenger engines had been amazing. She hadn't been in them for long, but the patterns and power arcs were incredible. She was already thinking about how she'd copy them to improve the *Marquis*'s capabilities. If they won today, the fight would not be over.

She could hear orders coming down from the bridge, occasionally from Choria herself. From what she could tell, the battle was going as well as it could, considering the sheer firepower the Stavengers had brought with them. She didn't know exactly which ships had been lost, but she knew she'd have to grieve them later. Right now, she had work to do.

They weren't currently close enough to a big gunship to do any damage to it, but the star-mage she'd been paired with had very detailed short-range perception. They were able to give her locations on enemy fighters and their trajectories, and she was able to reach for the electrical systems. She knew the rebel side used small fighters too, but their stingers always had protection from a bigger ship. Stavenger fighters were just thrown out as cannon fodder, their fleet commanders not caring what became of the pilots. Jonee tried not to think about the part where *she* was the one killing them. Working with her partner, she took down fighter after fighter, sometimes by draining their power, sometimes by overloading their weapons, but always making sure they wouldn't be able to hurt any of her friends.

The boarding klaxon sounded, and her star-mage put their hand on her arm. They were finally close to a gunship. Jonee had been in deep, so it took her a moment to focus on the other mage. She took the protein they offered her, barely even chewing before swallowing it. The recharge was immediate.

"Let's go, kiddo," the star-mage said. "We're going to need you for the door."

There were other electro-mages on the *Marquis*, of course, but Jonee was the best at frying circuits without rendering them unusable. She could get the door open, and then they would be able to close it again.

It was a short way to the hatch from her station. The star-mage gave her four more protein bars on the way, and by the time they got there, she could feel all of her toes again. Axel, now a captain officially, was there himself, passing out weapons and boarding suits, and keeping everyone level-headed.

"Open 'er up," he said to Jonee when he saw her.

The hatch was shiny and new, like the Stavengers had just finished building it when they sent it off to fight. Jonee wormed her way into the circuits, searching for the weaknesses built into every door. With the calories humming through her system, it was almost too easy. She didn't need all of her attention to do this, and she did love snooping through Stavenger electrical systems.

She found the trap at the exact moment she tripped the door circuit. In a panic, she shut the airlock behind her, leaving three-quarters of the boarding party standing in the corridor of the *Marquis*. Someone was shaking her by the shoulders, yelling. They hadn't seen it yet. They might not see it before it killed them.

The door slid open, and Jonee desperately reached inside for something, anything, that would protect her crew. There was a hissing noise she wasn't sure if she was actually hearing or if she was sensing in the system. *Protect. Protect. Protect.* She was deeper in the æther than she had ever been, and even though she was on the verge of panic, the way forward had never been more clear.

In a blaze of light, Jonee directed all of her will at the space where the door had been and hoped it would be enough to hold.

They lost two ships before Choria realized that the Stavengers didn't care about the survival of anyone they had sent to attack Enragon. It wasn't just the frigates and the fighters that were expendable. There were a lot of people on the gunships, and the Hegemony didn't care about a single one of them. Morgan felt sick to her stomach as she watched the explosions.

"The *Marquis*," she croaked after Choria had issued the order that no one was to board. "It's still attached."

"Get me Axel!" Choria demanded, and Ned rushed to comply.

"It's Troya, Captain. Admiral," the acknowledgement said.

Morgan barely recognized the voice through all the interference. "Axel's in the airlock. Jonee sealed it right before the door opened. Somehow, she knew. I can't see what's happening in there."

"Smoke?" Choria asked, fear in her tone.

"Light," came the answer.

"It's opening!" said a voice in the background.

"Get me a camera feed," Choria demanded.

By the time Ned had the feed running, the airlock had cycled open. Morgan watched the star-mage Jonee had been partnered with stumble back into the corridor, followed by a few familiar crew members, and finally Axel.

"Admiral," Axel wheezed, his face filling the frame. His voice was hoarse from yelling. "You're not going to believe this."

He moved out of the way, and now that the line of sight was clear, Morgan could see Jonee. Her feet were planted on the deck plates like she was rooted there, her hands held out in front of her. Filling the gap where the door had been and blocking out the toxic explosive gas that the gunships were rigged to release when they boarded was a shimmering wall of pure, somehow solid, light.

28.

THEY WERE STILL TRACKING down the last few Stavenger fighters, but for now, all was peaceful. The surviving rebel heavy ships began the arduous task of hauling the blown-out hulks of the gunships back to Enragon for salvage. They were a mess, but even a charred circuit board could be useful, if only when it came to understanding any new alterations or updates to the Stavenger tech. There was nothing left of the frigates that was worth retrieving.

The *Cleland* docked at the station, and Choria, Morgan, and Dr. Morunt met it at the airlock. The *Marquis* was still attached to the Stavenger gunship. Jonee hadn't come out of her ætherwork yet, so Dr. Morunt made sure to have medical support in place before they tried anything extreme. It wasn't a long trip back out to where the two ships hung in space, but it felt like forever. This was the first time Morgan had been away from Enragon, and even though she wasn't still attached to the station, she felt every millimetre of distance in her marrow. She knew that it could only be an emotional connection, but it was still anchored in her gut.

The familiar halls of the *Marquis* smelled like ozone. The ship had taken some damage in the fight, but Morgan was glad to see that everything appeared to be under control. Choria hugged everyone they met, though she was clearly antsy and wanted to get to the other airlock as soon as possible.

The air was crackling when they got there. Jonee hadn't so much as moved, though her chest rose and fell with every breath. Axel was standing behind her, and her star-mage partner was hovering protectively.

"Captain," Choria said. "Report."

"It's some kind of barrier," Axel said. "It's airtight, because none of the gas got through. When the Stavengers were dying, they tried to get through it as a last-ditch escape attempt, but it electrocuted all of them. One of their electro-mages even tried something, but went down like a bag of hammers."

"Is everything over there clear?" Choria asked.

"Yes," Axel said. "No life signs, and the atmosphere has reverted to normal."

"Then if Dr. Morunt is ready, get her out," Choria said.

Morgan twisted her fingers together as the med crew tried to bring Jonee out of her trance. Finally, after a whispered argument about why the Stavenger electro-mage had died, one of the other electro-mages from the *Marquis* gave her a shock, and that was enough. Jonee dropped her hands. The barrier disappeared. Then she collapsed into Dr. Morunt's arms, and he lifted her onto a gurney.

"She's not as depleted as I expected," Morunt said, attaching the IV.

"I gave her five bars right before she did it," the star-mage said. "We were going to board, so I knew she'd need them more than I did."

"She sent out an arc of electricity, but she didn't ground anything," Morgan said. "That barrier was static because *she* was holding it in place."

"We'll ask her about it when she wakes up," Choria said.

Morgan stood beside the gurney and picked up Jonee's free hand. Her pulse was strong.

"Let's go home," Morgan said, and was surprised to realize she meant it.

Two days later, as repairs continued and the supply line to Brannick cautiously reopened, Tasia finally cornered Morgan when everyone else was in operations with them.

"You found something," she said. "You didn't say anything because of the attack, but it's quiet enough now. Tell us what it is."

Choria and Ned were organizing rebel deployment. Vianne was on duty by the Net. Jonee, still pale, was sitting at a workstation sketching Stavenger circuits and firewalls on a screen and trying to remember what it was she felt when she'd called her barrier into being. They stopped when Tasia spoke. All eyes turned to Morgan.

"It's the signal I've been tracing. I assumed it was a remnant of something, leftover radiation." Morgan tried not to grit her teeth. There was no way she was going to explain this well enough because she herself didn't fully understand how it was possible. This was probably the worst presentation she'd ever given, and while she wasn't being graded, she *did* need them to believe her. "And maybe the signal we had at Valon was, but this is something else. It's too strong to be leftovers. And it's much closer than I thought."

"Do you think it's an actual shoal?" Choria asked.

It was the first time Morgan heard it out loud, and it felt wild and unbelievable. She had seen the data and checked it as much as she could in the time she had, and it still didn't seem real. Her conclusions couldn't possibly make it through peer review. There hadn't been a shoal of wild oglasa in generations, and everyone knew it. The farmed stuff was stretched thin and produced a lot of un-recyclable waste products, so Skúvoy was the only station that manufactured it in quantity. The real thing would be invaluable.

"I have no way of knowing for sure," Morgan said. "But that's the theory."

They weren't looking at her like she was completely nonsensical. They were looking at her like she'd told them something that was difficult to parse, but they were all doing their best to work their way through it. Because they trusted her word. Her research. They trusted her.

"What would a shoal mean for the disaster?" Ned asked. "I mean, do your parameters change?"

"When it was just a hint of a trail, I thought I might be tracing the disaster back to its source," Morgan said. "Now I'm not so sure. It's possible that there isn't a source, at least not the way we'd think about it. Instead, the oglasa go through some sort of change, and that's the sign that precedes everything else."

"So, if you find the fish, you'll have a food source and a timeline for the disaster?" Jonee asked.

"A short timeline, yes," Morgan said. "In theory."

Vianne smiled encouragingly. She knew as well as Morgan did that the theory was solid. Morgan had spent years on this, and now it was finally coming together. Even if the consequences were terrifying and it wasn't anything like she'd imagined, Morgan had been waiting for this moment for most of her life.

"You know," Vianne said, "I was sort of joking when I suggested stealing Argir's office, and I never really doubted you, but this is amazing."

"Thank you." Morgan felt a little choked up. "Katla doesn't get any of this, not even a scale, if it turns out I'm right."

"Well, you haven't been wrong yet," Choria said. "The *Marquis* is yours whenever you're ready to go."

Before she left the station again, Morgan went down to the infirmary to see Pendt. Her hair had started to grow back. Her hands were bandaged for protection, but Morgan assumed her nails were too. Her colour was definitely better, and she wasn't draining the IV calorie bags as quickly as she had been. But beyond that, there was no change. Pendt slept, and they had to go on without her. All they could do was make sure she was comfortable, and wait.

29.

THE *CLELAND* WAS FASTER, but the *Marquis* had better viewports, and for that reason alone, Morgan was glad about the ship they chose. The whole bridge crew was frozen in their tracks, looking out the window in sheer awe.

"How can there be so many of anything?" Ned said. "How can this be a fraction of what there *was*?"

Morgan couldn't even speak. Outside the ship, for as far as the eye could see and almost as far as the instruments could detect, were oglasa. Their silver scales refracted any available starlight, scattering brilliant patterns of light. They moved, and the light moved with them, undulating and rippling, like waves through the blackness. It was hypnotic. It was beautiful. It was endless.

"Tasia?" Morgan said, pulling herself out of her reverie.

"If we took one-tenth of that, we'd have ten years of food," Tasia said, blinking as she used the æther. "It wouldn't be exciting, but the processing plants back on Enragon are ready to go."

"We're expecting more rebels," Ned said.

"One-tenth of that could feed *Brannick* for ten years," Tasia said. "And the only reason it wouldn't feed Katla is that they're too snobby."

None of them had looked away from the viewport yet. They even spoke in hushed tones. There were just so many of them.

"Do your mothers know anything about fishing?" Morgan asked.

"I'm sure they could figure it out," Tasia said.

"My family used to fish, once upon a time." Morgan dragged her gaze from the window and looked at Axel. The captain was just as awestruck as the rest of them, drumming his fingers on his armrest as he sat, transfixed. "I'll do whatever I can."

They launched one of the shuttles to collect a sample, just to be sure. Morgan's equipment was set up in a corner of the bridge, working away. She had planned to keep an eye on it, but there was nothing that would change between now and getting back to Enragon, and she didn't want to stop watching the oglasa.

"I'm going to close the viewports," Axel said when the shuttle had docked safely back on board. "Otherwise, we'll never leave."

Morgan was not the only one who felt a tear run down her cheek as the metal shields came down. She understood why Axel did it and probably should have suggested it herself, but they were just so beautiful. Ned picked up her hand and squeezed it, and Tasia took the other one. They watched until the hatches closed, and the endless silver was shut out.

Then Morgan finally turned to her gear, confirming what she had suspected before she ever saw the wondrous sight. The disaster was imminent. She still had no concrete number, but she did know that it was going to be soon.

Deirdre took a bite of the first fresh-caught oglasa to come out of the Enragon processing plant in generations and wrinkled their nose.

"It's definitely healthy," they said. "But even your super-secret donair sauce that I certainly haven't figured out isn't going to make this stuff taste interesting."

"Then we'll keep trying," Tasia said.

"We're certainly going to have time," Deirdre grumbled.

The rebels had decided to maintain Enragon as a permanent base, rather than split off into their disparate cells again. A few would remain stationed on Brannick, which was being reorganized to function in concert with Enragon. Fisher wouldn't openly support the rebellion yet, but when the time came, everyone knew that Brannick and Enragon would stand together. Choria asked Morgan's permission to stay, which absolutely floored her.

"I have even less claim here than I do on Valon," she protested. "Why are you asking me?"

"Because you're an Enragon," Choria reminded her. "Old habits die hard. And because you helped get us through this. And because you found the first wild oglasa in millennia. And because—"

"All right, all right," Morgan cut her off, her ears turning pink. "You can stay. Of course you can stay."

Later, in her quarters, Morgan pushed the food on her plate around in circles rather than eating it. Ned was well into his second helping of dinner before she worked up her nerve.

"So, I was thinking about getting new quarters," Morgan said. "Real ones, in the habitation circle. These can go back to being a crash pad for whoever's on duty or whatever."

"I think that's a good idea," Ned said. "People like seeing you in the mess and at the market, or in the processing factories. If you lived with the rest of them, they'd probably be ecstatic."

"I still don't understand that," Morgan said. "I'm not special any more."

More rebels were coming every day, and they were bringing their families with them. Enragon wasn't going to be full for a long time, but the population was growing as word spread that it was safe and free. The Stavengers weren't done trying to stamp them out, but the rebels had kicked back in grand fashion, and now they got to rebuild.

"And yet they chose you anyway," Ned said.

He said it like it was obvious, but it hit Morgan in the chest like a brick. They didn't have to pick her. They didn't need her. But they wanted her anyway. She'd had so many plans, once upon a time, and this was so much better.

"There are a few options," Morgan said when she got her breath back. "And I just wanted to ask you if you thought I should go with one bedroom or with two?"

Ned stopped eating.

"I was going to ask if I could stay," he said. "Choria doesn't really need me, and it turns out I don't mind stations so much when I'm not . . . you know."

Morgan very much did know.

"Anyway," he continued, "we'll have to get Pendt back to

Brannick at some point, but other than that, I was hoping I could stick around. With you. Specifically."

"I'd like that," Morgan said. She felt lighter than she had in days.

"Then I think you should start with two bedrooms," Ned said. "And see where we go from there."

30.

THEY DID EVERYTHING THEY could and hoped it would be enough. They warned those who would listen. They prepared for a storm they could not name. And they waited.

When it happened, everyone knew.

Pendt Brannick woke up screaming. Dr. Morunt had a heart attack and barely survived long enough for his colleagues to resuscitate him. Tasia Furlough felt like she was alone in the universe for the first time. Jonee felt like everything was on fire, and then like nothing would ever be again. Choria Sterling gripped the chart in front of her and reminded herself that there were other ways to find home, if you practiced.

From one end of the station system to the other, æther-workers shrieked their loss. Riots swept through Katla almost immediately. Skúvoy cowered like a kicked dog, ready to turn on its master at any moment. The Hegemony couldn't pretend that nothing was wrong. Brannick, forewarned, tended their wounds.

Morgan held Ned where he'd collapsed on her bedroom floor. He was crying so hard she couldn't make out what he was saying, but she could tell he wasn't in physical pain. Finally, she made out one word, raw and stretched.

"Fisher," he croaked, and then he finally stilled and relaxed in her hold.

"Are you okay?" she asked, knowing it was a foolish question.

"A little dizzy," Ned admitted. His voice was scratchy, but he was already sounding better. "And . . . I don't know which way it is to Fisher. I always know which way it is to Fisher."

"It's that way." Morgan pointed unerringly at Brannick Station, her point of reference firmly beneath her feet. Ned looked at her, his eyes clearing. "More or less, anyway. I'd need a protractor to tell you how many degrees. But it's up from here. I taught myself to know where Brannick is from Enragon. I can show you, when you're ready."

"Thank you," said Ned, and pressed his forehead to hers. He stayed pressed against her. She could hear the beat of his heart, the hum of the station. The pieces of her world, not yet put together perfectly, but all of them within her reach.

It wasn't quiet. She wasn't ready. She didn't know what came next. But Morgan Enni had things to do.

EPILOGUE

THE BRIDGE of the *Harland* was full of old, outdated equipment. The ship itself was functional, but only just. And that had always been enough. For generations, the Harlands had made the difficult calls, had scraped by on the bare minimum. They had used their wits and their æther-work, and they carried with them not a gram of unnecessary weight. No one left the *Harland* alive, after all. Even their bodies were recycled, in the end.

There had been setbacks, of course. There still was no child with sufficient star-sense to take over as captain one day, despite numerous attempts to produce one. Most recently one of their own had selfishly betrayed and abandoned them, making it even more difficult to generate the crew the *Harland* would need. Yet through it all, the ship flew on, powered by the family that had lived on board for so long and little else.

Every electro-mage on the bridge gasped at the same time. Lodia Harland grabbed her head, a sudden pain lancing through her skull. Before she could ask what had happened, her sister began to scream.

"I don't know where we are!" Arkady Harland howled in absolute agony. "I don't know where we are!"

The full weight of it didn't hit Lodia until she reached for the æther herself and found nothing there. Arkady kept screaming.

In the infirmary, Sylvie Morunt lost track of the rations she was counting out. She tried to get it back, but the æther was gone and her gene-sense was useless. Moving with slow deliberation, she crossed the room and sealed the door, locking herself in with almost all of the food on the ship. Then her knees gave out and she sank to the deck. As the full magnitude of what happened hit her, she laughed.

And laughed.

And laughed.

ACKNOWLEDGMENTS

I wrote the first draft of this book in June of 2022 and edited it in June of 2024. In the intervening two years, I wrote four other books and published three of them. I bought a house. I put feet on my seventh continent. I turned forty. I learned not to measure my life in strawberry seasons. I forgot what every single character looked like. There are people who were here at the beginning who aren't here at the end.

Andrew Karre had a vision of how to make sure this book hit shelves. It was absolutely worth the detour. Josh Adams helped me piece together Phase 3 of my career, and I can't think of a better launch point. The Trifecta held my hand while I worried and laughed with me as I corrected two-year-old mistakes.

Thank you also to the team at Dutton: Julie Strauss-Gabel, Natalie Vielkind, Madison Penico, Rye White, Anna Booth, Rob Farren, Ilana Jacobs, Lori Thorn, and Maria Fazio. And to illustrator Jeff Langevin for delivering another banger.

Special thanks to Kristen Ciccarelli, Erin Bow, RJ Anderson, and new member of our local crew M. K. Lobb. It's hard to organize things, but I'm so glad every time we work something out and get together.

Amy M and Amy H both, in very different ways, made it possible for me to move into my dream home. Thank you for making it happen, from the paperwork to the hummingbird bush.

Chandra and Faith have been enabling Lake Magic since 2017, and I honestly don't know where I'd be without them, or the rest of the retreat crew for that matter. What the Chokshi Kraken hath brought together, let not publishing trauma put asunder.

This is the part where I usually thank Dragon Age, but I think we all know this is a Mass Effect book. Except for all the Dragon Age references. Really, it's an extension of my Arthurian fixation, which began in the summer of 1994, and not finding out how hilariously I was mispronouncing "Pendragon" until at least 1998.

This book is about thinking your life is small and realizing it's not. It's about choosing to fight when you had other priorities. It's about resisting, any way you can, even if it makes you a little uncomfortable. I hope your fight finds you.

Sky on Fire began in a little yellow cabin, the home of my heart, and was finished in a red brick cottage, the home of my soul.

AETHERBOUND

A *KIRKUS REVIEWS* BEST BOOK
A TOR.COM BEST BOOK

"A book for anyone who's ever underestimated themselves, and who had to find their people to figure out their power." —TOR.COM

★ "A close-knit, endlessly cathartic gem."
—*KIRKUS REVIEWS*, STARRED REVIEW

TURN THE PAGE FOR A SNEAK PEEK!

1.

THE FIRST TIME PENDT Harland saw the stars, she was five years old. She was watching her brothers play Spark in the crèche on board the *Harland*, where the Family children learned ship operations in the guise of competitive play, and the lines of alliance formed before teeth were cut. Pendt couldn't play Spark. Or, she could, but she lost every time and so no one wanted to be on her team. She couldn't make the cards light up yet, activating the necessary circuits to identify a match in her opponent's hand, let alone find the set in her partner's. She was a liability, and so she always sat out. On the bright—ha!—side, this gave her more time to study the less popular aspects of the *Harland*. While her brothers learned to run the engines, Pendt taught herself everything she could about interstellar travel itself.

It was a strange thing, knowing oneself useless at five. Space was dark and cold, and worked against life in most of its forms. For a human to be in space while also being a liability was dangerous, for the human and for everyone around her. Pendt did her best to stay out of the way, and to excel wherever she could. Her bed was always made the most neatly. She always scraped her plate the cleanest, getting every trace of protein from the meal. She cleaned up the crèche if her brothers or cousins forgot something, and she always volunteered to run errands when a messenger was called to run belowdecks. Pendt avoided the captain, but there was no avoiding the first mate: She was Pendt's mother, and they shared quarters.

The day that Pendt saw the stars was the same as every other day since the *Harland* had set out into deep space. Pendt had been born shortly after their departure and knew no world but the grey metal that lined the innermost hull.

Sometimes her mother was kind and warm—cuddling under blankets in those last few moments before the alarm went off and made them rise for the day—but more often she was the *Harland*'s first mate, and had no higher loyalty than to its captain. Her children must grow quickly, as their cousins had, and earn a place on the ship. Her oldest boy, Kaeven, was ten years old, and they went down like rungs on a ladder to Pendt.

All of the children tensed the moment Lodia Harland entered the crèche. As a matter of survival, all Harland children could tell when their mothers were being Family or Officer. The captain was rarely Family, but Lodia was softer, and with her there was always a dreadful moment of uncertainty. Today, as Pendt examined her mother's face, she found no answers there. Lodia was a strange mix of Officer and Family both.

"Pendt," Lodia said. "Come with me."

Pendt was moving by the time her mother finished saying her

name. Behind her, Willam found a match in Antarren's hand, and Rheegar immediately began to accuse the twins of cheating.

"If we can do it, and if it doesn't cost, it's allowed," said Willam, and Rheegar conceded the match with an angry glower while the twins crowed and little Tyro looked grateful he was also sitting out and wasn't forced to pick a side. Kaeven was too dignified for squabbling and stayed out of it.

For her part, Pendt felt nothing, no glimmer of the pull that circuits and spare parts always mustered in her siblings. Her youngest cousin, Karderee, sat by the door reading an engineering manual. He was eleven, and was too old for Spark now. Soon Kaeven would join him, and then they would both disappear to the engine room forever. Now Karderee settled for sniffing disdainfully at Pendt as she went to answer her mother.

"Good luck, little cat," he said, a sneer twisting his mouth.

In the early days of space travel, there had been a cat on board every ship to hunt vermin. Now there were environmental filters for that, and cats were an outdated luxury, another mouth to feed. Pendt was never sure if her family meant the name as an insult, though it did seem like her cousins felt that way.

Pendt raised her chin and took it like a Harland. Lodia squeezed her hand, just a little bit, and pulled her out of the crèche.

The *Harland* was a transport ship, specializing in living cargo. Primarily, they took workers and supplies out to the mines and brought back raw ore for processing. The ship was old, too old for the engines to propel it quickly. A new vessel might make the same run in half a decade, while the *Harland* was set to spend eighteen years in space. But what the *Harland* lacked in speed, it made up for with size. The new ships were fast and small, and so they couldn't carry the sheer bulk of materials and people that the outer reaches required. That was how the Harlands had made their name: each generation born into the cycle of travel with a captain to lead them and engineers to keep the power flowing. They never stayed still long enough to spend much currency, it was said, but they were worth a lot of it.

Despite the size of the ship, Pendt spent most of her time in either her mother's small suite, the mess, or the crèche. The medical bay was visited only in emergencies, and Pendt had rarely been ill in her few years. When she took messages below, she went only as far as the hard-seal door that prevented any of the paying passengers from gaining access to the ship. Conditions belowdecks could be very rough, especially as the years wore on and the food and water down there ran low. It wasn't a very safe way to travel, and it was only moderately safer for the working crew, so the door was sealed against any and all incursions. The only exit they had below was to space, and the only news they ever heard was messages from the ship's microphone. Pendt took the job seriously, mouthing the words written on the datapad she was given without really understanding them. The text was all times to destinations, perhaps meant as a morale boost and an indication that the bleakness would not last forever. When she spoke her words into the microphone, they were relayed or they were not. She had no way of knowing.

In truth, she knew very little about the ship or their mission, save that both were vitally important, though to whom she had no idea. Much of the galaxy was beyond her, which was only fair given that no one ever told her anything worth knowing, except sometimes by accident. She knew that the bare minimum of supplies had been brought along, and must be carefully dealt with. There were opportunities for trade every few years when the *Harland* arrived at a mining colony, but preparation and rationing were of the utmost importance.

"A generation ship is only as good as the next generation," the captain would say, both as praise and condemnation. This was the only reason Pendt could see why her mother had six children to the captain's four. Ten mouths to feed was a serious investment, and the captain expected them to pay off even if she was too busy to give birth herself.

Today, as Lodia pulled her into the lift, Pendt felt fear for the first time in her life. Space was always fraught with some measure of uncertainty—either the void would get her or it wouldn't—but it didn't truly frighten her. And despite their best efforts, she was not afraid of her brothers or her cousins. But something about today was different, and on a spaceship, different was usually a bad thing. The lift moved in response to Lodia's bio-code, not Pendt's, which was much more restricted.

Pendt looked up at her mother, a hundred questions on her tongue, but she saw that Lodia had fully become the officer as the lift began to climb. Harlands didn't speak to officers unless they were spoken to. Instead, Pendt counted decks. They passed engineering, which Pendt had only seen in pictures. It covered several levels, both due to the size of the engines and the number of operations controlled there. Everything from air and water to light and the intercom was routed through the power sources there and tended to by Pendt's oldest cousins and those born in Lodia's generation who hadn't reproduced.

Above Engineering was the deck where the non-Family crew members lived. Pendt had only ever seen the ones who worked in the galley. Anyone wishing to move to a colony could book passage on a ship like the *Harland* or try to get hired. The crew had better quarters and rations than those who just handed over currency and tucked in to enjoy the ride. Those passengers were kept below: out of sight, out of mind. The crew didn't necessarily know much about ships, so the jobs they did were the least desirable ones on board: cooking, cleaning, basic maintenance. The only exception was Dr. Morunt, a haggard-looking woman who had been added to the roster during a rare trip to Katla Station long before Pendt was born. Pendt never knew quite what to make of the doctor. She had a way of looking at her that made Pendt uncomfortable.

Last came three massive levels of stowage, where the captain kept the items she was delivering, the supplies she rationed, and, eventually, the ore she—or her descendant—hauled in from the stars. It was sealed almost as tightly as belowdecks, and no one was permitted in without clearance. Pendt had never been tempted.

The lift slowed, and then stopped at the bridge level. Pendt felt a swirl of emotions: dread, excitement. She had never been there, but she didn't know *why* she had been summoned. Not knowing was a weakness, and no weakness could be tolerated in space. Lodia released her hand and straightened to attention. Pendt copied her without thinking about it. Harlands stood up straight. As much as she could, and in all the ways that she could understand, Pendt tried to be the perfect Harland.

"Be good, little cat," Lodia whispered as the door hissed open.

Her mother's voice was half admonishment, half desperate prayer. Pendt never misbehaved and didn't understand why her mother might think she would start now, of all times. Pendt stood up even straighter, and willed herself to look as calm and old and capable as a five-year-old can look. Her back straight, Pendt Harland took her first steps towards the true centre of her small grey world.

Pictures of the *Harland*'s bridge didn't do it justice. The workstations gleamed silver under the lights, and the toggles and buttons and screens seemed to promise adventure. Pendt, used to only as much light as was required, blinked against the brightness of it. Important work must be done here, if the captain needed so much light to do it. Here courses were plotted and schedules were made, long-range communiqués were answered and sent, and all the most important decisions were made.

And the noises! There was the hushed murmur as two officers—some of her mother's other remaining cousins—did their work. The steady tone of the navigation system, beaming light back out to the stars. The hum, even now, of the engines.

And at the centre of it all, the tall, uncompromising figure of Captain Arkady, standing at her terminal and issuing commands.

"Pendt," said the captain.

Out of the corner of her eye, in the fraction of a second before she turned to face her aunt, Pendt saw a screen—no, it wasn't clear enough for a screen: It was an actual porthole. It was clear steel, as strong as the rest of the hull but transparent and *much* more expensive.

And through it, she saw a thousand specks of light.

2.

"IT'S BEAUTIFUL, ISN'T IT?" Arkady said, her own gaze slipping from Pendt's face to the stars.

"Yes, sir," Pendt replied.

The window was why her aunt commanded the *Harland*. She could tell, with precision and certainty, where the ship was in relation to the stars at each moment. Lodia could do the same thing, but her sense of direction wasn't as good, so she was only the XO. She could hold a course, but she couldn't set one. Pendt dragged her eyes away from the stars to her aunt's face with some effort, and Arkady nodded.

"You know," she said, "I can't play Spark either. Neither can your mother."

"I know, sir," Pendt said. "You two can feel where we are, like the Stavenger sky-mages before magic was purged. That's why you're the captain and why Mother is allowed to have so many children."

None of Pendt's cousins had star-sense, and so far, none of Lodia's children did either. For the first time, Pendt wondered whether her mother might have another baby, even if it went off plan. A ship full of engineers needed a captain, and without a captain, the *Harland* would be lost in the void.

"That's right," said Arkady. Her voice was calm and level, not commanding. She was almost, almost, an aunt, except that her shoulders were held too high for her to be entirely family. "Some give their hands to the *Harland*, and some give their minds. Can you give something for our ship?"

"Of course, sir," Pendt said. Her chest puffed out. None of her brothers had been asked to do something for the captain yet, and she was the youngest of them.

"Eat this," Arkady said, and passed her a four-gram protein cube.

Extra food was unheard of on the *Harland*. If Pendt was eating it, that meant someone else was *not*, and there were only so many calories given to a person every day. As captain, and because her work took so much out of her, Arkady received the largest share. She must always have calories to burn, because she must always use the æther to know where they were and where they were going. Pendt received enough to make sure that she grew, and nothing more. She wanted to eat the protein slowly, to savour the treat, but something in the atmosphere of the bridge told her that this was not the time to dawdle. The older cousins were disciplined, of course, but she could still feel them watching her.

Pendt put the cube on her tongue and then ground it between

her teeth as quickly as she could. She swallowed, and for the first time in her short life, felt the whisper of potential in her mind.

"Pendt"—Arkady's voice had changed. Now she was the captain entirely, and this was a command, not a request—"I need you to make your eyes blue."

All of her siblings had blue eyes, and most of her cousins did too, except for Tanith, whose eyes were brown. Pendt's eyes were green. She usually did her best not to think about them. She only saw her reflection briefly every day when she brushed her teeth. On a ship where everyone important had the same utilitarian haircut and variations on the same genetics, green eyes were enough to mark her as an outsider within her own family, and she had never liked that feeling. Still, she couldn't imagine why the *Harland* needed her to have blue eyes. She knew she owed the ship already, even if she was only small. If she could help, she would.

It was like Spark, a bit, only instead of looking at circuits for a match, she was looking at a code, and the code was inside of her. She had never understood the game the way her brothers explained it to her, but this made much more sense than their muddled attempts to include her in their play. She saw the paths of light, the same as they described them. There was even a touch of electricity to it, but there was something else too, something that Pendt knew in her heart even if she couldn't put a word on her lips.

She found the part of the code that made her eyes green, and focused on it. She knew what blue looked like, both in someone's eye and in the code, even though no one had ever explained it to her, because her blue-eyed cousin was standing close by. She reached for that blue, strengthened by the four grams of protein, and wrote it overtop of her own green code. It felt as natural as breathing to do it, but experiencing the change made her uncomfortable in a way she couldn't articulate. How could something so easy feel so wrong? Was she going to be the same person after this? What right had she to do it, and what right had her captain—her aunt—to ask.

She opened her eyes, and Lodia gasped, a soft sound that might have been a sob, except Harlands didn't cry. The captain's face hardened.

"Pendt, you must listen to me," she said. Her tone was unmistakable now. Arkady had stopped thinking of her as Family and saw her only as part of the *Harland*.

"Yes, sir," Pendt said.

She didn't know what she had done wrong. She had done exactly as Arkady asked. Maybe it was the wrong shade of blue. She couldn't see her own eyes, of course, but Pendt was sure she'd matched her cousin's eye colour when she'd changed the code. Maybe she should have gone with Arkady's shade instead. Maybe her aunt had wanted her to be more creative. Pendt tried reaching for the blue again, and she could see it just as clearly as before, but something inside her *knew* that if she tried again, without the protein, it would only hurt her in the long run.

"You must never use your gene-sense again," Arkady said, giving name to Pendt's curse. "Do you hear me? Never use the æther, unless I have given you permission."

"You mean until I get lessons?" Pendt asked. Surely there was a version of Spark for her to play, now that she knew what she could do. The colours called to her, choice beyond measure, and she couldn't answer that call. "I've been doing my best to instruct myself until—"

"I mean never," said the captain, abruptly cutting her off. It wasn't the colour. It was the fact that she could do it. "Your skills will not be useful to the *Harland* until you come of age. Until then, you will do what you are told."

Pendt wanted to cry, but some instinct told her that crying wouldn't help, and she clung to it, even as her Harland-ness seemed to fall away from her. If she was useless, then there was *nothing* that would help. She would be a blue-eyed burden forever.

"I'm sorry, sir," Pendt said. Her voice was very small. "I'm sorry I'm not better. For the *Harland.*"

"I am sorry too," Arkady said. She spoke like she'd already forgotten who Pendt was and didn't look in her direction. She looked at Lodia instead. "You're dismissed."

Pendt remembered nothing about the lift ride back down to Family quarters. Her mind was struggling to absorb everything she had seen: the lights and sounds, the coldness of her aunt's look, the way her cousins gazed right through her. Lodia didn't hold her hand.

"You only have bio-sense, nothing electrical or star-born, or even mathematical," Lodia said when she and Pendt got back to the Family quarters. "That's what gene-sense means. Before the æther was purged, the Stavengers called it grain-sense, and mostly used it for farming. We have no need of that here. It's not worth it to spend the calories on you."

Pendt said nothing. The part of her that wondered about

the future and dreamed about flying a ship with her siblings was dying, and the part that was growing in its place was a silent, waiting thing.

"You won't be useful until you're eighteen and can work legally under the shipborn rules," Lodia continued. "Then you can be hired out. Until then, you will be worthless. The captain will decide what you can do to earn oxygen."

Pendt understood only that she was useless, and that she didn't deserve to breathe as a result. She knew that eighteen was far away, more than ten years, and she knew exactly how many calories and how much atmosphere a person consumed in that much time.

Then her brain fixed on the word *hire*. They would get her a job on another ship. She'd have to leave everything and everyone she had ever known and go to a place where she wasn't Family. She would never belong again, and that was the worst fate she could possibly imagine. She wasn't much of a Harland, to her shame, but in all of her dire imaginings, she had never considered losing her name. She'd rather face the airlock.

The next morning, Pendt was taken to the galley instead of the crèche. She would miss the quiet times she'd spent learning about *Harland* operations, but she wouldn't miss her brothers. Or the way everything in the room reminded her that she was useless. Or the constant feeling of disapproval from whatever elder cousin was in charge of training. Really, she could read anywhere.

She was too young to be of good service doing maintenance, and the galley was moderately safer anyway, though Pendt was never sure if that had entered into Arkady's calculations. The children didn't get jobs until they were twelve unless they showed remarkable aptitude, and Pendt had no aptitude for anything. It was known immediately by everyone who saw her, family and otherwise, that her position was a mark of some terrible failure on her part.

The cooks made her stand on a stool to pass them things or carry pots that were too big for her. When she made mistakes, she was reported immediately for punishment. She didn't hold it against them. They would be punished far worse if they coddled her, and they had no reason to. Even shamed, Pendt was Family and they were not. That meant she was the Family's to use as they saw fit. Arkady ruled in the galley as much as she ruled everywhere else, and her edict regarding Pendt was wordless, but clear nonetheless. Still, she was small, and she was clumsy, so Pendt made many mistakes.

"There is nothing in the void," said Lodia as she locked Pendt into one of the supply closets for having dropped three grams of vege-matter on the galley floor on the fourth afternoon of her new life. It wasn't her last infraction. She didn't like the small space or the confining dark, but she was coming to appreciate the solitude. She'd been forced to eat the matter as part of her own rations, of course, so there hadn't been any waste, but such behaviour couldn't go unpunished. "You have to be more careful."

Pendt held her chin up and took it like a Harland.

Three days and two more stints in the cupboard after that, she overheard her cousins discussing if their mother was going to airlock her.

"It would be much more economical," Donalin argued. "Otherwise we're going to feed her all these years to bring us dinner. Usually, we make people pay us to do that, just for the privilege of being on our ship."

"She's still Family," Tanith said. She was sixteen, and there was something in her face that made Pendt think she knew a secret that would never even occur to her younger sister or any of the boys. "A Harland is always worth something, even if we have to wait for her for a bit."

"The captain has made it clear we're not to bother with her one way or the other," Jerrus said. He was the most practical of the lot, the most like his mother, except he couldn't feel the stars. "So, we won't, unless we get new orders."

"And you'd better set an example for her sibs," Tanith said. "Not to mention Karderee. They need to understand how fragile our balance is, and what Pendt's flaws might cost us."

That shut everyone up for a while. The Harlands were not afraid of space, but they were respectful towards it, and not a one of them, Pendt included, was going to tempt fate.

As she cleared plates from the table without being acknowledged by any of her relatives, it occurred to Pendt that she had one thing they didn't have: She had seen the stars.

She didn't see them again for a very long time.

The Recipe

The Recipe

Armin Wiebe

The Recipe
first published 2025 by Scirocco Drama
An imprint of J. Gordon Shillingford Publishing Inc.

Scirocco Drama Editor: Glenda MacFarlane
Cover design by Doowah Design
Author photo by Mike Deal/Winnipeg Free Press
Production photos by Dylan Hewlett

Printed and bound in Canada on 100% post-consumer recycled paper.

Production inquiries to:
arminwiebe954@gmail.com
www.arminwiebe.ca

Library and Archives Canada Cataloguing in Publication

Title: The recipe / Armin Wiebe.
Names: Wiebe, Armin, author.
Identifiers: Canadiana 20250259613 | ISBN 9781990738746 (softcover)
Subjects: LCGFT: Drama.
Classification: LCC PS8595.I3573 R43 2025 | DDC C812/.54—dc23

We acknowledge the financial support of the Canada Council for the Arts, the Government of Canada, the Manitoba Arts Council, and the Manitoba Government for our publishing program.

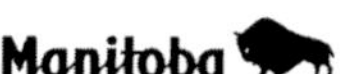

J. Gordon Shillingford Publishing
P.O. Box 86, RPO Corydon Avenue, Winnipeg, MB Canada R3M 3S3

For Lynne, Jenny, and Mildred

Armin Wiebe

Armin Wiebe's plays, *The Moonlight Sonata of Beethoven Blatz*, *Wine and Little Breads*, and *The Recipe*, are spin-offs from his fiction set in mythical Gutenthal: *The Salvation of Yasch Siemens*, *Murder in Gutenthal*, *The Second Coming of Yeeat Shpanst*, *Armin's Shorts*, and *Grandmother, Laughing*. *Tatsea*, set in Canada's subarctic, received the McNally Robinson Book of the Year Award and the Margaret Laurence Award for Fiction.

Renowned for the musicality of his dialect and dialogue, and his humour, Armin has done readings with Carol Shields, W.O. Mitchell, David Bergen, Sandra Birdsell, Louise Penny, Richard Van Camp, and Miriam Toews.

In addition to living and teaching in Manitoba, he taught for six years in Whati, Northwest Territories, before teaching creative writing at Red River College. Armin has served as writer-in-residence at Saskatoon Public Library, Parkland Regional Library, and University of Manitoba's Centre for Creative Writing and Oral Culture. He proudly makes his home in downtown Winnipeg.

Acknowledgements

While playwrights get the writing credit, plays are a collaboration. Rick Chafe and Rory Runnells made me rethink and discard the notion of an adaptation, and I initially wrote the opening scene for a workshop led by Yvette Nolan. Dramatists in Dotage (Brian Richardson, Sue Proctor, Bruce Sarbit, Jenny Gates, Kevin Longfield, Lynne Martin, Harry Nelken) shepherded me through the first draft. Suzie Martin provided valuable dramaturgy from a younger woman's perspective and led the first workshop hosted by Brian Drader and Manitoba Association of Playwrights. I thank Kelly Thornton of Royal MTC and Suzie Martin of Theatre Projects Manitoba for believing in the play. Director Ardith Boxall, dramaturg Brian Drader, and the talented cast have provided enthusiastic, insightful input throughout the workshop process. I must also thank Heidi Harms and Doug Reimer who served as accent advisors to dialect coach Tom Soares. A special shout-out to Rory Runnells of MAP who insisted that I write him a play, and to Theatre Projects Manitoba who has supported my plays ever since. And gratitude to my first reader and dramaturg, Lynne Martin.

Playwright's Note

A story is never the whole story; there is always a possible spin-off story. *The Recipe* is a spin-off from my novel *The Salvation of Yasch Siemens*, stemming from a slightly altered moment from the novel which quickly sprouts into a story of its own. While the novel is driven by Yasch's voice and point of view, the play is powered by Oata. If you have read my Gutenthal novels you have met Oata. If you have not, I am pleased that you are here, ready to meet this abundant woman who has lurked in my imagination for over forty years. Oata is (with apologies to Tennyson) a part of all women that I have met, and when story triggers occur to me, she sometimes appears with a context and then hounds me until I write it.

Although the play is fiction, *The Recipe* uses a real midwife's recipe cited in a paper by Conrad Stoesz called "'For women when their monthly period does not occur': Mennonite Midwives and the Control of Fertility", (*Journal of Mennonite Studies* Vol. 34, 2016 pp.105–122). When I heard this paper presented in 2015, I thought, "There's a story here," but I had no idea what it was—until Oata bugged me.

Foreword

When you read this book, remember that a playscript is a recipe for something wildly alive. It is a recipe for transformation. What you don't see on the page is the alchemical process that takes place. This recipe is a document for an alchemical journey of discovery. On the stage, you will see the spirit in matter.

Playscripts are not books, novels or short stories. They are maps, charts, incantations, designs for creating live art: theatre. In theatre, the actors must live inside the characters; find them, struggle with them, build them, bring them to life. Only then will they tell us the story.

The characters in *The Recipe* are deeply rooted in Armin's literary works and in the land itself. As a director, it is fascinating to watch actors climb into the skins of these literary figures. These characters are akin to classic ones. They are storied, venerable portals to the past and yet so modern, so vital! They are mysterious. *Can we break the code?* You should know that these characters willingly reveal their truths to the ensemble with abandon.

You should also know that a magical process will take place. The ensemble discovers they are playing in a world that is beautifully broad and disarmingly authentic. *This feels new.* The actors are finding their way in a strange new land. *How can it be so theatrical and so naturalistic?* The actors become intensely curious and bond with the playwright; just the right amount of deference to the writer as character expert is established. Armin is playwright, consultant, dialect coach, historian and creator. *Armin knows more about these characters than seems possible…*

Next the ensemble will discover that the characters know more than everyone, including Armin, and they will be our spirit guides. *These characters are wise (and foolish)*. Watch how they instruct the playwright; revelatory, vocal, hilarious, achingly truthful. Armin humbly reabsorbs all this new information, remaining in service to the characters and the ensemble. These characters are beyond the realm of their creator.

Together everyone in the room takes a collective plunge into another world.

I have been witness to Armin Wiebe's stage alchemy twice.

In 2011 when I was the artistic director at Theatre Projects Manitoba, the company premiered Armin Wiebe's first play, *The Moonlight Sonata of Beethoven Blatz*. While a rookie playwright, Armin was an award-winning novelist, a Manitoba literary hero; an established artist. His stories were set in this (fictional) Mennonite farming community in Southern Manitoba. It was abundantly clear that the world of Gutenthal belonged on the stage.

The work was inherently theatrical, the characters authentic, inhabiting a world that was, to many, unfamiliar but beautifully relatable and unmistakably drawn from the land, culture, and experiences of its creator. Even if you had never been to a Mennonite farming community, never heard the rhythm and musicality of Armin's mixed-up form of prairie English, you connected with it. The play's director Kim McCaw and Armin transformed the literary to the dramatic and *The Moonlight Sonata of Beethoven Blatz* was a smash hit. Other plays followed, including the dark and stormy *Wine and Little Breads* and now, *The Recipe*.

The residents of Gutenthal deal with flapping tongues, heartbreak, infertility, sexuality, being outsiders, social stigmas, death, loss and abandonment. With Armin's great guidance, they wrestle with internalized negativity from their community, face shame head on, take big risks, make mistakes and face their peers with bravado and sometimes compassion. They do this with humour, sarcasm, reluctant self-examination, and a tenacious hold on their wildest dreams.

Armin's characters exist between the turn of the last century and today. They bear witness to all the decades of their creator's life. They can exist in different times, storylines, and relationships as they explore issues of the day. In *Beethoven Blatz,* a young couple finds a creative solution to their infertility, and by doing so, empowers their own chosen community. In *The Recipe,* two young women find guidance from the silenced matriarchs and midwives of their own people and discover the power and possibilities of forging their own way in the community by working together.

Oata Needarp, Yasch Siemens, Sadie Nickel and Pug Peters are young adults circa 1960. They were created by Armin in 1984, reimagined in 2024, but were born on a windswept prairie in the late 1940s.They are time travellers. They share the wisdom of the ancients, the freedom and frustration of being outsiders, the potential consequences of taking responsibility for your actions, and discovering the power of choice.

Ardith Boxall

Ardith Boxall is a director and actor based in Winnipeg. She was the artistic director of Manitoba Theatre Projects from 2005 to 2021. Ardith directed the premiere production of The Recipe.

Production History

The Recipe premiered at The Tom Hendry Warehouse Theatre in a co-production between Royal Manitoba Theatre Centre and Theatre Projects Manitoba on November 7, 2024, with the following cast:

Cast

OATA NEEDARP.......................................Amanda Shymko
YASCH SIEMENS.......................................Toby Hughes
SADIE NICKEL.......................Rhea Rodych-Rasidescu
PUG PETERS..Aaron Pridham

Creative Team

Director ....Ardith Boxall
Dramaturg ....Brian Drader
Set Designer... Brian Perchaluk
Costume Designer .... Daina Leitold
Lighting Designer................................ Hugh Conacher
Sound Designer...Ashley Au
Fight Director ....Jacquie Loewen
Intimacy Director.. Aria Evans
Voice & Dialect Coach................................. Tom Soares
Assistant Lighting Designer.................Anika Binding
Assistant Director ....Alan Fehr
Stage Manager...Zahra Larche
Apprentice Stage Manager........................Devon Helm
Artistic Director RMTC........................Kelly Thornton
Artistic Director TPM................................Suzie Martin

The Recipe received development support from the Manitoba Association of Playwrights, Theatre Projects Manitoba, and Royal Manitoba Theatre Centre.

Oata (Amanda Shymko) and Yasch (Toby Hughes) watch Pug scramble for the steering wheel in *The Recipe*, a co-production with Theatre Projects Manitoba and the Royal Manitoba Theatre Centre. Set Designer Brian Perchaluk, Costume Designer Daina Leitold, Lighting Designer Hugh Conacher. Photo by Dylan Hewlett.

Through the screen door. Oata (Amanda Shymko) and Yasch (Toby Hughes) in *The Recipe*, a co-production with Theatre Projects Manitoba and the Royal Manitoba Theatre Centre. Set Designer Brian Perchaluk, Costume Designer Daina Leitold, Lighting Designer Hugh Conacher. Photo by Dylan Hewlett.

Sadie (Rhea Rodych-Rasidescu) asks Oata (Amanda Shymko) for help in *The Recipe*, a co-production with Theatre Projects Manitoba and the Royal Manitoba Theatre Centre. Set Designer Brian Perchaluk, Costume Designer Daina Leitold, Lighting Designer Hugh Conacher. Photo by Dylan Hewlett.

Sadie (Rhea Rodych-Rasidescu) confronts Yasch (Toby Hughes) in *The Recipe*, a co-production with Theatre Projects Manitoba and the Royal Manitoba Theatre Centre. Set Designer Brian Perchaluk, Costume Designer Daina Leitold, Lighting Designer Hugh Conacher. Photo by Dylan Hewlett.

Yasch (Toby Hughes) and Pug (Aaron Pridham) fight in *The Recipe*, a co-production with Theatre Projects Manitoba and the Royal Manitoba Theatre Centre. Set Designer Brian Perchaluk, Costume Designer Daina Leitold, Lighting Designer Hugh Conacher. Photo by Dylan Hewlett.

"Stop glutzing at my legs." Sadie (Rhea Rodych-Rasidescu) Yasch (Toby Hughes) in *The Recipe*, a co-production with Theatre Projects Manitoba and the Royal Manitoba Theatre Centre. Set Designer Brian Perchaluk, Costume Designer Daina Leitold, Lighting Designer Hugh Conacher. Photo by Dylan Hewlett.

Making the recipe. Oata (Amanda Shymko); Sadie (Rhea Rodych-Rasidescu) in *The Recipe*, a co-production with Theatre Projects Manitoba and the Royal Manitoba Theatre Centre. Set Designer Brian Perchaluk, Costume Designer Daina Leitold, Lighting Designer Hugh Conacher. Photo by Dylan Hewlett.

Oata (Amanda Shymko) says a final no to Pug (Aaron Pridham) in *The Recipe*, a co-production with Theatre Projects Manitoba and the Royal Manitoba Theatre Centre. Set Designer Brian Perchaluk, Costume Designer Daina Leitold, Lighting Designer Hugh Conacher. Photo by Dylan Hewlett.

Character List

OATA NEEDARP	Age 20, an abundant woman: someone living in a larger body
YASCH SIEMENS	Age 23, a landless hireling with dreams
SADIE NICKEL	Age 17, slender female
PUG PETERS	Age 22, cocky son of a farmer
PASTOR'S VOICE	Age 45, radio call-in preacher

Setting

A prairie farm between the Red River and the Pembina Hills c. 1960. Summer. Wide open space, suggesting fields, road, pasture, farmyard.

Farm kitchen with a screen door through which conversations take place. (Inside: hand pump, water pail and dipper, radio, crank pre-dial telephone, fridge, range. Outside: steps, a post for hanging milk pail, a yard light.)

Light: moonlight, sunlight appropriate for the time of day.

Sets: minimal, perhaps moveable, not cluttering. Light and shadow, possibly projections. More suggestive than tangible.

Language

The characters speak a mildly buggered-up form of prairie English. Their speech reflects the underlying Plautdietsch (Low German) patterns of their world. At times they use Plautdietsch words or anglicized forms of Plautdietsch words. Read the dialogue as written and allow an accent to develop naturally. Avoid imposing a caricature spoof accent on the lines. A PowerPoint pronunciation guide is available from the playwright: arminwiebe954@gmail.com

SUNDAY NIGHT. August. Moonlit prairie road. Pickup truck. No headlights. YASCH drives. OATA snuggles beside him. Dashboard lights.

OATA: Yasch, I need to talk with you something.

YASCH ignores her.

Yasch, I need to talk with you something.

Sensation of truck turning off the road onto double dike.

Where go you?

Jolt.

What want you on the double dike?

Bump.

Put on lights at least. Want you the Mountie to hold us up again?

Lurch.

Yasch, what's loose with you? Say me something.

Rattle.

Say me some—Düsent! There's a car!

Truck inches up to the back of a parked car.

Isn't that Pug's—Hey, you'll hit it!

Bumpers touch. Engine strains as the truck pushes the car.

What do you? Stop!

YASCH flicks on headlights. They see a bare-bottomed male scramble from the back seat and dive to grab the steering wheel to keep the car from veering into the ditch.

OATA: Gott im Himmel! That's a bare narsch diving over the seat!

YASCH slams the brakes. They watch as the naked male settles behind the wheel. The car starts up, spins tires, and lurches away in a flash of red taillights.

Huy yuy yuy! That was Pug Peters, not?

Truck idles roughly. Clink of bottles. Psst of bottle cap.

Is that beer?

YASCH: Want some?

OATA: Keep that stink away from me.

What's loose with you anyways?

You scare me, Yasch.

You would push a car with people into the ditch?

YASCH: Pug pisses me off!

OATA: And it bothered you not that I was with?

YASCH: I stopped. I stopped before I did them anything.

OATA: But if I wasn't with?

YASCH: Calls me dow-nix 'cause my Futtatje has no farm and—

OATA: Over that you would push his car off the dike?

YASCH: She was in the backseat.

OATA: Holem de grül.

Where you wanted to be.

With skinny Sadie Nickel.

Gott im Himmel, Yasch, after all we've done together?

And still you have your shorts all kroppijch over somebody that's fifteen?

YASCH: Seventeen. Sadie was in there with...with Pug's bare narsch.

Slurps beer.

And I no way even tried nothing with her. I just pitched and she played catcher and then Ha Ha Nickel fired me.

OATA: For fartzing around with Sadie.

YASCH: No! I told you I no way tried nothing with her.

OATA: Your milk sure tasted like sow thistle when Ha Ha sent you to seed for me after Foda's heart attack.

YASCH: I was feemäsijch mad!

OATA: Because?

YASCH: Sadie went with that two-faced Schwengel...

Swigs beer.

Seventeen just. Too young for me. Too young for Pug Peters.

OATA: But you want her still.

YASCH: Can't a person have dreams?

The truck engine sputters and dies.

YASCH: Dievel, I'm out of gas.

OATA: Skin and bones? That's your dream?

YASCH shuts off the lights. Moonlight bathes the scene. OATA casts a large shadow as she steps out in her pink tent dress (pink stockings, pink high heels, pink purse) and rotates, wide-armed, so her skirts rise.

OATA: Yasch Siemens, I thought you dreamed big.

OATA walks away from the truck.

She wipes her eyes with her sleeve.

What for did I wear high heels and nylons to Sunday Night Christian Endeavour anyways?

A crow caws. YASCH drinks and tosses the bottle.

YASCH: Oata, wait.

YASCH gets out of the truck, wearing blue suit with shirt and tie, slinks after OATA. OATA keeps walking as he catches up.

OATA: Pug is maybe right. Only a dow-nix runs out of gas and makes a woman walk home on the double dike in her best shoes.

OATA stumbles. Bends to take off a shoe.

YASCH: I-I didn't know.

OATA takes off the other shoe, brandishes both at YASCH.

OATA: Am I old shoes so soon that with me right beside, you chase after skinny Sadie?

OATA flings a shoe at YASCH. YASCH catches it.

YASCH: I meant not.

OATA: What is that dream you have?

OATA flings the other shoe. It bounces off YASCH and drops to the ground. YASCH stoops to pick it up.

I want to hear this.

YASCH: *(Cradles the shoes.)* Nah, well—

OATA: The well has water, so pump.

YASCH: I-I, how can I say?

OATA: With words, Yasch. Words like you made dirty verses about me in school.

YASCH: For that I shame myself and I said you sorry.

OATA: So say me something now.

YASCH: I liked to work by Ha Ha Nickel.

OATA: You didn't like working for my Foda last summer?

YASCH: No. Uh, I know we have hardly dug him under, but it made me dizzy to work for your Foda, always running back and forth for this wrench and that hammer. With Ha Ha I saw how things could be, and...and that made me want to do things like he did.

OATA: Why didn't you?

YASCH: I tried. I got up early, checked the oil, wiped off the grease, stopped drinking with the ball team, and I—

OATA: And you took Sadie to the games.

YASCH: I thought maybe if I worked hard for Ha Ha... he maybe could help me get a start...the kind of start the farmers' sons get, only...

OATA: Only what?

YASCH: Only Sadie leaves me by the ball game to go to the *Town Without Pity* show with Pug Peters and he brings her home real late and Ha Ha Nickel blames me for that and sends me to seed for you, and then after the funeral he says he doesn't need me no more.

OATA: So Sadie let you take the blame for Pug.

Says you that not something?

OATA walks away.

YASCH: Says me that?

YASCH slinks after her, a high-heeled shoe in each hand.

OATA: Are you so duhpsijch?

YASCH: Duhpsijch?

OATA: You can't see it?

OATA blocks YASCH's way. YASCH offers the shoes. OATA waves them aside.

Are you so dead?

YASCH: Dead?

OATA: So dead that you notice not what has happened with us?

Before Ha Ha fired you, and after, hasn't stuff happened with us?

YASCH: Nah well, you—

OATA: So it's my fault?

YASCH: You—

OATA: You drank my chokecherry wine.

You slept with me.

YASCH: You led me on.

OATA: You helped me dig my father under.

YASCH: I couldn't just claw out from you right when your Foda had gone dead. Not if I want to call myself a mensch.

OATA: And you could sleep with me again.

YASCH: You, you asked me in.

OATA: When you closed my Foda's eye in the hospital, I thought that meant something. I thought you showed me a mensch, as you say.

A crow caws. OATA turns away, stepping gingerly in her stocking feet. YASCH follows, offering the shoes. They reach OATA's yard. OATA spins around to block YASCH.

Why anyways came you back? Ha Ha Nickel wasn't paying you anymore, so why came you back to work for me? For no pay yet.

YASCH: Nah, nothing else to do and so much farm for a woman alone and—

OATA: And so you shovel shit out of my barn. You go to church with me in your new Sunday suit.

OATA waves her hand in his face.

You buy me a ring.

She pulls off the ring.

A ring, Yasch!

YASCH gapes at the ring. A crow caws. OATA slips the ring back on, turns and tromps up the steps.

And all the time you dream Sadie Nickel.

OATA exits into the house. Slams screen door and hooks it.

Yard light goes on and spotlights YASCH slapping at swirling insects with OATA's shoes.

YASCH: That puffed-up Peters! Two white moons in the brights. Funny, but not funny ha-ha for me. Not with you there, Sadie.

Lights go on in the kitchen. OATA paces, gazes at her engagement ring, pulls it off, stares at it.

OATA: How could I smear myself on like that?

She slides it back on, splays and flexes her fingers.

What made me think, I didn't think, I thought I could...

YASCH: Seventeen only. So I never tried nothing.

OATA: Am I like my Mahm in the mental home?

YASCH: Oh Sadie, you let that holy roll-your-own...

OATA: *(To YASCH, but he can't hear her.)* Why picked I a dow-nix like you to throw myself after?

YASCH: You know Pug couldn't even learn the shortest Bible verse, Jesus wept.

OATA: *(To YASCH, but he can't hear her.)* I threw myself after you. I did. I led you on.

YASCH: But big feet he had, biggest on the school yard. Biggest always leads, if you have a big farm.

OATA: But holem de grül, NEEDS a woman not sometimes?

YASCH: Oh, Sadie, I have nothing, but I would be you good, always.

OATA scrutinizes herself in a mirror: her figure, her ring hand on her cheek

Was I too careful, Sadie? Too slow? Wanted you I should try something?

OATA: Such bothered you not after some chokecherry wine.

YASCH: *(To OATA, but she can't hear him.)* But with you, Oata. Nothing careful, nothing slow.

YASCH holds OATA's shoes to his cheeks.

Chokecherry wine sure, lamplight in your eyes, noseful of Evening in Schanzenfeld perfume.

OATA: Heart clappering a hundred miles an hour.

YASCH: But what if your father had lived?

OATA: On the wine sofa. In the morning shine.

YASCH: Would we have looked in each other's eyes?

OATA: When a father goes dead...

YASCH: A person can't just claw away from such a thing.

OATA: You closed my father's eye. I didn't lead you with that.

YASCH: In the waiting room the black plan came.

OATA: What meant you?

YASCH: Can your eyes see that?

OATA: Did you not want Father to see us together, all morning messy?

YASCH: Is my plan really so dark?

OATA: But you clawed not away from me then.

Would any other Schluhdenz in this village have stayed?

YASCH: You put the ring back on your finger.

OATA: If I slip in a mud puddle, must I lie there till I drown?

YASCH: Sadie is maybe sour milk now, but you, Oata, your land. A knock at least.

YASCH knocks on the screen door with the heel of a shoe.

Oata, your shoes.

OATA starts toward the door, stops, shakes her head. She switches off the house light, then the yard light, leaving YASCH in moonlight on the steps.

She turns on the radio. Tweetering sound effect.

NEWS VOICE: *(On radio.)* A Toronto pharmacist has been convicted of selling condoms in his drugstore. Howard Fines faces a five-hundred-dollar fine and possible suspension of his pharmacist licence.

OATA changes stations.

Bar of transition music. They both listen.

PASTOR: *(On radio.)* Hello, this is the pastor speaking.

PUG: *(On radio.)* Hello, pastor? I have this problem, see.

OATA turns up the radio.

(On radio.) I have this fat girlfriend, see.

OATA freezes.

YASCH: Dievel!

YASCH raises the high heels like weapons.

PASTOR: *(On radio.)* Tell me more.

PUG: *(On radio.)* Well, she's after me always.

OATA gapes at the radio.

PASTOR: *(On radio.)* Yes?

PUG: *(On radio.)* When we're together alone, uh, she tries to make me, uh, do sinful things.

OATA strikes a glaring pose.

PASTOR: *(On radio.)* Sinful things?

PUG: *(On radio.)* And she's so big and strong, I, uh, have to do what she wants.

OATA slumps her shoulders, mouth agape.

PASTOR: *(On radio.)* I see. Why don't you stop going with her then?

PUG: *(On radio.)* But I lawve her!

Sound of caller hanging up.

YASCH: Dievel! Only Pug Peters says *lawve.*

YASCH attacks the air with the heels.

PASTOR: *(On radio.)* Oops, lost that caller. *Ask the Pastor*. Spruce 2-6661.

OATA switches off radio.

The clock ticks.

She tiptoes to the screen door. She watches YASCH flailing in the moonlight until he senses her watching.

They listen to each other's breathing.

OATA: You think that?

YASCH: That dirty son of a—

OATA: Do I make you do sinful things?

YASCH: I'll smash him one on the nose.

OATA: Blood on your new suit won't look so good.

YASCH: On his it will!

OATA: I've never seen you so—

YASCH: Damn manure spreader.

OATA: Don't swear. He smattered us both with his dreck.

OATA unhooks the screen door.

Let not the mosquitoes in.

YASCH enters, slams the screen door behind him, and assumes a combat stance, pink high heels in hand.

Yasch, I need to—

YASCH: That barn-holy roll-your-own churchy two-by-four creeping Judas donkey lizard!

OATA switches on the light, stares at YASCH and laughs.

OATA: A whole sermon you can preach. You're almost cute when you're mad.

YASCH: Not funny!

OATA: Is too! Funnier even than my father cussing out the Credit Committee over and under and three times around.

YASCH: Credit Union?

OATA: They wouldn't a loan approve to buy Ginter's two quarters.

YASCH: Holem de grül!

OATA: Tongues flapped the next day that the Kuhl brothers had bought one quarter and Rape Rampel the other.

YASCH: Farmers on the Credit Committee. Wouldn't borrow my Foda a hundred bucks to buy some weanling pigs. Said he wasn't of good character.

OATA: I made them pallbearers.

YASCH: Oh yes, I wondered.

He gestures questioningly with the pink shoes.

OATA: To carry him to his new land.

YASCH: You keep a sharp knife.

YASCH hands OATA the shoes. She takes them absent-mindedly as she keeps her gaze on YASCH.

YASCH: A funny thing on a sad day.

Sound of clock ticking.

OATA: Yasch, I need...how sad was it? That day, for you.

YASCH: How sad?

OATA: What thought you about? During the funeral.

YASCH: Oh mensch, so much thinking tjrieseled through my head...how can I say you...

Sound of crows through screen door.

OATA: *(Notices dirt on her shoes.)* Düsent, look what you've done!

YASCH: You took them off.

OATA: Now I must clean them yet. *(Grabs a rag.)* A woman tries to look pretty for Christian Endeavour and—shit, there's a scratch—See? Now you tell me where I'm supposed to find pink shoe polish on a Sunday evening?

YASCH: I can maybe get—

OATA holds her pink fingernail up to the shoe. Finds pink nail polish.

OATA: Maybe this. Think you it's easy to match everything with the same colour? It's not so simple being a woman, you know.

OATA applies nail polish to the scratch.

Don't think I'm doing this for you. Even barn shoes are too good for going with you. Good thing I took them off or they would be all grey, maybe yet with a broken heel. *(Holds up the shoe.)* Not so bad, I guess. So close to the ground, who will see?

OATA starts cleaning the other shoe.

YASCH: A pug-nose who phones *Ask the Pastor.*

OATA: Pug prickers me too, but listen—

YASCH: Just let me plough him good!

OATA notices her dirty stockings.

OATA: Düsent! Now I must wash my nylons yet. Just one pink pair I have.

While YASCH gawks, OATA takes off her stockings and washes them in the sink as she talks.

Yasch, I must say you something. I think maybe...uh... Pug Peters has his teeth in your pantleg. He knows you pushed his car. He knows you saw him with no pants. So he phones *Ask the Pastor*. Now he knows your bloomers itch with barley dust, and he will schnurks every time he sees you.

OATA hangs up the stockings to dry. The clock chimes.

Huy yuy yuy! Half-twelve already. I need to sleep so I'm wide awake when I see the lawyer.

YASCH: Lawyer?

OATA: About Foda's will.

OATA moves to the door to open it.

YASCH: Will?

OATA: Out before the mosquitoes come in.

YASCH: But you—

OATA: Mosquitoes!

YASCH hesitates, then slips out the door. OATA switches off the lights inside. YASCH heads off.

YASCH: Will?

OATA slips off her ring and peers through it after YASCH.

OATA: *(To herself.)* Yasch, I must say you something...

OATA slips her ring back on and hooks the screen door.

...but can I now?

OATA switches off the yard light.

Must I carry this alone?

OATA shuffles into the darkness of the house.

YASCH: Nobah Naze Needarp's will?

YASCH reaches his truck in the moonlight.

Isn't it Oata's land?

Sound of truck door creaking open.

Sounds of night prairie.

OATA'S SCREEN DOOR. Moonlight. SADIE tiptoes to the door. She smooths her hair and rumpled Sunday clothes She knocks lightly.

SADIE knocks a little louder. OATA shuffles into the dark kitchen in her night-dress. Without switching on the light, she approaches the door. She flinches when she sees SADIE. They stare at each other through the screen.

SADIE: Is Yasch here?

OATA: Here?

SADIE: I thought maybe... *(Slaps at a mosquito.)*

OATA yawns. Turns away.

Can I come in?

OATA raises her arms, drops them, takes an expansive breath as she rotates to face SADIE.

OATA: Why?

SADIE: Mosquitoes.

OATA: For sure in the night—

SADIE: They're biting me crazy.

Slaps at her arms and legs.

I need to talk with you.

OATA: What's so weighty you knock on my dark door?

SADIE: Please, Oata...I'm scared.

OATA unhooks the screen door and opens it a sliver so SADIE can slip through, then hooks it again. Switches on light, eyes SADIE's dishevelled appearance. Waves SADIE to a chair beside the door. SADIE sits.

Can I have something to drink?

OATA: Water good enough?

SADIE: Oh yes.

OATA shrugs. Yawns. Dips water from pail and hands dipper to SADIE. Watches SADIE gulp water. Clock ticks. SADIE smooths her skirt, crosses her legs, fingers a run in her stocking, fidgets, avoids OATA's gaze, turns to glance out the screen door. Drinks the rest of the water.

OATA: Is somebody outside? *(Takes the empty dipper.)*

SADIE: Oh no. I hope not. Who would be?

You, you were with?

OATA: With?

SADIE: With. In the truck?

OATA: Truck?

SADIE: Were you with Yasch on the double dike?

When the truck pushed the car. Saw you Pug?

OATA: *(Yawns.)* Something pretty near same as a pig's behind.

SADIE: Not funny.

OATA: What then?

SADIE: I was in the car.

OATA: *(Yawns.)* With the behind?

OATA sits at the table, props up her head on her elbow.

Why go you not home?

SADIE: Pug let me off by my corner and I got scared that maybe you and Yasch had blabbered it on the party line.

OATA: Or *Ask the Pastor*.

SADIE: Such you wouldn't!

OATA: Sounded like Pug Peters on the radio.

SADIE: Pug phoned *Ask the Pastor*?

OATA: Guess the Peters let the children play on the phone.

SADIE: Said he stuff about me?

OATA: Talked about sinful things.

SADIE: He didn't!

OATA: Said his girlfriend makes him do sinful things.

SADIE: No!

OATA: Has he a girlfriend?

SADIE shrugs, then tenses.

SADIE: It's late, I-I think.

OATA: For sure, almost ten after one.

SADIE: I-I mean...it's late... my time.

OATA yawns to cover her disquiet.

What should I do?

OATA: Such things your mother would know, not?

SADIE: Oh but no! I can't.

Some girls—

OATA: You have said this to some girls?

SADIE: Oh but no, just some girls said...

OATA: Gutenthal girls?

SADIE: Well, yeah.

OATA: Everything they would know.

SADIE: Some said that, well, they said your mother—

OATA: My mother would know about you and Pug Peters' behind?

SADIE: No no, not that. But some say your mother knows stuff.

OATA: For sure, mothers know stuff, yours maybe too.

SADIE: Stuff about what to do when...

OATA: When what?

SADIE: When a girl's time is late.

OATA: Something can be done?

SADIE: To make the time come.

I mean... make my period come. Your mother—

OATA: Why would Gutenthal girls blab such about my mother?

SADIE: In the mental home she is and—

OATA: Sadie Nickel, such dreck I will not hear from you. You make a nest with a pig's behind—

SADIE: *(Sobbing.)* Must I lie in that nest forever?

OATA unhooks the screen door.

OATA: Never before have you Gutenthal girls even said me a friendly word and now you come to me with such. Go quickly. I don't want to slap mosquitoes the whole night.

SADIE rises slowly, weeping.

SADIE: Please Oata, I-I'm scared.

OATA opens the door firmly.

OATA: Scary things it gives in this life.

SADIE exits. OATA hooks the screen door and switches off the light. She gazes out after SADIE.

(To herself.) Holem de grül, am I so stone-hearted I can't feel with that skin and bones?

She places her hand on her belly.

Such maybe would...Mahm, know you such things?

OATA shuffles off into the darkness of the house.

DOUBLE DIKE. SADIE walks unsteadily in the moonlight.

SADIE: Now that cluck's tongue will flap all over the party line.

SADIE stumbles slightly.

Shit!

She sees the shape of YASCH's pickup truck.

SADIE: Yasch?

Clink of bottles. Psst of bottle cap coming off. SADIE stops.

Drinking beer.

SADIE hesitates, then gingerly approaches the truck.

(Whisper.) Yasch.

(Louder.) Yasch.

YASCH turns. SADIE stands in the moonlight, her long thin shadow a marked contrast to OATA's abundant shadow earlier.

YASCH: Sadie?

YASCH stares at SADIE with a confusion of anger and pain and wistful, spine-melting longing. SADIE begins to weep. YASCH slides a foot to the ground.

SADIE: You won't tell?

YASCH: Tell?

SADIE: My folks.

YASCH: Tell what?

SADIE: You...I was with...why did you? ...why did you that?

YASCH: Pug Peters. Brings you home late. You let your old man blame me!

He fires me and lets you go out with that-that—

YASCH drains his beer and flings it away, opens another. Steps away from truck.

Where is that butt-naked Pug? Can't he even drive a girl home after?

YASCH chugs half his beer. Chokes and sputters.

Does the old man know that Pug lets the calf suck him off?

SADIE: I'm scared.

YASCH: Of Pug?

Of your old man?

SADIE weeps.

SADIE: I don't know what to do.

YASCH: What mean you?

SADIE: I mean, Pug—

YASCH: Dievel, that dirty—

YASCH gulps beer, starts to fling it, but it's not empty yet.

SADIE: Will you tell?

YASCH: Tell?

SADIE: Blabber it over the party line.

YASCH: I would never.

SADIE: Promise?

YASCH: Yeah, sure, but—

SADIE: But what?

YASCH: Your elders will wonder where—

SADIE: What can I do?

YASCH: Go home.

SADIE: Home?

YASCH: Before your old man catches you here.

SADIE: Would you take me?

YASCH: Take you? Now? When it's Puggish late, you want—

SADIE: Can you take me home?

YASCH: So they can blame me?

SADIE: Blame you?

YASCH: For making you late.

SADIE: Late?

YASCH: Anyways, can't. No gas. No job, no gas.

YASCH drains his beer and tosses it.

I would have been you good, always. I would have waited till…till you were, ready.

SADIE: Would you?

YASCH: Yeah.

SADIE: But you're with Oata engaged.

YASCH: Yeah.

YASCH grabs SADIE and kisses her hard until she shoves him away.

SADIE: What's loose with you jerks?

She starts away. Then stops.

Is it true what you said about Pug?

YASCH: Ask him!

SADIE: Liar.

YASCH gazes after her until she's out of sight.

YASCH: *(To himself.)* Düsent noch emol eent! I kissed her.

Are me the bearings loose?

What if she tells Oata?

KITCHEN. OATA shluffs back into the kitchen in her nightdress, restless. Switches on light.

OATA: Mahm, didn't you used to have...?

She opens a drawer.

Not here. No, the deep one, I think.

Opens another drawer.

Army and Navy...Eaton's catalogue... Mackenzie Seeds...this maybe.

She pulls out Grandmother's worn midwife book tied with a shoelace. OATA turns pages.

(Reads.) For when a woman's monthly... holem de grül, Mahm, it's true!

OATA traces the recipe with her finger.

(Reads.) Yellow muscat wine...nutmeg.

OATA gazes at the recipe, then reaches for paper and makes a list as she reads.

"Bury in horse manure for twenty-four hours." Horse manure? ...cloves... horses we never had, but that manure pile is old from Grandfather's time... cinnamon... yellow ginger... horseradish roots.

OATA runs her finger over the recipe, checks the list.

Should I?

OATA holds up her ring, then touches her belly.

Try to help that skinny Nickel?

Thoughtful pause as she smooths the paper with the list.

Mahm, is that why Grandmother had to go to court?

OATA hides the book in the drawer and leaves.

SADIE wanders in the moonlight.

DOUBLE DIKE. YASCH's truck bathed in moonlight. YASCH sprawled on the hood of the truck. Snoring. Faint idling sound of approaching car. Soft thud of bumpers touching. Truck jerks.

YASCH: What the dookkat?

PUG PETERS, dressed in western-style shirt with bolo tie and dress pants, sidles up to the truck.

OATA fades into the darkness of the house.

PUG: Hutz droat, Siemens, is Oata Needarp in there?

Schmausing in the truck on the double dike. After Sunday Night Christian Endeavour yet.

YASCH emerges from the truck slowly.

Squishy in there when the springs get rockin', eh?

YASCH: Dü dipstick!

PUG: Prickly, huh, Yasch?

YASCH eyes him, seething.

Barley in the bloomers. Big as a revival tent.

YASCH waits.

Covers the hay when it rains. Oata's hay, eh? You sneaky devil. Nobah Naze Needarp must be rolling in his grave over you and fat Oata. *(Sings.)* "Roll me over in the clover." *(Laughs.)* Ride 'em, cowboy. Lotsa bounce for the ounce. Feels good, not? Me, I like 'er slim, a willow for my willy—

YASCH hauls off at PUG. PUG ducks.

PUG: Jealous, Yasch, just jealous.

YASCH: Dip your stick and don't even drive her home after.

PUG swings at YASCH. YASCH ducks, then rams PUG into the side of the truck.

Dump her off so she can wander around in the dark crying.

PUG shoves YASCH back.

And you call yourself a mensch.

PUG: How know you that?

YASCH: She came here and told me.

PUG: Here? You lie! I let her out by Ha Ha's driveway.

YASCH: Told her you let the calf suck you off.

PUG: Dievel.

YASCH: Maybe phone *Ask the Pastor* about that.

PUG: Where'd she go?

YASCH shrugs.

YASCH: When Ha Ha Nickel hears about this, maybe a 12-gauge shotgun wedding yet!

PUG: You wish. Everybody knows you're riding fat Oata Needarp because you want her land!

YASCH lunges. PUG scurries to his car laughing.

Dumma Esel. You'll be clawing out for Mexico yet like your Futtatje!

Sound of PUG's car backing away.

YASCH: Yeah, just let the calf suck you off.

A crow caws.

Sadie's mad. Oata's mad.

YASCH slams his truck door.

Out of gas.

For sure Muttatje won't want to hear about this.

He trudges off.

MONDAY MORNING. MORNING SUNLIGHT. OATA steps out through the screen door, reading the LIST in her hand. She is dressed in the pink tent dress to see the lawyer. She has overslept. Cows mooing. Chickens squawking. Pigs squealing.

OATA: Oh, shit. Isn't Yasch doing chores?

She looks at her watch. She takes a step and stumbles over SADIE sleeping on her steps.

Düsent!

SADIE: Ouch!

SADIE raises her head.

OATA: Slept you here?

SADIE: What?

OATA: You didn't go home?

SADIE: I couldn't. I was—

Cows' mooing gets louder. OATA is frazzled. She waves the list in her hand as she talks.

OATA: Can you milk cows?

SADIE: Huh?

OATA: With a dress on and nylons?

SADIE: What mean you?

OATA: Hear you those cows? I can't be late for the lawyer. Can you milk for me, and feed the pigs and chickens?

SADIE: Huh?

OATA bends close to SADIE.

OATA: I maybe can help you, but I must go now. Pails on the post. Cream cans in the ice house. Give the blue milk to the pigs.

OATA tucks the list into her purse as she hurries off. Sound of car starting up and driving away.

SADIE pulls off her stockings and ties them around her neck like a scarf. Cows moo.

SADIE: Coming!

SADIE takes the pails and exits.

MIDMORNING SUNLIGHT. OATA'S YARD. SCREEN DOOR.

Sound of car pulling up. Engine stops. Click of car door.

PUG enters yard, dishevelled in his Sunday night clothes. He hesitates, takes in the scene, straightens out his clothes, then saunters up to the screen door. Knocks. Peers through the screen. Knocks again. Looks over his shoulder. Scrutinizes the yard. Knocks again. Peers more intently through the screen.

SADIE enters carrying two pails of milk, just in time to see PUG open the screen door. She watches to see if he will enter. PUG shoulder checks and sees SADIE. He closes the door.

PUG: Sadie?

PUG approaches her.

SADIE: What do you want?

PUG gets closer.

PUG: What do you here?

SADIE: Go away. I'm busy.

SADIE tries to go around him, balancing the pails.

PUG: Where's Oata?

PUG blocks her.

SADIE: None of your beeswax.

PUG: Where is she?

SADIE nods at his clothes.

SADIE: Don't you have milking?

PUG: Women's work. My sister does that.

SADIE: Figures.

PUG: What you mean?

SADIE: Let me by.

PUG reaches for the stockings around her neck.

Leave me alone!

PUG: Didn't you go home?

SADIE: What want you in Oata's house?

PUG pulls on the stockings, forcing her to step toward him to keep from spilling the milk.

PUG: Still mad?

SADIE pulls against the stockings.

C'mon, Sadie, it was funny, you know.

SADIE: Funny?

PUG: You hiding in the back seat.

SADIE: They knew I was there.

PUG: Just Yasch and fat Oata.

PUG gently drapes the nylons over her shoulders and leans in to kiss her.

SADIE: Don't! You'll make me spill yet.

PUG: Let's go park along the States ditch tonight.

SADIE: After you make me shame myself?

PUG: C'mon Sadie, we were having fun. Give me a smooch.

SADIE: Oata's cows feel smoochier than you.

PUG: You're cute when you get mad!

SADIE: Let go! I have to creamer the milk.

SADIE squirms out of his grasp.

PUG: Just a little smooch, Sadie.

PUG reaches for her again.

SADIE: No! Get away from me, you pig's behind!

PUG: I like your behind.

SADIE: And you call *Ask the Pastor* and shame me more!

PUG: Who said you that?

SADIE: Even Yasch would be me better.

PUG: Yasch?

SADIE: If you MILKED cows you'd know how to treat a girl.

SADIE escapes through the screen door. Hooks it. PUG raps on the door. He peers through the screen.

PUG: Where is Yasch? Hiding under the bed?

SADIE: Go let the calf suck you off!

Phone rings: two long, three short.

PUG turns and surveys the yard.

PUG: Hey, Yasch, your Futtatje is phoning from Mexico!

PUG grins, slams his fist into his hand, and swaggers off. Sound of car starting, spurt of gravel as car drives away.

NOON SUNLIGHT. In the kitchen SADIE rinses the milk pails. She steps outside and hangs pail on the post. Sound of car approaching. Sound of car stopping, shutting down. Car doors open and slam.

OATA enters yard. She carries a grocery bag and legal envelope and other mail toward the house. SADIE jumps up and opens the screen door. OATA walks past SADIE as if she hasn't seen her. SADIE shadows OATA into the kitchen.

In the kitchen, SADIE feigns disinterest as OATA sets out her purchases on the table.

OATA: Pull me some horseradish.

OATA sits down and rolls down a stocking.

SADIE: Horseradish?

OATA: Mäaradikj. Know you not English?

Rolls down the other one.

SADIE: Oh.

OATA: Three or four at least. I need the roots.

SADIE: Where?

OATA: Northeast corner, grows wild there. Rub the dirt off.

SADIE: Well, yeah.

SADIE exits.

OATA: Bratty yet, too.

OATA absent-mindedly winds the pink stockings around her hand.

Pink. Who decided pink?

Coming back to the present, she digs out the midwife notebook from the drawer and opens it. She runs her hand over her abdomen as she reads. She notices she is still wearing the pink dress.

Pink makes the boys wink.

OATA reaches for an apron, then turns away.

Enough with pink.

OATA heads off.

SADIE enters with the horseradish. She sneaks a look at the notebook but hesitates to get too close.

OATA re-enters, pulling her housedress into place. Her pink lipstick and nails stand out against the plainness of her dress. She bends over the recipe, without acknowledging SADIE.

SADIE: This enough?

SADIE tosses the horseradish on the table.

OATA: Half-gallon jar. The cellar!

SADIE: Yes, Mahma.

SADIE exits.

OATA: *(Calls.)* Bring two!

SADIE: *(Off.)* If I can find!

OATA examines the horseradish and checks the recipe. SADIE enters with two half-gallon sealer jars.

OATA: Wash the horseradish and chop the roots into little pieces. Oh shit, no yellow muscat wine by Brown Drug Company, just crackling rosé. *(Sighs.)* Must I go to Emerson yet to see if they have? *(Grimaces, stares at the recipe.)*

SADIE: Mom says if you don't have sugar use honey.

OATA: For sure, girl.

OATA exits. SADIE washes the horseradish and begins chopping.

SADIE: Eew! That's strong.

OATA: *(Off.)* Dandelion!

OATA enters with a glass gallon jug of yellow wine.

Mahm made it before she went to…we had to cut the flowers real fussy so no green mixed in. I figured chokecherry, but the recipe says yellow muscat, so dandelion should work better, don't you think?

SADIE: I guess. What anyways are we making?

OATA ponders how to reply, hesitant to spell it out.

OATA: Had you a visitor in the night?

SADIE: You mean? *(Shakes her head.)*

OATA: You want me to help, not?

SADIE: Yeah.

OATA: Your period, you want it to come?

SADE: Oh yeah, for sure.

OATA: You wouldn't want…I mean…maybe with Pug?

SADIE: Would you?

OATA: With Pug?

SADIE: With Yasch, I mean.

OATA: Chop it finer.

SADIE: Really, would you with Yasch?

OATA: Let's just think about what you need.

SADIE: Think you this can work?

OATA: I don't know. I remember one time…a girl came on a bicycle, a hot day, Mahm sent me outside. When that girl rode away Mahm was looking in Grandmother's book. This one. She sent me to the cellar for a half-gallon jar. Mahm said, go pick cherries in the far pasture. With a milk pail. Don't come back till the pail is full.

SADIE: *(Chopping.)* That stings.

OATA: *(Unscrews the jar lids.)* Use the tea towel. *(SADIE wipes her eyes.)* I saw Mahm with that half-gallon jar. She shoved it under in the manure pile. She looked scared maybe somebody would see. *(OATA takes the chopped horse radish.)* Two spoonfuls, it says. *(Spoons the horseradish into the jars.)* Strong for sure. It must, I guess. *(Fingers the recipe.)* One nutmeg. I have just ground nutmeg.

SADIE: One spoon, maybe.

OATA: Heaping, I think.

SADIE: Tablespoon.

OATA: For sure we want it strong. Don't we, girl?

SADIE: *(Hesitant.)* For sure.

OATA: Star anise. Two spoons.

SADIE: Mom puts that in noodle soup.

OATA: No noodles for this. *(Shakes jars to mix.)* Cloves.

SADIE: Like Lifesavers?

OATA: Maybe cloven hoofs.

SADIE: Huh?

OATA: One spoon, I think.

SADIE: You don't know?

OATA: Recipe's in German. Some numbers beside in English.

SADIE: Oh. *(Nervous.)* Did the girl come again?

OATA: Late the next night I was sleeping already, the house door creaked open. I heard a bicycle riding away, then the house door creaked shut. Cinnamon. Let's do two spoons. *(Adds it.)* Two spoons ginger.

SADIE: I like gingersnaps.

OATA: Not making cookies, girl.

SADIE: Did you ever, hear?

OATA: Never. Now the wine. *(Opens jug.)* One quart. The jar is two quarts, so fill it half and a schulps more. *(Pours the wine.)* Stir with the wooden spoon. *(Pours wine into second jar.)* Such a thing, a woman mustn't flap her tongue, about such a thing.

SADIE cups her hand over her mouth.

Want you people to know?

SADIE: Oh, but no!

SADIE sniffs a jar of mixture.

I must drink this?

OATA: Not ready yet. We have to bury it in the dung pile.

SADIE: Dung?

OATA: Horse dung.

SADIE: Oh. Shit.

OATA: Twenty-four hours. *(Looks at the clock.)* So tomorrow in the evening.

OATA sets out two glasses and pours dandelion wine, as SADIE stirs. Sunlight streams through the liquid in the jar. OATA hands SADIE a glass of wine and raises her own.

OATA: Schlooks!

They clink glasses and sip.

They stir in unison, creating moving sunbeam shadows. Clock ticks.

SADIE: What will it do?

OATA: What do you want it to do?

SADIE: *(Pause.)* Will it hurt?

OATA: Hurt your periods?

SADIE: Sometimes. An ache, sort of. Makes me want to go with a hot water bottle to bed.

OATA: Maybe you'll be lucky like that.

OATA takes a sip of wine, eyes the mixture. SADIE takes a careful sip. She's not used to wine.

SADIE: My mother, when I was still little, I heard her scream in the bedroom. I went to see. She yelled at me to go away. I saw blood all over the bed.

OATA pulls out the wooden spoon, holds it up as if to taste it, thinks better of it, and lays it down. She puts the lid on the jar and screws it down tight. She takes SADIE's spoon and closes that jar.

SADIE: Do you think?

OATA takes another sip of wine, then checks the recipe.

OATA: We mustn't flap our tongues about such.

She gazes at SADIE and takes another sip.

OATA: Says here you must drink two tall glasses morning and evening. With brandy.

SADIE: Brandy?

OATA: Such I don't have in this house.

SADIE: My mom maybe has some. She puts it in her Christmas cake.

OATA: I won't tell the church ladies. *(Sips the last of her wine.)* You can't drink this till tomorrow night.

OATA studies SADIE as if pondering a problem.

Why don't you go home? You can come back tomorrow with the brandy. You can't hide here forever. Soon they'll come looking for you.

SADIE: I guess.

OATA: Came anybody while I was in town?

SADIE: No.

OATA: Phone?

SADIE: Unless when I was in the barn.

OATA: *(Picks up a jar.)* Barley looks ripe. Need to get the swather ready. Foda bought new knives just before his heart attack.

SADIE: Dad showed me how to hammer rivets. And I swathed too.

OATA: I forget you have no brothers. You could work this off, I guess. But still you must first go home.

SADIE: Won't Yasch…?

OATA: You see him?

SADIE: No.

OATA hands SADIE one jar, then picks up the other jar, brandishes it at SADIE.

OATA: Say nothing to no one. No one.

SADIE: Oh but no.

OATA: What will you say your mom?

SADIE: I'm helping you.

OATA: No one must know.

SADIE: I know.

OATA: So to the stable and out through the dung gate.

SADIE: That a Bible verse?

They march their jars out the screen door.

TUESDAY EVENING. OATA'S KITCHEN.

OATA, in her "farming dress"(or perhaps bib overalls with rolled up pantlegs) washes the milk pails. She looks at the door as if expecting someone.

OATA: Two days already. I thought for sure he would come back.

OATA sits at the table and shuffles through a pile of mail.

She plays with her ring and gazes at the jug of dandelion wine catching the rays of the setting sun.

Was I too...? Is that how Yasch will act if we have words?

OATA picks up an envelope and tears it open without really looking at it.

But we had more than words. *(She stares at the letter.)* What! Three years arrears. How did I let this go by? I told Foda to not always wait till the last year to pay tax.

Sound of car driving up. Shutting down. Car door.

Now he comes. Better have a good story.

PUG, dressed for a social call, slinks up to the door and knocks.

OATA slips the will and tax letter back into its envelope. A fly buzzes. OATA grabs a flyswatter as she rises and saunters toward the door. She stops a few feet away.

You?

OATA stares at PUG through the screen. PUG pulls at the door, but it is hooked inside.

PUG: Uh, Oata, I want to talk with you.

Uh, I was wondering, uh, wondering if maybe, uh...

OATA: Really? Me? You want?

PUG: Nah, well.

OATA: I never would have— *(Sniffs.)* Aqua Velva yet too.

PUG: I mean, I want…

OATA: Why didn't you phone?

PUG: Phone?

OATA: Your elders have phone, not? They let you?

PUG: Let?

OATA: Let you use phone. It's good to phone first so a person can get ready.

PUG: What?

OATA: I didn't know. It's a weeknight and with getting ready for thrashing, I still have on—

PUG: That's what I—

OATA: A woman likes to pretty herself.

PUG: I want to see about renting the land.

OATA: Aw, and here, what with reeking your Aqua Velva, I just thought—

PUG: No no, not that.

OATA: You mean there isn't room?

PUG: Room?

OATA: In your car. I hear you have Christmas lights rigged up under the dash to shine on a girl's legs when she sits you beside.

PUG: Who said you that?

OATA: Gutenthal girls like to talk.

PUG: The land. Now that your Foda, I thought maybe—can I come in?

OATA: I like talking through the screen. It cools the air.

PUG: The mosquitoes.

OATA: That's why I keep the screen door closed.

PUG: Oata, a farm is too much for a woman alone.

OATA: A woman alone?

PUG: Well, your Foda is gone dead, and—

OATA turns her back and kills a fly.

And, well, I could farm your land and give you one-third share when the crop is in. If you let me use your Foda's permit book, you wouldn't have to do anything—I would do all the work for you.

OATA: Want you the barns too?

PUG: Oh no, just the granaries.

OATA: Why need you Foda's permit book?

PUG: Well, I mean, you wouldn't need it if—

OATA: Foda's permit book is good for this year's crop only. Next year I'll need my own permit book. Listen you never to your old man?

PUG: Nah, well, sure.

OATA: What crops would you seed on my land?

PUG: Crops? Well, wheat for sure, barley and oats, maybe flax—yeah, some flax for sure.

OATA: You got money for seed? Fertilizer? Chemical? Fuel? Machinery?

PUG: Well sure, I—

OATA: Want you to rent my equipment too?

PUG: Maybe, but I think I would use the old man's.

OATA: Will your old man co-sign the deal?

PUG: Co-sign?

OATA: Don't see any collateral, just a car with Christmas lights under the dash.

PUG: Collateral? What mean you?

OATA: The land isn't just some dirt for you to sow wild oats in.

PUG: Wild oats?

OATA: And can you show me the ledger from the last year you farmed for yourself? If you want to do a crop share deal, I need to know that you keep honest books.

PUG: Are you saying—?

OATA: You didn't talk this over with your old man, did you?

PUG: Not yet.

OATA: The land is not for rent. If I wanted to rent, it would be cash. Half up front before seeding, and half the tax too. Machinery and granaries extra.

PUG: That's robbery.

OATA: Call the RCMP.

PUG stands there gaping.

PUG: Just wait. You'll rent to me yet.

OATA: Just because your old man lets you drive tractor doesn't mean you're a farmer.

OATA slaps a bluebottle fly on the screen. PUG leaves. Sound of vehicle driving away.

See men only land?

OATA picks up the envelope with the will.

Mahm, what think you? Should we rent?

She stashes the will in a drawer and runs her hand over the jug of dandelion wine.

The will allows that, I think.

Faint knock at the screen door. It is almost dark. OATA sees SADIE with a backpack.

I thought you wouldn't come.

OATA unhooks the door.

SADIE: I had to hide before. When I saw Pug.

OATA: Wanted to take me out.

SADIE: No way.

OATA: Reeked of Aqua Velva yet, too.

SADIE: Blue or green?

OATA: Wants to rent the farm.

SADIE: House and everything?

OATA: Just the land.

SADIE: Oh.

OATA: Should he want the house?

SADIE: Uh, what for?

OATA: Put up Christmas lights maybe.

SADIE: Has those under his dash.

OATA: So it's true.

SADIE shows brandy bottle.

SADIE: See?

OATA: A full one.

SADIE: And Mom said it's okay if I stay with you to help for a few days.

OATA: She doesn't need you?

SADIE: No. Dad's taking her to Mouse Lake. Says his crop won't be ready for swathing till next week.

OATA: Sure can use your help.

SADIE on tenterhooks.

SADIE: It's over twenty-four hours.

OATA: That's true.

They step outside.

SADIE: Can we find it in the dark?

OATA: There's still some moon.

SADIE: Light enough, the moon. Full moon again soon, I wish.

SADIE and OATA move toward the manure pile in moonlight.

OATA: The pasture looks pretty in the moonshine.

SADIE: Yeah, I guess.

OATA: This manure pile was started almost hundred years ago.

SADIE: Holy dung.

OATA: Could be. Here, yes?

The women dig the jars out of the manure. They hold the jars up to the moon for a moment.

Mahm told me that the women would never let their men plough this pasture. The crocuses in the melting snow sure were pretty.

SADIE: Yeah, sure. You think this will work?

OATA: Maybe yes, maybe no, maybe rain, maybe snow.

They carry the jars back to the screen door and slip inside.

OATA turns on a light. They set the jars on the table. OATA wipes the jars. OATA holds one jar up to the light and gazes at the liquid. She shakes it a little and sets it on the table.

OATA tries to open the jar.

SADIE: Let me try.

SADIE loosens the lid and unscrews it. She sniffs the mixture.

OATA gets out a tall glass and a short glass, positions the tall glass and SADIE pours the mixture.

SADIE unseals the brandy and pulls out the cork.

How much, you think?

OATA: So much, maybe? *(Indicates depth.)* It's not Freshie.

SADIE pours brandy into the short glass.

SADIE: Smells strong.

OATA: Will burn, I think.

SADIE: Which one first?

OATA: The recipe didn't—the brandy after, I think.

SADIE anxiously picks up the glass, furtively looks toward the screen door. OATA hooks it and leans back on it. SADIE sips the mixture, swallows, grimaces, then with determination downs the glass, pausing for breath once.

SADIE: For sure not Seven-Up. That horseradish still burns.

SADIE reaches for the brandy.

OATA: Two glasses, it says.

SADIE: Oh.

OATA refills the glass. Sadie takes a swallow. OATA picks up the jar lid and toys with it, ponders whether to take the mixture herself.

OATA: Was it worth it?

SADIE: Huh?

OATA: With Pug?

SADIE: You mean?

OATA: Did you want to?

SADIE: Uh, sort of, I guess. It kind of just happened. Pug was pretty dringent and ...he used a safe.

SADIE takes a sip. Grimaces.

It wasn't altogether terrible the next time... and then it was harder to say no...even when he had no safe.

SADIE downs the rest of the drink.

No, not worth it. Where can a girl...you know, if the guy doesn't have?

OATA: Not from Eaton's catalogue.

SADIE takes a sip of brandy.

SADIE: Makes this taste good. *(Finishes the brandy.)* Uh, with Yasch?

OATA: Not altogether terrible. If no visitor comes, you drink more in the morning.

OATA screws on the jar lid.

SADIE: How soon you think?

OATA: The recipe doesn't say.

Now to bed. Tomorrow we fix the swather ready.

SADIE puts her hand on OATA.

SADIE: Can I sleep with you?

OATA murmurs and switches off the light.

They leave the room.

WEDNESDAY MORNING. OATA'S YARD. SADIE, wearing short cut-off jeans, hammers rivets as she replaces knives on the swather blade. Old tin bucket for the old knives. Small carton with the new knives.

YASCH, wearing farm clothes, shuffles up. He is shocked to see SADIE. Disoriented, he gawks as SADIE deftly uses the hammer and chisel to cut the rivets on an old blade, inserts a new blade and hammers new rivets. One blow lands slightly off target and the hammer glances off the rivet.

SADIE: Damn!

YASCH: Here, let me.

SADIE: Oh you. No, I can do it.

YASCH: What do you here, anyways?

SADIE: What looks it like?

YASCH: Who said you should?

OATA: *(Off.)* Sadie, how are you—?

OATA, bib overalls pantlegs rolled up, walks up holding a broken sprocket, stops when she sees YASCH.

YASCH: I can easy do—

OATA: Sadie's doing it.

SADIE: A few more. Then I'll put it back in.

OATA: Good. Then tighten the canvas and hook up the PTO and see if it runs smooth. And take the grease gun to the fittings.

SADIE: For sure. Broken sprocket?

OATA: Hope they have one in town.

SADIE: Should I start on the barley?

YASCH: I can do that.

OATA: Sure, you can start.

YASCH: I'll help.

OATA glances at her watch and eyeballs him until he gets nervous.

OATA: You can pick the peas and shell them. And make us something to eat. I should be back by noon.

YASCH: What?

OATA: Pick some lettuce and make salad with sugar and vinegar.

YASCH: What mean you?

OATA: And kill that big rooster and roast it. Then we'll have lots to eat for a few days.

YASCH: But Sadie could—

OATA: Sadie is swathing.

OATA starts off.

YASCH: *(Weakly.)* Oata? I need to say you—

OATA: Now?

YASCH: Uh...my...uh...can you borrow me some gas?

OATA: You leaving?

YASCH: No, but...my...truck's on the dike and—

OATA: Still? *(OATA stops but doesn't turn.)* Don't use the purple gas.

OATA leaves.

YASCH: Thanks, I—

Sound of vehicle starting up and driving away. YASCH nervously watches SADIE.

Sadie, let me do that. You can make dinner.

SADIE: I'm working for Oata.

YASCH: Sure, but—

SADIE: *(Hammering decisively.)* And stop glutzing at my legs.

YASCH: I wasn't.

SADIE: A woman can feel such a thing.

YASCH: Feel?

SADIE hammers.

SADIE: Pug wants to rent Oata's land.

YASCH: That Schwengel—will she?

SADIE: Maybe. Maybe not. *(Hard hammer blows.)* A rooster in the oven would maybe help her decide.

YASCH: Rooster?

SADIE: Still glutzing at my legs.

YASCH: I'm not.

SADIE hammers the last rivet and checks that the knife is tight. Picks up the blade and bucket.

SADIE: Suit yourself.

YASCH slumps as he gazes at SADIE's legs as she leaves.

YASCH: Can a guy help it when they're burned in so brown and so... rooster roasting? No sweat!

YASCH leaves.

SADIE steals into the KITCHEN. She starts to fill a thermos with water, then pauses as she eyes the jars with the mixture. Tentatively, she caresses a jar, then opens it, reaches for a tall glass, and after a moment of hesitation, fills it with the mixture. She screws the top back on the jar and studies the glass before raising it to her lips to take a sip. She grimaces at the taste.

Sounds of chickens squawking.

(Off.) C'mon, stretch out that neck.

Sound of a chop.

(Off.) Düsent!

OUTSIDE, YASCH scurries on with headless rooster flapping, splattering blood.

Holem de grül!

YASCH struggles to clasp the wings to the legs.

C'mon!

SADIE takes a swallow, looks at the glass with determination, then takes a serious multi-swallow drink.

YASCH notices blood on his pants.

Dievel! Oh shit.

Looks at the house, holds rooster out at arm's length. Cautiously approaches the door.

SADIE drains the glass and reaches for the brandy and pours a generous dollop. Takes a swallow. Cringes as the brandy burns down her throat.

Sips.

YASCH carries in the rooster.

SADIE: Blood on Oata's floor!

YASCH: What do you here?

SADIE: Pluck it at least before you roast it.

YASCH: Hot water.

SADIE: You should—

YASCH: I know! Can you heat some?

SADIE: Okay, but take that bloody thing outside. You want to wash floor too?

YASCH: I'll go.

SADIE: Make fire to burn off the pin feathers.

SADIE plugs in kettle. Readies a milk pail.

YASCH: Yeah, yeah.

YASCH hurries out.

SADIE: Didn't my dad learn you about planning?

SADIE sips brandy as she waits for the kettle to boil. The phone rings: one long, two short. SADIE answers.

(Into phone.) Hullo...no...not here...none of your business...gotta go.

SADIE hangs up.

Shit. Pug. What if he comes again?

Sips the last of the brandy and pours some more.

SADIE rummages in her pack, pulls out two baseball gloves, tosses them on the table, pulls out a John Deere cap and puts it on her head. The kettle boils. SADIE gulps the rest of the brandy. Clasps her chest as the burning liquor goes down.

Work already!

SADIE pours the hot water into the milk pail and carries the pail out, wobbling slightly as the brandy hits her.

The phone rings: one long, two short.

SADIE comes back in. She pours another glass of mixture. YASCH follows with the plucked rooster.

Phone rings: two long, three short.

YASCH freezes.

Isn't that your mother's?

YASCH: She'll answer.

SADIE: Took you the guts out?

YASCH: Guts?

SADIE: Yeah. Take the guts out before you cook it.

YASCH: I know that.

Phone rings: one long, two short.

The phone? I should maybe—

SADIE: Oata's not here. Do it outside.

YASCH: Outside?

SADIE: Didn't you ever see your Muttatje do it?

YASCH: Well, yeah—and give cats the guts.

SADIE: Here. *(Hands him bowl.)* For heart and liver and gizzard.

YASCH: Gizzard?

SADIE: The stomach.

YASCH: For sure, the stomach.

SADIE holds out a knife, blade first.

YASCH recoils.

Oh, yeah.

YASCH gingerly accepts the knife.

SADIE: Does Oata like the feet?

YASCH: Feet?

SADIE: If she likes the feet, then you should cut the claws off.

YASCH: I like feet.

SADIE: Chicken feet, I mean.

YASCH: Those too.

SADIE: Maybe preheat the oven while you do that.

YASCH: Can you do that? My hands are full.

SADIE: I'm swathing.

YASCH: Yeah, sure. How hot?

SADIE: Stop glutzing at my legs. Three fifty.

YASCH: Okay.

SADIE: Get that bird out of my face!

YASCH: The way you're swathing I'll have to cut the barley with the rooster claws.

SADIE: Can't a girl have a drink on a hot day?

YASCH: Put some ice in that Freshie.

YASCH leaves with the rooster.

SADIE: Shit!

SADIE finds a dish towel and covers up the jars, brandy, and the wine jug. She downs the last of the brandy, then washes the glasses.

Woozy, she sits at the table and props up her chin.

YASCH enters with the rooster and bowl of giblets.

YASCH: Lots of guts. Good thing Oata has three cats.

He gazes at SADIE, not sure what to do next.

Where's the roaster?

SADIE: My mom keeps it in the oven.

YASCH: Get it out for me.

SADIE: I'm swathing.

YASCH: In the house?

SADIE: Stop glutzing at my legs!

YASCH plops the rooster on the table, sets down the bowl, and opens the oven.

YASCH: Dievel, that's hot!

SADIE: Take it out before you turn it on.

YASCH: What do I do?

SADIE: Use gloves to take it out.

YASCH grabs the baseball gloves and grabs the hot roaster from the oven.

YASCH: Heesch, burns even through leather!

YASCH sets the roaster on the stove, removes the lid.

SADIE: Close the oven.

YASCH: I don't have three hands.

SADIE: Not like a woman, huh? Don't touch the rooster with those gloves!

YASCH: Shit.

Phone rings: two long, two short.

SADIE: Lots of tongue flapping today.

He drops the gloves and picks up the rooster and drops it into the hot roaster. He reaches for the lid, almost burns his hand. Grabs for a glove.

Aren't you going to season it?

YASCH: Season?

SADIE: Salt and pepper and stuff.

YASCH puts down the lid and looks for salt and pepper.

YASCH: Stuff?

SADIE: Parsley sage rosemary thyme.

YASCH: Like the song? Think Oata has?

SADIE: In the cupboard maybe.

YASCH reaches over the beverages and rummages in the cupboard, finds spices.

YASCH: Sadie, look. Prunes. My mom puts prunes on roast chicken.

SADIE: Whatever, you're the cook.

YASCH glances at SADIE and scrutinizes the covered jars and bottles as he seasons the chicken and places prunes on the bird.

Unsteadily, SADIE rises from the table, bends to pick up a baseball glove, plops down in the chair again, and pulls a ball out of her pack, and tosses it repeatedly into her glove hand to deflect YASCH's glances.

SADIE: Pour some water in, else it will get too dry.

YASCH: I know that.

YASCH adds water, then puts the lid on the roaster and shoves it in the oven.

The phone rings: one extra long, two short.

SADIE: Somebody really wants to tell Oata something.

YASCH: Maybe it's my Muttatje.

SADIE: Pick up the glove!

YASCH: Huh?

SADIE: From the floor where you let it fall.

YASCH: Hey, that's mine!

YASCH picks up the glove and slips it on his hand without thought.

SADIE: Forgot it at our place. Think fast!

SADIE flings the baseball at him. YASCH snags it reflexively.

YASCH: What do you?

SADIE: Pitch to me.

YASCH: Here?

SADIE: 'Course not, silly. Outside.

SADIE staggers out the door. Yasch looks around bewildered, then follows SADIE.

OUTSIDE, SADIE stumbles backwards to put distance between them, then crouches into a catcher's squat. She pounds her fist into her glove, almost losing her balance.

Come on, chucker, put 'er right here!

YASCH winds up and throws a slow pitch right into SADIE's glove. SADIE tosses the ball back nearly losing her balance.

That all you got? Put 'er here!

YASCH pitches slightly harder, still straight into her glove. Teetering in her squat, SADIE fires the ball back so it smacks YASCH's glove.

You pitching to a girl or something?

YASCH: Or something.

Pug wants to rent Oata's land, you say?

SADIE fires a grounder back at him, forcing him to drag his glove on the ground to scoop it up.

Wants he to get married?

SADIE: What for would he want that?

YASCH tosses the ball high like a fly ball and gazes with admiration as SADIE judges the ball into her glove.

YASCH: Who knows what such a Schwengel wants.

SADIE tosses the ball high into the air between them, both move, eyes on the ball.

YASCH/ SADIE: Got it!

YASCH snags the ball as they collide.

YASCH embraces SADIE.

Phone rings inside: one long two short.

YASCH: Uh Sadie, I-I must say you about Futtattje—

SADIE: *(Pushes away.)* You dizzy?

YASCH: What?

SADIE: You're talking funny.

YASCH: I didn't say nothing.

SADIE: You play catch with Oata?

Sound of vehicles arriving, shutting down.

YASCH backs away quickly.

YASCH: Here comes a curve!

Stee-rike!

OATA: *(Off.)* No! I said you no!

OATA holding new sprocket, followed by PUG, appears unnoticed as SADIE throws the ball high into the air.

SADIE: Fly ball!

YASCH eyes the ball, judging it, doesn't notice SADIE doubling over.

YASCH: Got it!

SADIE drops her glove, astonished, then dashes toward the house.

SADIE: Hip hip—hurray! Hip hip—hurray!

YASCH: Hey, where you going?

SADIE disappears through the screen door.

OATA: Huy yuy yuy!

OATA, swinging sprocket, hurries after SADIE.

PUG: What's Sadie—?

YASCH: What do you here?

PUG: What do you, Siemens?

YASCH: Thrashing time.

PUG: Oata lets you play catch with Sadie?

YASCH: You get fired?

PUG: Fired?

YASCH: Peters' farm has no work?

PUG: Come to make a deal.

YASCH: You the Watkins man now?

PUG: Very funny.

YASCH: Rawleigh? Oh I know!

PUG: Shut your—

YASCH: Tupperware! Party guy, huh?

PUG: Deal for land!

YASCH: You mean trade your car for the hole under the outhouse?

PUG: The whole farm. With crop.

YASCH laughs and tosses the ball high in the air.

YASCH: With what? Gopher tails?

YASCH catches the ball and fakes a pitch at PUG's head.

PUG: Laugher yourself if you want. This farm will be mine.

PUG picks up SADIE's glove.

YASCH: Oh yeah?

YASCH fires a pitch at PUG. PUG fumbles and chases after the ball.

Sadie would've got that easy!

PUG hurls the ball at YASCH. YASCH snags it, hurls it back. PUG grabs it. They continue playing catch, moving out of sight.

INSIDE KITCHEN. Sprocket on the table. Alternating sounds of SADIE moaning and laughing. OATA enters from a back room. She pauses as if a little dizzy. She picks up the sprocket and rotates it in her palms as she listens to SADIE's moans and giggles. OATA sets down the sprocket.

OATA: *(Calls to SADIE.)* I see you covered the jars.

She lifts the towel and measures the levels in the jars and brandy bottle with her finger.

(Calls to SADIE.) How much did you drink?

SADIE: *(Off.)* Enough, don't you think? *(Laughs, then slides into a groan.)*

OATA: Lots of brandy too, I see.

SADIE: *(Off.)* The horseradish is schentlijch strong.

OATA: Anyways, you have a visitor.

SADIE: *(Moaning.)* Hope visiting hours are soon over.

OATA: *(To herself.)* Such recipes, Grandmother, such secrets. And the men for sure, just women's stuff they'd say. *(Laughs.)* Always think they know everything.

OATA contemplates the jars, then takes a glass and carefully fills it with the mixture. She sits at the table with the glass but doesn't drink.

OATA: *(Calls.)* You know, Sadie, if I rented out the farm, I could move to town, be close to Mahm, get a job in the hospital, or I could move to Winnipeg, get away from all this. I could even take nurse training, learn to give needles. The world is bigger than Gutenthal, not?

From offstage, SADIE groans. OATA sniffs.

(Calls.) Did you put something in the oven?

SADIE: *(Off.)* I need some...

OATA: *(Calls.)* Bottom drawer, blue box.

SADIE: *(Off.)* Thanks, I'll give back.

OATA: *(Calls.)* It's a big box.

SADIE: *(Off.)* Was that Pug?

OATA: *(Calls.)* Now he says he wants to buy.

SADIE: *(Off.)* With what?

OATA: *(Calls.)* Old Peters will co-sign, he says.

SADIE: *(Off.)* That's funny.

SADIE enters unsteadily.

Dad said Peters is so deep in debt the Credit Committee didn't want to borrow him money for seed and chemical this spring.

OATA: What tongues don't yet flap.

SADIE: Uh...you won't tell Pug, will you?

OATA rises.

OATA: We tell no one. No one. If you must, you talk to me. Got it?

OATA holds SADIE's gaze.

SADIE: *(Grasps back of chair.)* I guess.

OATA: Not your mother, not the Gutenthal girls, no one, not ever. Only me, if you must. Bubblegum this isn't.

SADIE looks away and gestures at the glass on the table.

SADIE: I won't need more, I don't think.

OATA: Oh but no...anyways, what for were you playing catch?

SADIE: Huh? Oh, yeah. Yasch was glutzing at the jars, when he wasn't glutzing at my legs.

OATA: Oh?

SADIE: Even told me to put ice in the Freshie. He was getting too nosey, so I lured him outside to play catch.

OATA: Did he ask about the brandy?

SADIE: Had his eyes full with my legs.

OATA: You think fast, even when you're a bit drunk.

SADIE (*Groans.*) I don't feel so good.

OATA: Go lie down.

SADIE: But—

OATA: We can swath tomorrow.

SADIE hesitates.

OATA raises the glass and sniffs it, grimaces, and sets it down. She looks at SADIE.

OATA: You know, Sadie, this morning when I got up from the bed, you were still sleeping, like a sister maybe. It felt good, really really good, because we had to get the swather ready, and the combine. Just me and you.

The baseball slams into the screen door.

Holem de grül!

SADIE flees to the bedroom.

YASCH: (*Off.*) Butterfingers!

OATA goes to look. PUG steps up to the door. YASCH lurks and eavesdrops.

OATA: What do you? I said you no!

PUG: Oata, listen, I can offer you a good deal.

PUG surreptitiously flips the bird at YASCH.

OATA: Hot air.

PUG: I told you my old man will co-sign the deal.

A crow caws.

OATA: Deal? Half the price of land around here? Not one number written down. Nothing from the credit union. Who will hold the mortgage?

PUG: My old man.

OATA: The crow tells me your old man's pen has no ink.

PUG: What?

OATA turns away. YASCH flips the bird at PUG. PUG scowls.

Lightning. A thunder clap. Rain.

PUG flees.

OATA: When hot air hits cold it gives a storm.

YASCH bursts in.

YASCH: Dunna 'n blitzen!

OATA: It hails!

YASCH and OATA watch the rain and hail through the screen door. Abruptly, the hail and rain stop. The sun blazes hot.

OATA pushes out through the screen door. YASCH follows.

BARLEY FIELD. OATA and YASCH shuffle about in the hailstones, stunned.

OATA: Five minutes. Barley smashed and shredded.

YASCH: The wheat too. *(Gestures.)*

OATA: He was going to go that day.

YASCH: Huh?

OATA: Foda. Foda was going to get crop insurance. Then I had to rush him to the hospital and you came to help and we...I just didn't think about crop insurance...and now.

OATA picks up a hailstone, studies it, letting it drip.

So schentlijch hot and we get ice. *(Sarcastically.)* Maybe I should sell to Pug. Crop and all.

YASCH: That Schwengel bragged that you would.

OATA assumes a seductive stance.

OATA: All dressed up. Aqua Velva too. Christmas lights under the dash.

YASCH: You wouldn't!

A crow caws.

OATA: Too bad that pig's behind has no ink to sign a deal.

YASCH: If he had some ink, would you? Sell?

OATA flings the hailstone away.

OATA: That why you've been hanging around?

Because you think the land is mine?

YASCH: Nah, well, I thought about it for sure. Wouldn't it be yours now?

OATA: And dreaming about Sadie at the same time?

It looks not good, Yasch.

YASCH: Once it's dry, maybe we can still—

OATA: Jungtje, jungtje, see you not what we have here?

Can't even salvage this for feed! There'll be no money, Yasch.

YASCH can't find words.

I maybe could let the cows loose on the field to graze. Somebody would have to herd them so they don't wander off. But who? I give you some small things to do and I come home and you're playing catch with Sadie Nickel!

YASCH: Sadie wanted—

OATA: Sadie wants, Sadie gets? Is that how it will be? As soon as I turn my back you play catch with Sadie?

YASCH: No no, that's not—

OATA: Where anyways were you for two days?

YASCH: Uh...düsent noch emol eent!

YASCH takes off like his pants are on fire.

OATA: Dow-nix! Every time I need an answer to a weighty thing you run like a rabbit.

OATA hurls a hailstone after him.

Is that what a man is?

OATA picks up a hailstone.

What know I about men anyways?

Holds ice to her cheek.

I never had boyfriends. Boys just called me fatty fatty two-by-four. And my Foda...didn't handle Mahm so good.

How can I know what a man should be?

OATA hurls the hailstone at the sky.

But holem de grül, if you sleep with me,

if you buy me a ring,

and you agree to marry with me,

even if I lead you on

it can't be right that you think about skinny Sadie when I'm sitting you right beside!

OATA grabs another hailstone and presses it to her heart.

Can't you see how that hurts a woman?

Why stay I here?

OATA spreads her arms.

Gutenthal. Good valley.

Folds arms defiantly.

Not such a good valley for me. Not a good valley for Mahm. Not for Foda neither.

Picks up a bunch of barley stalks.

People always schnurksing behind our backs, tongues flapping like willow whips, even in the church.

But then Foda, who felt those whipping tongues all his life, whipped Mahm all the way to the mental home.

Flexes the stalks like a whip and whips her thigh.

Why thought I that you were different? Why thought I that a person from the wrong side of the double dike would grasp how such whipping feels?

Stops flagellating herself and holds up the ring.

What made me think that wearing your ring would make me fit in, give me some respect in the village?

Was I so lonely?

And now these whipped fields. And taxes not paid.

Grasps the head of the stalk and slowly rubs the chaff off the seeds and lets the seeds trickle from her hand. OATA presses her palm to her belly.

Is this...could it be...wages of—

Oh, what now?

YASCH hustles up carrying a willow basket and a cowhide blanket. He is breathless, trying to cover up agitation.

YASCH: Had the rooster in the oven, didn't want it to burn. Brought some lunch.

YASCH hands the basket to OATA and spreads the blanket on the ground.

The sun is so hot the earth is dry almost already.

YASCH takes the basket and sets it on the blanket.

Brought the rooster legs to eat. And some sugar and vinegar lettuce. Such a freaky thing. The hail missed the garden. Look, a ripe tomato. Sit and I'll give you a plate.

Nonplussed, OATA settles gingerly on the blanket. YASCH loads a plate with food and hands it to her with a fork. Then he pours cold tea into a cup.

YASCH: I almost brought the jar of Freshie, but it felt too warm for such a hot day, so I brought tea from the fridge.

OATA: That's not Freshie, not for drinking.

YASCH: I saw a glassful.

OATA: Not for men anyways.

YASCH: Oh.

Nervous silence. A crow caws. YASCH watches OATA assess the food with her fork. He picks up his fork, but is hesitant to dig in. He opens his mouth but fears to speak. Something more vital than food is on their minds.

YASCH: Oata, I-I must say—

OATA: Where were you for two days?

YASCH: Oata, I...on Sunday in the night—

OATA: I already know about Sunday—

YASCH: My Muttatje was shouting, "Liar, liar," over and over.

OATA: You lied to your Muttatje?

YASCH: On the phone. She was talking—

OATA: Let me say you something, Yasch.

YASCH: ...then she got really still—

OATA: Nobah Naze Needarp maybe wasn't the best farmer, but he talked with his fat daughter about why he seeded barley here and flax there—

YASCH: She—

OATA: Know you anything about me?

YASCH: Huh?

OATA: I liked Business Practice in school.

YASCH is confused.

OATA: Did you?

Hundred percent I got, and with the handbook from the ag rep I easy learned me how to keep the farm ledger. Know you what that is?

YASCH: *(Struggling to stay with his story.)* The phone voice still twittered from—

OATA: In spring I mostly drove the tractor because Foda had to rest when the pain shot up his arms.

Even after his heart attack, I would have finished the seeding myself.

But tongues flapped on the party line—

YASCH: Futtatje's Mex cousin—

OATA: The next thing I knew I had you underfoot, because men don't think a woman can do anything alone.

YASCH: This Mex cousin said—

OATA: Of course, being Oata Needarp in Gutenthal isn't always much fun so I figured I would have some fun with you.

YASCH: Futtatje had his arm around—

OATA: We had fun, didn't we?

YASCH: Fun?

OATA: For one evening I made you see past the picture you and the village have of me. Maybe we'd have been embarrassed in the morning and clawed away from each other. But Foda died, and you helped with the funeral and finished the seeding, and it seemed like it was good for us together.

YASCH: Futtatje had his arm around a Spanish woman.

OATA: You're not listening! And I thought there was a mensch behind the Schniggelfritz you mostly showed us.

YASCH: This Mex cousin said that the next day they found Futtatje— *(Breaks down.)*

OATA: Of course, now there won't be swathing—

YASCH: They found Futtatje with a knife in his back!

OATA: What did you say?

YASCH: My Futtatje is murdered.

OATA: Gott im Himmel!

YASCH: That's why I didn't come.

Silence. A crow caws.

I should have phoned you.

OATA: Your poor Muttatje. Believes she it's true?

YASCH: She phoned when I was getting lunch ready.

OATA: Just now?

YASCH: Just now the RCMP came to tell her they got the police report from Mexico.

OATA: Holem de grül! Why didn't you go home?

YASCH: Muttatje said I should stay.

OATA: Stay?

YASCH: With you.

OATA: Your Muttatje said you should stay with me?

YASCH: She was crying and mad at the same time it seemed like. She said, "That Schniggelfritz was like a dog chasing a car, and now he got his teeth into a tire and look what happened."

OATA: Such she said about your Futtatje on the party line?

YASCH: "Still, my man he was," she said.

OATA: Your father, too.

YASCH: Yes...and the last two days, talking with Muttatje, she talked how Futtatje couldn't quite make himself go where he thought he wanted to go. With no land, who was he? The last few years, she said, Futtatje got more like a dark cloud until this spring when he suddenly said he must drive to Mexico.

YASCH raises the jar of tea but lowers it without drinking.

And I felt like Muttatje was talking about me.

OATA: What mean you?

YASCH: Futtatje schnurksed about those who had more than him, who laughed at him for having to do foot-licking jobs to get by. I learned to schnurks like him. It helped me get by sometimes, but...I was shaming myself over him too. Oh shit, now I'm talking crazy.

Crows caw. Gust of warm wind.

OATA: Yasch, talking about what is inside isn't crazy. Only it's hard to find someone to listen, someone...comfortable, to talk to. You were comfortable to talk to, sort of. Only we didn't really know each other, not so that I could tell you about the crazy tjrieseling storm inside. But you were there when...and how anyways could I know how to talk such things when really I had been alone for most of my life.

Like you, I think.

YASCH: Oata, my Futtatje is dead...and...I-I can't cry.

Summer prairie sounds.

I can't cry, Oata.

Muttatje too...for two days...didn't cry, until just now on the phone.

YASCH sobs.

She said you are my chance to not be like Futtatje.

OATA: Holem de grül!

OATA struggles with this.

It's not so easy when a father goes dead. When people belittled him.

They laughed at my father. A farmer with no son. Like he wasn't altogether a man. You laughed at him.

YASCH: I did. To not be the lowest, I think. *(Murmurs.)* Some things an honest man can't lie about.

OATA: Said you what?

YASCH: Some things an honest man can't lie about.

OATA: Is that so?

A crow caws.

YASCH: It's true...it's not so simple...I-I mean, yes, I-I played catch with Sadie—

OATA: That I saw.

YASCH: After I killed the rooster, and Sadie boiled water—

OATA: So Sadie got the rooster ready?

YASCH: No no, Sadie just boiled water so I could pluck the feathers and then I took out the guts and she told me to switch the oven on.

OATA: Good thing for sure.

YASCH: And when I had the rooster in the oven Sadie said I should—

OATA: So Sadie made this picnic lunch for you?

YASCH: No no. I didn't even see Sadie when I made this ready.

OATA: So you made this all yourself? For me?

YASCH: For you. For us together.

OATA: Us? What is us?

YASCH: Um, us. I mean, you see, I bought you the ring. You said you wanted to marry with me—

OATA: And you?

YASCH: Me? What?

OATA: You want to marry with me?

YASCH: I bought you the ring, not?

OATA: And want you that?

YASCH: Well, sure, I want that.

OATA: And Sadie? Or another girl with skinny legs?

YASCH: Oata, I know I'm with you, engaged, and so I shouldn't like someone else. I know that that's wrong. I mean, I like Sadie very much... and dreams I had, yes—

OATA: You said already.

YASCH: Yeah, I know, I can hardly believe, how can I say—

OATA: Some things an honest man can't lie about.

YASCH: Nah, well, when I went with you to the hospital when your Foda went dead, that nurse told me to go to the waiting room, and there was a doctor magazine, and I read in it, oh Oata, I'm so black inside. I read that fat people often don't have long to live, and then such a black plan came into my head, that...that I would marry myself with you so I would...get your farm and then when you went dead from fat—

OATA: You would go marry yourself with Sadie.

YASCH: I come to you with a black heart, dark dark black. But Oata—

OATA: How dark can it get with black?

YASCH: I kissed Sadie. She came to me on the double dike...and...and I was so mad that Pug had... so I kissed her.

OATA: Did she slap your face like in the movies?

YASCH: No, but she was feemäsijch mad.

But Oata, I see now how wrong I was to do that to you, to Sadie, and I don't know if you can forgive me.

OATA: *(Sings.)* "Just as I am without one plea."

YASCH: What?

OATA: *(Sings.)* "O Lamb of God I come, I come."

YASCH: Huh?

OATA: And now you want me to hum it yet ten times through?

YASCH: What mean you?

OATA: We're not in a big revival tent here with a curtain in the front for the "I come sinners" to go behind.

YASCH: Revival tent?

OATA: A rooster isn't the same as a Lamb I come, I come.

YASCH: Huh?

OATA: Will I ever be skinny enough for you? Will you glutz at my legs the way you glutz at Sadie's or will you always be thinking of that skin and bones even when she isn't skin and bones anymore? Think you that a woman like me should feel lucky to have a Schludenz like you? Think you that I need a Schludenz like you?

YASCH: I didn't mean—

OATA: If I need some pants for this farm I just have to wait, and soon every pig's behind from here to Winkler will want to give me a ride in a car with Christmas lights under the dash. It's not just skinny legs that look nice in the shine from such lights. Even that lawyer was glutzing me over the whole time when we were reading the will.

YASCH: Uh...what says that will anyways?

OATA: None of your business really.

What's here for me anyways? People that schnurks at me and my family. A man that wants only my land, not me. *(Gestures with the chicken leg.)* So what is for me here?

Silence from YASCH.

When you didn't show up on Monday, and Sadie Nickel did, I figured pants don't need a man in them to run a farm.

YASCH is stunned.

Now this farm...always this farm has passed down to a daughter.

Sometimes there were no sons.

YASCH: Like now.

OATA: Safe on first.

YASCH: Huh?

OATA: Other times the sons died before the father died. But always a daughter lived to take the farm.

YASCH: Like your Mahm.

OATA: Safe on second. And none of these daughters were skinny Nickels. Going dead from fat doesn't run in this family. Not the women at least. The men who marry this farm haven't gotten to own it at all.

YASCH gapes.

So the farm's not mine to sell.

OATA rearranges herself coquettishly.

I can't even use it to maybe lure a man who has a farm already and would be happy to join his with this one.

YASCH: Whose is it then?

OATA: It's Mahm's.

YASCH: But she's...

OATA: Crazy? Listen, Yasch, this farm isn't mine. I don't even have to stay on it or take care of it.

YASCH: But what would—

OATA: So if I marry with you, where would we live? And what would we eat?

YASCH: You mean your Mahm won't let you live here?

OATA: I had a dream too. I knew I had to see the lawyer and after he read the will with me, I was going to see Mahm in the mental home and talk with her about what would be best. If you hadn't played bumper cars on the double dike I would have asked you to come with to make a deal to rent the farm from her.

YASCH: Rent? From your own mother?

OATA: Mahm must live too. The will says the farm can't be sold while she is in the mental home. I'm first in line to rent it if I want to.

YASCH: Want you that?

OATA: Until Sunday night I wanted that. I thought you would, too.

YASCH: I wanted that.

OATA: This morning, I was excited to fix ready the swather and the combine, with nobody to schnurks that I was doing it like a woman. Know you how good that feels?

As the scene progresses OATA's presence grows and glows like a diva singing her song so that by the time OATA rises from the blanket YASCH is bursting with desire for this abundant woman.

It feels like after a bad cold one morning you can breathe free and the air fills your lungs and you feel it go all the way to your toes and your fingers and your hair. It feels like a calf let loose in the pasture for the first time. It feels like coming home from church on a schentlijch hot Sunday and taking my stockings off and feeling the air in the shade wave over my legs.

YASCH: Hutz drot!

OATA I feel like that on this farm now, even with this hail.

OATA rises and rotates wide-armed gathering in the land around her.

OATA: So, Mister Yasch Siemens, what say you to that?

YASCH: Gott im Himmel, you look like you will fly up!

OATA: I must show you something.

OATA whirls around.

Not my legs, Dummkopp. Come, let's go.

OATA strides across the field, casting a long shadow. YASCH hurries his shadow after her.

PASTURE. MANURE PILE. Golden late afternoon light.

OATA: See this pasture.

YASCH: Yeah.

OATA: Never been ploughed.

YASCH: Never?

OATA: Grandmother said me that her Mahm told her the grass grew as high as people when they first from Russia came. Same grass the buffalo used to eat.

YASCH: Buffalo?

OATA: Just one time Great-grandmother, when she was fourteen, saw some buffalo over there beside the creek.

I will never plough this pasture neither.

YASCH: But you said it's not your land.

OATA: That's so, it's Mahm's. If she gets out from the mental home and sells, I get half the money. But she won't sell. When she dies, I get the farm. A woman has to think farther than next week.

YASCH: So the farm will be yours?

OATA: If I don't go dead from fat first.

YASCH: I-I didn't—

OATA: Not so funny when you hear it out of another person's mouth, huh?

YASCH is speechless.

OATA: Now's when the dung hits the fan.

OATA whirls around and points at the manure pile.

So what do you see?

YASCH: Manure.

OATA: Hundred years old nearly.

YASCH: Really?

OATA: Like gold, this stuff.

YASCH: Gold?

OATA: I don't have a crop, but I have this.

YASCH: You mean—

OATA crouches and digs her hand into the rich humus compost.

OATA: Lawn dressing.

YASCH: Lawn dressing?

OATA: In the city. People pay good money to put this on their lawns. I read it in the *Co-operator*.

YASCH: Holem de grül!

OATA: So maybe if I find pants with a man in them that has a truck, this farm could have some cash to get through the winter.

YASCH: You mean—

OATA: Know you such pants?

YASCH: Well, maybe if—

OATA: Chew this through. Taste it. Sniff it. Feel the manure fork handle.

YASCH is stunned with desire. Getting no response, OATA turns away and starts off.

I guess I'll go look in the phonebook. For pants with a—

YASCH: Oata. Oata come once here.

OATA stops. Turns slowly. Waits.

YASCH moves toward OATA, slowly, steadily. He moves in, throws his arms around OATA, and gives OATA the longest, suckingest, noisiest kiss. A crow caws. They come up for air.

OATA: Sounded like a cow pulling its foot out of the mud! At least you started it this time.

YASCH kisses her again until OATA wriggles free.

Okay already, there's shit to shovel.

YASCH grabs her and kisses her again.

YASCH: I know something better.

OATA: Don't want to shovel shit?

YASCH: Not for lawn dressing, well, maybe a couple loads, but wouldn't this lawn dressing be worth more if I spread it on your Mahm's hailed-out fields? Free fertilizer for us.

OATA: You can think past next week.

YASCH kisses her again and gazes into her eyes holding the embrace.

YASCH: We fit together like syrup in a curved bottle.

OATA: Huy yuy yuy, now you have words yet. But...

YASCH: But what?

OATA: What if syrup isn't sticky enough?

YASCH kisses her again.

SADIE: *(Calling, off.)* Oata!

OATA: Sadie will see us yet.

YASCH: Who cares?

SADIE calls from the screen door.

SADIE: Oata! I need to talk with you.

YASCH and OATA continue kissing. OATA wriggles away.

YASCH: Talk what about?

OATA: A woman just needs to talk with another woman sometimes.

Cows moo.

YASCH: I'll do the chores. Then I'll get the truck.

OATA: You do that.

OATA starts off, then pauses.

Uh, Yasch, when you finish that...I maybe need to talk with you something.

YASCH: For sure.

OATA heads to the house.

Safe on third?

OATA shrugs.

YASCH heads to the barn.

OATA'S DOOR. SADIE waits on the steps, anxious, hand on the screen door handle. She opens the door and follows OATA into the kitchen, hooking the door behind her. The evening sun streams in through the window lighting up the jars of mixture.

SADIE: Was that really...

you think it...

is it...?

OATA: You got your period...a heavy period.

SADIE: I-I just...

OATA: Be thankful. Go lie down in the bed. I'll bring you a hot water bottle.

SADIE: You are me so good.

They hug. SADIE leaves.

OATA gazes out the screen door at her domain listening to barnyard sounds.

Then she sits at the table, ring hand on the brandy bottle.

She picks up the glass of mixture and holds it up, lovely in the sunrays.

OATA sets it down,

slowly stirs it with her finger,

pondering.

End of play.

Enrichment Guide

This enrichment guide for The Recipe *was created and compiled by Patrick Derksen with contributions from Armin Wiebe; it was edited by Ksenia Broda-Milian for Royal Manitoba Theatre Centre. The material has been adapted slightly for inclusion in this book.*

THE RECIPE:

"A remedy prescribed by Dr. Wilhelm Toews of Rosenthal for women when their monthly period does not occur. Take 1 quart of yellow muscatel wine, 1 nutmeg, 1 loth star aniseed, ½ loth seasoned cloves, 2 solotnick fine cinnamon, 1 loth yellow ginger, 2 spoons horse radish roots. Mix this together in a jar and bury it in horse manure for 24 hours. Then drink 2 kopecke whiskey glasses of it, morning and evening with brandy."

MENNONITES AND MANITOBA

The Recipe takes place in a semi-fictionalized southern Manitoba in the 1960s. This area was settled by Mennonites from Ukraine and Russia as part of the historic "West Reserve" only 80 years prior. Only a few short years after arriving, many Mennonite villages and fields dotted the landscape, which previous settlers had passed by as being too swampy and/or grassy and lacking access to rivers and lakes. The industrious and hardy Mennonites were used to such challenging landscapes, and it became some of the most productive farmland in Canada.

While some Mennonite groups were resistant to technology, by the 1960s, most in southern Manitoba lived in a blended landscape of modern (driving cars and trucks, hosting radio shows) and pastoral (manure piles and folk remedies). Their previous tight communal approach to life was being overrun by commercialism and individual rights. Farms decreased dramatically in number, yet were increasing in size as poorer farmers sold their land to their richer neighbours. More people were working in industrialized and commercial settings, leaving their farming life behind. This all happened within the course of a generation, and many Mennonites struggled to process the rapid change in their traditional way of life.

The Plautdietsch (also known as Low German) language of the Mennonites was increasingly being replaced by English. Having no written form (until recently), it was (and still is) a constantly evolving language as Mennonites emigrated to Russia and then North and South America. What remained consistent was the element of humour and creativity in its many sayings and exclamations. Today it is more and more difficult to find fluent speakers of this wonderfully vibrant language.

Find out more about the language at
https://www.plautdietsch.ca/

or by watching a video from the Mennonite Heritage Village at https://www.youtube.com/watch?v=dFP5hsUHwUA

GLOSSARY

Dievel (DEEvil):	Devil
Dookat (DOOK aht):	rocking
Dow-nix (DOW nix):	good for nothing
Dreck (DR-RECK):	slop
Dringent (DR-RING yint):	insistent, urgent

Dü (DEW):	you
Duhpsijch (DUHP sijch):	doltish
Dumma esel (DUH ma EH zil):	dumb donkey
Dummkopp (DUM CUP):	dumb head
Düsent (DEW sint):	thousand
Düsent noch emol eent (DEWZint NOCH e MOLE EYNT):	"thousand yet one time once," an exclamation more powerful in its sound than in any literal meaning
Fartzing (FAR-RT zing):	farting
Feemäasijch (FUY MACE ijch):	bestially
Futtatje (FOOT ah tjeh):	little father
Glutz (GLUHTZ):	stare, ogle
Gott im Himmel (GUTT im HIM mil):	God in Heaven
Gutenthal (GOOT in TAHL):	good valley

Holem de grül (HOLE im di GR-REWL): "Fetch the Fear," an exclamation similar to "Jumpin' Jehosophat!"

Hutz Drot (HUTZ DR-ROAT):	hog wire
Jauma (YOW mah):	misery, pity
Jungtje (YUHNK tjeh):	little boy
knoppijch (KNUPP ijch):	knotty, knotted
Kuhl (COOL):	a surname
Mäaradikj (MEH R-RAH dick):	horse radish

Mahm (MAHM):	mother
Mahma (MAH mah):	mommy
Mensch (MENTSH):	man, person
Muttatje (MUTT ah tjeh):	little mother
Narsch (NAR-RSH):	ass, posterior
Nobah Naze Needarp (NOH bah NAZE NEE darp):	neighbour nose Neudorf
Oata Needarp (OAT ah NEE darp):	Agatha Neudorf
Rape Rampel (R-RAPE R-RAHM pil):	a nickname for a rapeseed farmer named Rempel
Schanzenfeld (SHANZ in FELD):	place name
Schentlijch (SHENT lijch):	extremely
schlooks (SLUHKS):	swallow, slurp
Schluhdenz (Scluh DENZ):	slob
schmausing (SHMOW zing):	slobbery making out
Schniggelfritz (SHNIG il FRITZ):	scamp
schnurks (SHNER-RKS):	snort
schulps (SHUHLPS):	splash
Schwengel (SHWENG il):	a lever, stick shift
tjrieseled (TJR-REEZ ild):	swirled, twisted

THE WORLD OF *THE RECIPE*

Playwright Armin Wiebe has written many fictional works set in the same world as *The Recipe,* the little community known as Gutenthal. While it is technically a fictional place, it is based on the many villages and towns found in southern Manitoba.

It's important to note that there are many, many divisions among Mennonites, even just in Manitoba. At the time of this play, a large population of Mennonites lived in northern Winnipeg, who were quite liberal and almost culturally indistinguishable from the general population. There were also Old Order Mennonites whose women were required to wear kerchiefs and who thought rubber tires and mustaches were sinful. Gutenthal seems to fall somewhere in the middle of this spectrum. Not only is Gutenthal an important part of the story, but we must see it depicted in a way that supports the world of the play. The land motivates much of the action, so this world is rustic and agricultural, filled with passionate people.

PRAIRIE GOTHIC

This play could be considered an example of Prairie or Western Gothic. This genre looks at the people and places from small towns and the surrounding countryside that goes beyond the veneer of a plain & simple life and reveals the dark undertones. Characters in Gothic literature are usually deeply flawed and often eccentric. The setting is often decaying or even desolate. Characters dress in muted tones; any bright colour stands out meaningfully. There is an element of the forbidden or sinister – even the unnatural. Characters have sinful secrets. There is usually a cultural or religious vacuum, where traditional values are questioned or disregarded. Poverty is so prevalent that it can be considered a character in the story.

The Recipe is very humorous, which accurately shows how downtrodden folk use humour to cope with their difficult lives. As famed preacher Chuck Swindoll put it: "Humour (…) is a God- given escape hatch…a safety valve. Being able to see the lighter side of life is a rare, vital virtue." While humour is not always present in the Prairie Gothic genre, one shouldn't discount a story from being part of the genre just because it is also funny.

Examples of Prairie Gothic include:

Literature

∞ Cormac McCarthy's novel *Blood Meridian* and his Border Trilogy

∞ *The Goodbye Family*, by Lorin Morgan-Richards (comic strips and animated series)

∞ William Faulkner's works, such as *As I Lay Dying* and *A Light in August*, while focused more on southern USA, have definite rural Gothic elements

Film & Television

∞ *And God Said to Cain* – dark western tale

∞ *The Power of the Dog* (2021) – a prairie setting with plenty of intrigue and family drama

∞ *Fargo* (the 1996 film as well as the TV series) is much more modern than this play, but its dark prairie humour has all of the elements of Gothic Americana

Music

∞ Johnny Cash was a master of the genre, with songs such as "Man in Black," "Sunday Morning Coming Down," and "Five Feet High and Rising." His more humorous songs, such as "A Boy Named Sue" and "One Piece at a Time" are great examples as well.

- ∞ The Handsome Family, especially songs such as "Far From Any Road" and "So Much Wine."
- ∞ Townes Van Zandt, with songs such as "Waiting Around to Die" and "Pancho and Lefty."
- ∞ Del Barber, with songs like "The Waitress," "Home to Manitoba," and "Right Side of the Wrong."
- ∞ Neil Young, particularly his albums *Prairie Wind* and *Chrome Dreams II.*

Other

- ∞ The video game *Red Dead Redemption II* is a Gothic Western that illustrated the gritty social upheaval of rural vs. urban life.

Themes and Topics

Parallel Monologues

A common dramatic technique is the monologue, where we can hear the inner thoughts of a character spoken out loud. There are some powerful monologues in *The Recipe*. However, there are times during the play where two characters seem to be talking to each other, but are essentially speaking monologues of their own. Neither of the characters seems to even hear the other, showing they cannot appreciate or even understand the other's point of view. This ends up being humorous and tragic at the same time. They are so preoccupied with their own thoughts that they fail to hear each other. While this serves a narrative purpose in character and plot development, it also is a comment on our society. How often does this happen in our own lives?

Independence in the 1960s

Those who lived through the 1960s witnessed a decade of revolution and assertions of independence. The World Wars had revealed how connected our planet was, for better and for worse. The international trade of ideas caused conflict, and the divide in political views became heightened (communist vs capitalist). The sixties became known as the "counterculture" decade, with numerous anti-authoritarian movements.

Some world events:

- ∞ 32 African countries gained independence from colonial powers between 1960 and 1968
- ∞ The Berlin Wall was constructed by the Soviet Union.
- ∞ The Voting Rights Act in the USA prohibited racial discrimination in voting.
- ∞ Protests against the Vietnam War reached a new height.
- ∞ Music became much more experimental as artists pushed the traditional boundaries, with artists such as Bob Dylan, Jimi Hendrix, the Beatles, and Janis Joplin.
- ∞ Fashion grew more casual (fewer suits and hats).
- ∞ "The Pill" is approved in the USA; Canada decriminalizes birth control and therapeutic abortion (although it would not be fully decriminalized until 1988).
- ∞ Martin Luther King delivers his famous "I Have a Dream" speech.
- ∞ *Silent Spring* by Rachel Carson, an exposé on the effects of DDT, spearheads the modern environmental movement
- ∞ Betty Friedan publishes *The Feminine Mystique*, which is credited for sparking the modern feminist movement.

- ∞ Youth increasingly seek a voice, adopting mantras such as "Never trust a person over 30" from Jack Weinberg and "I hope I die before I get old" from The Who.

Traditionally, Mennonites lived a conservative, socialist existence. This was demonized by Western countries such as the U.S.A. The Mennonites who lived in Canada were increasingly pressured to adopt more Western/capitalist views. This led to more opportunities to be independent, but it also meant their tight communal social safety net was getting looser.

The news of women's rights and feminism would likely have been sharply criticized by church elders and the general populace. But among young Mennonites, the counterculture movements would have been appealing and influential.

Choice

Every character in *The Recipe* is faced with important, life-altering decisions. Yet they all struggle to realize that they are making choices at all—tradition dictated many aspects of their lives. It was not without justification; the traditional way had carried them through many hard times. It was easier to follow the same well-travelled road. Choosing a new path seemed risky, so many opted not to choose to challenge it.

> *"You can choose a ready guide in some celestial voice*
> *If you choose not to decide, you still have made a choice"*
>
> —From the song "Freewill" by Rush

The women in particular struggle with understanding that they even have a choice. The role of women in Mennonite society was very clear: they are to be mothers and take care of the home. More and more women were working outside of the home, but this was in addition to these two crucial roles. This became known as "The Triple Day." It was difficult for women to see that there was room to make choices in their lives.

Women in the 1960s were pushing for some choices that we consider basic equality today, and spearheading movements that are still being fought.

- ∞ Health: Women should have the right to make choices about their bodies, health, and lives without fear, violence, or discrimination.
- ∞ Reproductive Rights: Women's reproductive rights include access to contraception, prenatal services, safe childbirth, and legal abortion.
- ∞ Equality: Women's choices are often limited, and they may experience reminders that they have limited options compared to men.

Women faced more rigid expectations of their roles in life and were discouraged from wanting more. As we see in this play, women such as Sadie and Oata push back in ways that are available to them, but they are secretive or considered outright taboo.

Women Supporting Women

> *"Sisterhood is powerful."*
>
> —Robin Morgan

The 1960s saw the rise of many women's rights groups—what is referred to as second-wave feminism. Groups fought for rights in education, health, the workplace, and even fashion and presentation in advertising. The movement continued into the 70s, 80s, and beyond.

Some notable examples in Canada:

- ∞ Canadian Voice of Women for Peace (VOW)–campaigning for nuclear disarmament and an end to war
- ∞ Women's Legal Education and Action Fund (LEAF) – focusing on legal rights in the Constitution

- ∞ Front de libération des femmes du Québec (FLF) – fought against the oppression of French-Canadian women by anglophone capitalists
- ∞ Canadian Association for the Advancement of Women in Sport
- ∞ Bookstores specifically for women appeared, including Women's Press (Toronto), the Vancouver Women's Bookstore, and the Northern Woman's Bookstore (Thunder Bay)
- ∞ Feminist magazines and newspapers–*Herizons* (Winnipeg), *La Vie en Rose* (Montreal) and *Branching Out* (Edmonton), as well as the mainstream *Chatelaine,* which had both English and French editions.
- ∞ Numerous unions pushed for women's rights in the workplace, with impactful strikes taking place. Grace Hartman became the first president of the Canadian Union of Public Employees in 1975 and was instrumental in creating the Royal Commission on the Status of Women.

In the course of this play, we see a microscopic feminist movement, representative of many of these larger issues.

Confronting Insecurities and Biases

We see the characters of this play engaging in activities outside of the gender stereotypes: Oata managing the farm affairs, Sadie fixing machinery, Yasch preparing lunch. Yet they all struggle with imposter syndrome as well: Oata thinks she needs to marry someone to manage the farm, Yasch feeling like he is not a man unless he acquires land and a wife.

Bias is a prejudice or unfair treatment of a person, group, or idea based on their characteristics. This might include race, gender, age, religion, or sexual orientation. Bias can be conscious or unconscious and can have negative or positive consequences. It is often difficult to notice our own biases.

Biases can be inward as much as outward, resulting in feelings of insecurity. If one believes that women are not suited for field work, for example, they become dependent on men to do it. Many of the biases we hold on to form our perception of the world.

Our brains are wired to categorize and sort. In other words, we are predisposed to bias. It takes effort to not fall into prejudices and generalizing perceptions.

For a fascinating look at how bias works in the human brain, see these videos and books:

- ∞ "Cognition - How Your Mind Can Amaze and Betray You: Crash Course Psychology #15" https://youtu.be/R-sVnmmw6WY?si=QUVJenf7yjot--Si
- ∞ "Why You Think You're Right – Even If You're Wrong" (TED Talk by Julia Galef) https://youtu.be/w4RLfVxTGH4?si=848ZytWMrIX_QtnT
- ∞ *Thinking Fast and Slow* by Daniel Kahneman
- ∞ *Invisible Women: Exposing Data Bias in a World Designed for Men* by Caroline Criado Perez
- ∞ *The Art of Thinking Clearly* by Rolf Dobelli

Discussion Prompts

Before Reading the Play:

- ∞ What preconceptions do you have about the Mennonite people?
- ∞ How has the shift from small family farms to large factory farms affected the culture and landscape of southern Manitoba?
- ∞ What recipes have been passed down in your family? Has this process predominantly involved men or women?

- How do the career options for women today compare to those in rural 1960s?
- "Pants don't need a man to run a farm." Why would this be a revolutionary idea sixty years ago? Is it a revolutionary idea even now? (Approximately 30% of Canadian farmland is owned and operated by women in 2024, according to Statistics Canada.)
- Emily V. Gordon said, "Women compete, compare, undermine and undercut one another—at least that is the prevailing notion of how we interact. Feeling on guard around other ladies is normal for a lot of women, and it's exhausting." Do you agree with this statement?

After Reading the Play:

- What details place the story in the 1960s? What details make it seem like Gutenthal is stuck in an even earlier decade (or century)?
- Each character in *The Recipe* struggles with important choices. Discuss how the story is influenced by the choices made by:
    - Oata
    - Yasch
    - Sadie
    - Pug
- At first, Oata considers Sadie a rival. What causes her to change her viewpoint?
- Mennonites are defined by their ties to their brand of Christianity. What role (if any) does faith play in this story?
- Does Yasch's infatuation with Sadie go beyond her looks?

- ∞ As Sadie talks Yasch through preparing the rooster, he complains, "I don't have three hands." Sadie replies, "Not like a woman, huh?" How does this statement comment on the perception that men do the "hard" labour?
- ∞ "Holem de grül, Grandmother. Such recipes... such secrets. And the men for sure... just women's stuff they'd say *(laughs)*... always think they know everything." Why would the women feel the need to keep their knowledge secret from the men?
- ∞ Are there are hints that Oata thinks about drinking the recipe herself?
- ∞ Oata tells Pug: "The crow tells me your old man's pen has no ink," meaning he doesn't have money to buy her land. Plautdietsch speakers delight in knowing and inventing sayings such as this. What were some of your favourite turns of phrase in the play?
- ∞ How could women take power in the patriarchal system of Mennonite society?
- ∞ Why is the second offer of marriage very different? How has the power shifted in Oata's and Yasch's relationship?
- ∞ What does it say about male relationships that the last interaction we see between Yasch and Pug is them playing a game of catch immediately after arguing and insulting each other?
- ∞ What feminist issues are tackled in this play?

Other Resources:

- ∞ *Daily Bonnet*, a satirical news website written by Andrew Unger that highlights 21st-century Mennonite issues. www.ungerreview.com/category/mennonitelife/
- ∞ Miriam Toews is an award-winning author of several books detailing contemporary Mennonite life, such as *A Complicated Kindness* (2004) and *Women Talking* (2018), which was also made into an acclaimed film.

- *Shelterbelts,* a graphic novel by Jonathan Dyck, illustrates the nuanced lives of Mennonites in southern Manitoba.
- *A History of Winkler* by Frank Brown, published in 1973, explores the history of the former West Reserve's largest settlement.
- *Living Between Worlds: A History of Winkler* by Hans Werner is an historical look at southern Manitoba's largest Mennonite community.
- *Mennonite History for Young People* series: www.plettfoundation.org/education
- "1963: The Beginning of the Feminist Movement," article in *The Guardian*, www.theguardian.com/lifeandstyle/2013/may/07/1963-beginning-feminist-movement

Sources:

- Playwright's website: http://www.arminwiebe.ca/
- History of Mennonite Settlement in Manitoba: http://www.mhs.mb.ca/docs/pageant/21/mennonite westreserve.shtml
- Low German/Plautdietsch resources: https://ereimer.net/plautdietsch/pddefns.htm http://www.arminwiebe.ca/FlatGermanLexicon.html A big thank you to Wes Reimer for help with translation!
- Julia Merkel, (2008). *Writing against the Odds.* pp. 25–27.
- Charles R. Swindoll, *The Finishing Touch: Becoming God's Masterpiece* (Dallas: Word, 1994), 220.
- "Why Women Compete With Each Other" by Emily V. Gordon (October, 2015) https://www.nytimes.com/2015/11/01/opinion/sunday/why-women-compete-with-each- other.html
- "Writing Prairie Gothic" by Cecelia Frey https://ceceliafrey.wordpress.com/2017/10/26/writing-prairie-gothic/ https://arsof-history.org/articles/v4n4_1960s_page_1.html

∞ "The 1960's: A Decade of Revolution" by Kenneth Finlayson https://arsof- history.org/articles/v4n4_1960s_page_1.html https://www.thecanadianencyclopedia.ca/en/article/history-of-birth-control-in-canada https://www.thecanadianencyclopedia.ca/en/article/womens-movements-in-canada-196085 https://en.wikipedia.org/wiki/Timeline_of_1960s_counterculture

About the Enrichment Guide author:

Patrick Derksen grew up in southern Manitoba straddling two worlds: his father grew up in the Mennonite community of Horndean, and his mother came from the French community of Letellier. As a result, his father referred to him lovingly as a "square-headed frog." He has been living in Morden for the past twenty years, working as a middle-years teacher. He has written several plays of his own, including *A Lighter Shade of Noir,* which has been performed all over the world. He is a proud member of Flatlands Theatre Company, which operates out of the P.W. Enns Concert Hall in Winkler, Manitoba.